STEEL
FRAME

First published 2019 by Solaris
an imprint of Rebellion Publishing Ltd,
Riverside House, Osney Mead,
Oxford, OX2 0ES, UK

www.solarisbooks.com

ISBN (UK): 978 1 78108 705 3
ISBN (US): 978 1 78108 704 6

Copyright © Andrew Skinner 2019

The right of the author to be identified as the author
of this work has been asserted in accordance with the Copyright,
Designs and Patents Act 1988.

All rights reserved. No part of this publication may be
reproduced, stored in a retrieval system, or transmitted,
in any form or by any means, electronic, mechanical,
photocopying, recording or otherwise, without the prior
permission of the copyright owners.

This is a work of fiction. All the characters and events
portrayed in this book are fictional, and any resemblance
to real people or incidents is purely coincidental.

10 9 8 7 6 5 4 3 2 1

A CIP catalogue record for this book is available
from the British Library.

Designed & typeset by Rebellion Publishing

Printed in Denmark

STEEL FRAME

ANDREW SKINNER

SOLARIS

For AGB
who used to tell me stories about flying.

ONE

THE AIR IS heavy with sweat and moist with shipboard rot, mixed so thick that I'm starting to think I'd rather choke than keep on breathing. Hell, there are times I think I might try it just for the change of pace.

The clammy atmosphere settles slick across my skin, presses in on my eyes and ears like I'm halfway drowned already. It dulls my hearing until all I have left is the heartbeat-throb in my temples, and the deep echoes the air seems to carry all on its own. The ringing of our chains and the rumbling press of our bootsoles on the deck. The tremors match a marching count, just like everything else down here.

In this place, the march is all that matters, and there's nothing we could do to challenge it that wouldn't cost us blood or broken bones. We could try to hold our ground, maybe shake the order if we were brave or stupid enough, but the shackles will always hold it better.

And the chain gang does the rest.

It's a beast built on all of our worst impulses, running on fear and fists and clawing fingers. It's a warden's work done by prisoners, and it'll beat the fight out of you every day. You can resist, of course, but the gang will chew you up, break anything that will not bend, and fight itself ragged over what's left. The best choice is to comply, but you have to abandon any hope of making it out the way you arrived. Worse, you have to join in. The rules are simple, but they only work if everyone pulls their weight, and once you understand that—once you know your place among the cogs and grindwheels—you become part of the machine.

We understand. I understand. I've been part of a machine before. I hold the beat because I know better than to try anything else.

It only takes one. One of us to miss the step, to lose our place, and the rest of the gang topples over us. Through us, if our luck's running low. Chances are, the steel is the only thing that'll have a say in how it all turns out, and you can do better than hoping the chain will show you mercy. This old tether wraps everybody on this stretch, holds us straight, and keeps us from fighting back. It makes us measure every step, forces us to set our movements to the rhythm, humming a tune that's just enough to keep us all in line and all in time.

The loudest hum comes from a big Palmirran by the name of Salt, dead ahead, the next one up the chain from me. He's colonial gene-stock, engineered around a chest full of lung and muscle. More muscle than lung, but his airways have more power than the rest of us stitched together, even singing for our lives. He shakes the space around him, setting the whole world to a song that only he seems to know for certain. The chain gang has caught the tune now, and it follows us everywhere.

It came with us off the barges from Kiruna, and now it trails us through mouldy corridors and acid-etched spillways, past pressure heads locked with massive hydraulics, between huge magazines and air-gapped blocks of armour plate.

A squad of long jackets guides us deeper, matching our pace and setting the path ahead. They belong to the company; you can see it on shoulders stitched with NorCol's heavy logo-blocks, sleeves tracked with unit insignias and assignments, cuffs embroidered with a warden's gate.

They watch us through breathermask goggles, and swing steel batons from their hands, not speaking unless we give them reason to. We don't, for the most part, but I can almost hear them carrying the song on the other side of their filters. It seems Salt's odd tune is infectious.

And the echoes get longer with every step.

Long enough now that we're starting to lose the returns. We're floors deeper now than where we began, though I couldn't tell you how far. There's nothing keeping track, and the bowels of this old ship look the same as anything NorCol has to offer. The same grey paint, thick and prone to flaking, streaked ruddy where rust brews and blisters underneath. Cloudy bulbs mark the walls on every eleventh step: every one that's still alive is matched by a neighbour that flickers and spits, and another that leaves its sector in the black. The moist air puts a sheen on everything and a haze around every source of light.

There's no sign of where we are in all this murk and shadow. I could take a chance, ask the wardens, but I prefer to keep my face in its current configuration. I swing my step but keep the rhythm, swaying left when the chain sways right, and craning for a sign of the boat we've landed on. A name would be good, but I could use a number just as well, maybe trade it up and down the line until someone recognised it. Anything's better than what I've got, and what I've got is close to nothing. A general sense of size. The length of corridors, and the height of hatches.

From what I can see and hear, we're somewhere under the maindecks, aboard a tub that's got reason to have more than one kind of deck. An assault carrier, or maybe a big destroyer. A shellboat, maybe, but I don't think I've gotten quite so lucky. The walls don't have company markings yet, but wherever we are, NorCol wants us in line and out of trouble.

They've certainly put the effort in. It takes two to beat a chain gang: one to hold the nose and the other to whip the tail. The wardens know that just like we do, but they've surrounded us with company boots, and made our escorts into a statement of intent. They're here to watch us walk and kick our shins when we start edging off the narrow.

They've been with us twenty, thirty minutes now, if I had to guess. We've come most of a K from the hangar where we arrived. The going is slow, but we could've stretched that distance if it was what we meant to do. We didn't, and we don't. Wherever we're going, there's something like death waiting near the end. And even if there wasn't, there's an art to moving in chain, and slow is the only way to do it that doesn't cost you skin.

There are two heavy rings round my ankles, joined in the middle. The chain runs up from there and around my throat, where it's cinched with a padlock. The lock rubs against my chest, an anchor that's been left in the water a little too long, gone to feathering rust and sea-green scale so thick you'd have to crack your way in just to reach the keyhole. Not that it would do you any good without the Christs-damn key. I've never seen it; not on the day they put me in chain, standing on the block in Kiruna's lime-and-concrete quad, and not any time since. I'm starting to think it doesn't exist.

Chainlinks run back down from my collar, and connect to another pair of ankle hoops in front of me, tight around Salt's huge shins. It's the warden's insurance; if Salt tried to make a run for it, the line would pull tight around my throat and drop me to the deck face-first. Assuming he didn't topple in the process, he'd have to carry me, deadweight and dragging, gagging on my collar. On another convict, that would be a problem, but Salt's nearly twice my size, and heavy even by colonial standards; he's got muscle enough to drag me for several K in any direction he decided to go. I'm lucky. He chooses to be here, as much as anyone chooses to be anywhere. Looking at him, you know they wouldn't have gotten him into shackles unless he'd meant them to.

Even now, he could snatch a warden before the others caught up, snap a spine or crack a skull before they could do anything to haul him short. And he knows it, and knows they know it too. He knows to save the threat for when he needs it, and spends the rest of the time walking to the same tune as anyone else; carefully, and with a little extra chain in one hand. The slack comes from the part of the line that joins his feet to my neck, gathered up loose and wrapped around his fingers. If something snagged when he took a step, he'd let it swing, and save me from scraping myself up off the floor. I do the same for the con behind me, and he does the same for those behind him. The links go both ways; you do what you can, and the others won't go tugging at your feet.

"Chain gang," comes the call from up ahead, "halt!"

We're tethered throat and ankles, the first strung forward and the other one back. There is no *stop*—not any more than there's a *go*. If we want to walk, we have to work our way up to speed, and wind our way down again before we come to rest. Even with a cliff edge up ahead, momentum would carry us four steps and change before we could stop ourselves, and that's without the little hobble at the end.

The jackets wait us out, but they've done this all before. When we're finished dragging our feet, they herd us tight together, and someone shuts an airlock behind us, one of the sergeants testing seals on a door up ahead. We're pressed tightly now, and I can't see much past Salt's shirtless back. I watch his ink instead.

His skin is almost the colour of clay, and colonial tattoowork looks down on me from between the crags of his shoulders. There are tallies and banners for every war he's fought, and dark marks for every rebellion he's helped put down. Odd symbols trace lineage down his spine; a dawning sun for his home fleet, and a curved eclipse for his home ship. From there, it trails into stars and constellations, showing his place among the squads that were once his brothers and sisters. Those last few end in ragged scars, skin and ink lifted out with a combat knife.

There's a hiss, and I yawn through the change of pressure in my ears. The airlock is obvious now that we're in it, built just shorter than a whole gang standing on top of each other. It's narrower than the corridor behind us, but wide enough that a pair of NorCol jackets can push their way past, jangling keys to hand. The cons keep clear, rest their shoulders on the nearest wall, and give me a moment's eyes on where we're going.

MAS-HANG C

says a yellow stencil on the door, whatever that's supposed to mean.

[ALL BERTHS]
AUTHORISED PERSONNEL ONLY

The two jackets get working on the locks ahead, and the rest of their squad walks the line, rattling our shackles and checking the links around our necks, reminding us who's in charge.

Thunder stops them dead, shaking the floor beneath our feet. Somewhere on the decks above us, something huge roars to takeoff.

I trade glances with Salt over his shoulder, and look back over my own. The man behind me meets my eyes. He's another ex-jockey, just like Salt and me, but this one looks like he hasn't seen a steady meal in years, or a shower in twice that. His skin is sickly pale, and his muscles run rangy. Lear, he's called, to match the ugly look in his eye.

"Hangar," he says.

"Burning hard," I reply. "Big enough that it needed launch-assist."

"Big bird," he agrees. "Wide throat like that, probably a corvette."

"Or a lander. LCA Scudderbox."

"The only reason to fly a 'box is if you've got marines on station."

"Which means there's a garrison."

He clicks a finger. "Which means we're riding a carrier, at least. Big enough to haul wings and armour." He spreads a grin, and crews it with ugly teeth. "Maybe they have birds for us."

As the engine sounds subside, I can just about hear the edge of something else.

"What was that?" I ask.

Lear blinks at me. "What was what?"

A low rush, almost a whisper. This time from around us.

"That."

Salt turns as far as he can manage and offers us a smile. "Didn't you hear?"

"Hear what?"

"They say there are clouds outside."

THE JACKETS DON'T leave me time to ask. They're winding us up already, and the line responds on instinct, working through the beginnings of another halting march.

The back of the line decides it. When the second-last con has slack on the neck behind them, they punch the shoulder ahead. Half a second more, and the next con does the same. A shiver works its way through the line until each of us has checked lengths, and made ready for the walk.

The front stamps a boot.

One, two.

The rest of us join in, eyes closed.

One, two.

We wait for the beat, let it carry us along. Salt wakes his ancient tune again.

"Chain gang," comes the call, "march!"

One, two.

Right foot, left.

The first in line steps wide, and the rest of us shuffle along behind, more to keep the timing than because we're moving yet. The next steps out, and the chain keeps creeping.

When we were still new to this, we'd put our hands out, waiting until the one ahead was a full arm's distant before we leant into the stride. Now we do it by feel and tempo. Heartbeats pump and bootsoles roll like tank tracks. We are the machine.

The wardens steer us through the stencilled door I saw before, and then another, sealing each one shut behind us as we go. A few steps in darkness, then light creeping in from ahead: at first, it's barely as bright as the halls we've been crawling through, but it warms quickly, becoming a sunrise up ahead.

13

We stop before it dawns. There's a groan and a shuffle, too sudden for comfort. We bump and stagger and trip. A few collide, or scrape knees and knuckles. Judging by the shouting, someone has fallen over themselves near the front, and the line has to wait while they find their feet, find the rhythm all over again. Another two steps, and there's another stall, another stumble.

Twelve steps after that, and I see what's cut them short.

Christs above and below.

Where the hell *are* we?

Our little tunnel ends on a doorstep, and our low ceiling cuts away. We go from a cramped hole to a cavern, the ceiling suddenly a thousand metres up. We manage to keep the march for a few more beats, but the sudden rush of air and noise rips the song away, leaves us lurching across the threshold and blinking at the bright and chaos.

The hangar is bigger than anything I've ever seen, under NorCol's name or otherwise.

Hot winds blow thick with engine wash, pierced by screaming gunship throats and the guttural flares of shuttles, clouds of fighting craft taxiing through the iron heights above us. Thrusters glow hot enough that I can feel them on my skin, nearly half a K away.

Steel canyons spill out across the horizon, warships nestled within. I count six corvettes in dry-dock, and one massive destroyer at rest: *Okula*, by the markings on its upper decks. A demigod of Open Waters, guns stowed for now. Its hull sparks with welding lights, and its char-black engines gape. Service drones whir and wheel between its masts, swarming around the six-limbed assemblies that climb its cliffside plates.

I don't realise that I'm staring—none of us do, not until there's an angry jacket yanking on our chain. Even then, the wardens have to work to get us moving. Salt has lost his song, and with it any chance the rest of us had of holding firm. We are lost without the marching-count, and every movement ends in a stutter or a trip, grazes smeared bloody on the deck. The jackets stamp alongside us, trying to force a little rhythm back into the line, but it doesn't do us any good, and so they drag us out instead.

Out between the scaffold-limbs of giant cranes, and under a rail-engine that rolls on electromag tracks as wide as I can step. We cross a yard full of flatbed hulks, bunkers full of fuel and one-eighty tonne pallets stacked with munitions. The cranes reach above us, trading monstrous caskets through the air.

After the yard, four lanes of active rail, but the wardens have to hustle to get us across. Huge hauler-engines tear past, forcing us to stagger and choke to clear the path before they catch us. One whips past so close it singes hair and skin in a gale of acid-tinged exhaust.

Halide arrays hang from gantry-tops, arranged like temporary suns, lighting roads and alleys in selective daylight, limning huge hulls in silver. Red strobes mark the legs of the cranes and the bodies of the engine-cars, and add a little crimson to the smog. Nighttime fills the places where the lamps can't reach.

We drop in and out of huge shadows, and march past lines of NorCol marines in bluegrey battledress, all squared up and waiting for the gunboats circling overhead. We pass pillars of steam, duck through sheets of rain from the clouds brewing near the ceiling. Containers rise in patchwork cliffs on either side, stencilled in the marks of a thousand minor companies, dotted here and there with the crests of the great corporations that marshal the darker parts of human space. The gods of old Steyr and ancient Raytheon, of powder-makers and wars that never end.

We stumble through it all, struggling to find a beat. Our ears ring with all the noise, and our sweat runs thicker in the steam. It's been a while since any of us has had anything to drink.

There's more concrete and tar and bonded plating, machines bigger than anything I've ever seen, but most of it's forgotten as soon as we've passed by. My eyes are clouding, merging everything together into a parade of storms and shadows.

Somewhere in the middle, we cross into a clearing. A little

circle of open deck, rimmed by scaffolds and ringfence and barbed-wire coils. A line of metal hoops has been welded to the floor.

"Chain gang, halt!"

But we're already slowing. This is different. The wardens are pulling away.

I look up in time to be blinded.

Someone sweeps a spotlight down the line and leaves me blinking. I clear the spots in time to see heavy silhouettes emerge from the dark on either side: NorCol marines, walking the line and locking our chains to hoops on the deck, rattling our padlocks to check that they're still intact.

They aren't as rough as the wardens were, but there's steel where they had grit. These are soldiers.

I look around, but there's no sign of what we're doing here.

"Welcome to *Horizon*," says someone I can't see, loud enough that it rings in my ears. It takes a second to find the source, a line of bullhorn speakers two storeys up, bolted around a rusty scaffold rail.

Salt's still looking, still blinking.

"Up," I whisper.

He follows my eyes, mumbles his thanks.

A pair of white gloves catch the light, pearly on a filthy handrail. There's a row of teeth in the air above them, just as bright, ratty eyes and over-comb.

Someone turns a lamp on him.

Now that I can see, the man himself is clean and starchy. A little beacon in the grime that clings to everything else. The uniform says he's Colonial Authority; deep grey with rings of gold over his cuffs and braid around one shoulder, gilded epaulettes and collar-tips. There are medals across his chest, but all I can see from here is the glint.

I lean over. "Know him?"

Salt gives me side-eye. "Think I know everyone?"

"You were colonial."

"He's Authority. I was Navy, remember?"

"Guessed I'd give it a try."

One of the soldiers homes in on our voices, but we've got our hands up before she reaches us. She's wearing NorCol's turquoise armour-plate, with a field-blue overcoat. A helmet hides her face, internal systems light her eyes orange through the visor-slit.

"Shut it."

We don't argue. Not with her, and not with the nasty little carbine in her hands.

Beady-Eyes is too high to notice us. "My name is Durer," he says, the words buzzing as the speakers reach their limits. "For those of you who haven't guessed, I am here on behalf of your beloved Authority. Here to make sure that your transfers go as smoothly as possible."

"That's what they call it, then?" I whisper, once the trooper's turned her back.

Salt chuckles. "Call it 'transfer' when what they mean to say is 'sale.'"

"Don't know about you," growls Lear, right by my ear, "but I'd better be expensive."

The carbine finds us again, this time with a finger on the trigger. "Quiet."

I offer her a glare, but Salt does a better job. It comes with the altitude. He's got a whole head and shoulders on her, gun or no gun.

The grunt holds the look, but Durer speaks before she has anything to say.

"To begin, I need confirmation that all of you are here of your own free will." He leans on the last two words like there's a punchline coming. It doesn't. "If not, now is the time to make that plain."

No one moves, and no one speaks.

Durer rolls his palms on the handrail, rubs those cotton gloves oily. "Well?"

More nothing.

"There is no penalty for doing so," he says, monotone, like

he's reading from a script. He laughs suddenly. "But you came a long fucking way just to turn yourselves around."

The chain-gang stands where it's been put. The soldiers don't say anything. No one shares the laugh.

Durer's disappointed. He watches us for a few seconds more, like he's expecting something. Whatever it is, he doesn't get it. He sighs, filling our ears with static.

"I am required by law to give you one hour to make up your minds." He holds out those filthy hands. "Or until I'm satisfied that none of you have been brought here without your clear consent. Conditions of sale and all that." He looks us over. "I think we'd all prefer the latter, correct?"

We don't reply.

"Oh, for Christs' sakes. Raise your hand if you'd rather die out there"—he aims a finger into the distance, at the hangar-locks where shuttles come and go—"than in one of my cells."

I raise my hand without a second thought, and Salt does the same. I can't see much past his bulk, but Lear and everyone behind me has arms in the air.

Durer claps his hands. "Ha! Excellent!" He leans back, and glares at someone short and faceless standing to the side. One of NorCol's administrator corps. A bureaucrat, here to inspect the goods. "There you are," says Durer. "All volunteers, as stipulated. Happy now?"

If there's a response, it's too quiet for us to hear.

Durer turns back and hangs over the handrail at us. "The law entitles each of you to due process. That would normally get in the way of our little arrangement, but today is your lucky day." He straightens, rests a hand on his chest. "Today, *I* am due process."

"Nice to meet you," growls Lear, just loud enough to carry.

There's a quiet second while the chain-gang decides if it's going to duck out of the way or stretch to get a better view. I decide on option one, and so does the con behind Lear. We're waiting for NorCol's boots to come crashing down on us, to haul Lear up by his collar and bloody his lip, maybe break a rib or two.

But Durer puts an end to that before it starts. He shrieks with laughter, filling the air with spit.

"He's insane," mutters someone down the line. At first, I look for the con who said it, but the voice has an edge of filters to it, and a husky NorCol accent. I find the source wearing a company coat, standing near the marine from earlier, both looking just as uncomfortable as the rest of us.

Durer finds himself again, but it's a minute before the snickering stops. He takes a sleeve to the dribble on his chin. "Excellent, excellent." He comes about, blinking like he's forgotten where he is. "What was I saying?"

The administrator leans in, but we don't hear them speak.

"Oh yes. Of course." He shakes himself out, favours us all with an ugly smile. "I am required to inform you that if you proceed from this point, you will forfeit your usual rights and protections under the Articles of Colonisation. Your legal status as a citizen will be suspended indefinitely, subject to the conditions of transfer, et cetera, et cetera." He waves the last of it away. "Raise your hand if you don't get it."

We watch, but no one moves.

Durer pulls himself up on the rail, feet dangling. "This is it! Your last chance!" Another sickly giggle. "*Who wants out?*"

The echoes take a moment to die, but the chain gang keeps its peace.

Durer drops back to the floor, apparently satisfied. The administrator is saying something, but he's already lost interest. He nods, and yawns into an oil-soaked glove. "Yes, yes. Whatever."

A few words more, and he's watching us again.

"That about does it." He puts an open hand out above our heads, holds it there like a greasy benediction. "As presiding colonial officer on this ship, I hereby suspend your citizenship until such time as your sentences are complete, or you die during the term of service. As of right now, you are all property of the Nor Collective." He licks his lips. "Good luck."

TWO

THE CHAIN-GANG TENSES, watching the soldiers on either side. It's us and them, and the Colonial Authority has just relieved us of our rights.

We're still waiting for the fight when shadows part, and a few pairs of troopers step into the light with buckets in their hands. They slosh water up and down the line, running it out in deep ladles. They spill it over our chins and our shirts and across our blistered skins, but each of us gets a fair measure of the company's generosity.

It's shipboard-stale and almost unbearably cold, but for a few moments, it's the only thing that matters in the entire universe.

At the end, we find ourselves under the eyes of a short man in a pair of red overalls.

"Folau," he says, in a voice to match his size. "Anyone here by the name of Folau?"

"Folau!" adds a nearby marine, more loudly. "Is there a Folau here?"

"Thank you, sergeant."

The line doesn't move. We're still recovering, still gawking at the man who came to find us. His eyes are small and sharp and crow-footed at the corners. Engine grease inhabits every wrinkle, but misses the bristle-brush moustache perching on his lip.

"Is there an Arko Folau here?"

"Arko Folau!" yells the sergeant. "Show yourself!"

"Who's asking?"

The chain gang chuckles.

I don't know too many people on the line. When you're locked up, you cluster around familiar things. Mannerisms, for the most part, language and accent close behind, and anything else that gives you something to relate. Salt is colonial, while Lear and I are corporate, but all three of us were jockeys once upon a time, and it's easy enough to see. We picked each other out in the first few seconds after we met, and after that, we kept to ourselves. We spent our time on the barges together, and before that on Kiruna station. Before that, on the shimmer-ship that brought us from the edge of familiar space, launched from a silo on Syndamere. Before *that*, in Reveley Prison, sharing tables in the mess, and watching out for each other on the yard.

If you know where to look, the line is full of little cliques like ours. Former soldiers, pilots and mercs, bloodhounds and hunters and helix-tricks. There are a few plain ol' convicts in the mix, a handful of thieves and murderers added in for good measure, but they're even more obvious than everyone else.

Most of us don't know more than a bare handful of the others, but *everyone* knows Folau.

I don't know what he did before he ended up on the chain, but wherever it was, it burned out any sense of fear he might have had before. Wouldn't be much of a problem if it was anyone but Folau, but his brain has a direct line to the muscles that move his face around.

The moustache looks him up and down, takes a breath to speak, but Folau cuts him off.

"Gonna have to find a bottom bunk somewhere else, old timer. I don't play with pensioners."

The moustache puts out a hand, stalling the sergeant's armoured fists. "*I'm* asking," he says, with as much volume as he can manage. "I've got record here that says you were a greaser. Civilian crew of the CAV *Kei River*. Is that correct?"

"It is. So what?"

"I've got a knuckledragger crew that's short one times mechanic. You want the spot?"

"Shit, yeah."

The moustache nods, flaps some fingers at the sergeant. "Get him out of there."

The sergeant waves a couple of marines up the line, one of them with a pair of bolt cutters in their hands.

"Chin up," says the other.

Folau glares at them.

"You want it or not?" asks the moustache.

Folau turns his glower into a grin. "Do your worst."

They grab him by his hair, yank his head to one side while they pop the lock at his neck. They take another off at his waist, and cut through the shackles on his feet. Arko Folau takes a moment to enjoy his freedom, shaking his boots and running hands up and down his shins. The moustache isn't waiting, already walking away.

"Hop to, convict," growls the soldier with the cutters.

Folau skips into a run, still grinning like a jackass. He tussles Salt and I along the way, earns himself a kick in the shin that nearly trips him over. He and Salt were both colonial, even if they didn't share a boat or branch of service. Still, there's enough familiarity to earn Salt a single-finger salute as Folau turns to catch up.

"We'll miss you too," rumbles Salt.

We watch him jog to catch the old mechanic's silhouette, already fading from view. One of NorCol's jackets splits off from the rest, and follows the two of them away into the dark.

For the first time, I realise that there's a queue.

The next one steps up to where moustache was standing before, and I can already tell what she's looking for. She's got the same long coat as the soldiers do, but hers is unbuttoned, and there isn't a uniform underneath. Instead, she wears the conductive under-layers of a flight suit, matte black with silver plugs where her jacks and spurs connect. She's got the jockey swagger, you could see it from a K away.

Her balance shifts as she walks up to the line, always changing the spacing between her feet. It's something Average Joe Bio has to work to understand. Bio's got instinct, and that little shiver in the back of their ear that warns them if they're about to tip. Keeping balance isn't so much a thought as a feeling.

You lose that once you've been jockeying a while, though. Your machine has gyros and reactive masses and terrain-modelling software, entire subsystems dedicated to keeping it upright and mobile. It rubs off on you after a while, and you start forgetting the habits that made it so easy when you were the only one doing the work.

Whoever she is, she's been at it a long time. She's twitchy, and her skin's so pale it's translucent, her platinum hair buzzed on either side around the metal plugs above her ears. You need surgery to get them installed, boreholes drilled through your skull, but they'll give you a clean feed past anything.

She's got rank, too. A captain's marks on her collar, and a pair of ace's pins on her lapel. Ace and double-ace.

It's probably the only reason she wears the coat. Without it, the NorCol grunts wouldn't know when they were supposed to be saluting. A strip on her breast reads *Hail*.

She takes a moment to focus on us, like she's waiting for her optics to adjust. "There are three jockeys on this line. Please put up your hands."

And there it is.

Moustache got first pick, but he was always going to, just on the off-chance they'd snagged an engineer. Real skills are worth their weight in blood and tungsten. Folau's not an engineer, but the company will take what it can get. There's a lot of money in the shallows, and safety too, so most greasy fingers don't travel any further than Rimir. Wherever we are, I'd take a bet that we're a long way out from there. Open Waters, definitely. Frontier country.

A jockey's worth less than the chance of finding someone with qualifications, but we're more expensive than pilots or gunnery, and almost triple what you'd get for a ground-pounder.

I put up my hand. Salt and Lear do the same.

Salt nudges me, catches my eye and sends it down the line.

"Ha."

There are two others, right near the front, waving their hands like idiots.

Hail sighs. "*Three* jockeys." She looks us over again, and decides to start at the front.

The first one up is a con called Todd, and I recognise him in an instant. He's been trying to walk like a jockey for as long as he's been on the chain. He's got the unfocussed look, the hand-eye delay, but he doesn't understand what they are. He seems to think he should swing wide and out of sync with everything, stuttering like the jockeys in the flicks. He doesn't know what it's like to concentrate on everything you do, just to be sure that you're the one actually doing it.

Hail marks him in a second, shoots him down. "Next," she says, already coming about.

"Hey," growls Todd. He starts forward. "Get back he—" One of the marines steps on his chain; he's airborne for a second, body and soul, before he finds the deck with an ugly thud. A NorCol boot keeps him where he is.

The next con drops her hand before Hail even gets there. She's some no-name who's been trying the same tricks as Todd, with a little less noise but a little more skill. She recognised the three of us for what we were, and went to work on Salt. Tried a smile and then a little skin, then a little more, but the old colonial brushed her off. After that, it was Lear, but she ejected before it got too far. She tried me last of all, but it was half-hearted. Must have figured she'd have better luck with the boys.

She had more of a chance than Todd ever would. She used to be a privateer for Sigurd or something, and had enough flight-time that she knew what a jockey looked like. And what one didn't look like.

Hail nods on her way past. "Good move."

She finds us. "Name?"

"Salt."

"Just Salt?"

"Just Salt."

"No surname?"

He rolls his shoulders. "Lost it."

She bites. "Where?"

"Dakar Phradi."

Jesus.

The chain gang gapes at him. The NorCol crews do too.

"Unit?" asks Hail.

Colonial Navy, 3rd Expeditionary, attached to the CNV *Babylonian*. He doesn't have to say it. Anyone who's more than ten years knows the story. The first human brush with something we genuinely couldn't explain.

I'm staring just as much as the rest of the line, but I can't hold him up on not telling me before. The chain-gang isn't a place for sharing.

"Lost that too," says Salt.

"The 3rd is all gone," says Hail, cool to the touch. "No wreckage. No survivors."

"Not gone," rumbles Salt. "Just lost."

She rolls with the punches. "What was your charge?"

"What else?" he chuckles. "I survived when I wasn't supposed to. Cowardice, obviously."

She watches him for a moment more, but it looks like she's made up her mind. If he was faking, maybe he'd have chosen a less interesting lie.

"All right," she says, as her eyes switch targets.

And find a lock on me. "You?"

"Rook," I say. "Eyo Rook."

"Unit?"

I start with "NorCol," and wait a heartbeat after that, but Hail gives nothing away. No special treatment for one of their own—not that I'm surprised. "Ten-Seven-Seven Mechanised. C-SAR."

It's pronounced *see-sar*, and it stands for Combat Search and Rescue. Can-openers on angel wings.

She nods. "The helmet is yours, then."

"Helmet?"

"Later." There's a strange edge to her look. "What was your charge?"

Here I was hoping I could get past without her asking me. I grit my teeth, and spit it out: "Two counts damage to property, one count desertion."

The first count is for damaging company equipment, and the second is for damaging an employee. Me, in this case. I damaged myself, and damaged my machine in the process. I've got some nerve-damage from where it saved me, even when I didn't want it to.

It's the long way round for saying that I lost the plot one day, stretched past breaking. It's a code: 'desertion' doesn't mean running away; the three-count is what anyone else would call a suicide attempt.

Hail holds my gaze a moment more. "And?"

"Two counts of murder."

I wasn't myself.

I expect more questions, but all she does is nod and take aim at the rangy shape behind me. "Name?"

"Jonathan Lear."

"Unit?"

"Didn't have a name."

"Where?"

Lear smirks. "All over."

Hail growls at him. "Which company, convict?"

"Loh Kustar."

"You were a Locust?" She sounds surprised. I would be too, if I hadn't spent a few weeks tethered to the man.

Loh Kustar is a tiny company, with just a few thousand machines to its name. I jockeyed with NorCol for most of a decade and only ever met two of the things: cheap commercial frames clocked well past the safety margins, bulked with after-market parts, salvage, and homebrew steel like nothing you've ever seen. Their jockeys are even rarer than their machines, and the stuff of crazy stories. Lear's are crazier than most, but I've got a few of my own.

I watched a Locust dodge a bullet, my bullet, at less than fifty metres—point-blank, when you're six storeys tall. I watched a wingmate crater himself trying to match an impossible turn, a machine that was nearly all engine outperformed by a flying scrapheap.

Lear nods. "Dragoon. Pattern 19, revision 6." As if that should mean anything to anyone.

"Charge?"

"Criminal conduct in a time of war."

Hail crosses her arms. "You were convicted of a *war crime?*"

Lear holds up a handful of fingers. "Crimes. Plural."

"What did you do?"

"What the company wanted me to do, instead of what it was telling me to."

That seems enough for her. Hail has weighed us up, done the dance. But there's one more thing.

She puts eyes on us, suddenly crystal clear. "Did you choose to be here?"

Lear rattles his chains. "Well, we didn't just wander in."

Hail holds her ground. "I need you to spell it out, convict. Right now. Do you mean to be here?"

I frown at her. "We took the deal, if that's what you're asking."

Salt nods. "There wasn't much to lose."

Hail almost smiles at that. "You'd be surprised." She waves to the crew with the bolt cutters. "Get them out. I've got what I ordered."

IT TAKES THE cutting crew a moment to decide where to start, but with Salt and Lear for company, it was always going to be me.

They work with calm detachment, break the damned lock on my chest and give me back my feet, all in just a few seconds. Seems they don't know where the key is either. They leave me to rub the blister on my collarbone and to find my stride without the chain.

The next choice is harder than the first. In the end, they decide on Salt. I would too: he could do you just as much damage with his chains on as he could without, and he doesn't give them any reason to change their minds. He leans so they can reach his throat, keeps every movement slow and obvious. When they're done, they step aside to let him through; he hasn't given them any trouble, and they don't offer any themselves. They're already sizing up Lear.

Salt finds me in Hail's shadow, the both of us standing taller now without the weight around our necks. "Still alive?" he whispers.

"Enough to regret it. You?"

He nods back at Lear. "Enough to enjoy the show."

NorCol armour crowds the chain, weapons free. No one is looking forward to this. If any one of us was going to make a play, the jackets figure it might be him. Somewhere else, something in it for him, and they'd be right. But he's also not stupid; I've watched him counting heads, and half-heard the mumbled calculations. Every outcome is the same.

The marines call in a few extra hands, and move in circles so there's always an open line of fire. A hair out of place, and they'll light him up where he stands.

Lear keeps his peace, hands up, palms exposed. He holds perfectly still as they pat him down, stretches his greasy neck for the cutters, and even manages to smother that awful, everpresent smile.

The jackets watch him long enough to see him out of arm's reach, and a second longer to be sure he isn't coming back.

"Where to?" he asks, once he's caught us up.

We look back for Hail, but she isn't waiting.

WE FOLLOW HER back into the noise, but there isn't space for questions. It's enough work keeping stride and not tripping over ourselves.

A pair of marines swing out behind us, and keep a few paces clear. To begin with, I figure they want the distance. Nothing's dangerous like a con with idle hands, so they spread themselves out, and give themselves time to react if we decide we're going to make a break.

A few minutes further out, and I'm not so sure. They're starting to trail, jogging every so often so they can keep us in line of sight. They slack a little more after that, only drawing level when Hail gives us a minute to breathe. Even then, they spend the time picking at their boots and staring into nothing, looking at everything but the three of us. I keep waiting for Hail to tread on a couple of toes, maybe get in their faces a little bit. She's seeing it just as well as I am, but she doesn't seem to care.

"Hop to," she says, but it's only aimed at us. "We're a long way from our birds."

She starts along the same path that brought us in, through the loading yards and across the huge rails again, but the familiarity doesn't last long. She turns without warning. The three of us follow, but we can't help trading glances. This place is full of blinds and gulleys, and NorCol's jackets haven't turned the corner yet.

It would be so easy to get ourselves lost, and hard to get found again. Or it would be, if we all had shit for brains.

We turn as one and run to catch her heel. We're jockeys, after all. We can put our hands up if we have to, but none of us like the idea of fighting on our own two feet. Even if we did, it would be just a matter of time before NorCol ran us down and stretched us out where all the other cons could see.

We find Hail waiting for us, a couple of turns ahead, with arms crossed and half a grin. The jackets roll up a moment later, hands on their weapons and easy on their feet. Two more edge out of the shadows, carbines ready.

She waves them off. "It's all right. We're clear."

It takes them a moment to relax. "Understood," says the one with rank. The carbines turn away, leaving us with the original two. Now, they keep right on our heels. This isn't like the wardens from before. Relaxed but awake, and here because the company wants the certainty, rather than because Hail thinks she's in for a fight.

She'd asked us if this was where we meant to be, and we'd said it was, but that wasn't enough. She had to give us the chance to run, to throw it all away.

Looks like we've passed the test. The first one, anyway.

And so she takes us deeper.

We stagger down a staircase carved into the concrete floor and take a ladder several storeys down. We walk through channels made to carry water, sewerage, and shipboard waste, then along corroded walkways that look like they're sinking into the spoil. We find a hatch at the end of it all, and swollen paint and flaking metal make us force it open. We try hands and elbows first, but Salt takes the load on his shoulders, pushes through in a cloud of rust.

The other side is all bright light and rushing noise. We spill out into a canyon: pale, metallic cliffs that climb a hundred metres tall on either side. The dry dock's empty now, but there are still signs of the things that were here before us. Engine tests have left long, black streaks across the walls, and ugly ruts mark the floor, worn by massive landing-gear.

The high walls channel sounds from all across the hangar, turning them into a single, endless wash. The noise leaves me dizzy, sweeps me along with it. This place wasn't built for humans.

We duck through an exhaust vent and follow Hail up to the tops of the containers. We walk across gantry-ways and scaffolding, then drop back down to the hangar floor. It's hard going. The pace is drumming me close to exhaustion, and I can see that the other two aren't doing much better. Salt and Lear hunch like they're still wearing chain, and walk with that strange half-limp you get when there's shackles around your feet.

I've managed to get my neck straight and my shoulders back, but every time we turn a corner, I find myself marching again, Salt's blasted tune still stuck in my head.

I fight it, but it takes work. I hum a NorCol shanty, and match Hail's stride for a few steps, now a little faster, then a little slower. I have to concentrate on breaking the rhythm, but it never seems to last. I look up to find Salt and Lear moving to the beat still playing in my head, humming just loud enough to hear.

Lear notices it, takes his eyes off the floor and gives me a lopsided grin. He immediately snags his boot on a break in the decking. He catches himself before he's tipped too far, turns the fall into a stagger.

"They've fucked us up," he observes, turning his foot over in the light. The crack was wide enough to swallow a boot, but he got away without leaving any skin behind. "Haven't they?"

It's a little too bitter for me, but Salt works a chuckle. "We're jockeys, Lear. I haven't walked this straight in years."

"Not like this. Feels like I'll be wearing shackles 'til the day I die."

"It gets better."

We look up to find Hail watching us, a hand on her hip.

"It won't happen tomorrow, but it'll happen."

A concrete platform rises behind her, the letter C stencilled on one side in bright yellow, tall as I am and almost as wide as Salt. A monorail train waits for us at the top.

Hail plugs a thumb over her shoulder. "For now, I need you to get inside."

"Where are we going?" I ask, without thinking.

Hail watches me. "Does it matter?"

It does, I realise.

I spent three weeks on a windowless shuttle to get here, months before that to reach Kiruna station, wherever the fuck that was relative to everything else. The most of two years, if you count the time I spent in limbo, waiting for someone to buy my time.

All that, only to be dropped into the bowels of a ship that I didn't know existed, in a place that no one's bothered to name. I don't know where I am; not on this ship, not anywhere. I don't even know what the stars look like outside.

"It matters," says Salt, before I can reply.

Hail almost smiles. "All right. At this moment, we're standing on the starboard edge of Hangar C. You three are transferring to my unit, based in D-Lower."

"There are four hangars, then?" asks Lear. "Three more like this?"

"The NCSV *Horizon* has twelve master hangars, A through L, and they're all the same as this one. A through C are dry-dock and transitional, six corvettes and two destroyers apiece. D through F are where the shells live. G and H are the hives where the fighters hold up at night. The rest are modular bays, configured on demand."

Christs.

"Where *are* we?" I ask.

"This is Hangar C—"

"No," rumbles Salt. He steps forward, arms crossed over his chest. "I've never heard of a ship this size. Not even in the Authority. Not anywhere."

"*Horizon* is one of the original six; one of the dreadnoughts," says Hail, without so much as a blink, "and the largest warship ever built."

"But where the hell are we?"

The jackets step up, but Hail waves them down. "We are holding anchor in Open Waters, beyond the frontier. Where, exactly? I couldn't tell you. It's deeper than you've ever been before, and that's all it pays to know for now. The rest we'll fill in later, when you can handle it."

"I've been deeper than most," I say.

"Been swimming all my life," says Lear.

She meets our eyes, one after the other, but she doesn't give an inch. "You haven't been deep like this."

Lear bites back. "How would you know?"

"I know because *Horizon* is it. Because you are now further from the Origin System than anyone else in human history."

"Where?" asks Lear, his voice catching just enough for us to hear it.

"Wouldn't help if I told you."

The floor shakes, and another train appears in the distance, following another line through platform C. It howls past, a blur of white and turquoise, a rush of ozone-stink. Hail doesn't look back. She's watching the three of us, the wind catching streamers of her hair, tugging at the collar of her coat.

For a heartbeat, I catch the edge of something else. A scar, curved around her throat. Little bubbles of tissue where her skin snagged between the loops of a chainlink collar.

The train shrieks away, leaves us alone in the quiet.

"Because *Horizon* isn't on the map."

THREE

THE TRAIN IS plain inside, every flat surface stamped with NorCol's blocky logo. Glossy seats line the walls on either side, with thick red restraints ending in heavy silver buckles. I've seen lighter belts in a fighter-pilot's chair.

By the time I make it in, Salt's already claimed a place, taking up two seats and most of a third, having to slouch with the wall as it curves into ceiling.

Lear folds himself into a seat nearby. There was never much of him to begin with, but there seems even less when he sits down next to Salt. He draws his feet up and rests his chin on a knee. I set myself down across from the two of them, and Hail stands between us, a hand looped through one of the straps hanging from the ceiling. The other seats stay empty.

"Where'd the shadows go?" asks Lear.

Hail sways as the train begins to move. "Back to their posts."

He offers her an ugly smile. "Aren't you worried?"

She returns the smile with teeth and flips her coat back around a service weapon on her hip. It's the kind NorCol issues to all its jockeys; nine shots in the mag, single-stack, barrel wide enough to fit your finger. Not enough to fend off another machine, if that's what brought you down, but it isn't made for that. It's designed to keep the vultures off your back if you eject, and to give you fangs if someone tries to pry you out of your pod. She's probably got it running composite shot; made to shatter if it hits anything airtight or important, but more than enough to make a mess of a smartass con.

She rests a hand on the grip. "Aren't you?"

Lear eyes the gun. "Not while we're getting on so well."

Hail pulls the coat straight, smooths it out. "Have they told you how this works?"

"More than the Grey did?" asks Lear.

"More than the Grey did." She nods. "Durer is a piece of work, but he's just the Authority's local mouthpiece. A few months ago, you were taking up space in an Authority cell, eating Authority chow and breathing their air. Now you aren't, and the chances are you never will again."

"How much did we cost?"

She raises an eyebrow at him, but he doesn't shrink from the question. He lets his feet down to the floor and spreads his hands out on his lap. "We may be cons, but we three are premium." He nods at me. "I've only bumped into NorCol S&R once before, but they flew my ass off. Made me work for my supper." He clicks a finger at Salt. "And you got a survivor of the Third-Christs-damn–Expeditionary itself, lost to fucking aliens or something. I mean, fuck, we're hot stuff, aren't we? Gotta be expensive."

"I don't have a number."

Lear looks her up and down. "But you've got an inkling."

Hail doesn't blink. "Sales come up by the block, and the Authority mixes it up so the corps don't get to cherry-pick. An engineer eats as much as a jockey does, and about as much as a dock-hand or a driver or anything else. Breathes the same, just for good measure." She rolls a shrug. "We paid more than the usual."

"You mean, you bribed someone."

"We added a little gravy, and increased the chances we'd get something worth keeping. The fee was for everyone on the line, though."

"You must end up with a lot of cheap meat."

Hail glowers at him, and he matches it.

"What? I saw the rest of that gang. Hell, I lived and breathed

36

with 'em. A lot of human waste in there." He snorts. "Is this how NorCol keeps the furnaces running? Just stack a bunch of no-names together, grind 'em up for fuel?"

"It could be…" I say.

"…if you keep this up," says Salt, finishing the thought.

Hail cuts through it. "How much did they tell you?"

"The same thing they tell everyone else, as far as I can tell." I roll my head back, feel the kinks clicking loose in my neck. "Recruiters get us out on the yard for an hour, give us all the same lecture. We sign up, they say, and do some dirty work for one of the corps. In return, we get to stretch our legs, and the Authority knocks a little time off our sentences."

"Why do you think that is?"

"Economics. We're cheap."

"Speak for yourself," grumbles Lear.

But Hail is shaking her head. "Why do you think they take cons, specifically?"

"Because the deeds are *dirty*," says Salt, stretching arms out on either side. "And we're in jail already."

But Hail's look pulls me short. "Mercs do most of that stuff already, don't they?" I ask. "Mercs and Werewolves and Dagger Chaks."

She nods. "Even if they didn't, the companies always find someone up to the task. They found you three, after all, and all in the same block. Neat coincidence, don't you think? They can scratch just about anything out of the grime." The car sways, but she's rock-steady. "This is about something else."

I understand. This is about dying.

"What happened to the others?"

Hail locks her eyes on me, but doesn't answer right away.

"It's a fair question," says Salt. "Four jockeys, counting you; that's the normal flight size. You're picking three of us up in one go, which means that you're missing three units. All of your stick. What happened to them?"

"They died."

"Worked that out already," I say. "How bad?"

"Honestly?" she asks.

"If possible."

"Not as bad as it could have been, but bad enough. We got split up, and a Sigurd crew pounced on them in the storm. If there were ejectors, the wind carried them away."

"Storm?" I trade glances with the other two. "What do you mean, *storm*? Where are we?"

She leans in. "How much *did* they tell you?"

"About this place?" I cross my arms. "Nothing, apparently."

"I'll start at the beginning, then. One, the Authority doesn't touch your sentences. They keep rolling, same as before."

Lear blinks at that. "What? The recruiters said—"

"That you'd get your time cut?" Hail laughs at him. "You thought it would be that easy? Murderers and war criminals and anything else you can imagine, and they just let you out early?"

"That's what they said."

"Well, from where you're sitting, it'll definitely seem like they did."

I sit up and glare at her. "What does that mean?"

Hail opens her mouth to speak, but a siren interrupts. The car brakes hard, and she has to fight to stay on her feet.

"What's going on?" I shout, but it's lost to the noise.

"Belts!" yells Hail.

The car stops dead as we yank at our restraints. Lear gets his closed in a moment, and I'm not too far behind. Salt gives up after a few seconds—the belts are made to fit NorCol employees, not colonials. He braces himself against the seats, one boot pressed hard against the other side of the aisle, arms spread wide.

Automated shutters roll down across our windows, but not before I get a look outside. NorCol uniforms sprint across the open docks below us, and giant walkers kneel, driving anchors into the floor.

A few jackets are caught out in the open. They drop to the deck and put their hands over their heads.

Something clatters under the floor, like locks being driven home.

"What's going on?" I finally manage.

Hail pushes herself back in her seat and closes her eyes.

"Tide," she says. Just as it hits.

It starts with a bubble in my stomach; the kind you get when you're breaking atmosphere and started edging micro-gee. My inner ears tell me that we're turning, that the floor is becoming the wall across the walkway from me, and that I'm strapped to seats on the ceiling. Belts float in the air around me, coiling like they're in freefall. It lasts half a heartbeat, less.

And then it's done.

At first, all I can hear is the rush of blood behind my ears. Everything else come in a second later, but choppy, like it's being filtered through a turbofan. The shutters climb our windows, and patchy light creeps in from outside, the air around us suddenly thick with dust. Lear is exactly where we left him, his grip denting the seats. Salt hasn't moved far, but I can see raised veins and sheets of sweat. He held himself in place through all of that, boots and fingertips and sheer force of will. Hail is looking out the window.

I follow her gaze. "What the fuck was that?"

Outside, steel screams and sirens wail, smoke rises in the distance. Containers lie scattered across the hangar floor, cracked open or perched on piles of wreckage. A crane lies on its side, neck broken. Fire crews tear along the hangar's internal highways, and drones swarm above, lines of foam spewing from their nozzles. A shuttle hangs loose in the gantries above, gushing fuel that falls like rain.

"Christs," mutters Lear.

"Christs is right," replies Hail, eyes unfocussed. "That's another one."

"Another what?"

She doesn't look back at me. "Tide. A string of gee waves, starting smaller than you can feel, but ramping up to one huge burst, exponential. The last one big enough to give you a feel like flying."

"You said 'another.'"

She nods. "The first was about two weeks ago. The outstations figure they're coming from somewhere deeper in."

'Deeper'?

But Hail's changed focus again. She perks up, listening to something I can't hear. Someone is calling in over the net, piped in through the wetware in her ears. She sheds her restraints, stands to pace the train. "Then I need you to get someone to override this car. We're still clamped," she says, stooping to look out the windows again.

The locks clatter beneath us and the train pulls off, sudden enough to make Hail stumble. She collects herself and keeps pacing as if nothing happened. "Thank you. We're moving now; ETA is a couple of minutes. Try and contain it until I arrive." She cuts the line with a blink and slumps back into a seat. "Hold on," she whispers.

I pop my restraints, and wave a hand to catch her eyes. "What's happened?"

Her face is dark for a moment, then outlined in stark white light. We've hit a passage between the hangars, and the windows fill with tunnel-black. Halide lamps skip past us, drawing her features silver, then burying them back in shadow again. She watches me, her eyes bright in the glow, beads of light in the sudden gloom.

"The Juno's broken loose."

WHERE HANGAR C was a valley, D is a ravine.

D's walls are half a K away, but you can't see much past the huge single-berth blocks that close in around us, skyscrapers flipped through ninety degrees and anchored to the hull on either side. Self-contained hangars, with their own crews and life support, munitions stores and fire suppression.

Each one is made to hold a single shell: the machines we've been brought here to fly.

I've seen others like them before, but never so many. There must be two hundred blocks in here, probably more. Heavy hatches mark the sides, airlocks nearly thirty metres tall, with loading pads on every doorstep like floating balconies.

There'll be locks on the hulls as well; they can expose each block to the vacuum outside, or seal it off again on demand. Launching shells is dangerous business and catching them is even worse, so the ship seals every unit off from the others. If things go wrong, *Horizon*'s crew can isolate a block and void all the air until the fires go out. The jockey just better be holding breath.

"Here is fine," says Hail, to the voice in her head again.

I look up in time to watch her stand, bracing herself as the train tests it brakes.

"Fine for what?" I ask.

"Shortcut," says Hail. She's already up on the seats, one boot on either side of the aisle. She rams a fist into the ceiling and something pops; the panel breaks loose on the second hit, shedding paint-chips and dust. She coils, then pounces, pulls herself out by fingertips.

I find my feet as fast as I can and scramble up behind her. I don't have the muscle to jump as high as her, but I kick out and hunt for grip. It's slippery, but I've got enough to support my weight.

Hail looks down at me, coat billowing. "Stay here!" she yells, just audible over the rush. "Get off at the next platform! Someone will pick you up!"

"Like hell!" I yell, and keep pulling until I've got my chin level with the roof.

I'm burning up, feeling half like death and the rest like falling. But for the first time in what feels like forever, I've got some control over where I'm going.

Hail frowns at me for a moment, and I match the look with a glare. She shakes her head but offers me a hand anyway and hauls me up without a sound.

A NorCol gunship slows to a hover just above our heads, vents and fins twitching as they correct, the pilot holding steady with barely a metre to spare. Two jumpsuits hang from the slide-door, all helmets and combat cladding.

"You first!" yells Hail, waving at me for their benefit.

I step up and the jumpsuits pull me clear in one smooth move, throw me into the compartment behind them. Hail arrives a heartbeat later, and they lock us down with practised hands. The pilot turns the boat around on a hair and pulls away hard enough that I'm counting gees.

Salt and Lear watch us through the hole in their ceiling.

"There a shell loose?" I ask, as loud as I can. It's just enough to hear myself shout.

Hail jams a headset down over my head, does the same for herself.

"Say again."

"What happened?" I say, too loud for the sudden quiet. "Sorry."

She shakes her head and misunderstands me. "The next platform is ten, fifteen minutes away," she replies. "The elevator to our blocks is ten more after that, assuming there's no one in the way. I can't wait for that."

"And there's a shell loose?"

She nods, and holds up two fingers. "Second time."

"Operator?"

She shakes her head. "Not for a while."

"It's moving without a jockey on board? What about internal logic?"

"Autopilot and IL will shut down when you ask them to, and we're asking," she replies. "This is different."

"Different how?"

"That's the problem. We don't know exactly."

She looks like she's about to say something else, but the gunship pulls around hard, crushing us into our seats, then throwing us back against our restraints as it stops itself dead in the air. The slide-doors roll back and the jumpsuits loom over us, breaking the clasps on our belts and hauling us out of our seats. They salute Hail on the way out but ignore me. I return the favour. I'm watching Hail and plotting my own way down to the deck below us: a landing pad, attached to one of the huge sub-hangar blocks. She's moving in a second, and I have to sprint to catch up.

We drop into a crowd shielding their eyes and ears as the gunship pulls away. There's a security detail up front with rifles in their hands, but they don't hold us up. We have to shove our way through a line of silver coats behind them; a fire-crew, watching and waiting, whispering to the suppressor drones hovering nearby. They slow us down, but they don't mean to. They probably sortied when the tide hit, but something's keeping them from getting at the problem, left them milling around on a blast-hatch, trading glances and awkward laughs, looking up at the block's main doors looming over all of us.

I soon see why.

Hail and I push through the hatch that closes the block off from the rest of D.

Standing between us and the airlock to the hangar itself is a shell, almost as tall as the main doors. My heart skips at the sight of it, but it isn't a Juno.

This is insurance, standing tall like there's a jockey in the saddle, nearly seven storeys of jagged armour and control surfaces, shaped mostly like a human being. Thrust-vector spines run out from its shoulders and jut from the back of its beaklike head. Enamel-white paint coats most of its skin, turning to NorCol's turquoise on the tips of its fins and the hard corners of its hull. It stands with its feet spread, and the gates to its missile tubes open on either side of its chest like ruffled feathers. It's missing the usual weapon mounts on its arms and shoulders, traded for something that looks like it used to be a signal mast or supporting strut—a piece of *Horizon*'s massive architecture, ready to swing like a club.

The shell is an M661-E, 'Decatur.' It's recent, probably less than a decade old. Which explains the strut.

A gun is only as good as the rounds left in its mag and the rate of its action. Once upon a time, arms manufacturers built with close quarters in mind, issuing their machines with combat drills, lances, and massive knives that could hold ground if the fight ever got toe-to-toe and bingo ammunition. As the guns got better, and the ranges so long that you'd never see the hits, they stopped issuing iron and started building for speed and eyesight instead.

And Decatur here is the latest and greatest at that. It's made for fighting distant specks and little echoes on its scopes, PHADAR sparks and heat-ghosts against background nothingness. Anything closer by, and it has to improvise. The strut is heavy enough, even if the machine wasn't made to wield it. In the hands of a shell, *any* shell, it'll do as much damage as they need it to.

Assuming the backwash from those missiles doesn't fry us first.

Hail is yelling at someone when I finally catch her up.

"There was nothing we could do," says a shape in a fireproof suit. He pulls the hood clear, revealing a deepset welder's tan and a faceful of beard. A knuckledragger, judging by the machine oil that lives in his pores. "Crew tells me they were opening the storage casket on your request."

"It was overdue for overhaul. *Years* overdue."

"It's overdue for the scrapyard, Hail."

"Just tell me what happened."

"The tide happened. It cracked the door on the casket with the shell still inside. Snapped the hinges."

"And now it's just *loose?*" She takes a breath, lets it out. "What about containment?"

The knuckledragger shakes his head. "No luck. We've tried magnetising the floor, but the Juno's old. A lot of freaky alloys in there."

"Envelopes?"

"No shields yet, and won't be for a while. Generators are still warming up."

"That idiot is going to kill us."

They turn to look at me, but I'm not looking back.

"Tell that jockey to close their fucking tubes," I growl, waving up at the Decatur. "They're going to smoke us."

The beard jerks a thumb at the airlock behind him. "You going to fight that thing, then?"

Hail hauls him short. "Do it."

He glares at me. "And who is this?"

"One of mine," she replies, without a moment's hesitation. "She's also right. Get those tubes locked, right now."

"If the Juno decides it's taking down the doors, this machine is all that's standing between us and getting pasted, Hail."

"Won't do us any good if we're dead already, Kadi."

He holds her look for a moment longer, but he's already sunk, and he knows it. He blinks, and the implant displays in his eyes come to life, irises aglow with orange holographics. He blinks a few commands after that, and listens to someone speak inside his ear. His face contorts. "Then you'll have to make do," he tells the short straw on the other side of the line. "Get them shut."

The Decatur glances at us.

"You heard me."

It shifts its grip on the mass of steel in its hands, but locks its tubes.

"That's better. Look lively."

It turns back to stare at the door, shifting its feet. The movements are sticky, like there's a nugget at the wheel.

"Tower wants you to make a call," says the knuckledragger, eyes back on us. Hail takes a breath to respond, but he waves her off. "I know you've got a special arrangement, but that's why *you* are the one doing the calling. Either you find a way to shut it down"—he puts a thumb over his shoulder—"or Tower tells *him* to shut it down for you."

"WHO WAS THAT?"

Hail unscrews a blackened bolt and hands it back to me. "The beard? That's Sul Kadi: chief maintenance and technical support, big-boy knuckledragger for this sector of D. In theory, he belongs to me, but he's professional NorCol."

"And doesn't like taking orders from a con?"

The chuckle is bitter. "No, but he'd be a bastard even if I wasn't." She tosses me another bolt and leans in to start working on the next.

It's hot work. We're crouched in one of the ducts connecting the block to its primary life-support systems. There are six others, and together they're enough to handle all the airflow the block could need. One by one, the gauge is just wide enough for us to move on our hands and knees, to sit on our haunches maybe, but not a whole lot more. Just a little too tight for prising our way through a filter-grate.

"What happened to it?"

"The Juno?" Another bolt pops loose, five more to go. Hail drags a sleeve across her forehead and offers me the wrench. "It belonged to someone I knew. Beast of an operator. Something of a local legend, so long as you had clearance to know about it. It's his rep that keeps the machine alive, not mine."

"How did he die?"

"Bad luck, because it wasn't skill that did it. A Sigurd machine hit him, rail slug, hole this size." She measures it out between her finger and her thumb, and aims her eye through the middle. "The Juno didn't feel a thing, even managed to fly itself back home. The round didn't damage anything mechanical."

"But it buttered the jockey."

She leans back against the duct, catches the next bolt when I toss it to her. "Took longer to wash the cockpit than it did to fix the hole."

"And you kept it shuttered."

"Since the moment it got back. I knew it wasn't for the best, but every time we boot it—" she breathes in, out, holds her hand for the next bolt. "Every time we boot it, it pumps the cockpit with hard audio. A couple of techs got their eardrums burst."

"It was trying to drown them out."

"It succeeded. Once they were clear, it slammed the locks on its hatches and went dormant. It took most of a week just to beat the locks, and longer to get it shut down properly. I wanted to start it again, but without a jockey—"

Somewhere up ahead, metal shrieks as it bends. Huge footsteps shake the ground, and something spills across the hangar floor. We can hear rivets forced from their sockets, spat out like shrapnel.

Hail helps me roll the last of the bolts, our hands locked together on the wrench. We're both panting by the end, but her gaze is full of fire. She's back at the grate in a heartbeat, prying at it with her fingertips.

I catch her arm. "Why are you doing this?"

She glares at me. "You heard Kadi. They're going to kill it."

I don't let go. "Why? Why this machine?"

She deflates, but you wouldn't know it from the look in her eye. "Juno was a strange series. They were built in the earliest phases of the Cluster Trials."

Before we realised that putting consciousness into war-machines was a bad idea.

"It's insane."

She shakes her head. Shakes all over. "No, but that's the problem. It knows exactly where it is, what it is, and how far it's come. It remembers everything."

"It remembers *him*, doesn't it? That operator of yours."

"It does."

"All right."

"All right?" She stares back at me. "Why are *you* doing this?"

"A knuckledragger just threatened you, out in the open, and didn't split his lip on the deckplates. Can you think of any boat where the jockeys would watch that go down? From a 'dragger?" I almost laugh, but it's too bitter for me. "Ever served on a boat where you wouldn't have to drag someone off him?"

"There'd be a riot."

"Exactly." I meet her gaze. "I'm part of your flight now, right? I have to live here, in all of this?"

"You are. You do."

"I have to live with fucking Sul Kadi?"

That earns me a smile. "You do."

I nod. "I've got your wing."

Steel slams into concrete, hard enough that we can feel the impact. The ducts rattle around us. Hail is back at the grating in a flash, but I'm with her now. We inch our fingers around the corners, lift it out into our hands. We flip it over on its corners and feed it back the way we came.

Hail risks a glance around the corner. "Ready?" she whispers.

"What's the plan?"

"I try talking."

"And if that doesn't work?"

Her smile is grim. "That's where you come in."

"Power supply?"

"The reactor is stone-cold, so it'll be running on a hard connection to the ship."

I take a breath. "Where does it connect?"

"The Juno's storage cradle. You run for that." She points. "If you can't reach that"—her fingers turn, ninety degrees—"you try for the maintenance boards. Whatever you can get to first."

"How long after that?"

"The batteries are designed to handle life support and mindstate continuity in an emergency. They weren't meant to keep the machine at speed." She weighs it out, eyes closed for a moment. "It won't be spending anything on keeping a jockey alive, so I'd say thirty seconds. Maybe a minute."

I nod, and try to fill my lungs. "All right. That's it, then?"

"That's it," she replies, and puts an eye around the corner. "Ready?"

"Ready."

"Good." Hail sets down on knees and fingers like a sprinter. "If that doesn't work, I want you to run."

THE JUNO STANDS in the furthest corner of its little hangar, near the heavy airlocks that open into space.

It's smaller than I was expecting, head and shoulders shorter than the pale thing standing outside. Where the Decatur was slender and prickly, all jagged edges and deflection zones, the

Juno was built to take hits up front. Thick armour lies in bands across its chest, and wide panels cover its shoulder joints. Ablators have been bolted over every flat surface: thick ceramic and moulded metal plates, made to break away under fire.

Some of the plating is new, but most of it isn't. The hull used to be covered in burgundy paint, almost the colour of a scab, but bullets and shrapnel have cut through to the steel in a thousand places. Dust has ground it smooth wherever metal rises to an edge, and thin scars crisscross its body: a record of glancing railgun strikes.

The shell is staring at its hands.

I glance at Hail, put out my hands, imitating it, frowning.

She's crouching between the wheels of a flatbed hauler, flipped on its side. She's about ten, fifteen metres clear of me, but she reads the motion easily enough. She shakes her head helplessly.

I look back at the Juno. A heavy-duty plug clings to the base of its neck like a parasite, the thick cable trailing along the floor and into a massive casket, set into the wall behind it.

That's the cradle. An empty negative, hollow in just the right shape to fit every part of the machine itself, and able to take its weight while the knuckledraggers shut it down and fiddle with its joints. Ladders and scaffolds run up on either side, and maintenance terminals flicker, flashing warnings.

The power cable runs into the middle of it all, where a matching plug connects to Hangar D's power grid. I've never known a Juno before, never had to work the connections on one either, but I've jockeyed on a Volkov. Most of one, anyway. A trainer, gutted down to legs and hindbrain with a saddle strapped over the top. I got my jockey's patch on that thing, earned all the usual scars in the process. Earned a few other things too.

They say Junos and Volkovs fought each other across the slopes of Olympus Mons, mixed in with Coyotes and Callistos and Ultras and things no one remembers the names of. The fittings are all from the same generation, with the same heavy breakers all painted rustproof red. I know where I'm going.

I swallow and risk a glance at Hail. She's watching the Juno, but it hasn't moved from where it was. It works its huge fingers, turning its palms over in the light.

The Juno is old, older than the trainer, than almost anything else I've ever had the chance to fly. It was built at a time when every design expected weapons to fail, mechanisms to freeze solid, or jam with dust under alien skies. They used to issue shells with swords back then—blunt, flat, heavy things that barely deserve the name. They used to strap massive shot-cannons to their hulls—short range and nasty, with three whole moving parts, including the bullet.

When the Juno closes its hand, the fingers form a battering ram.

I look back at the huge door leading back into the ship. Kadi and his goons haven't moved on it yet, and all of the locks are still in place. Good thing, too. If the Decatur makes it through, that young blood better have his A-game ready. Juno's coming out swinging.

Hail waves to me, catches my eye. It's my turn.

"Quickly," she hisses.

I take a breath and push off as hard as I can. The sprint is heartbeats-long, and Hail has to catch me at the end, bringing me down in the lee of the hauler. My chest burns and my throat aches, more from the rush than the running. I let myself pant, and Hail doesn't interfere.

This is what it feels like to be alive. I'd almost forgotten.

I find Hail's eye and give her an A-OK. She nods, then points to her eyes, then downrange to the machine.

She'll watch my back.

She mouths the word *Ready?*

I nod.

Hail holds five fingers up, and mouths *Five*.

One finger drops.

Four, I reply. I turn away and get ready for the run, keeping time in my head.

Three.

Two.

I push off.

I've made it ten steps when I hear a crash behind me, and the shriek of steel on steel. I risk a glance over my shoulder, just in time to see Hail roll out into the open, bringing her hands up above her head. The Juno is struggling to pull a fist clear of the flatbed wreck that used to be our cover.

Shit.

I keep pushing.

"Over here!" yells Hail. "Look at me. Look at me!" Her voice echoes around the dock. "*Look at me*. Remember who I am."

There's another crash. I'm halfway to the cradle when Hail shouts again.

"Rook!"

I change direction on instinct, turn hard enough that it nearly twists an ankle. The flatbed's cab whips past me, trailing cable and twisted scrap, spinning as it hits the floor. It crumples in the corner, just ahead of me.

"Right!" shouts Hail. I almost don't hear her. "Turn right!"

I see it. An emergency access, just wide enough for me. I turn, put my shoulder to the door and let momentum carry me through. At the speed I'm going, it's like hitting a wall.

I come down hard on the other side and lose my footing halfway through, rolling off hands and knees. I look up to see the Juno hunting for me, forearm just too wide to clear the doorway, fingers trailing sparks where they gouge the floor.

I scrabble on all fours, hurl myself clear as a huge hand clamps shut, less than a metre from my feet. It pulls away, and the doorway fills with a heavy metal face, three eyes in a line down one side, each as big as my head. The Juno glares at me, massive lenses whirring in their sockets, trying to get a fix.

I can hear the focus-rings grinding together, like something's caught in the mechanism. I can see the cracks, too. One eye is an empty socket, and another is lined in shards of broken glass. The last is still intact, but mirror-fissures run across it, crackling as the machine tries to focus. The Juno's blind.

It pulls away, and heavy steps roll into the distance. I can feel each one, rumbling up through the floor.

"Christs," I manage.

And a hand closes on my shoulder.

I WHEEL AROUND, heart in my throat and fists in the air.

Hail steps back. "Easy, easy."

It takes me a moment to swallow my pulse. "You scared the shit out of me." I frown at her. "How'd you get in?"

Hail shrugs, gestures down the corridor behind her. "This is a saviour bay, compartmentalised in case there's a breach on the hangar side." She looks down at the claw marks in the floor. "Juno's onto us."

"I don't think so. I don't think it knows who we are."

She rests a hand on her hip. "You, maybe, but I've known that machine for as long as I've been on this ship."

I shake my head. "That wouldn't help. It can't see us."

She frowns. "Didn't look that way to me." She offers a hand, hauls me to my feet. "Come on, let's get clear of this door."

I follow her through another airlock, and help her roll it closed behind us. We don't want the Juno skipping wreckage through the gap. A few corners later, and we've got several layers of concrete for cover, air to ourselves and a moment to think.

Hail leans back against the wall, shakes her collar out. "You said it can't see us."

I trace a finger around one eye. "It looks like it took a hit to the face. Optics are shattered. Not enough to blind it completely, but enough that it doesn't know who or what we are."

She growls. "The head must've been loose in the casket, got thrown around when the tide hit." She takes a breath, measures it out. "Dammit, Kadi."

"So what do we do?"

"How bad is the damage?"

"I only saw the port-side. Two lenses completely destroyed, the other still in its rings, but cracked."

She rubs her eyes. "It should have sensors and scopes left."

"They're long-range. Terrain and ranging won't help either. Good for fighting another machine, but at this distance, it can't see more than shapes and shadows."

"So what do we do? That Decatur isn't getting in here."

I smile. "It won't have to."

The glare softens, but only by a hair. "Tell me what I'm missing."

"Earlier, when you picked us up—you said there was a helmet. What did you mean?"

For a moment, I'm sure she's going to wall me out. Then something gives. "It came in a few days ago, E and O guy dropped it off. The package had my name on it, but no return address. There was a note with it, handwritten, asking that I hold onto it for a while. I recognised the unit number when I met you."

I laugh, despite myself. "He thought I was being stitched up. Probably still can't believe that I did what I did."

"Who?"

"Antique by the name of Troy. Head knuckledragger for my old unit." I shake my head, but I can't bury the smile. "Such a goddamn sentimentalist."

Hail's eyes find their edge again. "And what does your helmet have to do with the Juno?"

"You said it remembers everything, right?"

"Everything."

"Well, it'll remember this."

FOUR

THE GREAT COMPANIES have a lot in common. Efficiency is one. Their operations stretch between stars and employ billions of human beings; it's exactly what you'd expect. A kink in the system means a tidal wave further down the way, and so they build in straight lines, network their employees, and layer everything with lube.

Ruthlessness is another. The companies survived where governments could not, back when humanity was taking its first steps out of the Origin System. Every employee gets the same history lesson when they sign up: the Colonial Authority might be the big dog now, but it was the companies that kept the species afloat while Earth's little empires set themselves alight. What they won't tell you is that when the unified government finally caught up to the company seed-fleets, it found entire systems inaccessible, radioactive, and clouded with the wreckage of a thousand corporate wars. The companies are still at it, but it's small-scale now, where the Authority's dreadnoughts aren't looking or are too distant to intervene.

The companies share a common history, but the devil's in the little secrets they've learned on the frontier. NorCol's closest competitor is Hasei Haldraad Deep Space Engineering. They aren't as big, their total displacement maybe two-thirds of what the Collective can bring to bear. They're no less of a threat, though. Hasei builds for speed, and they're the best at it: everything they touch is faster, lighter, and sleeker than

55

anything the competition can provide. It sells itself on that, and I've seen the adverts up close.

Well, I haven't *seen* them, exactly. I've caught blurs and flickers on my scopes, tracked machine-ghosts almost too fast to follow. I've even fought a few, if that's what you can call it. Staring at my instruments and hurling shots at distant pinpoints, hoping I'll get lucky.

Hasei sells steel and stability, but there are others on the frontier. Companies that trade in time and expertise, offering solutions to every kind of problem you can imagine. If you want something done, and you want it dirty cheap, you get Loh Kustar on the line. The Locusts are always on the news band, propping something up or stamping it out. The results are never pretty, but there's always results. Sigurd-Lem is almost the exact opposite. Not quick, not cheap, but put up enough capital and their R&D departments will do you miracles and black magic.

But if you need something survived, you buy Nor Collective.

Back before there was an Authority to speak of, back when Sigurd and Hasei were still subsidiaries of the ancient Bayern Corp. Back when the Marr hit Sevastopol and flash-fried the new colony from orbit, the only thing still standing was the only NorCol machine that got there in time. It's *still* standing. The survivors turned it into a monument, high on a plinth made of ash and concrete dust. You can even go and see it, so long as you stay behind the radiation shields.

NorCol builds for the future. It's their motto, but most people don't understand what that means. It isn't some feel-good tag line, it's a promise. When the stars go dark, NorCol'll be around to watch it happen.

You can always count on NorCol, come rain or shine or afterglow. When one part fails, another takes the load, then another. When you finally kill one of its machines, there's another ready to walk across its corpse. Redundancy's what the company does best.

*　　*　　*

AND JONATHAN LEAR is using some of that redundancy now. At least, that was the idea. Hail lost the line to Kadi almost an hour ago, and we can't tell if the nets are down, or if he just isn't picking up any more. Worse, we can still hear the Juno moving around right outside the door, ready to butter us the moment we step outside. We took a risk just getting here, and we're not about to try it again. Not yet, anyway.

We've had to get creative. Hail has got rank and contacts, but only a few of them are willing to tread on the right toes to reach us. She's still a con, after all, and Tower's got her way down on their priority list, too busy cleaning up the tide-damage to bother with us. In the end, only one of them came through; a name I don't quite catch, and a rank I'm sure I don't hear right. There's no way Hail knows a whole Werewolf by name.

Whoever she's got on the line, they've just enough clout to get my chain-mates diverted to the roof of this block. They've snagged a knuckledragger crew as well; flight mechanics for the most part, assigned to stations that don't need them right now. A crew that's just fitted Lear into the auxiliary air supply.

"Where do you think?" I ask, running my fingers down the wall. There's a vent near the floor. "Here?"

Hail watches something in her eye, a projection plotting out the nearby air ducts behind the walls in amber holographics. "Not here." She pauses for a moment, blinks at something. "That one."

I look up at her, turn to match her gaze. "Which?"

She steps past me, puts her hands on a metal locker and tips it to the floor with a crash. Behind it is a heavy grate.

"There."

NorCol's engineers built every block with a backup life-support system, but that wasn't enough. Extra ducts run alongside the backups, with their own breather units and filters, big enough that they could keep this little hangar running through just about anything, come siege or sabotage or catastrophic accident. There isn't much to the vent itself, and it's nowhere near big enough to handle air for the whole hangar, but it isn't intended to. It's still more than what a few scared knuckledraggers would need if there was a fire in the block outside.

We sit down on either side of the vent and listen. It's all we can do. Hail's wrench is where we left it—

Somewhere back the way we came. Back behind a half-blind war machine.

"Is he through yet?" asks Hail. She isn't speaking to me. "Understood. We've just found the exit."

Hail's contact is somewhere above us, standing with the 'draggers on the roof. The air ducts are built to NorCol standard, wide enough to accommodate one full-sized vacuum suit, helmet and all. Hangars are full of dangerous things, and there's no point pumping air in if the people inside are busy dying of something else.

The crew has just finished taking apart the big breather module at the end of the shaft. Lear is somewhere between us and them, hauling my old helmet down the duct. As it turns out, the Locusts build their jockeys thinner than NorCol builds their suits.

"Hear that?" whispers Hail.

I crouch near the grating. For a second, all I can hear is the blood moving around behind my ears. I glance up at Hail, but she's got her eyes closed, listening. I inch closer. I can just about hear the rustle of clothing, the edge of someone breathing. A boot hits the side of the duct. There's a sound like a curse, turned to a hiss as it echoes down the duct.

"You there, Locust?" I ask.

We wait in silence for a moment and are rewarded by a long, rattling scrape. A length of steel bursts through the grate, tearing through the filter-mesh.

"Wrench," says Lear, somewhere behind it.

I pick myself up off the floor. "I guess I deserved that."

A smile tugs at Hail's lip, but doesn't make it all the way across. She pulls the wrench free and starts popping bolts. Together, we lever the grate out in a few seconds and pull Lear up by his hands. The helmet trails behind him on a line of cord. He swings it up where I can catch it, clicks it free of the little clasp on his belt.

"Thank you," says Hail.

Lear puts up a finger and goes fishing through his pockets. His hands surface with a pair of calorie-bars, flavour: grey. "Hungry?"

We are. The bars are hard and fibrous, and it's best if you don't think too hard about the taste. NorCol has taken planets and founded cities on this stuff, but that doesn't mean anyone likes it.

I hadn't realised how hungry I was until I started chewing.

Lear waits us out.

"What convinced you to do it?" asks Hail.

"Two jockeys stuck on a pad with only ourselves and a few lost 'draggers for company? Fuck that." Lear shrugs. "Although, it turns out that Folau's been moved to the same crew that came to help us with the break-in. Took the breather apart for me." The Locust gives us a bastard-grin. "As it turns out, I'll do anything to rain on Folau's parade." He nods to the helmet. "That the one?"

I hold it up and look it over for the first time in two years, probably longer. I don't even know any more.

"Yeah." I breathe in, let it out slowly. "This is the one."

It's emerald green, but covered in scratches that turn pale and dirty where they run through to the armour underneath. The visor looks seamless from the inside, but the outside is made of eight glassy plates: layers of bulletproof composite fused across the front. They make it look like it's glaring at you.

Brass badges perch on the brow. A jockey's winged lightning, and the service bars that mark NorCol's professional corps. Silver stripes run down the left ear, engraved with the name of every unit I've had the displeasure of serving in. The one at the top doesn't even have letters any more, worn down until all you can see are the outlines. The one at the bottom still shines:

Nor Collective.
Battlegroup Odessa, Overgroup 6.
1077th Mechanised, 19 Wing. C-SAR.

My unit.

While it lasted.

An iron angel stands out on the right ear, painted there by a jockey called Sun. She gave it a sword and a shield and wings with too-long feathers that curve around the back. There used to be an inscription underneath.

I turn the thing over and show Hail and Lear the ancient logo on the base.

"You got that off a *Volkov*?" Lear frowns at me. "Seriously?"

"Seriously."

"How'd you get it?"

"Trained in one, back before I got my patch."

He gives me side-eye. "And they let you keep the helmet?"

"I didn't give them a choice." I roll it over in my hands, and feel the weight again. "That machine nearly killed me. Burned me enough that I spent a long time wishing it had." I heft the helmet. "Without this, I'd be dead."

Lear nods at that. Jockeys are superstitious at the best of times, no matter which company's cap they wear when they're out of saddle. I've got the helmet, and it looks like Hail has the Juno. If it wasn't for his time in chains, I'd bet Lear would have a few charms of his own. We carry our wars with us.

"How does this help? They're saying the Juno's running blind in there."

"Not blind." Hail's look is grim. "But close enough."

"Its lenses are damaged, but at least one of its eyes is still together. It can't recognise faces"—I balance the helmet on one hand—"but it'll recognise this."

Lear's eyes widen. "They were competitors. You know that, right? This is off a Volkov, the original block-buster"—he aims a finger at the wall—"and that is a *Juno*." He taps the helmet. "As far as that machine's concerned, this is the enemy."

"It was civil war," says Hail. "There wasn't any difference."

THE HELMET HISSES in my ears. It's trying to test for pressure, but there's nothing to keep the seal intact. The neck-ring grasps at the collar of my shirt, hunting for the steel rim that would normally close the system. All it finds is fabric. It shreds a little, experimentally.

Pressure test failed, says a little window, projected across my visor. *Please exercise caution.*

Even without a suit, the helmet-smells envelop me. Iron and saline, and a little of my own blood, still bedded in the lining. There's fabric polished yellow and brown by the sweat of a few thousand hours in the saddle, the hint of something musty, and the plastic stink you get on anything with breathing tubes. The helmet's had its filters replaced more times than I can count, optics changed out about as often. The holographic layers and projectors are a few years old, but not nearly as old as the steel bucket that holds it all together. The networking and primary pilot interfaces are newer, all NorCol standard. I've replaced the inners twice, but I always find an excuse to bleed into the damn thing before the week is out.

All that, and the work of three different mechanics, and it seems I'll never get rid of the smell of burning flesh.

I take a breath and work the lump around in my throat. I look back down the corridor at Hail and Lear, crouched and ready to sprint for the casket. The lock in front of me leads into open air, with nowhere to run and nothing for cover.

They'd better be quick on their feet.

I cue the transmitter with a blink, and the helmet picks it up. "Ready?" I ask.

"Ready," says Hail, through her inbuilt systems. She can hear me through her wetware bridge, piped right into her head, but I don't have that kind of luxury. Her voice crackles in through the speakers near my ears. "On your count."

"On my count," I repeat, steadier than I feel. I cut the microphone and take a moment to slow my breathing down to something approaching normal. Give me a machine, and I'll fly it to the end of the world. Just don't leave me on my feet.

Christs. I don't remember it being so claustrophobic in here.

I have to swallow the acid rising in my throat, beat the urge to hurl this damn thing clear of my head. It feels like it's drowning me.

"Rook? Are you all right?" Hail is right by my ear, and so far away.

I clench my fists and force my lungs to work.

"Rook?"

I nod, but it's a little too quick, shaking the helmet around on my head. "Sorry. One moment. I—"

I swallow. I don't know what I'm doing. This is a bad idea. "I'm looking for a net."

I blink at that. I don't know where it came from. It's a lie, but a heartbeat later, I realise that it's a good one.

Hail nods. "Understood."

I call up a window on my visor and blink my way through the helmet's networking options. It doesn't have much in the way of range: maybe ten metres or so, and then only through open air. It's designed to give you initial access and handshaking to the machine you're going to be jockeying, and the first few strands of connection before you actually plug yourself in.

I cast a quiet net, broadcasting my service numbers and ID.

Is anyone out there?

Something returns.

It's quiet, barely enough to register, but I can feel it. I don't know how much the Juno can see, but it knows I'm here.

"On three," I tell Hail.

She and Lear lean into the airlock.

"One."

Breathe in, breathe out.

"Two."

I take the door ahead of me by its handles and put a little force on the lock.

The "*Three*" dies in my throat, drowned by a sudden rush of air-pressure, and a shriek of rolling steel.

Behind it, almost an echo, is Hail.

"Kadi?"

But there's no reply.

"*Kadi?*" again, shouted into nowhere.

And something giant moves outside.

I pull on the door with both hands, feet skidding on the deck, kicking hard to beat the gout out of these hinges. They don't give without a fight, but I've got some to spare, boot jammed against the frame and knuckles straining. Three tugs and I've bought enough room to push my head around the corner.

The Juno rests on one knee in the middle of the hangar—a mountain of armour and hydraulics, dark eye-sockets waiting near the peak. I feel its attentions shift to me, but only for a moment. It shutters the little net my helmet casts before it, cuts the connection to the jockey's suite in its cockpit. Kadi has killed any chance I had of breaking through. I'm just another threat now: mapped, categorised, de-prioritised.

And that dull gaze has moved already. It's looking up at the hangar doors, and the tall shape walking through them.

The other machine steps into the light, pale and glimmering turquoise, craggy plates arranging themselves for impact, deflector surfaces in bloom. The Decatur is a wall of strange geometries and stencilled livery, branded by the Nor Collective.

The machine is big enough, strong enough to fight its way clear of one ancient shell; all it has to do is stand there, let all that armour do its job. But the jockey's twitchy. They bring that rusty signal mast up in an awkward grip: worth its weight in extra steel, but only if the operator has the skill.

Hail is shouting, but there's nothing she can do. If Kadi can hear her broadcast, he's ignoring it. The Decatur spreads its stance, improvised club loose between its fingers.

I expect the Juno to find its feet, to come in low and fast with those hammer-fists up, but the old machine doesn't move. At first I think it's waiting, trying to make sense of the blurry, half-familiar thing trespassing in its hangar.

No. That isn't it. I can see the way it's hunched itself, one arm just out of sight. The old shell is holding something, sheltered behind the mass of its body.

The Decatur takes another step closer, but its jockey drops the foot too hard, clumsy and loud, shaking the ground beneath us. Whoever's riding saddle is way out of their depth, and the fight hasn't started yet. The next step is so far off-line it nearly dumps the shell across the deck. The machine catches itself on the hangar-side, forces itself straight and steady, but I can see it wasn't the operator who reacted. They're flubbing it, losing connection.

Every jockey in the room can see how this is going to go.

I can hear Hail switching channels in the background. Trying to explain, for all the good it'll do. The Decatur straightens as its operator finds themselves again, flares all that plating, taller and wider, as if it can scare the Juno into submission.

But the threat is only as good as it looks, and that old shell is blind.

"Christs-dammit, Kadi, it can't see what you're trying to do… Kadi? *Kadi?* Why won't you listen?"

Somewhere behind her pleading, almost silent, is something else. It isn't a voice, not exactly.

What are you? barely an echo on the net. I think I'm the only one who hears it.

The Decatur tilts its head, as if listening to something. Not the whisper in my ear, but something loud and coarse.

"Take it," growls Sul Kadi.

Hail is right behind me. "No! *No!*"

The pale shell slides one leg forward, the strut raised over one shoulder. Muscle moves beneath its massive plates, ready to put all that weight behind the swing.

But it's off balance, overextended. And slow. Way too slow. Blind as it is, even Juno sees it coming.

The Decatur brings its weapon around and down. The Juno stands into the blow, one hand still clutched to its chest, the other raised, angled, and ready to ride the impact. Metalwork skips from its armour in a shriek of steel and a shower of sparks. The signal mast tears and buckles, folds under its own mass, turning to deadweight in the pale shell's hands. There's no damage done to Juno, just paint and surface wear.

And Decatur's now in range.

The Juno steps in close, kicks the other machine out at the knee, comes down hard on the joint and rides it into the deck. Plating bends; the Decatur tries to save itself, swivelling the knee well past human-possible, but there's no way the jockey can recover in time. They're down on Juno's level now, and there's a beating on the way. A massive fist swings up and under, connects. Even with my helmet over my ears, the impact leaves me deaf and gasping.

That pale chestplate nearly caves. It holds, just, buffers blowing out before the impact can break the Decatur's bones, but the Juno isn't aiming to kill. It's been at this a long time. It understands. Without a weapon of its own, and only one hand free, a real fight would've been over in seconds. Instead, it plays to its strengths, and the other machine's weakness. It doesn't have to beat the mass of armour and deflectors—breaking the jockey will work just fine.

And so it aims to blind and maim, to leave the operator sucking for air, blinking at the shock. That first punch landed just metres from the cockpit, and the next one finds centre-of-mass so hard the armour cracks, raining splinters down across the deck. Strike-surfaces rattle in their housings, primary armour systems ringing like church bells, even from all the way out here.

It works. The jockey reels, tries to throw the shell backwards, but that old monster is so close it's probably all they can see. Screens full of Juno, instruments blaring, the jockey does exactly what you'd expect: they panic. They're losing their connection to the machine, and the twisted leg can't hold their weight, but it doesn't stop them thrashing. Something tears, something else fails with a whine.

There's a weird prickle in the air as the jockey pulls the plug, and a sudden rush as the shaped explosives wake beneath the Decatur's plates, skipping sparks and cutting steel around the outline of an ejector-pod. It's the machine's mind-state, saddle, and operator all in one, tearing free of the shell. Huge rockets swell to life inside the machine's deep chest, ready to hurl them all to safety. Ready to wash the hangar with fire and exhaust, damn anyone standing nearby.

Bastard.

I throw myself back behind the lock, but there isn't time to wrestle the door back into its frame. The best I can do is find cover, jam my knees around my ears, force my eyelids shut, and brace my arms across my vitals. I'll pay with skin, that's for sure, but there's every chance that I'll live. Enough to claim some of Kadi's teeth when this is done, anyway.

I hold my breath, but nothing comes. No burn, no sudden concussion.

A second passes in the quiet. And another, before I'll risk an open eye.

Something bright flashes across my visor.

EJECTOR FAILURE
ABORT
REPEAT: EJECTOR FAILURE, OPERATION ABORTED
ALL POINTS RESPOND

If someone calls, you go.

Into the fire, if that's what it takes. Into the wind, even if it's blowing full of hate and cinders. Towards the screams, if they're lucky. Into the quiet if not.

Over decking that's slick beneath my boots, crackling and sharp where shattered armour fell. Through air that stinks of fuel and scorched iron, rippled by heat-shimmer and hazy with smoke.

If someone calls, you go. That's the way it works. 'These few for the many, this one for another. These things done, so that there may be life.' A grand oath, for a fucking can-opener. But some habits die hard, and NorCol drilled them deep. I was up and walking before I knew it, and out the door before I'd decided what to do. My training keeps me moving, but it doesn't stop me feeling like I'm about to choke. Doesn't stop me wishing I had more than just this helmet, or that I didn't have to do this on my own two feet.

Get the plug, I send to Hail, hoping she'll pick me up. If she replies, I don't hear it, but I can't spare the moment to check. It's all I can do to keep myself from tripping up. Ready to turn and run, but still not looking back.

I walk a line into the lee of the teetering Decatur, too compromised to move. The plates have bent so badly that the cockpit is probably trapped by its own supports. The retros are still sparking, hot enough that I can feel them from here, but there's no burn.

Decatur, M661-E. Made for gun duels and firefights, smart and fast. Optimised for long rails and warhead strikes, trading heavy metals and solid-core kinetics with targets so far away you can barely make them out against the stars. Good at taking needle-hits at range, deflecting blast-blossoms and hypervelocity shot.

Not so much against mass and swinging fists, apparently.

The pale machine tries to watch me, but I don't meet its gaze. Dipshit. I keep pushing. I can't stop now—hell, I can't even slow down.

My world darkens in the shadow of the Juno, all faded crimson and webs of silver scars. I feel that gaze again. Feel it take my breath away.

I can hear the movements of its massive body. There are other sounds, but I'm not listening; it's static, interference. *Noise*, even if it echoes with my name. In that moment, all I know is the grind of steel on steel, joints shifting where huge fingers make a fist.

Six eyes try to focus, and sensor-pulses ring.

But I don't stop.

I feed my own systems out like a jockey waking a machine. Like there's nothing out of place.

I send my voice across the net. "Present," I tell the shell, the word as steady as I can make it. "Present yourself."

The Juno stands tall, but it can't make those lenses work. It doesn't respond to my requests for operator access. I watch it tense, that hand still sheltered near its chest.

"Present," I repeat, loud and clear. My heart beats itself against my ribs.

The Juno takes a massive step. Glass falls from its shattered eyes.

"Present."

Something heavy shifts across the net. Handshakes and ciphers, the kind you might expect one shell to send to another. It isn't a conversation. Not quite.

There aren't any words, but I know what the shell is trying to do. I understand.

What are you?

I fight the urge to look back at Hail and Lear. They must be most of the way to the plug by now. I swallow.

"Your operator," I say. "Present your cockpit lock."

The Juno watches me. One fist unfolds.

Another cluster of code flows out on the net. Requests, queries.

Am I broken?

"Yes. Your optics are damaged."

It considers this, turns its palm over in the light.

I can see what it's been holding. A little sparkle of glass.

The machine peers at the remains of an eye. What little it could save.

"Use mine."

The Juno looks up.

I open the connections to my helmet optics, rethink, and open everything. I kill the firewalls on my central systems and clear the encryption on my thoughts. It's what a jockey would do for their machine, and so I do it.

It's the most difficult part of this job.

The shell will give you eyes, but you have to trust them. It'll give you fists and fire, and feet that'll walk through hell, but you have to let it keep the balance. It'll give you wings, and in return, you have to let it into you.

I'm not special. I made lower-middle in boot-camp, and sure as hell didn't set any records, but this is one thing I've always been good at. While the others had to dose to find connection, had to tug and fight and dig their spurs, I've never had trouble sharing the inside of my head.

It feels like coming home.

The Juno watches my systems unfold themselves across the net, open and vulnerable. It reaches for one connection: a little camera in the join between visor and helmet. The machine doesn't touch anything else.

A small light flashes green in the corner of my eye. *New connection established,* says my visor. *Streaming to remote device.*

The Juno is very still.

The other fist unwinds. The shell touches its face, rolls fingers across the empty spaces where eyes should be. It feels the pits and scars on its hull, and finds the fresh weld in the middle of its chest. It's just a little thicker than my thumb, and still silver, not even painted over yet.

I quietly curse Sul Kadi.

I am broken.

I've never seen a shell do that. Damage assessments, yes, more times than I'd like to count—but they're always clinical and robotic. Hardware abstractions testing to see where functionality begins and ends.

This is something else.

There is a hole. It touches the railgun wound. *Here.*

"Let me fill it."

I twitch, surprised at my flapping tongue.

The machine doesn't move. I step closer, even as everything else is telling me to run. My pulse runs so fast it hurts.

The Juno moves slowly. It closes the hand around the remains of its eye, and sets itself down on one knee. The way it would when a jockey gave the order to present.

The operator's lock clicks open.

"Don't move," whispers Hail, somewhere far behind me.

They're going to pull the plug. They have to. It's the only way this doesn't end with another fight and another wreck. I look up at the Juno.

And it looks down on me. It isn't watching Hail and Lear climbing scaffolds in the distance. It's right here, waiting for something.

Oh.

Of course.

"My name is Rook."

FIVE

I'VE BEEN ALL over on NorCol's tab. *All over*, from the core to the bloody fringes, and across the border more than once. I've spent nearly all of that time hustled from one unfamiliar tub to another—never to anything the size of *Horizon*, but across every configuration of deck and bulkhead and hull that you can imagine, and a few you'd have to guess at. Century ships built by ancestor-engineers, and grandline vessels with lore and legends of their own. Fractal-shapes cooked up by neural networks and R&D acid trips. Nightmare-things built using stolen secrets, cold-forged from starlight and emptiness.

Some things change, others stay the same, even on a monster like *Horizon*. Even on a boat like this, bigger than anything and teetering on the edge of nothing, I don't need a map for what I'm looking for. I follow passages I have no reason to recognise, steering by gut and instinct first, then by sound and smell. It's a rumble in the distance, filling every vent and passage full of echoes and familiar scents. It's a wall of noise when I find it, and a wash of heat and steam.

The chow hall is exactly what I'm expecting, exactly where I expect to find it. Long tables all in stainless steel, benches crowded with uniforms. Point-lamps glare from the ceiling, lighting cones through the low haze. One side of the hall is all countertops, the space behind them opening into the industrial workshop that NorCol probably calls a kitchen.

Half of Hangar D's jockeys sit on one side, and half of its knuckledraggers keep to the other. A few tables mix near the middle, but they keep it personal—pilots and technicians paired off and talking shop, ignoring the odd looks they get from either side.

Hail, Salt and Lear have claimed a table to themselves, and they wave me down as soon as I clear the door. At least, Lear does. Salt has his head on the table, and Hail only looks up once I'm in range.

She spares me an eye. "Sleep all right?"

I roll my head around. "I'd forgotten what a bed felt like."

"I'll take that as a no."

"You'd be right."

"And the suit?" asks a familiar voice, just behind me.

I turn to find Arko Folau with a trayful of oily eggs in his hands, a jug of black coffee balanced on the corner.

"Better than the sleep."

On the surface, my new flight suit is much like any other I've worn in NorCol's service. There's a conductive sleeve underneath, full-body, with fluid lines to keep you warm or cool or whatever it is you need. Over that, thick fabric mesh run through with strands of artificial muscle and covered in bands of soft armour, turquoise on a grey background. Composite plates are tucked in against my ribs, under my arms and over my shoulders, lining my hips and moulded to cushion my spine. If our shells take a hit, the inertia can kill us before the bullets do, and so the company pads our suits, covers them in carapace.

On the surface, you wouldn't know anything was different, but I can feel where someone has tweaked it. Brand new, the suit should feel like a straitjacket. Too slow and too heavy, while its little mind gets used to wearing you.

But this one moves like it knows me.

I raise an eyebrow at Folau. "Your doing?"

He smiles, and drops himself into the seat next to Lear. "You're welcome."

Lear looks up from his chow. "What're you doing here, knuckledragger? Need a map?"

Folau ignores him and gets busy on his breakfast, working his fork like a shovel. "You see, you noticed," he says, talking through a mouthful of scramble, waving a finger at me. "Unlike my favourite Locust here. Did the same work on his suit as I did on yours, but it seems he doesn't even need a helmet."

"What's that supposed to mean?" growls Lear.

Folau grins at him. "Your skull is plenty thick on its own."

"Fuck you."

"Later, honey." Folau taps his shoulder, right where a suit's central processors would live. "I tweaked them, added a little homebrew. Defaults are for dipsticks."

"Sounds like you've been busy," says Hail, through a cloud of caffeinated steam. "How'd the swabbing go?"

"Swabbing?" Folau rolls his eyes. "No idea what you're talking about."

She grins at that. "Good thing you were so busy tweaking their suits. Newbie knuckledraggers usually get the whole hangar floor to themselves."

I sit down across from Hail. "Thank you, Folau."

He tips his brow at me. "You're welcome, jockey." He elbows Lear. "See that? Courtesy from my colleague over here."

Lear loads his fork with a bubble of something grey and oily, flicks it between two fingers. He scores a direct hit, right in Folau's ear.

"How are your implants doing?" asks Hail, over the noise that follows.

I set my helmet on the tabletop. "Medical pulled the last of the plugs out before I hit my bunk last night."

I blink life into my eyes and a holographic display opens up, right above her face. I spread one of the menus with a glance and offer her a connect. She accepts, her eyes aglow for a moment as the request pops into existence where she can see, fading again as her devices pair with mine. I twitch as she filters in, a little weight settling against the front of my skull. Once

Lear and Folau have finished flapping at each other, I do the same with the Locust. He reads as a wingmate, his position recorded, and medical data traded between us. Annoying right now, especially from Lear, but we'll need to be used to it by the time the shooting starts.

I flinch at the connections. It's been a long few years. "They're still a bit raw, apparently." My temples throb.

Lear looks up, but his eyes flicker and spark. He falls back, clutching at them. "Not as raw as mine," he manages. He paws at the little streak of blood running down his lip. "Fuck." He collects a napkin to bleed into.

Salt stirs like a mountainside and flicks another napkin across the table to Lear.

I glance at him. Lear is wearing a suit just like mine—just like Hail's, if you don't count all the rank and tabbing. Salt is something else.

"Didn't they have anything in your size?"

"'Good morning,' you mean." A blink, and his eyes glow golden, offering another connection to our net. His steady heart beats somewhere under all of it, just out of hearing.

"Something like that," I reply. "Couldn't NorCol find you anything that fit?"

He holds his hands up for inspection. He isn't wearing the armoured gauntlets, just the soft gloves that fit the conduction layers underneath. They look thicker than mine, even with all of my hard casing counted in.

The rest of his body is covered in metal bands, with chunky bolts like lines of blisters down the sides. A fibre-mesh runs underneath, ruddy orange between slate-grey steel. It's the kind of gear you'd expect if wars still happened on foot.

"Folau had to dig it out for me." He nods to my helmet. "Probably older than that bucket of yours."

I shrug. "It does what it needs to."

"So does that." Hail points to the yellow stuff on Folau's tray, then waves me off my seat. "Go. Get some breakfast into you. We've got a long day ahead."

"Longer than yesterday?"

She watches me, her gaze suddenly a few degrees colder. "No. But yesterday shouldn't have happened the way it did, and it won't again. It's been dealt with."

I hold my ground. "What does that mean?"

"Whatever you want it to," she replies, low and toneless. "The Juno's safe."

"After everything that happened?"

"The damage is on Tower. They sent a nugget to do a jockey's work, and they paid for it in steel."

"And Kadi?"

Her jaw tightens. "He's been dealt with too." She tilts her head at the kitchen. "Go on. I need you eating."

"It's good," offers Lear.

Folau nods, shedding crumbs. "Hate to agree with Locust here, but it *really* is. They've got real fuckin' eggs, chief."

I frown at him. "Chief?"

"That's you." Hail leans back, takes some of the edge off her gaze. "Standard practice. You had the highest rank before, so you're the first in line for it now. You're my new flight chief. Congratulations."

"Also, we didn't want it," says Lear, behind his bloody rag.

Hail raises an eyebrow, but Salt stirs first. "He makes it sound like there was a vote. There wasn't." He tips his head. "Congratulations."

Congratulations. Ha. First in line if Hail bites dust. First to take the reins if she gets wounded, or gee-locs through a turn. Lear made it sound like a joke, but he's right. It's a rough job, and anyone who had the option would pass.

Somewhere along the line, I remember to say, "Thank you."

Hail raps a knuckle on the table. "Now get yourself fed."

"Aye aye," I reply, and my stomach tugs at me.

The chow line is immediately familiar. I collect a tray, and shuffle my way past sloppy eggs, spicy vitro-sausage wallowing in artificial grease, pale cheese, black beans, and folded flatbread, still hot and floury. NorCol's grey nutri-bars have fuelled the company through more fights than anyone cares to count, but they aren't made for comfort. In NorCol's holds, that's what breakfast is for.

The company's soul is right here, floating between bubbles of imitation gristle. I don't waste time filling my tray before tracing my way back through the noise. I set down across the table from Hail, but I can't hold her eyes. I have to focus a little too hard on operating my fork, but it all goes down fast enough.

I probably don't chew as often as I should. "Christs. It's delicious."

"Go for round two," says Hail. "You're going to need it."

Lear follows me back for one of his own, and Folau helps us manage a third tray after that. We mop up, and wash it down with caffeine darker than night and thick as tar.

Hail watches. "Better?"

"In every way."

"Good." She crosses her arms on the table. "When you arrived, I asked you how much they'd told you."

"Nothing," I mutter. "Less than nothing."

She nods. "Standard. Then you asked me where we were."

"You didn't give us much of an answer." I pick at my teeth between speaking. "'*Horizon* isn't on the map,' you said."

"That's because it isn't."

"Where are we, then?"

"That's the trouble," she replies, without hesitation. She's given this talk before.

Salt spreads his hands out on the table. "Simple question, Hail."

"Complicated answer," she replies. "And useless without the right context. I told you that the Authority doesn't touch your sentences, you remember that?"

Lear grumbles. "Should've known."

"Why would they do that?" I clear my throat, try again. "Why go through all the trouble? I saw the paperwork—reduction of sentence is guaranteed, even if you don't make full term."

"Did you read it? I mean, actually read it."

I frown at her. "Of course I did."

Hail raises an eyebrow, but there's half a grin beneath it. "Is that right? Do you remember what it said?"

I go and open my mouth, but I can't find anything to say.

Salt swirls his cup, watching the reflection. "Ah. I see."

"You remember?" Hail asks him.

"Fine print. Something about the duration of sentence, relative to what it would have been." He furrows his brow. "It's subjective, then?"

"It is."

Lear rolls his eyes. "What the hell does that mean?"

Hail smiles at him without warmth. "They don't take years off your sentence. It just feels shorter."

I don't understand, and I say as much.

"As I say, it's hard to explain, but much easier to show you." She turns on her seat, looking for something behind her. She picks out the moustache from yesterday, seated among his knuckledraggers. "Remember him?"

We do.

She nods. "Good. That's Vikram, maintenance and scheduling for D-upper."

Folau pulls a face. "What's he got to do with anything?"

"How old do you think he is, exactly?"

"Fifty?" asks Lear.

"Eighty," says Folau. "Definitely eighty. No, wait. Ninety? A hundred?"

Lear sniffs at that. "Not much good with humans, are you, greaser?"

Folau shrugs. "Two hundred? Three hundred? Throw me a bone here."

"Fifty's good," says Salt.

I roll my hand. "Late forties, with some wear and tear."

Hail shakes her head. "Folau is right. His first guess, anyway."

Lear scoops dark caffeine out of the bottom of his mug, waves the tarry finger at Hail. "I call bullshit. No way he's a day over sixty."

"Biologically, he's just had his fifty-eighth birthday," says Hail. "*Horizon* medical could probably confirm that." She leans back again. "Like to guess how long ago he was born?"

Salt smiles gradually. "More than fifty-eight years ago?"

"It's difficult to be sure, but yes. Vik's fifty-eight years old, *subjective*. Only, if you were one of NorCol's bean counters back on Destiny, you could look up his payroll, his ID, and see that he was born on this ship about eighty years ago. Eighty and change, if you're counting from the outside. If you're counting at one gee."

"You said he was born here—" I trail off. "No shimmer jumps?"

"He's never left this ship. And *Horizon* has been anchored the whole time. No heavy acceleration. No shimmer."

"How?" asks Lear.

"Not *how*," says Hail. "I probably couldn't explain it to you anyway. What's important is *where*."

"And where are we?" this from Salt.

She puts up a finger. "Give me thirty seconds." With that, she stands, and wakes the displays in her eyes. "Read you, Switchboard. Mind getting Obs for me? Thank you." She looks into the air above our heads, taps her foot. "Morning, Rorke, Hail here. Yes." Another pause. "I need clearance on an Obs pod, as soon as you can get it for me."

Her expression twists. "I'm asking nicely. This can be as difficult as you want it to be."

She grins at the ceiling. It's brutal. "Oh, you *know* I would."

Another pause, and the smile loses all the harsh edges.

"That's the correct answer, Observation. Thank you." She blinks the glow away, and focusses back on us. "We've got clearance, but the window is short. We'll have to run." She raps a knuckle on my helmet. "Bring your buckets." She spares a glance for Folau. "Sorry, greaser."

He shrugs in his overalls. "I'll find my own way."

Hail doesn't wait for us to stand. "Come on."

We have to jog to keep up.

Salt pats Folau on the shoulder on the way past. Lear ruffles his hair. Folau replies with a well-exercised finger.

I catch Hail first. "Where are we going?"

She doesn't break stride. "To take a peek outside."

I EXPECT US to take another train. Everything on *Horizon* seems to move that way: monorail engines hurl themselves through the air over our heads and shriek through tunnels below our feet. The endless noise follows us throughout the ship.

We skip across a rail yard, between the cars of a massive train, but we don't board. There's a backlog. A Decatur lies on a flatbed, its feet peeking out from under an oil-stained tarpaulin. One of its hands has broken free of the rigging and dragged across the rails next door, leaving white scars across the steel. A crew of knuckledraggers is wheeling a crane around to lift it back into place.

We don't take that train, or any other, but pick our way between the rails, catching a cargo-lift as it passes our level. It's an open platform, wide enough that the Juno could stand in the middle with its arms outstretched.

A group of NorCol overalls watch us from between a cluster of walking loaders, passing comments we can't quite hear. Hail glares downrange, and they turn back to their smokes and bickering.

"What's their problem?" asks Lear, flexing his fists. "Don't like jockeys on their deck?"

Hail spits. "Jockeys aren't a problem, convicts are."

It's the same when we clear the lift, sixteen floors up. A checkpoint wants our IDs and an explanation. It happens again when a NorCol jacket and his troopers pull us over, wanting to know what we're doing so far from the hangars.

Hail waits for them to drift out of earshot before she explains. "We're the bottom of the ladder. To the regulars, we're worse than the stiffs who work the bilge lines. At least they have the sense to stay out of sight."

"Why?" I ask. "There must be cons all over this ship."

"There are, but didn't used to be. Used to be all professional."

"But now we're the ones who get the fighting done?" asks Salt.

"They don't replace the full-timers on this ship any more, and the original units are too small for live ops. They're spectators now, for the most part."

He smiles broadly. "Nothing like watching from the sidelines."

I chuckle at that. "They're jealous of *cons?* Christs."

"That isn't all of it." Hail ducks under a security boom that hasn't moved in so long the rust has gummed it shut. She waits while we follow her in through the dust. "There aren't that many full-time jockeys left. Chances are, if you see a shell walking around, there's a con in the saddle."

"So what? A jockey's a jockey."

She shakes her head. "It isn't easy knowing someone who was in a chain-gang just a week ago could literally crush you under a thumb."

"So why don't you?" asks Lear, with a nasty grin. "They can only arrest you again."

"It's tempting," says Hail, not looking back, "but NorCol's got a couple of monsters on payroll, for moments just like that." She stops us short. "Here we are."

Lear squints into the dark. "If you say so."

Her eyes glow. "We've hit the first lock," she says to someone else.

The corridor lights up, bulbs bursting to life around us to show an airlock hatch looming over us. It stirs.

Bolts rock and seals part as the pressure equalises. Huge hydraulics add to the racket, whistling to match the creaking of the hinges. The door slips loose of its collar. It's easily three metres thick—more of a plug than a door. Six bolts rest inside, each gleaming pin as wide as my arm is long. There's a chamber on the other side, crowded with just the four of us inside.

"Helmets," says Hail, pulling her own bucket up and over. "Quickly. We're cutting this close."

The rest of us follow suit. The helmet lock finds my collar, and this time it has something to dig its teeth into. It slides into the neck-ring and bites down, gears cycling as it locks itself around my throat.

Pressure test in progress, says a window in my visor. Air hisses past my ears. *Pressure test complete. Sync with embedded systems?*

'Embedded' below the surgical scars on my neck and behind my ears.

I blink and follow the little prompts as I see them.

My eyes feel it first, straining as the visor's optics try to focus, the view blurring at first, but turning crisp as it finds a match.

With the helmet sealed tight, all I should be able to hear is my own breathing and the wheezing machinery that keeps the air pressure up. My wetware compensates for the silence, feeding in sound from receivers built into either side of the helmet. There's a moment of vertigo, and my ears pop like I'm coming down from altitude. It plays with my balance, but I've got the sense to swallow and wait for my body to adjust.

It always feels like this. Like the steel has sprouted ears on my behalf.

My heartrate appears in the corner of the visor: steady, but faster than I'd like. Core temperature and blood pressure show up just beneath it, all normal enough. In the background, the suit takes stock of itself, working out the remaining O2 in its reserves.

There's one more thing before the connection is complete; a little number appears in the middle of it all, right between my eyes.

00.00, it says.

That's the pilot-sync, measured in percentage points. A record of how deep a paired machine can reach into my head, and how far I'm reaching out. The closer you are to zero, the more you are yourself. The closer to a hundred, the more you're something else.

The last two digits flicker, just for a fraction of a second.

Somewhere far away, I can feel the Juno look up from where it stands.

Hail's in my face before I can make more of the thought. "I said, are you sealed?" Her voice arrives direct to my ears, a repeat hitting my thoughts just as quickly as the sound finds the speakers. It's like there's an echo in here, one heard, one projected across the inside of my skull.

"Sealed," I say, my voice strangely hollow.

"Sealed," says Lear, his own echo running close behind.

"Sealed," grumbles Salt. "This is going to take some getting used to."

I look back at him. He's wearing a bucket that actually deserves the nickname. Heavy bands run across the front, leaving only a narrow slit for the visor. Three camera-eyes cluster together on one corner, red lenses like a colony of blisters.

"I'll get someone on the case," says Hail. "We should be able to find something smaller, fudge the seals until they fit."

Salt raps a knuckle on his jaw-plate. "I'll take the suit as intended, thanks."

Hail shrugs. "Your call." She turns on her heel. "All right, Observation. We've just hit checkpoint 2. Good to go."

The door slides back into place behind us, and the one ahead unwinds, mechanisms chattering. We follow Hail onto a narrow walkway maybe ten paces long.

A steel ravine stretches into the distance on either side of us. We can't see the floor, we can't see the ceiling, and the narrow horizon is cloudy with dust. Another door waits for us in the metal cliff ahead.

"Where are we?" I ask.

Hail smiles at me. "Between *Horizon*'s primary armour plates."

We pass four more.

At the end of the line, we find a room, completely bare except for a single lamp in the ceiling. Must be the oldest thing I've seen on the ship so far. A crust of olive-green paint and corroded metal joins the lamp to its housing.

At first, it looks just like anything else that's been around a few years, painted and re-painted every few maintenance cycles. It's probably the same crew that does it—I doubt anyone else remembers where this is.

Looking closer, I realise the paint has been burned into place.

Hail faces us. "I need all of you to switch your filters on, full adaptive."

I nod and cycle my visor settings. The world goes black for a second, and I blink again, scaling it back into grey, and finally into something closer to the way it was before.

"Ready?" she asks.

"Ready," we reply, one after the other.

She nods, and I can just see the edge of her glowing eyes through her visor glass. "We're here, Observation. Checkpoint 7."

Silence for a second.

"Got it," says Hail. "Pull the covers."

Behind her, the wall splits across the centre. Two heavy plates roll away, and for a second, I'm blinded by the light. Every filter that can close, has.

My systems slowly compensate. Little details emerge from the murk.

I'm expecting a window into Open Waters; the deep-field curve of dark and distant stars.

I don't expect the clouds.

"Christs," I whisper.

Hail chuckles at that. "As far as anyone can tell, they didn't have much to do with it. Either of them."

Heavy glass holds the wall behind her, armour-treated panes as thick as my forearm is long. Behind that, a bubble of blue-tinged shield envelopes. They billow.

On the other side is a sea of wind and storm, cloudbanks thousands of K tall. They eddy and coil, forming little twisters that tear across the flats. Massive squalls live in the shadows, dark hearts curdled into storm cells, trading lightning across the open.

Gales whip past our window, close enough that I can see the texture. Streamers trail from the crags in *Horizon*'s hull, making the old dreadnought look like it's put down in the middle of some cold, ancient desert. Only I can't see any sign of hard ground below us, and nothing to mark where the currents end and the void begins above. Open air condenses where it touches cold steel and turns to the same silvery stuff as the clouds behind it.

A radioactive dawn hangs in the middle of everything; a rush of fire and curving light, flickering between the wind-walls, turning the storms to backlit shadows. I have to work the zoom on my optics to get a better look, but from out here, there isn't much past the wash. I can see that it isn't a star, nor the core of something that used to be one.

There, the streams spin so fast that they glow under friction, colder orange and pale blue around the edge, but turning white hot near the rim of something else, curving away under gravity. The light spills out across the valleys between weather systems, streaks into the gaps and ravines, painting everything orange and red and purple, or shrouding it charcoal black. There's more, turning static just on the edge of what I can see.

Even through the shields and layers of filtered glass, my suit is ticking off rads.

"They say it's artificial." Hail takes it in with a sweep of her hand. "Everything you see. The clouds"—she taps a finger on the window—"and the Eye."

The radiation counters in my visor are starting to climb, and the suit chirps at me, concerned that I'm not looking for cover. When I don't move, it flashes a warning at me, tells me to get out of the way, to get myself behind something dense and wait for medical attention, but I can't pull myself away. Hell, I can barely close my eyes.

"How they know that"—she shrugs—"I have no idea. But it behaves like nothing you've ever seen, or ever will again."

I can feel the fear resting in the pit of my stomach, but it's drowned out by the glow. Even with the suit doing everything it can to keep the light from baking my insides, filling me up with tumours and tremors and who knows what else, I can't help but stretch myself out in the warmth.

"We're holding orbit about a quarter of the way between the Transition Point and the outer sectors of the Eye."

"Transition Point?" asks Salt.

"If you hadn't guessed it, you're some way out to sea, convict." She rings a fingertip against the glass again. "Distance is a messy thing in here. The Transition Point is easy to find on this side, so long as your velocity is right, and you're working the right equations. It's easy enough to get back to normal space." She cocks her helmet at the Eye. "It gets more complicated when you're reaching for *that*. Every company's tried getting closer, but no one has ever made it anywhere near. Not that I know of, anyway." She traces an outline with her fingertip, where light curls around things we can't see. "All we have is the rim, and it looks like you can't reach that either, no matter how hard you push your engines. You always stall out, or find yourself turned around."

I'm only half listening. The light holds me in place, wraps me up, washes in through my eyes, past them until it's all I can see.

This is what it feels like to fly.

Not the turn and burn inside an atmosphere; a dirty curve of air and dust that doesn't do it justice. The void isn't much better; you can push yourself to the limit, pull so much gee that you're splitting veins under the pressure, and all you'll ever get is the pinprick scatter twisting past your cockpit.

This is what it should be.

Carried on winds that run forever, over clouds that rise like wave-tops on an endless sea.

I feel Hail's hand on my shoulder. "We don't have long, I need you on point."

"Sorry." I find her silhouetted. "Thank you," I say, out loud, but it isn't meant for her.

3.29, reads the counter in the middle of my visor.

The Juno has followed me out, kept just the echo of a connection between our systems. It filters in through the corners of my eyes. Something half remembered, and the feeling of wings and engine fire. Falling forever, or diving to impossible depths, fading away as the counter drops back to almost nothing.

I don't feel the room tip. I don't feel myself lose connection to the floor.

Hail catches me by my shoulder, hauls me up and fills my visor with her eyes. "Are you all right?"

I have to blink the sparks away. "Head rush," I manage.

It's a lie, but Hail doesn't say anything more. She watches me. I swallow and wave her away. "I'm okay. I've got it."

She raises an eyebrow, but in the end, she leaves me to stand on my own two feet.

"I don't understand," says Lear. "Any of it. How does this change anything?"

Hail sets herself between us and the window. "Everything on this side of the Transition Point is part of an accelerated frame of reference. At this altitude, every second you spend is longer by a little less than a third of what it would be. If you fly deeper in, towards the outstations, it gets heavier. Fly back out to the Boundary, and it gets lighter."

Lear cocks his head. "Longer than what?"

"Longer than a second at 1 gee."

"NorCol doesn't touch our sentences," says Salt, "but it doesn't have to."

Hail nods. "You're buying time. Twenty-four hours here is thirty and change at Old Earth standard. Ten years gets you a good return on whatever you'd have to spend in a cell somewhere else, assuming you live that long."

"Some nasty flying out there," says Salt, leaning for a look over the edge.

"You have no idea," says Hail. "On this side of the Transition Point, there are four competitor machines for every one of ours." She points upwind at something we can't see. "Hasei has a dreadnought called the *Orphan Source*." She does a moment's calculation in her head, marks something else, this time up and to the left. "Sigurd has the *Demiurge*." Now to the right. "Two Locust carriers hold near Rorschach: the *Pacal* and *Aeryn Sun*. Not as big as the dreads, but sharp enough." One last time, down below. "Esper Kinetic has a converted seedship called the *Immemorial*." She crosses her arms. "*Horizon* is the biggest by a long way, but don't make the mistake of thinking NorCol is alone out here."

"Where's the Authority?" This from Salt, doing his own calculations.

"Outside, with a capital O. Other side of the Transition Point, where it's sane." Hail jerks a thumb over her shoulder. "It's mad out here. They tried their luck after Sigurd made the first transition, but their losses weren't sustainable. The companies have a better tolerance for it."

"For what?"

She shrugs. "Grinding each other to a paste. Flying headlong into monster storms."

"What could they possibly want out there?" asks Lear. "What? Don't look at me like that—there has to be something of value. That's the way these things work."

"Stepping stones."

We turn to watch Hail again. She lines us up and marks something we *can* see. A little dark spot against the glow, and a thin strip of shadow out behind it.

"See that?"

We do.

The clouds shift around it, but it doesn't seem to move.

"Is that a rock?" asks Lear.

"No," I say, "it's matching our orbit. Look."

But Hail shakes her head at me. "Other way round, and yes—you could call it a rock. It looks like one up close; a rock for all that you could tell the difference, but it won't behave like one."

"Artificial," I reply. "That's what you said. You called it artificial."

"That's because it is. That and almost every scrap of rock out there. Built, engineered, whatever. There are four more above us and eight behind us, all moving at the same speed. All keeping the same orbit from the Eye, for what that's worth in a place like this."

"*Horizon*'s moorings."

"Everything sinks towards the centre, given enough time. Everything except these rocks. Without them, the storms would have us all over the place, and *Horizon* would have to burn just to keep from sinking. We don't know how they do it, how they keep their altitude, but we stopped trying to figure it out a while back. Truth is, we need them."

"There are others, then?"

"Thousands. Hundreds of thousands, millions. Some are small, no bigger than this room. Others are bigger than *Horizon*. Some aren't much more than balls of dust, but NorCol's found things that look like hangars, weather stations, cathedrals, and shapes we don't have names for. So far, everything we've found has been uninhabited, but we're still paddling in the shallows. A little deeper in, that might still change, we might find something that makes sense of all of this. But the truth is, we don't know much of anything. None of this is human-origin, but nothing is natural either. That's it. That's what we've got." She offers us a nasty smile. "This is your new day job, convicts. You are my new recovery team."

"Recovery? You mean like—"

"Like the diplomatics do? Yes, only the Authority has too much on its plate to keep a Diplo crew flying out here, so the companies have taken over. Whatever anyone will tell you, NorCol is here to pick the bones of a dead civilisation. Same goes for everyone else." She takes in our expressions, softens her smile just a little. "Welcome to the froth."

SIX

RIGHT FROM THE moment I open the door, I can feel the Juno watching me. It's back in its cradle. Someone has salvaged a new door for the front of it—stripped off something obviously intended to hold a Decatur. It's supposed to be a form-fit, with hatches and windows; instead, it's angular, all crags and odd geometrics, with ragged holes cut into the sides. And whoever put it back up took the time to weld a couple of deadbolts over the top, locked them into the concrete on either side. The welds are still black.

I look up at where the Juno's head would be, hidden behind the ugly panelling. I can feel its eyes.

I'll get you out of there.

I march on the nearest NorCol uniform. "You."

He looks up at me, blinking.

"Name?"

He gawks for a second before catching up. I can see the fight brewing, even before he knows it himself. The hairs on his neck stand up, and some dry comment perches on the tip of his tongue, something about jockeys minding their own business.

I hold my ground, work my fist. He wouldn't be the first knuckledragger I've laid out on the deck. "Something wrong with your hearing?"

"Avery," comes out in a choke.

"Avery," I repeat, filing the name away. "Who put those locks on my machine?"

89

"Kadi," he says, without a moment's hesitation.

He flicks a glance at my helmet. I've got it resting on two fingers, hanging by its chin guard. Three kinds of bonded composite, metal plating over the top, combat marks and badges jingling. The skull-bucket in the middle of it all is built to take a bullet, front and centre. Probably worse than bullets, but I've never had reason to test that.

His eyes check off the helmet and skip to my waist. Different units have different loadouts, but he can see the big pistol on my hip, and he'll know about the nasty sawback blade in the small of my back. I can see the calculations rolling around inside his head.

His job doesn't count much fighting, and you can see that from a K away. His fingers are fine, covered in clear oil, rather than the muck and grease you'd get on a mechanic. His patches mark him as the senior 'dragger for this block, but by the look of him, he'd be happy to be left alone with the avionics.

He's already worked out I wouldn't go for the knife or the gun. That would be too much.

No. He's seen the same thing before. A bar fight, probably. A jockey panting in the middle of it, heavy helmet like a bloody wrecking ball. Avery maps his teeth out with his tongue, like he's taking a moment to remember how many there are and what they all feel like.

If there was going to be resistance, it evaporates. After all, this isn't even his fight. Sul Kadi seems to be in charge, but Avery is the first point of contact. Kadi can only shit on him when he's got the time and inclination, and being the boss knuckledragger means that he's almost always bingo on both. Avery will be attached to this particular block. He'll have to deal with me every day.

"I'll pull the locks," he says, already spinning on his heel. He wrangles a pair of greasers on the way, snaps at their heels.

"Already the big dog on deck," says a familiar voice. "Didn't take you very long."

I turn to find Folau, or rather, half of him, leaning out from a tangle of wires and belt feeds. It looks like part of the fire-suppression system, the casing bent around the Juno's fist.

"Didn't take you long either."

He sketches a gasp. "What are you suggesting?"

"That thing's scrap, at best. Whatever you're doing isn't going to save it." I lean in. "But anyone looking for their newbie greaser might miss that you were here."

"Are you making out that I'm anything but a model em-ploy-ee?"

"Seems that way, doesn't it?"

Folau grins at me. "I guess it does. That a problem?"

"As you were, greaser."

He disappears, gets back to whatever it was he was doing before. "Aye aye, chief."

I shake my head and leave him to it. Knowing Folau, he's probably overqualified for whatever Avery has him doing.

The other knuckledraggers are fighting and sweating on the scaffolds around my shell. Whoever put the bolts in did it quick and dirty, like they were trying to sneak it in while Hail and I were on the other side of the hangar.

I grind my teeth. Kadi doesn't have much to worry about from fresh meat like me and he knows it. I'll have to find some way of returning the favour, make sure everyone's clear on where they're standing.

I'm still simmering when I look up and find the Juno looking at me. It's only half a head—three eyes down one side, peering through an awkward gap in the steel. The lenses are perfect now, and I can feel them on me.

I pull my helmet up and over, run through the seals and pressure checks. I let it settle and blink my way through a sync.

20.01, says the counter in the middle of my screen.

28.12

The floor falls away under me, and the hangar block spins with my head at the pivot.

31.48

I swallow hot spit and fight to keep myself standing. "Too soon," I manage, gasping. "Too soon."

24.17
11.62
5.59
1.00

And I can breathe again. My head feels lighter than the rest of me, and my vision clouds around the edges, but I'm still standing.

The Juno is a subtle pressure now, like a finger resting on my skin. I can feel its eyes on me, but not much more than that. It's the feeling of someone close by, or a light breeze on your neck.

"Thank you."

The machine warms at me.

Christs, I've missed this.

Avery interrupts my thoughts. He's got his crew knocking the big bolts free with hammers, the steel shrieking as they go. I grit my teeth and turn away. I'm not sure I can watch.

I push through the airlock separating the block from the rest of Hangar D, then onto the pad, looking out at the flipped city where two hundred other shells live. It's close enough that I can feel the Juno still, but too far away to hear the clanging.

Hail finds me there.

"There are others, you know."

"Other shells?"

She leans against the guardrail next to me. "Lear and Salt have brand new Decaturs. I've got a line on one more, if you want it. It's the M661, variant F. Factory-fresh. Paint's still tacky."

But I'm shaking my head before I've even decided how to answer. "I can't."

Hail nods but holds herself steady. "There's a Spirit as well, if you want, same as mine. Six-forty-four, M-variant. Heavily modified for ops in the froth, and probably one of the fastest machines on *Horizon*."

"I can't."

10.79, says the counter, just a heartbeat before it drops back to 1. The Juno is listening to us.

Hail crosses her arms. "Why?"

ANDREW SKINNER

I'd say it was the machine itself. Kadi needs an excuse to get rid of it, and Hail will do anything to keep it. A jockey using it for day-to-day is the only way to keep it on our deck. But that would be a lie.

"What is your score?" I tap my visor, right above the place where the little counter flickers on my display. "With the Spirit, I mean. What kind of sync do you get?"

She cocks her head. "Enough for high functionality. I get mid-seventies in flight, solid. Peaks around eighty-one, eighty-two under load. I've hit eighty-five in a fight."

I look back at the huge airlock, made to take a shell. "How far away do you think we are? From the Juno, I mean."

"Not counting the walls?" She blows out her cheeks. "Thirty meters. Forty maybe. Why?"

"What kind of sync would you get from this far out?"

Her eyes track along the ground. "This far out? Single digits, probably. With all the metal in the way, three to five percent, if I'm lucky." She watches me again. "What has this got to do with anything?"

"I flew a Spirit with Ten-Seven-Seven. From here, I'd probably do a little better than you, but I'd had that machine a long time." I turn back through the access-door. "Let me show you something."

I lead her out onto the launch-rail, halfway between the Juno's casket and the airlock doors. The machine tracks us.

"How far, do you think?"

She eyes it. "Fifty metres. About the same as before."

I nod and test the hangar's local net. "Avery?"

One of the overalls looks back. "What?"

"Get clear."

He hesitates, on the edge of mouthing off, but I'd bet that he was part of the crew that went behind my back, did work on my machine that I hadn't authorised, Kadi or no Kadi. Another jockey might have taken matters into their own hands, made an example of one so all the others understood. I'll let him go with a little PT.

"Understood," he mutters.

I wait for them to hit the deck, then spread my feet, take a deep breath, and stiffen all the muscle in my core. I close my eyes, and whisper, "Carry me."

31.44

The floor speeds away. My head feels like it's pulled free of my shoulders. My chest fills with fire, and makes me want to choke. My arms lock up, and my knees tremble.

48.09

62.13

My lenses shift in their focus-rings, trying to bring the world back from the blur. My reactor chamber reads a temperature spike, and pressures climb. My hydraulics flex and my fists stir in their housings. My wings press themselves against the cradle.

88.71

I can't hold it. I have to catch my head before I drop it. My stomach turns and my throat constricts. I don't hear the sound of tearing metal up ahead, or the shouts of the technicians.

2.43

I find Hail above me, holding me up by the webbing on my suit. Behind her, the cradle stands open, scaffolds scattered across the floor, the crew clear and watching. One of the lock-bolts has broken free of its mounts, landed end up on the concrete. The Juno stands in the midst of it, unsteady, a hand on its forehead.

Just like me.

"Christs," says Hail, eyes on me, then on the machine. "How did you do that?"

I have to gasp for air. "I can *hear* it."

IT SMELLS LIKE war in here.

And I'm barely through the door. I've got both feet on the ladder, and my back against the wall of the operator's airlock, listening as the outer hatch winds shut below me. My helmet would normally filter it, but my suit is trading air with the

Juno's own supply, sucking it in through one-way valves in my face plate.

There's the smell of oil from the hinges, and a sharp tang of hydraulic fluid. The plastic stink from the shell's air scrubbers, and the mix of solvents and surfactants that keep mould from growing in its lungs. There's plain old grease under everything else, but then, there would always be. The more of it drifts in, the more I recognise.

Hot metal mixed with body scents; a little acid underneath and a little iron overtop. Saline and blood and burnt propellant, acrid fuel and ozone. Other things more difficult to wash away.

Meat. Carbon. Fire.

Death.

A lot of it.

An amber hazard lamp spins in its socket, and a little panel informs me that the hull is back under pressure. I work the lock above my head, and climb the last of the ladder into the cockpit. The inner door shuts without my help, cutting the yellow light away to nothing.

I stand in the heart of my machine, swallowed in the warm and dark. I take a deep breath.

This is home.

"I'm ready."

Bulbs chatter and come to life: little ones hidden in the walls near my feet, bigger ones hidden in the tangle of cable above everything else. There are three or four directly overhead, giving the narrow cockpit a patchy yellow glow and leaving deep shadows in between. Even with the sickly lighting, the cockpit looks how I would expect, considering what you can see on the outside of its hull.

As without, so within. Exposed metal and chipping paint, every part built dull and heavy and over-engineered, built and rebuilt over generations.

I run my fingers down the wall. "You're an old bird, aren't you?"

Chunky welds plug holes in the pressure vessel, probably

matched by others even thicker on the armour outside. I count four breaks, all about as big as railgun slugs. Four dead jockeys, if I had to bet.

"And you've been through hell."

The counter spikes, and a log-stream scrolls down the side of my visor. It remembers thousands of operations, keeps the kill tallies from each one. Gun-cam feeds, mission replays, transcripts of everything its jockeys heard and said. Medical records.

Through hell, and back again.

I breathe more of the Juno's air and feel more of its hull, soft as I can with my fingers numb inside their gloves.

I trace oil stains between clusters of bolts and open ports. The more I look, the more patches I find. Some are just the welds, but others have metal plating fused crudely over the top. Cables run between newer components, and the stand-ins for things that couldn't be salvaged or replaced: jury-rigged substitutes hanging from cages and cable ties. Air filters jut out from sockets that don't quite fit them, joined with tape and solder and expanding foam.

In the middle of it all, is the saddle.

It's a little bubble of calm in the chaos, clean, and if you didn't know what to expect, completely out of place. It looks just the way it sounds; curved and padded, shaped like it was actually built with a human body for reference. It rests in its own little depression, half a metre below the cockpit floor.

There's a rut on either side of it, just wide enough to take your boots. In the flicks, they put jockeys in bucket seats as if they were pilots, or make them stand on open decks with their arms outstretched, as if the shell had the brains of a marching band and they were doing the conducting. They don't understand the way a shell works.

It needs to *feel* you move, and so it gives you space, but only as much as it can spare. There will be impacts, and gee high enough it'll turn you to bone-flecked jelly. So it gives and it takes away. It gives you space to move, but closes as much as it can around you, pads you so that you won't die the first time you take a turn with your engines burning.

I've missed this.

"I'm ready," I say.

The saddle rises from its hollow, and one of the consoles pops out of its sockets so I can step past. One foot in the well, and the other over the top. I slide my weight back in the saddle and it takes the load, moulding around my hips and fitting itself around my knees on either side. I do the dance, the little shake-and-shimmy when the saddle doesn't know you yet. It adjusts, and a little window pops up in the middle of my visor, asking what I think.

Continue calibration?

I shake my head. It doesn't feel like my old one did, but, "This will do for now."

I close belts around my waist and over my hips, anchoring myself in place. Muscle fibres in my suit run taut, offering something solid for me to rest against. They're the strongest part of the suit, made to keep me from folding over under load, but able to respond when I need it.

New user profile created, it replies. *Begin jack assembly?*

I let out a breath. "Do I have to?"

The window doesn't move.

"All right, all right."

I hate this part.

YOU SIGN ON the dotted line, and the first thing the company does is take a pound of flesh. That's not code for boot camp.

I went from feet on the street to my first round of surgeries in less than a week. They put me under without a word, and pulled my civilian wetware out on the same day they put the proprietary stuff in. They didn't bother to wipe the old OS; they just wrote it over, left some of the peripherals running in the background while the old implants went dead. I read the log from a company hospital bed two days later.

They changed the projection lenses in my eyes in a hundred and forty seconds a piece. After that, they cut into my chest, twelve minutes flat from first incision to full transplant. A new networking suite, haptics, biometrics, and a handful of stuff that NorCol tries not to advertise. Six minutes and thirty-three seconds later, they had all of my new wiring set and stitched into place without so much as a bruise.

For the most part, it was one-for-one. For everything the surgeons took out, they put something else back. My body had carried the standard 'ware for long enough, built up muscle and diverted arteries to fit. The company would have lost too much time on rehab if they'd carved out any more real estate, and so they gave me an upgrade instead. They pulled out the implants I'd worn since my early teens and replaced them with corporate gear.

There were a few exceptions, though.

They cut in just above and below each knee, made incisions on the outside of my thighs, right where it turns numb when you hit it on something. Another pair on each hip, right on the joint. Three more near the base of my spine. All just under the surface of my skin. NorCol's surgeons traded out for engineers, who went to work embedding stainless plugs in every cut, and filling them with nanite strains, made to bond me to the metal.

They look a little like electrical connections: one socket-ring inside another, the connection itself about as wide as a hair. The surgeons came back and stapled the plugs down, treated them with something that would turn the broken skin into scar tissue.

After my

—crash, if that's what you want to call it—

After I'd gotten myself arrested, while I was still locked into an infirmary cot, Internal Affairs brought a wetware tech into the room. I had both hands cuffed to the bedsides, already relieved of my weapons and network permissions, but the tech was there for the last of the company's property. She locked each plug down with a metal cap that needed a certain kind of key. Then she shut me out of everything else, and buried half of my memories under a company cipher.

Last night, medical opened my ports again.

It wasn't pretty. They had to take a scalpel around the edges, trimming back the places where the skin had grown across the ports. A medic cleaned them out afterwards, practised hands working like it was the kind of thing they did every day. The swabs came away with black blood, clear pus, and something that looked and felt like flakes of rust. I got a shot in the arm full of antiflam and antiseptic, but I don't know how much it's going to help. Now that I'm back in the saddle, my ports feel raw and swollen.

I take a deep breath and blink my way through a couple of prompts. My flight suit shifts, lines its own valves up with the plugs in my skin.

"All right," I tell the shell. "I'm ready as I'll ever be."

It hesitates. I smile into my helmet. "I'll survive, old bird."

The counter skips a beat. *You'd better.*

The saddle shudders, drops down into the hollow in the floor. Consoles inch closer as the space arranges itself around me. Armour shifts to compensate, internal airlocks and buffers closing tight. The shell settles, the cockpit maybe half the size it was when I climbed inside. Bulbs flick off in the corners and along the floor, leaving me alone in the dark.

Shackles close around my ankles, pulling them tight against the saddle. I can hear the jacks themselves, servos whining as they move around me. Little feelers with hypodermic tips. Even if I could see anything past the edges of my visor, I wouldn't go looking for them.

I don't feel them connect.

A dull throb warms my muscles and rides my spine, growing hotter every second. The plugs shift, and I can feel them moving. Their needle-tips will be splitting now, tiny filaments spreading out, burrowing in. I wish I didn't know what it looked like.

I get a flash of silver across my eyes, and pain lances through every part of me. The Juno holds back as I twitch and shudder and burn. I've been shot before, and it's easier than this. At least your body has the sense to go into shock.

Establishing connection...

Christs-dammit.

The Juno floods my veins with painkillers and trauma-blockers, and the ache fades, leaving me cold and panting. In its place, the hot shadows of where my body thinks it ought to hurt.

Connection established.

The first time is always this way. Always. The saddle has to get a feel for your pathways, and every jockey is different. The best way to understand you is to make you hurt, to follow a map of blazing neurons.

Converting signal. Begin transference?

But I'm still shaking. "Give me a second."

The shell is very still.

"All right." I grit my teeth and jam my eyes shut. "Go."

I die from the waist down. One moment, my legs are throbbing, feeling bruised; in the next, there is nothing. No sense of anything below the belt-line, just the oldest parts of my brain wondering why I'm not bleeding out. I drift, and try to swallow the panic building in my throat.

Transferring...

I really hate this part.

The pilot-sync gives the shell a way in, lets it in on what you mean to do and how you want to do it. At first there's a delay, the shell always catching you up; but when you've been at this as long as I have, it's like your own body.

But it's only half the solution. What happens when you can't quite feel your feet? When you're wearing thick shoes, or you've got pins and needles? You hit your toes on everything, that's what. You trip over yourself, catch your feet. So they cut you open, give you an extra set of nerves. So you can *feel*.

The floor of the hangar comes in cold and pitted, rumbled with the passage of distant trains. I can feel our weight, but it isn't spread evenly. We have one foot forward of the other, balanced where one of Avery's crew was changing the bearings in our ankle.

Transference complete, says my visor.

After that, the counter climbs quickly.

40.13

65.92

97.00

It holds, and the limiters keep it there. I feel like I could make a hundred if I tried.

But I might not come back.

I breathe in, let it out slowly. "Carry me," I tell the shell.

Merging with operator systems...

Shadows gather in the corners of my eyes, inching across until they swallow everything I can see. The Juno's body wraps itself around me, melts me down and casts me back in steel. Hydraulics flex like muscle. We feel each other.

The shell stretches out and relaxes back, to fit my posture. Our reactor shudders like the heartbeat in my chest, turbines cycle, fuel rushes like blood.

My pulse slows, and the machine cools around me. My vision shifts in time with the lenses in our head, finding focus on the ugly hangar outside. We adjust our feet and work out fingers. Our wings stretch out behind us, phantom limbs tied to muscles in my shoulders.

Merging complete.

I am alive again.

WE STEP INTO our starting blocks, left foot first. The block closes to our ankle, shackling us in place. One of Avery's ground crew steps up and does a manual check on the bolts and rails. The shell has its own sensors, but some habits die harder than others, and some will live forever.

The knuckledragger gives my Signal Officer an A-OK. The SO is wearing a void-suit, fireproof and armoured, with a full helmet over the top. He should be able to speak right into my ears, but he does something else instead—something older than this ship. Older than NorCol, if you're in the mood for counting.

He clears the deck on our left side and spells out a message with a pair of orange lamps.

Port side locked.

The shell and I lean forward, rest ourselves on knees and knuckles as we fit our right foot into the other block. Folau is on it, and he pats our hull on the way past.

"Clear!" he shouts to the officer up head.

The SO waves our right side clear, signals us again: Starboard locked. You are set.

"Understood," I send. "Thank you."

The ground crew trails away and begins sealing themselves into launch shelters on either side of the rail. The SO does one last check to make sure there's no one left on deck.

"Good hunting," he replies.

He fades away, and the rest of Hangar D folds in. Warbling radio chatter from a thousand different places: pilots calling in, jockeys calling out, ground crews and munitions mumbling into their mikes. *Horizon*'s traffic control wades through it, trying to keep order in the chaos.

The Juno throttles the noise back down to echoes and whispers, and finds me three connections in the blocks nearby. I can feel the others in their machines, three little pressure points arranged across the sides of my head. Salt is closest, and his contact presses hardest against my skull.

The Juno and I pick him up on our sensor-web, and my displays mark him out, a golden silhouette projected up against the wall. His prickly machine rests on the other side, sitting straight in its starting blocks, hands on its hips.

"What's the hold-up?" I ask.

The silhouette looks over at me, watching a projection of its own. "Waiting on a hotfix." It taps a finger on its knee. "I stepped a little too quickly. Looks like I made a dent."

Lear skips in. "He nearly buttered one of his crew."

Salt's shadow looks back at something the Juno and I can't see, past the wall of his hangar. There's too much steel for us to make it out.

"I lost my balance for a second. Just a second." Salt sighs loud enough to carry. "I'm a little rusty, as it turns out."

"I'm sure the knuckledraggers appreciate that."

"Damage?" I ask.

"All green. I'll be good to go as soon as the SO clears me."

"All right." I take a deep breath. "Any other problems?"

"I'm handling it. Sync is holding steady at seventy-eight percent. Just gotta get used to wearing it, is all." His silhouette gives an awkward thumbs-up. "There we go. Crew is clearing out. My machine will be good to go in two."

"And the jockey?"

Salt chuckles. "He'll just have to do."

"Fair enough." I try to get a fix on the shell behind him. "Lear?"

"Never flown anything with parts that matched."

"Ready to go?"

"SO signals all-clear. Locks are holding and rails are open." I can almost hear the grin. "This is going to be good."

At the end of the line, Hail's slender machine waits in its blocks, every system reporting. I can't see her with my instruments alone, but her shell is reporting every little detail. Enough for the Juno to sketch her out for me. Her posture is perfect.

"We're ready for launch, captain."

"Thank you, chief." There's an edge in her voice. "I need you faster than this. You get leeway today because we don't have time to drill, but that's it. I need a clean run."

"Aye aye," I reply. "We'll get it done."

The silhouette nods. "Get us clearance."

"On it." I hook myself back into the noise. "*Horizon* Tower, this is Recovery, two-eleven. This is Recovery flight two-one-one. Come in, Tower."

For a moment, all I've got is static.

A voice crackles in. "Good morning, two-eleven. This is Tower, and for the next"—there's a pause—"oh, eight minutes or so, I will be your flight control. You can call me Bell."

"Bell Tower?"

"That's the one. You looking for clearance?"

"Yes please, Bell."

"Confirm; you folks ready to fly?"

I send a ping past the other shells, one last time. They call back.

"Ready to go."

"Good. I've got an opening on the way. Warm those engines, it's cold outside."

I breathe in, let it out slowly. "Let's go, old bird."

My heartrate spikes hot and sudden in my throat, throbbing against the inside of my chest. I can almost feel the muscles contract, pounding in time with the pulse of our reactor. We flex our wings and I kick for thrust, flooding our engines with fire. The shell creaks as it strains against the launching blocks.

We slack off. Our engines are awake now: warm to the touch and waiting for us to call them back again.

The other machines do the same, blinking infrared in the corners of our eye.

"SOs report all-clear," says Tower. "Voiding."

My skin prickles, and the Juno's sensors read a sudden drop in pressure. Vents open up across the ceiling, sucking *Horizon*'s precious atmosphere someplace safer.

"Hangars report null-atmo." A timer appears in my eye. "Launch window opens in one minute, thirteen seconds." The floor rumbles as huge hydraulics work across the outside of the hull. The wall ahead of us splits down the middle. There's a sudden chill through my nerve-jacks, but the Juno holds it back. I shiver, but it isn't because of the cold. "Airlocks open."

A strange sunrise dawns on us. Dark winds blow.

"Get a grip," says Tower.

It takes me a moment to understand. Three metal chocks stick out of the deck, connected to rails under the floor. There's one on either side where our feet connect, and one more in the middle, with a handle just about big enough to fit the palm of a shell's hand. We lean forward and wrap our hands around the grip, crouching low, engines hot. Confirmations pop in and out of sight.

"Charging."

The rails crackle. We can feel the static.

"Confirm airlocks clear. Rails charged."

For a moment, we are together in the storm.

"Kick it, jockeys."

I reach for power, which beats in my chest. Our engines burn hot and loud. The rails spark and the starting blocks fire, shrieking as mag-drives hurl us towards the lock.

My suit fights the sudden gee, artificial muscle holding tight as the hangar blurs past on either side.

We hit the wind.

SEVEN

W<small>E FLOAT</small>.

We flare our wings and cut our thrust, waiting for flaps and stabilisers to bite. The breeze whistles past, and dust patters against our hull. The extra drag is chewing up our airspeed, rattling the cockpit as we cut through banks of cloud.

And then it goes still. We break through the cloud tops and into a sudden canyon between mountains of storm. I can't tell how big they are from here; there's nothing to measure them against. They might go on forever.

Between them is the Eye.

From here, all we have is the glowing rim and the strange currents that mark its edges. It feels closer out here, bigger without *Horizon*'s shields and armour in the way.

The glow catches the clouds, turns them red and dusty gold. We can feel it on our armour, but I'm glad we're so far away. Incandescent streaks blur the horizon, and equatorial storms tear at each other in the distance. It's what Hail calls the Storm Border; the break between the hot rim and the cold froth, inhabited by vast hurricanes and swarms of dark twisters. They trail hazy ribbons of cloud, bleeding out across the endless dawn.

The glow dims long before it reaches us: before it even leaves the bubble of lensing, distorted light that hugs the Eye. Even with all of our armour, and the crystalline composites built into the cockpit walls, I'm tingling.

I know it's just my imagination, but I keep the rad-counters out of sight anyway. The Juno's got my veins flooded with DeClide strains and Pepper Blue. They wouldn't stop the gales from stripping me of my skin, but our hull holds that out. The drugs make up for the places where the armour struggles, keeping me from catching tumours, or frying in the particle wash.

We are steel.

I can feel sheet ice on the contours of our hull, and all the warmth inside it. I breathe air past my helmet filters, but not all of the feeling belongs to me. It mixes with the rush of dust against the shell and makes it seem like I've got the breeze against my skin.

We let the cold wind carry us.

I work my fingers around inside my gloves. By the Juno's count, we've been flying five hours and change, and my creaking knuckles confirm it.

"Has it really been that long?" I whisper.

A timer in my visor adds another few decimal places, counting the picoseconds now.

I roll my eyes, and the helmet picks it up, tracking the movement across my internal displays. "Very clever," I say, but the Juno knows better. I don't quite bury the smile.

The cockpit shivers, and I look up, just in time to catch the edge of something solid in the cloud. I can't place the shape, but we have more than cameras and lenses. Our ranging systems read the change in density, flicking augur-strobes and PHADAR through the dust and converting the echoes into a shape I can understand.

The nerve-jacks sting, and I ask for antiflam. I blink my saddle through a reset, and let the jacks go to work. The painkillers numb it down, but there's a flash of sensation through the haze. Just for a moment, I can feel gravel beneath my feet and sand between my toes, course and cold and a little bit tacky.

They're both hallucinated and exactly real, translated from the ranging suite into familiar forms and feelings. Other systems report, filtering in through our eyes. There's solid ground out there. An island in the sky, the size of a small moon, its edges lost to cloud tops.

We're here.

"All right." I breathe deep. "Let's get dirty."

We push stabilisers out against the wind, shuddering as the plates fight the drag, and our windspeed plummets, giving us time to work our hands and legs free of their flight configuration. My visor reads the change in sync; we'd let it rest in the sixties for the flight, but now it climbs back past ninety. That kind of score is high for any jockey; high for me, and I'm the one doing the flying. I could probably cross my arms and let the Juno run on just my thoughts. I've known a few jockeys who worked like that—some of the best in the business, but a couple of mediocre ones too. Sometimes it's a skill, sometimes a knack.

I can feel how the Juno listens to me. Skill, knack: whatever it is, it's closer than anything I've had before.

For now, our limbs come alive around me, suddenly loose and responsive. I spread my arms. Outside, a pair of red fists move as if they were my own.

We throw them out for balance as the ground comes screaming closer, loosening our legs up to take the hit. The flaps close, and our engines spit thrust to counter the stuttering wind.

The sand rushes up to meet us.

We flare our wings just a moment before we hit and burn so hot it turns the stone glassy beneath us. Touch down's hard enough to rock me in the saddle, but light enough we don't lose reaction time. We kick pressure back into our legs and skip across a desert the colour of rust, engines glowing and ready to pull us back into the sky.

We tug our weapon from the mounts in the small of our back, and it expands in our hands. TaiBir Strategic, SSG-080-7, 258mm.

My eyes spark, and the weapon's extra senses hunt through the rush of dust around us. They lay the world out in golden holographics, tracing the curves of sand dunes and the hard stops of distant cliffs, marking red threat-vectors in between. Crosshairs float across the open, following the muzzle of our rifle, and an ammo counter rolls off in the corner—eight huge rounds in the magazine, thirty-two in reserve.

We stare into the murk, but there's nothing to see.

We hold very still, waiting for returns from the ranging systems. They're mapping everything they can touch, feeding it back into our projection. A wireframe valley opens across my visor, the real thing still hidden by the dust.

The cockpit creaks as we settle under gravity. We let the engines slack, and they tick and chatter as they cool.

The weapon comes back with nothing.

I let the air out of my burning chest, listening as the breeze whips and howls outside. A minute more, and the currents begin clearing the haze away, the dust running in smoky streamers from the edges of our armour. The sand is thin and powdery for the most part, but it gums around our lenses, reminding me of ash.

The Juno shakes itself irritably.

"All clear?" I ask.

No silhouettes detected.

I nod and we stand straight, folding our wings over on our shoulders.

A little world stretches out ahead of us, bathed in patchy Eye-light and covered in strands of cloud that linger between the peaks like fog. This rock is supposed to be artificial, but it doesn't look that way. We've landed in a shallow valley paved in stone, with little sand dunes piling up across it. A ridge rises in the distance, turning a circle most of a K away.

We chose this spot from a surveyor's hasty maps, and now that we're down and walking, I can see we chose well. As far as I can tell, this is the closest thing to open ground for a long way in any direction. Cliffs rise on the horizon, faults in the stone exposed under pressure. All around them is broken land: the cracked surface of the object, flexed apart by tidal forces. Crevasses run through the rock like arteries.

The surveyor who found this thing sent one of his drones into the cracks—a break in the ground maybe a meter wide at the top. It fell for nearly a minute before the signal cut out.

Then he found something else.

Hail showed us some of his video logs: helmet recordings and hull-cam feeds from a bony old man called Aoki. About halfway through, he mumbles something about a 'Lighthouse.'

I see it now.

It stands in the distance, high above the hills, completely still and impossibly thin. It's made of the same ruddy stone as the ground beneath our feet, but it's still pristine. Unmarked by the wind that scours everything else.

It glitters in the light.

I call up Aoki's charts and match the marker to what I'm seeing. There isn't a name for the strange shape ahead of me, but then, this hunk of rock doesn't have one either. All it has is a number: Object KA6769. That's it. None of the companies have claimed it yet. NorCol's probably aiming to put their label on it, and that's why they sent us. They want a feel for the place, a sense of whether it's worth the time and trouble.

I look up at the Lighthouse.

They want us up close and personal—augurs and samples at minimum. Better yet, they want one of us to take a step inside.

I grind my teeth.

Whoever draws the short straw, it better not be me. I'm made for open skies.

We set our rifle to passive sweep/sentry and pan our lenses across the valley. NorCol's here first, by the look of it. I scan the crags just in case, but nothing rises to meet us. We dropped down fast, letting the passives watch for threats—much as I like flying, there's nothing for cover when you're riding the breeze—but it looks like we're alone.

We turn and glance up at the sky, and I wake our nets, pinging the three shells still overhead. They're slowing already, mapping the space around us with their augurs. Their sensors are stronger than ours, and louder too. Much louder. They've got three hundred and thirty K to go, but it sounds like they're right next to us.

I smile at the contacts. "Taking your time, aren't you?" Hail must be losing hair.

We turn and survey our own private desert. "All right, old bird," I whisper. "Let's go for a stroll."

SOMETHING CATCHES OUR eye, a silver spark against the red-grey sand. We run our sensors across it, but it comes back dull and cold. There's no sign of a power source, no markers of anything made to explode. Augur returns come back clean.

We drop to our haunches and brush the dust away with our fingertips: a hunk of metal, cut like an armour plate. Flicking a corner out of the ground, we lift the whole thing out in one go.

Bright orange paint runs thick across one side, chipped on the edges and pearly where it burned. I roll it over.

It came off of a shell, if I had to guess. Thinner than ours, light and curvy where ours runs thick and flat. Whatever it was, it's long past dead. Trails in the paint show where shrapnel cut through it. Glancing, but hard enough to shatter the join where this plate met another.

We bring it up to our eyes, let our sensors get a taste, but there isn't much to show. I blink a few snapshots anyway, and skip the plate back to ground to get a better grip on the rifle. We drop to a knee, look out across the dunetops, spread the vents on our back and let the wind cool our engine sinks, trim our noisy augurs back to passive. The hills are cold and silent, and we do our best to imitate them.

But it doesn't help the tingling in my throat.

We wait in the quiet, eyes on the sky. A minute passes by, then another, just as empty as the first.

I'm about to stand—to push power back into our limbs and our augurs back across the open—when something heavy trips the edge of our senses. A deep echo on faraway cloud, and a shadow against the peaks and Eye-light.

We freeze everything we can spare, but toggle our joints on and off in brief, quiet bursts. We roll huge rounds through our magazine feed, and slowly shift our sights across the sky, steadying ourselves for the recoil to come. We sample engine emissions, catch ghostly returns and a whisper of hostile networking. Our lenses trace a shape I've never seen before.

Four arms and a sinuous hull, curving through the currents. Four huge wings, arranged across its spine, ending in fine feather tips that catch the Eye-light glow. A pair of huge vents trail heat and exotic particles and reactor signatures that read like the last moments of collapsing stars.

I kill our ranging, anything that reaches out from where we are and could be followed back. I drive the Juno lower, angle our lenses so nothing can reflect.

We hold our breath.

Even at range, the silhouette must be twice the size of any company shell I've flown or fought or seen. Hell, I've never even heard rumours of shapes like this, and jockeys like to gossip.

I ping the other shells above us, the signal as tight as I can make it.

"Contact, type unknown," I send. "REC." Recommend extreme caution.

Watch yourselves.

Hail clicks back. "Wait for the rain."

THREE MACHINES BREAK the clouds, full combat drop.

Ranging systems lead, and PHADAR crackles against the stone around me, echoes a thousand channels wide. Invisible and silent to human senses, a wash of noise and strobes to the machine. I pick my flight out, their outlines blurring as they pass in front of the Eye. The Juno puts up a hand to shield me from the glare, mechanical reflexes dimming the feed as light streams in between its fingers. Not *our* fingers; not just then.

For a heartbeat, the shell is all its own. We relax the hand together, and set it back on the rifle's grip.

The new arrivals circle. They've taken the long way round, keeping to prevailing storms and deep-weather cells. Now they drop with the Eye at their backs, little specks against the fire, using the glow for cover as they fall.

It's the trade-off. Decaturs have guns so big it would take two Junos just to lift one off the ground, and massive reactors to power every shot. Our own power plant isn't much bigger than my little fleshy fist, and it's quiet even by those standards. It's what you get when you're building shells in the middle of a civil war: cheap and compact, stripped down to whatever will do the job.

The new machines are different. They've got three hundred years of prosperity behind them, and alien secrets plundered from the dark. They come down faster than I can follow, throwing up dust and sand around their engines, vents glowing cherry-red inside. Spines and wings and stabiliser flaps open as they fall, but they don't have to wait for the wind. They descend on solid thrust, buoyant for a second before they hit the ground. We catch edges of them through the haze; yellow flashes of reflective hazard-strips, and armour full of angles in the light.

Our augurs pick a Decatur clear of the murk. It's a menacing assembly of ablative plate and thrust-vector blades, the prickly silhouette outlined in amber holographics. As the dust clears, it steps out into the Eye-glow, weapons level.

I can see down the throats of open missile tubes. A pair of assault cannons makes up most of one arm, barrels peeking out above its left hand. The right arm doesn't carry anything, but it isn't made to. A pair of crackling railguns is mounted on the shoulder, sweeping out ahead.

Its sensors howl into the distance, scouring sand and sky. Even the returns are deafening.

"Clear?" asks Salt, his footsteps rumbling through the stone, in through my jacks, up through the soles of my feet.

Hail's Spirit strides into the open. It's sleeker than Salt's machine, but you can see their shared ancestry. Her legs are a little longer, and her armour a little lighter, but it isn't made to take fire the way a Decatur is. It's shaped around clever fire-traps and deflector-surfaces, intended to slip through the storm rather than weathering it. Narrow wing tips fold around her shoulders, and a slender accelerator weapon rests in her hands.

It's almost exactly the same as the machine I flew with the 1077th, but Hail's is modified. It doesn't have a face; no eyes or visor-bands, just a smooth dome, pitted with little sensor-spots. Featureless, but close enough to a human head that you can feel it when it looks at you.

"Clear," she replies.

"Clear," says Lear, a second behind. "Where'd the chief go?"

We put out a hand to catch his eye. "Here."

It takes him a moment to find us.

"You are loud," we tell him.

His machine shrugs. It's the same model as the enamel-white shell I met on my first day, just inside the Juno's hangar block. The same jagged edges stained turquoise at the tips.

This one has a pair of silver rings around its wrists. We all do; they're NorCol's bond marks, made to look like we're still wearing shackles, even out here. It's a kind of plausible deniability—we're the dog-hounds brought in for war and not much else, and the company wouldn't want us confused for actual employees.

If the silver wasn't enough, massive stencils mark our chests and shoulders, painted black on the pale shells and yellow on mine. A grinning skull with *VIII* on its forehead. The death's-head insignia of the 8th Penitentiary.

"You called in a contact," says Hail.

"I did," I reply, "but I can't confirm it. I lost it before you broke the clouds."

"Maybe we scared it off," says Lear.

"Maybe I didn't see what I thought I saw. The more I look at the log—"

"The less sure you are?" asks Hail. "Froth does that. Let me see it."

I push the signatures across our little net.

"You're right," she says, a moment later. "That looks like a shadow to me."

"But I've never seen a silhouette like that."

"The other companies have frames designed for deep-froth.

Big, built for pressure. Surveyors and observation platforms, mostly."

"An observer, then? That'd explain why it turned tail," says Salt.

"We are loud," mutters Lear. His machine shakes itself out, as if its joints were stiff. "Heavy too. Christs-damn, is this thing heavy."

Salt's Decatur revs a bicep. "Think muscle, convict. The steel's got your back."

Hail cuts across them before Lear can bite back. "Keep everything you collected. We'll pass it on to Obs for classification."

Lear nods across our little desert. "Is this the right place?"

"Looks that way," I say. "Not quite what I was expecting."

"I hate it already."

Salt chuckles. "Doesn't look like enough to hate it, Lear."

"I'll make do." He aims his rail at the shadow on the horizon. "That's our object, then?"

I follow his gesture. Aoki's Lighthouse looms. "As far as I can tell."

"It gives me the creeps."

Hail's shell straightens. "We'll deal with the creeps later. Looks like we've got the right place." The Spirit glances over at me with its faceless head. "If Rook's shadow was a surveyor, we'd better get moving before anyone else shows up."

"It might be a bit late for that," I say. I push an image across the net: the chunk of armour from before.

"Dammit," she mutters. "Looks like Hasei beat us to the punch."

"It's the right shade of orange."

I pile on the rest of my readings, and the other shells share it amongst themselves.

"Where'd you find it?" asks Lear.

"Right where Salt's standing now. No sign of the owner."

Salt's machine checks the dirt between its feet. "There's nothing here now."

"Could it be driftwood?" I ask.

"Difficult to say, without the rest of it." Hail surveys the dunes. "Lear."

"Here."

"I heard 'Kustar trains its jockeys to track, old style. Any truth to that?"

His shell raps a knuckle against the side of its head. "Well, we didn't have anything so fancy as this."

"Rook, you and Salt"—Hail's shell puts two fingers out in front, shaped in a V—"take right and left, hunting pack. Eyes open." She glances back at Lear. "You're on me, Locust. Get sniffing."

I take the starboard flank, and Salt moves to port, almost hidden by the dunes. Lear and Hail are at the point of the V, and we're the tips. They guide us as we advance, Lear watching for a trail, Hail coordinating.

It's NorCol standard: if one of the flanks trips an ambush, the survivors are already facing the fire, arranged in a gunline.

Salt finds something first, and it doesn't kill him. He's almost all the way to the ridgeline when he calls out, pushes a stream from his hull cameras. The window in my field of view shows a pair of tracks cut deep into the stone, the treads of thin, three-toed feet. Around them, scratchmarks and fallen rock.

"Hasei must've been aiming for the flat," he says. "Same as we were." He tags a waypoint in the middle of the screen. "Paint here." It comes into focus; streaks of neon orange, marking the places where the ground cracked but didn't shatter, gouging steel. The feed turns, picks out something else. A trail of scratches, and furrows cut into the talus.

"The slope was too steep," I say. "Looks like they slipped."

"Rolled, looking at the mess."

"Hold up," says Hail. "We've got something."

I look back and find Lear's shell next to her, up to its elbows in the dust. It stands, rolling sand between its fingers.

"There's three of them here. Maybe four."

"Show us," says Hail, tracking the horizon.

The pale machine crouches again, and I trade Salt's camera-feed for Lear's. I watch through his eyes as the Decatur dusts the ground with turquoise fingertips. Delicate, if it wasn't so huge.

"See the burn patterns? Here"—he taps a finger on the ground, picking out a line of glassy circles in the stone—"here, and here. Hard burn. Too fast for wings, and about as heavy as us." His shell looks back at us and spreads its hands as if to measure. "Big fuckers."

I look over at Salt, then back at Hail and Lear. We picked this spot because it was about the only flat ground we could find for nearly fifty K in any direction.

The Lighthouse rises up ahead, and the broken armour lies where I left it, just behind us.

"They were being shot at."

The other three look at me.

"The main group put down just the same as we did. Smack in the middle, where the ground was as flat as it was going to get." I blink a marker over Lear. "They're coming in fast, combat drop. The fire starts"—I close the first, set another over Salt—"and whoever's still flying turns out of the incoming."

"And into the slope?" asks Salt. "You wouldn't do it on purpose."

"Someone takes a hit, right where I'm standing," says Hail. She glances back to where I found the plate. "Sends that piece of armour nearly two K backwards, in a straight line."

"Looks that way," I say.

"Railshot?" asks Lear.

"Too small. Rail'll kill the jockey, maybe knock out something important"—the Juno touches the little weld in the middle of our chest and my counter trembles—"but the hole's not very big. Whatever hit our friend here tore them apart. A hardround of some kind, wide calibre."

"Bullets." Lear's shell roots around on the ground. "Then there should be…" He trails off.

"What have you got?" asks Hail, not looking back, her weapon still scanning the horizon.

His shell spools its engines. "Step back."

Hail clears the space beside him, and Lear burns short and sharp. Nothing like his landing, but enough to kick him up in the air for half a second, wreathing him in dust.

He lands, gives the wind a moment to clear the haze, and pushes another feed for us to see. The bare stone's been shattered. Heavy bore.

"Hasei wasn't alone," says Hail. Her shell looks up toward the valley head. "And the fire came from the Lighthouse."

The Juno and I drop to our knee and sight our weapon up at the tower. I can feel the others do the same.

"It's quiet now," says Salt. "No returns on anything but stone."

Lear perks up again. "The tracks end right here." The Decatur stands and aims a finger downrange. "If that thing lights up, where do you run?"

"Front," says Salt, "get yourself into the crags. Rush them."

"Flank," I say, "lose them in the dunes. Come around."

"Down," says Hail.

We look back at her.

The Spirit stands on the edge of a chasm, a wide crevasse where the dunes come to an end, becoming a slow waterfall of dust.

I edge closer and risk an eye into the break. It's all rock for the first few metres, but there's something underneath. A ceiling in cross-section. A vault made of something that looks like brick.

There's a massive chamber beneath us. Beneath all of this.

"Hush," says Hail.

Her shell begins closing its connections, one after the other, leaving just enough to mark her out on our displays. It vents silver mist from the sinks on its back, bleeding heat into the breeze. "Five minutes." She nods to me. "Rook, you're next. Nice and quiet." Salt and Lear. "Thirty minutes clear, and you two are the lightshow. Whatever happens, you come calling. Loud as you can make it." Her voice falls to a whisper. "Cover me."

EIGHT

The Juno and I stand in the breeze, watching the crags. We'd be watching the Lighthouse too, but the other machines do a better job, so I leave them to it. I'm twitchy enough as it is, watching the little timer in the corner of my eye. Five minutes feel like they've stretched to an hour.

We look over our shoulder at Salt's Decatur.

"My turn. See you in thirty."

His machine knocks an easy salute off the corner of its head. "Good hunting."

We've already vented our engines through and through, but now we shutter our networks, kill any extra systems that might be making noise. Anything we can spare.

"You ready, old bird?" I whisper.

The counter jumps and ceilings out at 97, as high as the limiters will let us go. Our reactor-heart beats quickly.

"Thank you."

We step up to the edge of the crevasse. It feels darker now we're standing on the brink, looking down for any sign of Hail. She's in there somewhere, and I half expect to see her headlamps, but she knows better than that.

I take a breath and inch us towards the break. A second timer is running already, counting down to the fireworks. Lear and Salt couldn't go quiet even if they tried, so they give us a head start. Time to get our eyes on target, maybe smoke out whatever's creeping down below. These two are insurance.

Twenty-nine minutes and they drop in, all sound and fury, *Ride of the* fucking *Valkyries*.

The Juno and I take one last sweep and kill our augurs. The drop is short enough that we won't need engines to slow the fall, but we pop our headlamps on. Anyone watching'll see us easily enough with all the Eye-light streaming down the hole; with my torches on, there's a chance to make it mutual.

"Let's go."

We pull our wings close, flex hydraulics, and leap into the open.

We fall for less than a second before we hit dirt and turn on our heels, optics wide and our finger on the trigger. We stand on a mountain of dust, a column of light pouring down around us, our twin hearts pounding.

We spend a few beats getting our bearings, riding overclock and adrenaline, then kill the lamps and run blind into the dark, steering through the memory of what we'd seen, coming to rest in the lee of a massive pillar.

At least, I hope we do.

Our eyes recover, and night-vision systems fill them with greenscale and static. The pillar looms over us; it's made of the same brickwork textures as the ceiling above.

We set a shoulder against it and guide our weapon through the dark, panning across a vaulted cavern, the valley above us supported by a forest of pillars. Nothing moves between them, but then, all we've got is optics.

More of the pillars stand in rows, glowing in the light streaming through the crack above our head. They look like they run forever. Everything we saw on the surface rests on this.

We shift our aim and edge our way deeper. It's quiet; I'd gotten used to the wind brushing up against our hull, but there's only the faintest breeze down here. I can hear the Juno's insides move around me, joints shifting, everything set to the gentle rhythms of its powerplant. The noise of my breathing, the rush of blood behind my ears.

The cockpit is icy, even with my suit doing its best. Our

engines are inert, and we shut more of the machine down whenever we stop to check our bearings, leaving joints limp and systems silent until we need to move them again. We can't spare the heat to do anything more than that, not down here. We'd light this place up in infrared, an orange blossom against the silver-purple sand.

Some parts of us are better at dealing with the cold than others.

We measure our steps as quietly as we can, following our compass, edging closer to where the Lighthouse rises. More comes into focus as our eyes adjust, but I almost prefer the blur and darkness.

Little shadows stand on the floor around our feet, peeking out through the dust. They're statues, I realise, once I get the lenses dialled in close enough, barely taller than me. If I didn't know better, I'd say they were rearranging themselves when we look away, suddenly still when we sweep by them again.

Just nerves. I haven't hunted in a long time.

And this place isn't helping. I've never been so deep in Open Waters.

A little shiver creeps in through my feet. We turn, weapon tight to our shoulder. "What was that?" I whisper.

A window opens in one corner, tracing out a little map of all that we've seen so far. A red spot pulses in the distance, marking the source of a tremor in the stone beneath us. Short and soft, but there nonetheless. A footstep.

"Give me full immersion. All of it."

The Juno hesitates. *Are you sure?* asks the display.

I almost chuckle at that. "No," I say, but I blink past it anyway.

The shell gives me a moment to breathe. My ports still hurt, but that's what I get for leaving them a couple of years.

"Go," I say, before I have time to change my mind.

The jacks die under me. I tick and shudder as they roll through a reset, but there aren't any filters this time. The Juno gives me something to hold onto as I lose the feeling in my legs.

And then as they come alive.

The ground is there beneath my feet. Soft dust mixed with some kind of crystalline gravel that makes my soles ache. I can feel the gentle vibration that courses through everything in this place; the endless wind that grinds against the surface above.

And then comes the cold.

I howl into my helmet.

The Juno pulls back, tries to throttle the feed.

"No!" I have to force it through my teeth. "No," more clearly this time. "Wait."

This isn't real, I tell myself. I know it isn't.

Breathe in, breathe out.

This isn't real.

I imagine my feet. They're right *here*, inside a pair of thick, frostproof socks covered by soft inner shoes, inside a pressurised suit, inside steel-shod boots. They sit in a cockpit, within our hull, behind armour and insulation and more armour after that. I imagine every layer, rolling through them in my head, and cocooning myself in the middle of it all. I have to force my body to disbelieve. I'm out of practice.

It's most of a minute before I can keep my breathing steady. A window opens on my screen, and sketches my trembling heartbeat across it. It's the Juno's way of asking *Are you all right?*

I hold cold air in my lungs, let it out slowly. "I'm okay. I'm okay."

The window lingers for a moment more. *If you say so.*

But I'm not watching it. Or anything.

I can feel what the machine around me feels, translated one for one. I can feel footsteps.

I blink through a systems check one last time. Our vents are open, our engines cold; you wouldn't know us from the dust.

We take a gentle step together, and then we wait, listening for the echoes in the stone. We adjust, spread our weight, placing our feet down heel-to-toe. It'll do.

"Let's go."

We pull our weapon close and push deeper into the dark.

ANDREW SKINNER

* * *

HUMAN SPACE IS full of shells. Clumsy loaders on every dock, hauling luggage or supplies, working the lines that carry fuel and water. Spidery things that spark and flicker out beyond the airlocks, weld-light picking them out against patchwork hulls. Industrial hulks that live where cities turn to factory blocks, metal hides tanned by furnace glow.

Most people have never seen a machine like mine. Not colonial citizens, nor company employees. They might catch one in passing, see a shell flight lining up for transit, but it would always be from a distance. Always in peacetime. We are military-grade. Even little Juno is three or four times heavier than any of its civilian relatives, and that's without the weapons systems and the slabs of armour plate.

With all of that, we creep, our steps almost silent. We have to be. For as long as machines have done the fighting, war has been a game of hide and seek. The Juno's ancestors perfected it on Martian soil—the Knights of Argyre, fighting Coyotes and Vandals and Volkovs in the bloody-orange mist.

Back on the chain gang, Salt told me stories about the tracked monsters that fought in the time before that, when Unification was still a couple of lifetimes away. Back before the second Apollo, when the entire species was still stuck on the same rancid ball of dust. They jousted across Earth's ancient streets, hunting each other through the ruins of a planetwide city.

But none of it was new. The machines inherited it from us; tens of thousands of years hunting each other in the undergrowth, across the tundra and savannah, through the rubble. Holding our breath and trying hard not to step on anything that might give the game away.

Always listening.

I can hear another shell now, somewhere out ahead. I can hear it measuring its steps, using soft pads on its feet to keep the vibrations down. There's a moment's silence, then another footfall, another quiet second just behind. The jockey is choosing their path carefully, stopping to place every step. Sometimes the sound is dulled by sand drifts. But I can hear it.

Whoever's in the saddle, they know they're being listened to. They would; there's no way that they didn't hear Salt and Lear touch down outside, and there was every chance we'd find our way down here. At least they didn't get caught out in the open.

Not that it helps. Whatever it is, it's heavy—heavier than a Spirit. The Juno and I work our way closer, one foot in the front of the other. We don't have the armour for a stand-up fight, and our rifle needs a good eye to place the shots, but we have something else. The Juno is lighter than any shell built in my lifetime, and then some. Right now, it's almost silent.

We find them first.

We almost don't. It's a shadow against a background of shadows, even in the low-light. It's tall, almost three-quarters of the way to the ceiling, and it's full of straight lines; all solid plate, nothing made to break away. It could almost be one of the pillars.

I switch the feeds to infrared and our eyes strain for a moment, peering into a wash of blue and purple and silver-grey.

And yellow.

A tiny patch of it, straight ahead. It's the outline of a hand, warmth bleeding out between its knuckles, clasped around the grip of something cold. Fingers are always tricky, difficult to cover and even trickier to armour. Even then, this jockey's good. The machine is only half a degree above the cold—blink and you'd miss it.

We don't.

We set our sights on it, right where the top of its hull meets the superstructure, turns into a neck and cheekbones. We rest our finger on the trigger. I can feel the massive rounds in our magazine, hot and heavy. Black-tips, made for cracking shells.

Don't move.

We freeze.

The words hover in the middle of my vision. No voice, text only. It's a tightline transmission—a thread of light thinner than a human hair, aimed directly at the Juno's receiver, locked with a NorCol cipher.

"Origin?" I whisper.

The Juno pops a little window across the bottom of the display.

NCH221-107. Captain Hail, C.

I squint into the dark. "Where?"

Locating source...

A marker appears, almost directly behind the machine ahead of us. Another shadow, near-invisible even with my IR working hard. I flip to low-light, then back into thermal again. I can just about see the curve of the Spirit's bulbous head. Just.

The Juno and I aim a reply, careful not to clip the machine between us. *How many?*

Two, says Hail.

See one. My twelve. Other?

Your ten. Eight hundred metres.

I can't see anything. *No visual on two. Options?*

Have blindside, Hail replies.

The back of the hull, the awkward armour around their engines and between their shoulder-blades. *Blindside* is both a place and an intention.

We'd cut through it from two directions at once, hope to force an ejection before its sibling could respond.

But I see something else. *Timer,* I send.

Three minutes and change until Salt and Lear bring the noise.

Hail sends a wordless confirmation.

I hold my breath and watch the nearest shell creep, listening for its own phantoms in the darkness around us. It's a hundred metres away, less. Spitting distance, so far as a shell's concerned.

It's a Mirai, of Sigurd-Lem. A little older than the Spirit, but it could probably take both of us in a stand-up fight.

It's shaped like a person, and moves like one: at least, more than the angular, functional things NorCol likes to fly. Stubby wing surfaces rest around its shoulders, but they're folded in tight. A combat shield covers part of its left arm, a slab of armour with explosive bands bolted across the front. An assault cannon rests in its hands, massive magazine blocks joined to either side. High-gain lenses pattern its head and shoulders. There'll be others spread out around its body, top to toe. When I look out, I see what the Juno sees, visual feeds rolling in through two rows of optics in our skull. The Mirai lives in a flood of inputs, every limb and joint with its own set of eyes.

But it hasn't seen me yet.

I take a deep breath and let it out again. That's three companies on the same, tiny scrap of rock. So much for 'uninhabited.'

At least there are only two of them. We glance to our left, trying to see if we can pick Hail's other contact out of the gloom. One shadow gradually resolves out of the others, outline blurring as it moves to take a step. Another Mirai.

Something glints. An eye. Then another. My heart stops.

Shit.

It's looking right at us.

I bury the urge to twitch, to kick for thrust and skip back into cover. I want to turn, to get our muzzle on target.

Instead, we freeze, cold as the void, completely still.

And there's nothing but open air in the way.

THE WORLD OPENS up behind us.

I kill my low-light just in time. Screamer-flares erupt and infrared needles strobe through the dust. Every channel bubbles with white noise and signature-mirage. Two massive shocks run through the ground as Lear and Salt fall from altitude, weapons hot, their massive augur-arrays crackling through the air.

Hail's already moving, bracketing the Sigurd machine in front of me. Lines of plasma trace her shots, leaving acid afterimages in their wake. The Mirai is whip-fast, already halfway round, riding the impacts on its shield. We don't have time to join her; the other shell's drawing a bead on her machine, levelling its ugly auto at the nearest thing it can see. It still can't see me; it's doomed already.

The Juno and I tack past Hail and her engagement, line ourselves up, and kick for thrust. The gee throws me back in the saddle, easing as we float on engine burn, buoyant for half a second. We land so close the Mirai's black hull is all we can see. It tries to turn, spinning hard to bring its guns to bear, but we've already got it collared. We close our wrecking-ball fist, bring it down on the auto's heavy barrels. Steel meets steel with a thunderclap and a wash of sparks in the darkness, and the weapon spins loose in the air, hovering in a cloud of shattered armour and the Mirai's broken fingers.

The shell reels, fighting for purchase in the dust, but we've hit too hard and too fast. It works to keep its feet, grabbing at the secondary on its hip, but we use our rifle like a lance, slamming the barrel against its throat, bending the armour underneath.

98.38

I don't feel us pull the trigger, but my skin sings in the imaginary heat. For a second, the entire world is a pocket of fire and smoke and boiling gas. The flash is blinding, the picture playing over when I blink my eyes. I see enough. The round cuts through armour plate and insulation, but doesn't find its way to anything soft. The Mirai slides, feet spread to keep it balanced, leaving massive tracks in the stone between us. Our weapon ejects, cycles, and we haul it level in our hands.

The next shot slams the rifle back against my shoulder, tearing clean through mangled armour, arcing into brick and mortar beyond, spraying frag and burning propellant.

97.08

The shell stumbles, and its head spins away in a rush of fluid and atmosphere. Oil spatters and air turns silver in the cold. We catch the machine before it topples, pull it up by its ruined collarbone, jam our barrel against the hull, right over the cockpit.

97.00

I roar at the thing in front of us, all channels open. "Eject!"

The jockey hesitates, tries to raise a hand. We rest our muzzle against a joint, and take a whole arm clean at the shoulder, riding the recoil on gritted teeth and adrenaline, slamming our barrel back against its chest.

"Eject!" as loud as I can. "Christs-dammit. Eject!"

A massive casing rings against the floor.

"Eject!" My throat is raw. We press, feel the armour creaking under pressure.

The shell goes rigid, and explosive bolts squirrel around its hull, up and down and under its arms, popping welds and peeling armour. The machine splits, and retro-rockets wake inside, spitting fire past the cracks.

The Juno and I skip clear in time to watch the cockpit burst free, trailing fuel and cable.

The Mirai doesn't have its jockey any more, but it still has a little of its hindbrain left behind. The mindless body drives toward us, clawing through the air, sacrificing itself to keep us from the little pod bouncing away across the dust. The Juno and I oblige.

We kick out, plant our foot against its chest, ride it down to the ground. The hull opens up below us, shattered machinery suddenly bare where the cockpit used to be. Point blank, our rifle nearly cuts the thing in half.

We let it die.

My head is a rush and my lungs are raw. My skin prickles in the cold, but I'm burning inside. I've never made it past the limiters before. Never broken the magic ninety-seven. It feels like I might tip myself out, right here in my helmet. The Juno and I shudder together, darkness creeping in through the corners of my eyes.

A voice brings me back from the edge. It's Salt, shouting something I can't quite hear.

The line runs clear for a single, terrible second.

"Lear's hit!"

NINE

INSTINCT CARRIES ME the first few steps.

A gunshot rings out in a crowded place, and most people run the other way, trample each other trying to reach the doors. It's the sane thing to do, programmed into anything with a spinal column and a decent set of eyes.

Some run the other way. Maybe they don't know better, or they don't put much on their own lives, but they turn where they stand, and hurl themselves at the glare.

Stupid habit, I know.

I had the instinct to begin with, but NorCol drilled it deeper in. I crewed a company medivac for a while after basic, before I had the spurs to work a shell. I was on NorCol's tab, and they weren't going to let me off easy.

I flew an ambulance with an armoured snout and open doors, spin-guns mounted out the sides and bloodstains worked into the deck. It took me a few months to pass the trials for a jockey's patch, three months and three weeks after that to get myself a shell, but my job didn't change. My Spirit tore pilots out of flaming wrecks, collected ejectors before they burned up in the air or buttered themselves on the ground.

It was always the same. You hear a shot, you hear someone cry out, and you drop whatever you're doing. If there's a wall, you break your way through. If there's someone in the way, you push them aside. You turn and burn and pound dirt as hard as you can.

But I can barely move. I'm freezing up.

No. Not again.

44.31, says the counter.

I've been high functionality for nearly an hour now, riding the wave and feeling steel. I've gone higher than I've ever been before, swallowed in the glow of our reactor.

Now I'm just cold.

At first, I try fighting, straining muscles as I work to get the Juno moving in time. It's like wading through syrup. Everything is heavier than it ought to be, numb and stupid and out of time. The Juno pulls away from me.

40.00

It bottoms out. Forty is as low as you can go without losing sync. I struggle and cramp, but there's nothing I can do to find my way back.

It's happening again.

I'm going to watch them die.

Breathe.

It feels like a gentle breeze between the pillars. A shiver through my jacks.

Breathe.

And don't get us killed, I add, silently.

"I'm back," I whisper. "I'm back. I'm sorry."

The counter rises slowly. We could sync in a second, but the machine slows it down, gives me time to watch it climbing. Long enough to get the message.

Easy now.

"Thank you." I shake one hand out, work my fist against the cold. I shift the imaginary weight of the rifle outside, stretch the other set of fingers. We vent the heat of the fight, trim our nets back to something quiet, blink our lenses to clear the dust away, and bring the weapon to our shoulder. "Ready."

86.15

The Juno and I move on the balls of our feet, sprinting from pillar to pillar, crouching behind dust drifts and fallen masonry. We follow thermals between the vaults, map recoil-shocks through the floor and echoes off the ceiling. There's no wind or noise or glowing Eye-light, nothing to interfere.

We find their footprints before we find the machines themselves, then sparks and glimpses off their plates. A firefight wakes across our narrow horizon, fills the world with shadow verticals.

A shell flashes in and out of the darkness, right on the edge of what we can see. It's Salt, a flash of white plate and erupting weaponry, tracer-tracks and railgun sparks. Hail moves nearby, a ghost in the dust and gunsmoke.

A dark shape moves through the haze across from them, lit by muzzle flash. It's the Mirai from before, missing its shield and burning bright in the infrared, still alive despite Hail's best efforts.

It's a stand-up fight, toe-to-toe by shell standards.

I swallow the weight in my throat. If the Juno hadn't caught me, I might have lost us our feet. Now it slows me down. We don't have the armour or the power to jump into the thick of it, so we play to our strengths. Ducking under sections of ceiling fallen low between the pillars, darting from one tall shadow to another, trying to get a lock on Lear.

We keep our passives open, but we're mostly rolling blind. There's hot tungsten and depleteds in the walls, and they simmer when I switch to infrared. Burning propellant bleeds heat into the air, and the dust glimmers where it's been turned to glass by hypervelocity shot.

There's a slope I hadn't seen before, running downhill from where the Lighthouse seems to be. At least, that's what it looks like.

If we were out in the open, we'd have a better view, but then, an open field would have seen this fight done by now. Three on one, with space to manoeuvre, and we'd have spread the Mirai's wreckage all over.

Instead, it rides out the barrage, dodges bullets between the pillars. Its quick feet and fine sights keep the NorCol machines ducking for cover. Hail and Salt aren't pushovers, though. They turn the handle on the grinder, wither the ancient masonry under a stream of arcing fire.

No place for a Juno.

So we work the edges, keep our head down in the dust. The Sigurd machine may have eyes everywhere, but there's still a jockey in the saddle, soft and fallible.

We sprint between the pillars and drop into the lee of some broken stonework. At least, that's what I think it is. We level our weapon over the top, sighting on the chaos ahead, but it's a full ten seconds before I realise what we're leaning up against.

A distant muzzle flash lights it up, and I find myself looking down on a hulk of orange plate. We start back, and the Juno rides the rush, already sighting down for a shot.

But the Hasei shell doesn't move.

There's a huge hole in its chest, scorched and curled around an ejecting cockpit-pod. The Juno's sensors can't find a mind inside the shell, and there are no nets or reactor activity. It's still warm, though: dead less than half a day, if I had to guess.

We listen for the ping from its ejector, but wherever it is, it's keeping quiet. Its wingmates might have picked it up already, but there's every chance that the jockey just wants clear of the fight. I wouldn't blame them.

The Juno and I settle back against the dead machine and aim a tightline into the distance. *Friendly on three o'clock. Running cold. Check fire.*

Hail flashes back. *Understood. Checking fire.*

There's a line of light, almost unbearably bright. A railgun strike cuts a pillar in half, spilling glowing brick and metal sparks across the open. It's too big to be anything but the Decatur.

Don't forget to tell Salt.

I CAN SEE Lear. He was trying to make a break, looking for an angle. Locusts are famous for pulling rabbits out of hats, helmets, and plain old holes in the ground, but it looks like his luck cut short. His Decatur lost its left leg just below the knee and its right arm at the collarbone. He's pushed his wing-mounts out, spreading the blades for cover. They aren't doing him much good: they're nearly half gone already. His hull is holding up, but there's no telling how much longer that will last. He's stranded in the middle of the noise and light, stretched across his own personal no-man's-land.

Still alive, at least.

Hail and Salt are working to get close enough to get a grip on his machine, to drag him back from the brink, but the Sigurd jockey is good. Every time they break cover, or start looking for angles of their own, the Mirai brackets Lear. The shots aren't aimed, not yet, but that isn't the point.

A few shots hit, and Lear loses a couple of feathers, starts shouting back to Hail and Salt.

The tactic is as old as war itself. You aim to wound, not to kill, and force the other side to work their calculators. They can trade their wounded for a shot at you, but the field isn't level: they might lose more in the process. They've still got to draw a bead, but you've got your sights dialled in. Whoever's lying on the ground is getting buried, and there isn't much anyone can do about it.

Nothing Hail and Salt can do, at least.

The Juno and I inch closer, rising every time another load of munitions screams across the breach. We're quiet as the void and about as cold, using the hot noise for cover, dropping back when the air stills and the shadows flood back.

We're all optical, squinting at the dark and feeling our path with the Juno's sensitive feet. It's all we can do to keep from blinding ourselves. The low-light can't react fast enough to filter out the muzzle flash, and the infrared has to fight through a haze of boiling smoke. We can see the edge of a dark hull up ahead, but we don't need more than that. We can feel its heels as they slam against the ground, ringing to the weight of its shots.

And they get louder with every step we take. The Juno and I stop and settle against a pillar. We level the rifle out, and the feed comes in from our sights. It can handle the brightness a little better, and its eyes are keener than ours—more specialised. It cleans up the feed as we wait, and gives us a look at our target. A mirror-black carapace, covered in silver stencils.

SIGURD-LEM
XIV
REIVER GROUP B

There are a couple of Sigurd's glyphs underneath, but none I can read. I understand the markings underneath them, though. Kill tallies, scratched into the steel around its throat. Twenty-eight plus eleven. Twenty-eight shells sunk, eleven assists. Whoever's jockeying that thing is the fucking Grim Reaper.

The marks flicker in the glare of its muzzles, flashes outlines where the Juno and I can see them. We rest our sights where its neck meets its shoulders. Our rifle works through the targeting equations and plots the shot out in amber. A holographic Mirai tumbles, resets as the simulation works out the cleanest hit. The corrections come back, and we adjust. The weapon tells us to spread out feet, and shift the butt against our shoulder. We straighten and take a step to steady ourselves.

Our foot rings against something steel and we freeze.

The Juno risks a glance out of the corner of our eyes, and we find a patch of orange paint in the dust, lit up as another explosion rumbles through the ground. There's another piece of plating just beyond, about twice the size, folded over on itself. More of them spread out, buried in the sand, mixed in with a trail of ruined machinery and insulation. We shield our face with a hand and flick back to low-light, just for a second.

Oh no.

In the middle is a tangle of fabric and foil. A closer look shows limbs at strange angles and a helmeted head, twisted all the way around. The shapes are wrong, and make the body seem longer and thinner than it ought to be.

The jockey.

Crimson ice spreads out around the body, and the ejector-pod lies where it fell, torn open around massive bullet-holes.

They killed a jockey.

I grind my teeth.

They killed a jockey. Not out on the field, working their machine. Down in the sand, out of action.

We look up and straighten our weapon, but there's no dark shell up ahead. The Mirai is gone.

Fuck.

We launch ourselves to our feet and shoulder past the pillar, jogging first, then sprinting. We open our passives as wide as they will go, wake a few augurs from their sleep. They all come back with nothing to show. We drop to our knee, and I curse myself in silence.

It saw us. We got distracted, and it saw us.

Something clicks in the back of my head.

I push the Juno back into a run, and it lets me take the lead, not understanding. We leap across a fallen pillar, circle back the way we came, and find the Mirai in the middle of it all, right above Lear's machine.

I don't wait for anything more. We go hot, and I kick for so much thrust it picks us up, hurls us out of cover. We hit the ground running, keep on burning.

The Mirai leans down, and picks Lear's mangled shell up by its hull.

Hail and Salt are circling, but they don't understand. They're playing by rules that don't apply. They've got their weapons free and ready, but they don't shoot, not with one of their own in the way.

I wake my nets. Every single one. "Get out of there!"

The Mirai glances back at me, but it doesn't take aim.

It holds Lear up, presses its auto against his hull and opens up. The shots throw the ruined Decatur around, flapping like a target on a line. Lear pulls his ejectors, and the bolts start cutting him free, but the Mirai is too fast. It drops its weapon, plunges its open fist through Lear's cracked hull and tears his cockpit free. It rides the wash of his ejector rockets, holding on tight, fingers wrapped around the Decatur's heart and soul.

We land our first shot, right above the Mirai's shoulder-guard, but we're too far away. The bullet sparks off the armour, but the big machine barely moves. We send another round, cycle, and ride the recoil once again. We burn, running hard as the old Juno can handle.

Hail and Salt stand their ground. Lear is exposed, but he'll still be alive in there. They're waiting for a call. Waiting for the Sigurd jockey to admit the game's over. They think Lear is leverage, to be traded for a safe flight out.

But the call doesn't come.

"Get him out of there!"

Hail doesn't look at me. "We've got it under contr—"

The Mirai presses Lear's cockpit between its heavy hands. The pod shivers. Then it shatters.

OPERATOR DOWN.

OPERATOR DOWN.

OPERATOR DOWN.

The words scroll down the corner of my eye.

98.97

We're already flying, already riding the curve back down to earth. Our engines burn so hot that they're screaming warnings in my head. Our rifle matches the sound. We shake, caught between the recoil and thrust. We rain fire over the remains of Lear's machine, coming in so fast we catch sparks of burning armour in our eyes.

One bullet goes in the Mirai's chest, a second in its forehead. One in its hip, and another snaps its elbow back at the joint.

We're still riding momentum when our first punch lands, hits so hard we mangle our fingers on its hull. We draw back, slam into it again, shatter the rest of our fist behind it. The impact's so loud it hurts my ears inside my helmet. We plant another shot, point-blank against the outline of our knuckles in the steel.

The dark machine staggers back and falls over itself, chest buckled and ejector marks already showing under its armour.

*   *   *

WHO THE FUCK—

   —who the fuck—

   —kills an ejector?

Nobody, that's who.

Sometimes there's blood on the sand, we understand that; it's the name of the game. Once you pull the plug, though, that's it. You are no longer a hostile. Keep to yourself and any company machine will give you a pass. We're all jockeys at the end of the day. Don't do unto others, and they won't do unto you. It's been that way for longer than I've been alive, longer than anyone cares to remember.

There are *rules*.

I disconnect, dismount, and drop clear of the operator's lock. I pull my service weapon from its holster as I march across the dust.

I hurt all over, but that doesn't stop me. Hell, it doesn't even slow me down.

The ejector-pod is the same colour as the machine that held it. It rings in my ears, Sigurd's recovery frequencies singing loud and proud now that I'm close up. There are other sounds too. My heartbeat, deep and heady. My ragged breathing, hissing in my helmet. Hail and Salt drop in through the speakers, but I don't know if I hear them.

97.31, says the little counter in the middle of my visor, fading in and out of my vision.

I make for the thick hatch that holds the back of the pod shut; the one that keeps its cargo safe and sound. It won't stop us.

The Juno reaches over me. *I reach over her.*

It grips the hatch with its good hand. *I grip the hatch with my good hand.*

We spread our feet, and tear.

Metal splits around our fingers, bolts pop and hinges fail. Atmosphere boils in the vacuum.

I step into the breach, weapon drawn.

She steps into the breach, weapon drawn.

"Stand up!" I howl. "Stand up where I can see you!"

"YOU HEAR ME?"

My voice rolls around inside my helmet, leaves me alone in the cold with my pounding heart and heaving lungs. I inch my weapon past the broken hinges, and into the airlock behind it. I realise I can't see the saddle.

A steel column stands in the way, splitting the narrow walkway in two. There's something similar in the Juno, and variants in almost every shell I've ever flown. It doesn't look the same, but I know what it is and what it does. You could call it a vertebra, one big link in a chain that supports the machine body, and carries the thick cables and conductors that run into the base of the saddle.

I shout again.

"Come out with your hands up!" It sounds shrill now that my heartrate's running flat. I stand in the quiet another thirty seconds, making sure my channels are open. There's nothing from the Sigurd pod. I shut them down, open them again, and clear every channel I have access to; I cycle back through the Juno's transmitters, and boost the sound of my voice across every frequency I can reach, raw and unfiltered.

Still nothing.

And I'm running out of fire.

"Stacking up," says a voice in my ear. It takes me almost a whole second to process the words. I spin at the weight of a glove on my shoulder and Hail steps back, one hand in the air, the other carrying a weapon like mine.

Her Spirit rests on one knee behind her, its little airlock cycling as it stands again. Salt's shell moves through the dust in the distance, weapons crackling, panning through the shadows.

Hail catches my eye. "My shell's set for overwatch. It'll cover us," she says as the slender machine turns away. She rests her free hand on my shoulder; there's power in the grip. "Stacking up."

I nod and turn to face the broken hatch. "Take right," I whisper across our little net.

She taps my shoulder again. "Go."

I pass the column, following the narrow walk along the inside of the cockpit-pod. Hail curves back on the other side.

A dark suit meets us in the middle, still in its saddle. We face it, weapons level with its helmet, fingers on triggers.

"Hands up!" I shout.

The jockey doesn't move.

"I said, hands up!"

Nothing. We stand in the quiet, staring at our reflections in the visor-glass.

"Look," whispers Hail. She reaches out and runs a finger across the collar.

I glance at her, but the Sigurd jockey doesn't react.

She brings the glove back, works the fingers together where I can see. "Dust."

Not the mix of ground steel and burnt insulation you'd get from inside a crash, and not the stuff floating around the ruddy desert outside. I do the same as Hail, leaving a streak across his visor. The dust is dark and tacky, the same oily glaze you'll find inside any machine, no matter who's doing the flying. Grease mixed in with tiny paint-chips, metal powder, fuel vapour, and regular old filth. It folds together into a sheen that clings to anything it touches, prone to collecting on any unmoving surface.

Hail and I trade glances.

"You think—?"

She shrugs.

His strange cylindrical helmet lolls to one side, covered in the same strange muck as the rest of him. Nothing strange about that, not on its own. There are times when the company will put you on a long-haul flight, or send you out on a couple of ops back-to-back. You can spend a couple of days in the saddle, catching sleep while the machine takes care of business in between. You always come out of those trips dirty; it's what you get from being inside a living, moving machine. What's strange is his gloves.

You can get your fingers dirty, sure, but there's a pattern to that. Nothing collects on gloves.

There are switches to flip and buttons that need pressing. Even when you've got high-sync, even when the whole shell is one big phantom limb, there are some things that need a human touch. The oldest parts of any machine, usually: hatch locks, backup instruments, pressure valves. And that's not counting the thousand times you'll touch your visor, subconsciously trying to wipe away the sweat on your forehead, or reaching for an itch you probably shouldn't be trying to scratch. But his gloves are just as soot-covered as the rest of him.

I lean closer, and Hail gives me an eye. "Let me try something."

She watches me for half a second more, but doesn't move just yet.

I feel it too. Like I might wake him up.

I rap my knuckles on the visor. My glove leaves a mark on the glass, moves the helmet. He doesn't stir. I make a fist and hit hard enough to rock him back in the seat.

I flinch, and Hail frowns at me. "What is it?"

"Nothing," I lie. My fist feels like I've broken it, like there's something loose inside.

It takes a second for me to realise why. The Juno and I hit so hard that we broke its hand and sank a Sigurd shell in the process. I'm still feeling the echoes of that moment. I switch hands and shove him back, a little more carefully this time. Something gives underneath the suit, soft and spongy.

I start, nearly fall over myself.

Hail catches him, and looks back at me. "Are you okay?"

But I'm not watching her. In the light from her helmet-lamps I see ice inside his visor. The glass is silver-grey with frost. Ice.

Inside his helmet.

I find my feet. "Look."

"Christs."

I reach under the helmet's chin, feeling for the emergency

release. They work on pressure; if there's air inside, it won't break the seal until there's air on the outside too.

If it's empty—

The helmet pops loose without a fight, almost dropping into my hand. We can see the patch on his chest now. The jockey's name is Dane.

Dane doesn't look up as I pull the helmet clear. He can't. He stares straight ahead, eyelids puckered around a pair of open sockets. His skin is a deep red, and almost rubbery. It flakes in places, and cracks where the ice has turned it black. His jaw hangs open, stretched tight over empty cheeks.

Dane has been dead a long time.

"No gunshot wounds," says Hail. "Suit's still intact, by the look of it." She checks his chest. "Trauma plates are still green." She dials her headlamps up, runs them across Dane's withered face. "Freeze-dried, rather than frostburned."

I nod. "Dead before the cold got in."

"Impact?"

I shake my head. "He's still in the saddle. If the gee was high enough to kill him, it would have messed his connections up with it."

Hail shrugs. "The shell seemed pretty functional to me."

That's one way of putting it.

I peer at the nerve-jacks still locked into his legs. The suit is torn around them, and crimson crystals show where they shredded muscle and skin underneath. "Too fast for freezing and too clean for impact. He suffocated."

Hail's eyes glow in the light of the displays inside her helmet. "No holes in the hull. And he didn't die today." She looks up at the ceiling. "This thing was flying hollow. No air, no jockey."

"Worse than that." I guide her eyes to the bloody jacks. "He choked, and the saddle held him while it happened."

TEN

I SIT ON the Juno's knee and drink from the little tube in my helmet. The water is warm and my skin is cold, but I'm not sure how much of it I feel. Not sure I'm feeling very much of anything right now.

I hold up my right hand and turn it over where I can see. It's the one thing I *can* feel. My knuckles throb like I've just thrown them against a concrete wall.

I tell myself it's all in my head and look the glove over for signs of damage. There aren't any, and I can move the joints easily enough, but when I do it feels like there's a loose bone, shattered just like the fist we used to break Sigurd's machine. I know it isn't real, and that it's just an artefact of the operator's feedback systems working a little better than they should, but that doesn't help the ache.

I look up at the Juno's glassy eyes. "I'm sorry, old bird."

It glances at the stump of its hand. We hit so hard we crushed the fingers flat, fusing them with the rest of the gauntlet underneath. The shell gives a little shake. A shrug, if you know what you're looking for. And there's a stream of pilot-status queries, the kind you do before takeoff, or when you've lost connection and the machine can't feel where you are...

Oh.

The big eyes watch me. *Are you okay?*

I'm not sure I have an answer. Not sure I could put it all together even if I did. It's been a while since I've had to do what I did today.

I've pulled bodies out of cockpits full of holes, more air than armour, and I've burnt my flesh-and-blood hands in white-hot fires. I've done every kind of recovery that NorCol cares to train its S&R crews for, and then I've done them again and again until they all blurred together into one long rush of pain and dying. I've done things the company's instructors could hardly imagine, let alone prepare me for.

There's an informal chatter code among rescue corps: 'DTW,' Dead in The Water. It means everything and nothing, all at once. Catastrophic failure of the pressure-vessel, or the lucky pinhole shot that goes clean through. High altitude fragmentation, atmospheric shock, or a whole airframe splattered across terra firma.

It was a DTW that got me sitting here, on the inside of an alien rock, orbiting something nobody's ever heard of before. Three of them, actually. And there was nothing I could do.

Worse, I was the one that led them into the fire. It wasn't intentional, but you tell that to your own unit while they're busy burning up. I was cleared of their deaths, but that didn't help. The filings in my court martial called what came afterwards a 'rampage,' which I suppose is accurate enough.

Christs, my hand hurts.

Lear was Dead in The Water, but that doesn't mean anything on its own. He wasn't a bloody stain or a twist of skin and cartilage or anything. That would have been easier; I've cleaned half a dozen cockpits out by hand, done the bucket shift through human wreckage maybe a dozen more times on top of that. You zone out, and your hands keep running on automatic.

When Salt found Lear's body, well—

Lear was still Lear.

I'm glad I couldn't see his face.

He's with Salt now, wrapped in a couple of silver blankets we stripped out of an emergency survival kit. Salt's flight suit is thicker than mine or Hail's, thick enough to handle the kind of cold that would freeze us both to death. It'll keep Lear whole until we can send him off. Hail says NorCol doesn't bury cons, but we'll see to him ourselves. Jockeys have their own rituals.

Salt is around here still, humming that old tune of his across the net. Habit makes me follow along, though my helmet mikes are off. This one's just for me. I close my eyes and let it carry me.

I don't hear him stop.

"What would you have done?"

I almost miss it. I blink and find Salt's heavy suit standing in the dust below me, looking up. I swallow and open my nets, but it's a moment before I can speak.

"I got there as fast as I could. I—I just—"

He stops me short. "No. You did everything you could. The fault, if there is any, is ours, Hail's and mine."

"Don't say that."

"It has to be said, and I'm saying it. You saw it coming. Hail and I were fucking bystanders."

Even when we were still in chain, still bolted to the low decks of a murky prison ship, I don't think I'd ever heard him so bitter. He breathes loud enough that I can hear it, almost feel the changing pressure in my ears.

"I'm gonna wear that one a long time." He clears his throat, and looks back up at me. "When I asked you what you would've done, I wasn't talking about Lear." He nods at the dark pod, lying in the trench it carved through the dust. "What would you have done if that Sigurd jockey had been alive when you found him?"

"Shot him." It's almost too easy to say.

Salt nods. "Me too." He turns on his heel, wakes the dust around his boots. "Come on."

I sit up. "Where are we going?"

"To find out why."

WE SET DOWN near the first Sigurd wreck. I didn't see where the ejector went, but I remember my way back to the shell. In the end, Salt tracks the pod back, following a thermal shadow only his big eyes can see. It's resting up against a pillar, the snout buried in fallen brickwork. The Decatur dusts it off with its fingers while Hail and I dismount.

"Want me to open it up?" he asks.

Hail looks up at him. "You're a gun platform, Salt. Stick to what you're good at. Cover us."

The pale machine turns away, rail crackling. "Aye aye," he says, a little acid creeping in.

Hail's already at the hatch, and I pull in behind her. She tries the lock-handle first, but it doesn't budge.

"If there's a key, we're missing it."

She spares me a glance, then looks up and blinks at her machine. The Spirit leans over and taps one of its slender fingers against the hatch.

Hail nods, turns and waves me back. "Get clear."

We drop into the dust, and the shell sets down on one knee, clenching a fist. I shy away, but I'm expecting this to work the way the Juno would. I haven't flown a Spirit in a while.

It draws a bead, and lands a punch that's just exactly hard enough. It rocks the ground beneath our feet and spills dust from the pod's armour, but where the Juno and I would've crumpled it under our fist, the Spirit lands a hit dead centre, warping the door and popping the bolts. It leaves everything else intact.

Cockpit pods are built to ride the sudden gee as they eject, to drift through storms and atmosphere until someone picks them up, but that means less than you'd expect. They'll take a hit from just about anything a human being could carry on their own, maybe even a glancing shot from a shell, but it isn't enough to stop the Spirit, not now. Hail's machine pulls at the buckled door, hinges holding maybe ten seconds before it all falls clear to the dust, trailing cables and twisted metal.

Hail and I stack up, but she's in the lead this time. I line up behind her, slap her shoulder to signal *Go*. We rush in guns drawn, circling around through a pod almost identical to the first. We find a jockey in the same black flight suit as the first, and she's just about as dead. Judging by the body, she's been cold as long as her wingmate has. She's got the same odd tears around her jacks, the same frost in her visor-glass, and nothing else to say what killed her.

"I don't know what we were expecting."

Hail nods, but it's a moment before she replies. "She didn't fly all the way out here with a hollow shell on her wing. Same goes for the other one. You talk, you trade nav and obs and ranging."

I tap my helmet. "You'd notice if there was no one home."

"You would. And you'd turn back. Especially if they'd been dead as long as this."

"If these machines were *just* hollow, it would be easier to deal with. These two flew here with dead bodies in their saddles. They *took off* like this."

"Maybe they weren't the ones flying."

I holster my weapon. "You think the shell did it? All on its own?"

Hail shrugs. "It wouldn't be the strangest thing I've seen." She flicks her safety on and turns back the way she came. "Let's get out of here."

Salt watches over us as we make tracks for our machines. "Aren't they supposed to turn back? Hollow shells, I mean. Aren't they supposed to head home?"

I shrug, and the Juno mimics it, before I've even sat down in the saddle. "It probably depends on the company."

Hail comes up on the line, her own shell swaying gently as its jockey comes back into focus. "No, Salt's right. Leaving a hollow on the field is a waste of a shell."

I guess so. "Difficult to kill the jockey without breaking everything else along the way."

The Spirit nods. "Which means that if the machine survives, it's probably taken a big enough hit that it might as well be dead. It's more cost effective to get the hardware back home, jockey or no jockey."

"But there'll be some things that keep them around."

"A friendly machine under fire, maybe, but it'd have to be

pretty grim. Something the shell figures is more valuable than itself."

"So that's half of it, then." Salt's Decatur peers into the dark. "What's valuable enough to keep two hollows in the line of fire?"

"Probably the same thing that got Hasei into the mix."

Hail's machine glances over its shoulder. Even without eyes, the expression is clear enough. "We don't know how long ago that was. That plate you found might have been driftwood."

"It wasn't."

The Spirit spreads its hands. "Even so, a scrap of armour and some bullet holes isn't much to go on."

Now Salt is looking at me too. "It *isn't* much to go on." He doesn't make it all the way to asking.

We come about. Even with the pain in our hands, I'm beginning to think that I only feel alive in the saddle. "How about a whole shell, then?"

I'M THE ONE who made the offer, but it's the Juno who remembers the way. We backtrack across lines of heavy footprints—our own, already disappearing in the little breezes that creep across the floor.

The Hasei wreck is where we left it; there's a deep furrow where we set our knee and used the dead shell for cover. Now that I've got the time to look, it's worse off than I remember. It was killed in a stand-up fight, withered by the steel wind. There's a little body heat left, but only just enough to show in infrared.

There's something else, behind the warmth. Something that sparks and tingles on our skin.

"Reactors are bleeding," says Salt, just behind me. "They hit it hard."

Hail peers past him. "Any sign of the pod?"

The Juno looks over to where the Mirai had been before we lost it.

I have to turn our head. My first instinct is to point the way, but our damaged right arm cramps at the thought and our left hand's full of rifle, so I blink a quick marker instead. I don't want to look too hard. "Over there. Look for Hasei's colours."

Hail vaults the wreck and follows our faded footsteps between the pillars. The pod flashes into view under the Spirit's lamps, fading again as she turns to look for the jockey. Or what's left of them.

"Christs," she whispers.

The line is silent for a moment.

"This is what you saw, isn't it?" The Spirit clenches a fist. "You were here"—it looks over its shoulder—"and we were over there." The angle changes. "Which puts that Mirai at twelve o'clock. Maybe half a K." Her shell looks down suddenly as it hits something in the sand. An orange plate skips away into the dark.

"We kicked foot that same piece of scrap." The Juno and I roll up behind her, adding our headlamps to the scene. "And this is what we saw."

An ejector pod, opened up by massive gunshot wounds. They're close-range and methodical.

Hail breathes deep. "Lear wasn't the first."

"Not even the second," growls Salt.

I'm expecting his pale shell right behind us; the helmet adds a vector to his voice—tweaking levels to give direction—but always keeps the volume high enough to hear. When we look back, there's nothing to see. Infrared brings him into view a few hundred metres clear. Five reactor-cases light up around him, warm sparks on a field of purple and grey.

Salt stands in the middle of a wasteland. Carbon streaks mark the stone around his feet and draw little glassy circles where burning munitions baked the dust. The pillars around him are still standing, but worn down from thick trunks to narrow cores by a gale of hypervelocity shot.

There should be five wrecks to match the five powerplant units, but I'm not sure I could point them out. Even with Hasei's bright colours and Sigurd's mirror-black, it's impossible to tell where one machine ends and the others begin. The companies aren't in the habit of colour coding the insides of their shells, and what's here has been carved up, spread wide. Give us a week and we still wouldn't find it all.

The reactors didn't fare much better than the shells that carried them. Two are still intact; one of Sigurd's little suns, one of Hasei's silver supernovas. Two more are almost there, but hairline cracks run across them, their contents haemorrhaging into the cold. One has lost containment, both heart-chambers compromised 60-70%. It doesn't hurt us; our skin is thick and our parts are sturdy, but that doesn't stop the strange sparks across our eyes.

Putting a hole in a reactor-case is difficult, breaking one more so. Easier to kill the flesh and blood riding in the saddle.

If the cores are out in the open, casings cracked and shattered, then—

"What happened to the jockeys?"

The Decatur aims a finger, raises markers on the net. "Two Sigurd ejectors. One—and two."

The first is almost close enough for us to touch. "Clean break. No damage."

Salt marches on the other. "More of the same. Hatches sealed. No squealers."

No emergency beacons, no radio, not even a strobe light. Nothing. An ejector can keep a jockey alive for days, assuming nothing leaked or was damaged in the fight: but it's the last ditch. They have to survive everything else dying around them, and the chances are they haven't. And if they have, someone still has to find them.

Ask a jockey how they'd like to die, and most will opt for hot and fast and flying. If you weren't a jockey, you'd assume it was an ego thing; that's what we signed up for, right? A blaze of glory, rendered in burning steel and exploding magazines. But that couldn't be further from the truth. No one wants to burn to death, even if it's what we all expect. It's just better than the alternative.

Every so often, a patrol will turn up an intact ejector, a mummified jockey still resting inside.

Fallen pods are where we keep our nightmares.

"It's cold."

Salt rumbles. "Hollow?"

"I'd put money on it."

Hail hangs back, watching. "Any orange?"

"Over here." Salt's words turn to a growl. "Christs. Tally one."

"It isn't a tally if someone murdered them," says Hail. Her voice doesn't have Salt's distant thunder, but that almost makes it worse. "We've got five cores and three pods. Find me the other two."

Something orange catches our headlamps. Dammit, I really want to look away. "Got number four over here." The Juno pulls us away, aims our eyes at something else. I let it. "Jockey tried to run on foot."

Hail doesn't let me drift. "Just need number five."

I take a deep breath, and the shell matches the feeling, the little ember of our reactor warm inside our chest. We pick through the wrecks, but it looks exactly the way I'd expect.

Hasei and Sigurd tripped over each other in the dark and tore each other to shreds. We find dead missiles, and a couple of live ones too, tipped from their tubes. Piles of unusual brass, and a few of the rounds themselves. Long tracks from railgun shots. Armour in sheets and fragments, whole limbs and severed fingers. One of Hasei's hammerheads, still intact, wide eyes peering up at us from the dust. But no ejector.

"I'm not seeing anything."

"Keep looking. It has to be around here somewhere."

"I've got it," says Salt. "One moment." We watch as he traces something we can't see. His shell is hot and loud, but it's got eyes like nothing else. "Dead and cold, just like the others," he says, but: "You'll want to have a look at this."

ELEVEN

ONE MACHINE SHOULD look just the same as any other; after all, the wind doesn't care what badges you're wearing so long as there's a point in your snout, a curve in your wings, and enough fire in your engines to keep you up and flying. You'd think the companies would all just find the meanest shapes they could, build them over and over, pausing only to change the paint scheme.

They don't. NorCol's design bureaus like slopes and crags, tips like beaks and spines like feathers. Sigurd rounds its edges, fits everything into brutal frames that look like they could break you down by hand, and covers them in that strange mirror-finish that hurts your eyes. Hasei likes bright colours, and silhouettes that don't make sense until they're upside-down and pulling twice your gee.

There's a reason for it: adaptation.

The Articles give the Colonial Authority final say over any volume of space that happens to contain a human being—at least, that's the theory. They're supposed to be what keeps us all in line, the biggest stick in human space, but they can only reach so far. The companies all keep colonies of their own, so far from the shallows that they might as well be a different species. Cities staffed with citizen-employees, managers who run their own boroughs, and governors with seats on the companies' massive boards.

When you're that far out, there isn't much the Authority can do to keep the peace, and the companies will always find things to squabble over. On the frontier, that usually means solid ground. Stable worlds are rare, and even then, they have a habit of being deserts, only just fit for human life, give or take a few decades' terraforming. There are a few that are shear with ice, and even fewer where it melts for more than a moment every few months or so.

There are temperates, but only two that are anything like the little blue marble that started this mess in the first place. Jotunheim is one, and Sigurd-Lem holds it tight. Kildare is the other, and it's NorCol's crown jewel, out of bounds to anyone and everything. A pair of dreadnoughts watches its skies, and a trillion extra stars mark the minefields out beyond. It has two moons, but knowing the company, they'll be all dug out, innards replaced with anti-orbital batteries so big they'd sink a planet.

It's a prestige project, and I'd put money on Jotunheim being Sigurd's version of the same. Held up where employees can see but never touch, like some blue-green kind of heaven.

Shells aren't built for the crown worlds. There's no point. Nothing can come close enough to threaten them, not without being turned to vapour a thousand times over. We're made for the hard ground on their borders, and the places they mean to keep but don't have the raw firepower to *hold*. The deserts and tundras and volcanic wastes where their factory-cities live.

That's where the quirks come in. Each company has its own mix of fire and dust and dirty ice, weather patterns and atmospherics you have to live somewhere to understand. The hardware gets made to match; everything from a whole living shell to the boots its ground crews wear around their hangars, built to take advantage of every quirk and peculiarity.

Once you've been flying long enough, you start to notice it. Everything is easier when there's friendly ground beneath your feet, and hostile skies always seem to rattle you around. It creeps into everything, even the things that ought to be the same. After a while, you start to notice it in the competition as well.

Show a jockey a silhouette, and we'll probably tell you who

built it. If we can't, we'll have some handle on where it lives, and the colour of the skies it's used to flying.

The same goes for the ejector-pod coming into view ahead of us. It's missing its skin, and most of its internals are spread around it in the dust, but even with all the damage, markings hidden by dust and carbon-score, it only takes a moment in the glare of Salt's huge lamps.

They're Hasei brand. The pod, and the jockey too.

The ejector landed at an angle, beached on a sand drift. A Mirai followed it but didn't bother getting in close to make the shot. The pod was propped up like a target. High-cal rounds tore through the roof, nearly broke the whole thing in two. A few shots went wide and buried themselves in the dunes on either side. A few went high and hit the wall behind it.

Salt stands close and pans his big lamps up and down. The wall runs floor to ceiling, made of the same bricklike stuff as the pillars. It's still solid, but you can see where Sigurd's munitions struck. There's light on the other side.

"What do you think it is?" asks Salt, running fingers across the surface.

"A bulkhead, maybe," says Hail, picking her way across the remains of Hasei's shell.

"No," I say, "it's the foundation."

Hail and Salt look back at me.

"Check your bearings, count your steps. The Lighthouse is right above us."

The both of them go quiet, waiting while their machines do the guesswork.

"And when you're done, you can take a look at that."

They turn, following the marker I've just planted in their eyes, then take a second to work the angles, trying to find a bullet hole that'll give them the best view. They crane, trying to get a look at the thing resting in the sand on the other side, but they don't need any more than a glance. It's mirror-black, with familiar curves and stencils.

"What is it?" asks Hail, as much for herself as the rest of us.

"I can't tell from here, but one thing's for certain: it was built by Sigurd-Lem."

WE LINE OUR shells up against the wall. Salt's machine gleams up ahead, casting craggy shadows in the light through the bullet holes. Hail stands right behind him, not much more than a shadow in the glow. I'm behind her, still listening for any sound on the other side.

My jacks don't tell me anything we don't know already. We've been at it ten minutes or so, Hail and I listening for vibrations, Salt cycling those huge eyes of his. As far as our instruments are concerned, the space beyond is sterile. That doesn't mean we're taking any chances.

The Juno and I would always have been at the back of the line—we're both the lightest, armour-wise, and the slowest. That probably wouldn't have stopped us before, if it wasn't for our hand. We've got the rifle balanced on our wrist, with enough grip to get two shots off, provided we aimed the first one low and worked the trigger fast enough. After that, we'll be lucky just to keep a handle on it.

The Juno works the machinery in our right arm, flexing mechanical muscle that doesn't feel connected to anything on the other side. My hand tingles and my heartrate climbs in time with the heat of our reactor. I understand the message.

If we can't shoot, and can't fight the muzzle for control, we'll just let the whole thing go. Your average jockey fights from so far away that they'll almost never see the opposition in person, and the companies build shells to match—machines like the Decatur in front of us, with a pair of rails so long that he has to fold their muzzles back for the breach. They're deadly at range, but they don't do so well when you're stepping on their toes and aiming a battering ram at their chin.

Besides, we don't need the hand to work. We just need it to hit.

Grit your teeth, and don't give them anything.

"Ready?" asks Hail.

"Ready," Salt and I reply.

"Countdown," she says.

A red light blinks in the corner of my eye. A little tone plays in my head.

It flashes, and the sound keeps time.

Ding, ding, ding—

—deeeeeee—

It turns green, but Salt's already on the move. One step forward and another to the right, burying the foot in the sand. He drops his left shoulder and slams it into the wall. Ruddy brick explodes around him and dust fills the air.

Hail's Spirit zips through the haze after him, vanishes just as quickly as the Decatur did.

We throw ourselves out behind her, into open air and Eyelight, panning our weapon across a bowl of powdery sand. At least, the Juno does. It rides the transition, filters shielding its lenses as they adjust to the brightness. I'm out of practice, and not so lucky. The sudden change rides down the feeds, flows across my skull.

It's raw, and painful enough that it dumps me back in the saddle. There's still an edge of what I had a moment before, flashes of what the Juno can see as it turns across the open, hunting. Echoes of Hail and Salt on the network.

Clear left.

Clear right. All clear.

Fading away into a wash of static.

It leaves me cold and aching, my eyes desperately trying to adjust to light that isn't there. It makes me dizzy, cutting back and forth between the Juno's steady senses and my own. The machine makes the call; it drops me back into the dark with a blinding migraine and a surge in my stomach.

00.00

I can't see.

It feels like my heart has stopped.

The Juno finds me there, watches over us both while the

connections reset and the saddle pumps me full of stims. Two are drugs I recognise: ModAlign and Neuregen. You can't reboot a human being, but you can get close. They flush me down a tunnel, cloud my vision, wash my skin in shivers and sweat. Then they snap me back, root me in place. The counter flickers in the middle of my eyes, and the rest of the world filters in around it, like it's using the little light as an anchor. The numbers come to rest where they should be, but they're a long way short of the limit. I know we were higher when Salt breached.

Seems there's a reason they put a cap on it.

"Rook?" is the first sound I hear for certain, followed by the dull rumble coming in through our feet. Hail stands in the middle of our vision, looking down on us.

"Lost you there for a second. Everything okay?"

"OSEv," I croak. Operator Strain Event. It's when a jockey hits the wall and dips into shock for a heartbeat or two. It isn't a lie, but it isn't quite the truth. I'm not about to tell her that I've been running past the limiters.

I clear my throat, force myself to breathe. "It's under control."

Her shell nods. "We're in the clear. Take it easy." There's a pause, and something that might be a sigh. "You're going to need it."

Why—

The word doesn't make it all the way to the tip of my tongue. The Lighthouse opens up above us, galleries spiraling all the way to the top of the tower we saw outside, framing a distant spot of the passing sky above us. The wind flows in through the gap, and follows the corkscrew down to the ground. An eternal hurricane spins around us, powered by the Eye itself.

It's moulded the floor around us into a bowl. A small patch of stone shows right in the middle of it, but the dust climbs up against the wall, giving everything an awkward slope. Drawing us toward the centre.

A hunk of Sigurd steel lies in the sand—a narrow capsule, sealed tight and covered in company glyphs. It isn't alone.

A statue stands over it, buried to its shins in the ruddy sand. It's made of the same stone as everything else in this place, features ground down by the perpetual whirlwind. It has two arms: one ends abruptly, shattered at the elbow, and the other has a hand with six long fingers, wrapped around the handle of something that could only be a sword.

It's tall, but that only exaggerates the curves of its limbs, the strange set of its spine. A pair of wings rises from its shoulders, tips curving around to meet each other in the middle above its head like a giant halo. Its face reminds me of Hail's Spirit: smooth and unnerving, with the lightest hint of features underneath.

It lost a chunk of its chest in the impact that claimed its forearm. Directly behind it, there's a hole in the Lighthouse-wall, clouds swirling out beyond.

"What do you think it is?" I ask.

Hail breathes deep. "Where would you like me to start?"

"It's a shell," says Salt, matter-of-fact.

We look at him.

"Care to explain?" asks Hail.

His Decatur rolls a hand over at the joint, spins it around on top of its wrist. "This machine is base-human. Arms and legs, fingers and toes, almost all in proportion, but exaggerated."

"We don't have wings."

"We weren't built for flying; we made ourselves again, with wings on our backs. There's still something of us in the design, it's just hidden under things that are made to fit a purpose. We don't understand *that*"—he nods at the statue—"or at least, we shouldn't..."

"But we understand purpose." I see it now. The wings, the thrust-vectors down the sides. The hull bulged where a cockpit might be. "I bet if we went around, we'd find the engines."

I can feel him smile at me. "A shell's a shell, even if the bones aren't the same."

"What is it doing, then?"

We glance at Hail, but she holds her ground.

"A shell is made to fly and fight. There's as much 'purpose' as you're ever going to get. What's it doing? Just standing here and staring at nothing?"

"Watching," I say, without thinking.

It's in the pose, stance wide and weight spread across its feet. It's in the set of the wings, like the statue's getting ready for take-off. It's in the angle of the sword; low, not attacking, but ready.

It's in the set of its head, straight and level, looking at something.

At the Eye.

"And waiting."

"Careful."

But Hail waves him off. "We've been over it, Salt."

All over it. No trace of explosives, no sign of radiologicals. Sigurd's little capsule has skin so thick we had to ramp our augurs to the limit just to keep them from bouncing off. Every reading came back with the same blurry circuitry, and the flicker of a tiny power source in the middle of it all.

The Spirit edges closer. "Unless there's anything else you'd like to suggest?"

Salt hesitates, but we all know how this is going to go.

Our sensors didn't come back with much, but one thing's for sure: this little pod isn't killing anyone today. It doesn't have any guidance fins or engines. No fuses, and no kind of warhead that any of us can see. It's not a mortar or a mine, not a torpedo or an IED. Nothing that will sink one of us with it.

Hasei and Sigurd were fighting over something else.

"Didn't think so," she says. Even if Salt and I had anything to offer, I don't think she'd let us another step closer. She hadn't known Lear all that long, but that changes nothing. She's the one with the officer's stripes, and she'll be feeling the weight of them now. I've done the same several times before—put my neck on the line to stop them getting any heavier. "Cover me."

Salt and I hold our positions, fingers on triggers and eyes on the sky. Hail takes the last few steps and sets her machine on one knee, spreading a hand flat against the capsule's metal skin.

Now there's something you don't see every day.

She leans in, and her shell quivers. If I didn't know better, I'd say it was a shiver riding her spine, or a sudden twitch of nerves. I do know better, though. Her machine is slowing down, and doing everything it can to make itself quiet.

I always thought it was a Search and Rescue trick. You lean against whatever it is that you're about to pry open, and make use of the most sensitive surfaces of your hull—your hands or feet. S&R would use it to check a shuttle that looks like it's still pressurised, or a machine that's dead but not broken, with the jockey still inside.

Palm's best—you press it flush against the other hull, as close as your machine can manage. And then you listen. For the first few seconds, it'll sound like you're underwater, but that clears up quickly enough. That's when you take the other hand, and knock. If you hear an echo, it's still got pressure. If it rings like a bell, whoever's inside is holding their breath.

The capsule is only just big enough to take a single human being, assuming they didn't have to breathe for long, and didn't need all that much to drink. But then, Hail probably isn't listening for air. As much as she trusts her instruments, I'll bet that there's a pit in her stomach just like mine.

If it's a warhead, there'll be a solid core. If it's solid, she'll hear it easily enough.

I grit my teeth. Gently now.

The seconds pass, cold and quiet.

"All clear," she says, finally.

I have to work the cramp out of my jaw. "What is it?"

Hail offers us a feed from her hull cameras.

The capsule's body is almost perfect, still lined in Sigurd's mirror-finish. The metal has deep gouges in one end, but we already know where those came from. The Juno and I look up at the statue, and the ragged hole in the wall behind it.

"It hit hard."

"There's more." Hail gets her fingers underneath it, rolls it over in the sand.

A white barcode, stencilled across the casing. There's a serial number underneath, and a few markings I don't recognise. Under that, though, is something I do.

ALL-PTS-EMERG

Emergency, emergency, all points respond.

It's the call you make when your instruments are screaming at you, when every warning light is burning itself out, and there's nothing you can do but watch.

Under that is something else.

SLS 67617
DEMIURGE

"Christs," Salt and I whisper, almost all at once.

He recovers first. "It's a distress beacon."

"From Sigurd's fucking mothership."

Hail holds it up where we can see. "It has a serial number and locator frequencies. Just like I'd expect."

She takes another step, stops short.

"What's wrong?" I ask.

The feed zooms in, Hail's lenses working hard to pick something out of the paint. I find the edge of a word, etched into the side with a chisel. The scratches aren't deep enough to find the metal underneath, but they break the smooth mirror coat.

Salt peers over her shoulder. "What does it say?"

The Spirit collects a handful of reddish dust, and rubs it into the cuts.

DONT LET THEM TOUCH YOU

TWELVE

HORIZON TAKES ME by surprise.

It starts with a shadow: a dark mass in the distance and a lingering sense of weight. Then the first signal mast breaks the cloud cover, steel tips cutting the froth like there's a forest underneath. Ranging and augur stations pop out every few seconds, mixed in with silo doors and the barrels of a hundred thousand guns.

The dreadnought filters in, but it doesn't feel like we're coming up on a ship. We've dropped into a misty canyon, where the cliffs are edged in silver. Sentry-machines watch us from hangars in the crags.

All of that, and I didn't know it was there until the prow broke the cloud tops. Another thirty seconds or so, and I'd have hit something. Not that the big ship would've noticed.

I wish I could pop my helmet and rub my throbbing eyes. I've been staring at nothing but cloud and empty space for what feels like weeks. Long enough that I'd miss the biggest ship ever built.

A few hours' sleep would've fixed it, but I've been wide awake since we set off. I've tried every trick I can think of, and that's with a decade in the saddle. No one sleeps like a jockey; even upside-down and trailing fire, we'd still find a way to shut our eyes. Or at least, I should. I've got a prickly headache, and the kind of creeping, restless itch that makes it impossible to sit still. The Juno has a supply of stims and trauma-blockers, but they're made to keep you running; the machine could keep me awake forever if it wanted to, or it could shut me down so hard I wouldn't wake up without an IV and medical supervision.

So I stay awake; awake and wiry and wishing that I'd tried some of the painkillers about eight hours ago. At least I wouldn't have the ache keeping me company.

Worse, I'd forgotten that the Lighthouse was downwind. Anywhere else and we could break atmo, coast in the vacuum for a bit; here, we fight the currents. It took us five hours to reach our objective, but we've spent nearly twice that getting back, and it's all been thick and turbulent.

It's not just the wind. Hail has managed ten whole words since we left the Lighthouse. Just enough to put me in charge of getting us back to ground. Salt hasn't been much better, but it's not the same. He's quiet—you can almost hear the brooding—but Hail's silence has mass. It sucks at your ears, presses up against the sides of your head.

"You there, Tower?" I ask, more to ease the hush than anything else. My voice sounds about as raw as I feel, and the words come out croaking.

"Read you, two-eleven." It's Bell Tower again. I can feel the Juno silently responding to her nets, handshaking with the ranging stations, trading ciphers with the turrets on either side of us. The last lines of point-defence relax into their housings, and missile-tubes seal themselves against the breeze. "Good hunting?" she asks.

I swallow. It hurts. "Negative, Bell Tower. We lost one."

There's a pause. "A shell?"

The question isn't out of place, even if it feels that way. No one kills ejectors.

"Shell and jockey."

I can hear her take a breath. "Who was it?"

"Lear. 211-B."

"Understood." Her voice is suddenly clinical, like something's flipped a switch. It's the kind of tone every decent operator has in their back pocket. When there's a fire on deck, a hole in the hull, you hope that you'll get someone on the line who speaks just like this.

Have no fear. We are in control.

"Do you have him with you?"

"We do. 211-C is carrying."

"Copy, two-eleven. Clearing priority approach to D-Lower. Waiting on ground crews." There's an echo of someone speaking, like they've turned away from a microphone. "Crews report and flashes are up. SOs are ready to receive."

I breathe in, let it out slowly. "Thank you, Bell Tower."

"No problem, two-eleven." Her voice picks up, just a hair. "Steady as she goes."

With that, she's gone, replaced by the dull monotones of the SO and ground crews calling in, going to work. The Juno replies before I can find the will to speak, pushing stock responses across the net.

I touch the saddle. "Old bird."

The counter drops, but it doesn't feel like I'm losing grip. The connection turns to haze, loses resolution until all I can feel is the wind on my skin.

"Thank you," I whisper. It warms at me.

Hail doesn't let me float. "Don't tell them."

Her voice comes from nowhere. It's just as ragged as my own, but she has the same cold steel that Bell Tower had a moment ago.

Salt asks the question before I can. "Don't tell them what, exactly?"

"About the hollow machines." She clears her throat. "Don't tell them about the hollows, or anything else we saw. If anyone asks, Sigurd's jockeys died on impact."

I almost bite my tongue. "They'll think we did it. They'll think we broke in and—" I trail off.

"And shot them?" The steel takes an edge. "That's what you were going to do."

I stutter, but Salt has my wing. "There's a line between thinking and doing, Hail."

"Maybe so, but no one will judge you. As far as any NorCol

badge is concerned, Sigurd murdered one of our own in cold blood."

"And so we took two eyes for the one we lost?" growls Salt. "Like hell."

"Maybe we did, maybe we didn't. Maybe we just hit them so hard they didn't survive the landing."

"Why?" I manage. It carries, but only just.

"I need time. Time to do some digging on this before NorCol brass finds out."

"Digging?"

"Talking, mostly. I know a couple of other cons who might have something we can use. I've put out a call to one of them already, and they need space as much as I do." I hear her swallow. "Things aren't as simple as they were when you were full-time, Rook. Jockeys and crew will understand, but the company doesn't care about Lear. Worse than that, three shells are worth less than four, and the same goes for three jockeys. If there's a reason to send us out chasing ghosts, the company will take it, especially now that it's cheaper putting us out in the line of fire." There's a pause. "I don't see any reason to go looking for hollows until I know what this is about. When we do—and we will, I promise—I want it on our terms."

"I don't like it."

"Neither do I," says Salt.

"There isn't much to like." Hail lets out a breath. "I'm asking you. Asking, not ordering. Give me time to figure this out. Today hasn't been easy, and it isn't about to get better."

I frown into my helmet. "What do you mean?"

"We dismounted," replies Hail, like I ought to understand.

I don't.

"Think about it. We got out of our shells and put boots on alien soil." A marker pops into my eyes. Right ahead, on the lip of the hangar that's waiting to take me in. "See them? The crew with the aprons and hoses? They're decontam."

* * *

THEY'RE WAITING FOR me when I drop from the operator's lock. A line of rubber gloves and face-guards, boots wrapped in disposable covers. They've got NorCol uniforms underneath, and blocky sidearms on their hips. They're still soldiers, but with strange grey aprons that cover everything from their necks to their toes.

One of them steps up as I hit the ground, motioning for me to widen my feet and put my arms out on either side, all routine and automatic. He sees me tense, but it takes him a moment to read my reaction. He's already reaching, and I don't have enough to tell him off. I just need a second, a second longer than they're giving me.

I just need a second.

The trooper freezes when he sees the Juno stir behind me. I catch a flash of wide eyes behind the visor.

He retreats, puts his hands up, defensive. "Easy, easy."

But one of his squad is already starting forward, ready to put me down. Riding on adrenaline, and all the stories she's heard: haywire shells still half-jacked into their operators, machine and jockey still coming down off the combat rush. Not human-friendly yet.

The squad's sergeant tracks my eyes. "Hands off, private. You will lose, con or no con."

The private teeters on the edge, but the defiance doesn't look like much when the Juno starts working its healthy fist, massive joints sliding around in their housings.

"Did you hear me? Stand down, private. I am not cleaning you off the paving."

The visor stares at him. "Yes sir," she manages.

"What was that?" He taps the side of his helmet. "I didn't copy, private."

The rest of the squad is staring.

"Yes, sir." A little louder this time.

The sergeant nods, turns back to me. "Apologies, jockey. We need to sweep you, but the company's got me minding children at the same time. We're going to try and keep it civil." He growls at his squad. "Aren't we?"

"Yes, sir," they reply, loud enough to echo.

"I hear you lost a pair of wings today. Some of us were a little fast on the uptake there, and I know you need the space right now. Let us do our jobs, and we'll be out of your way. We don't want any trouble."

I watch him, but it's difficult to get a read with his eyes behind the glossy visor. "Neither do I, sergeant." I'm aiming for steady, but I get hoarse instead. "How is this going to go?"

"By the book."

"What's in the book, sergeant?"

He nods, back in familiar territory. "We're decontam and collection. We start with a once-over for particulates, and anything you picked up during the dismount. That's your boots, for the most part, but we have to sweep the whole suit." He cocks his head at the private with the death wish. "She's the pat-down, but I can find you another if you want."

I glare downrange, but it's half-hearted. She's a nugget if I ever saw one, treading fight-or-flight now that she's on the toes of a military shell. The eyes tell me 'fight' was what came up first, fading now that someone's pulled her short. "Is she going to do anything stupid?"

The sergeant matches my look, but adds in acid. "Are you going to do anything stupid, private?"

The private shakes her head a little faster than she should, rattling her helmet around on top of her head. "No, sir."

"There you go." He spreads his hands and feet like a jumping jack. "Just like this, and we'll make it go as fast as we can."

I cross my arms. "What about the hose?"

One of the jackets shrinks back where I can't see.

"Last step. Once we've cleared you of the obvious stuff, we hose the flight suit and clear the runoff." His shoulders drop at the look I give him after that, like he's expecting a fight, but he continues. "After that, the suit goes for final decontamination."

I hold his gaze.

He spares half a glance for the Juno. I can feel it watching him.

"It's protocol," he says. He finds a little iron in his spine, puts an edge on his voice. "I can't allow you to enter the compartments without decontam, and that's the rules talking, not me. It's either you and the suit, or it's just the suit." Not that he could stop me, and he knows that well enough. His body language is strangely hard to place, but he doesn't seem to be looking for a fight. His voice softens. "Believe me, you don't want to be inside when they scour it."

I almost smile at that. I've been through a crash cleanup once before. My unit put down in the wind of the Novgorod's attack on San Leneira. We didn't know it was biological until we got the call from the colony itself. When we got back to NorCol's carrier-group, they pulled us up on the runway, and fried the pathogen off of our shells. They did the same to us in our suits afterwards, out on the open deck. It wasn't enough to kill us, but it definitely felt that way.

"The helmet stays."

The sergeant looks me over, an odd look in his eye. "Understood. We'll dee-see it here and now." He has to turn on them before they move. "You heard me. Hop to."

The private steps up first and her squadmates follow her in, holding long green lamps like batons. They sweep the lamps up and over my arms, down my sides and around my boots, watching for something in their visors. They stop twice, fishing tiny pieces of gravel out of the seals where my boots meet my shins. After that, one helps me balance while the other checks the soles of my feet, picking between the treads with a little silver tool. They pull a handful of dust out of the boots, dropping each speck into a clear box with seals on the top and stencilled warnings on the sides.

The hose comes next. Three NorCol jackets, two with long-bristled brushes and a third with the pipe in hand. I flinch, expecting the worst, but they move even faster than the first crew. Their hands are steady and their motions are practised, working the suit down quickly; no comments, no stray glances, quick and professional. I can see why the nugget got pat-down duty. The hose crew are good at what they do.

They do three passes over my helmet: the first with water, and the second with spraycans—some kind of soap. The crew stands back, watching as the soap sizzles, clouding my visor with foam. After that, it's the hose again, set to high pressure.

"Helmet," says the sergeant, offering a hand.

I nod, and blink my way past the locks. The seals pop with a hiss of escaping air, and the suit goes limp. I twist the helmet off its ring and haul it over my head. The air is icy against my hair, bitter and salty from whatever it was they used to wash me down.

I hold it out for him, but pull it back. "Lose it," I say, a thumb over my shoulder at the Juno, "and we'll kill you."

It's a whole second before he decides if I'm joking or not. He tugs at his covers to get at the jacket underneath, showing me a name: *Andrade*, embroidered light blue on a dirty tab. Beneath that is a strip of unit markings. He might as well have given me his home address. He waits for me to read it. "That won't be necessary."

The private is back, but she's keeping her distance now, gaze slipping from the sergeant, to me, to the machine watching over us all.

"Whenever you're ready," she whispers.

I break the clasps around my neck, and two more behind the collar. "Your turn."

She fumbles the rest of the way down my spine, and offers her shoulder for balance as another of her squad helps tug me clear of the armoured outer skin. Arms first, and the chest-plates with them, leaving me standing in black conductives from the waist up. I don't have gloves any more, and so the private pulls my boots for me, taking turns with the other trooper to prop me up along the way. Together, they thread me out of the last of the flight suit and set me down on dry ground.

When I look up, the rest of the crew is already cleaning up, pushing ruddy water along the ground with the hose. The sergeant stands off to one side, my helmet in one hand, a silver blanket in the other.

He offers both. "I knew the last jockey who worked it." He nods up at the machine above us. "The Juno. Didn't think I'd see it fly again."

"You used to be decontam for this bird?"

He gives me that strange look again. "Something like that."

I pull the blanket around my shoulders and take the helmet on its straps. I feel almost feverish. "Thank you, sergeant."

He shakes his head, but motions for the other corner of the hangar. "I'd get clear before they start."

I turn to see another crew approaching. Their hoses look like the kind you use to put out fires, three jackets to a line, and instead of spraycans, they have pressurised tanks.

I look up at the Juno, and it looks down on me. I can hear the tick of systems rolling down inside my helmet, and only just feel the last nets shuttering. The connection slips away, but not all at once. The Juno's watching me.

See you soon.

COME WITH ME is scratched into the ceiling above my bunk, through layers of industrial grey paint and red rust-proofing.

To the bottom of the sea, says the wall below it, written in a different hand, but cut just as deep. You can see where they made it all the way to the steel; it must've been a nail or a chisel.

My compartment is sparse. There's a single bunk, a locker for my things, and about enough room to swing a jacket over my shoulders, assuming I didn't mind grazing a knuckle along the way. The walls would be bare, but generations' worth of jockeys have decided otherwise. There's a skull and crossbones etched above the door, *Abandon all hope, ye who exit here* along the top of the frame. All around is the same scuff and crap you'll find on any company boat: kill tallies and salty one-liners, military-grade philosophy and bad Seymour Decker jokes.

Decker doesn't cheat death, he wins fair and square.

The prison shuttles had their own versions of the same, etched into grime and rust and whatever else was in reach. NorCol's monster-ship isn't any different.

Come with me, to the bottom of the sea.

The walls keep a roll of who has come and who has gone, a century's history scratched by hand, into paint that covers untold years more. A pair of shackles stands out near my locker, next to the name *Sajjan, H*, and what looks like a prison term. There are six other jockeys by their names, ranks and units filled in where they had space. Someone etched a tombstone into the paint near the foot of the bunk, inscribed it with a name you can't read any more, hidden under fresher coats of paint. Others followed suit, counting their losses, never forgetting. There must be thirty of them. A little graveyard where the jockeys have kept their dead.

One of them was an artist, it seems. A little Juno watches me from the other side of the room, probably about as tall as my hand stretched out straight, carved with a knife-tip.

DONT LET THEM TOUCH YOU

It was scratched just the same as my walls were, unsteady and improvised.

Sitting up on the edge of my bunk, legs crossed beneath me, I flex my aching hand in the light. There's no broken skin, and nothing worth calling a bruise. It feels like I'm nursing a fracture in there somewhere, twinging whenever I try to move it around, but there isn't any swelling, and nothing to explain the hot throb keeping me awake.

Well, maybe one thing.

I lean over the end of my bunk and fish a ball of socks from inside one of my ship-side boots. The socks are NorCol's blue-grey, coarse, and almost comically thick. Ships' decks are always cold—there's no getting around that—just not the kind that gives you frostbite. The company might be callous, but it understands human beings just enough to know that it ought to insulate the living quarters. The same doesn't go for hangars, though. Shells don't feel the cold.

I look at the little Juno.

Not unless you let them.

The socks go on first, and a thick pair of fatigue greys. A pullover comes from my locker, and I grab one of NorCol's long coats off the hook behind my door, let it settle on my shoulders. The coat is almost brand-new, complete with my unit tabs and an embroidered strip that reads *ROOK* in dark capitals. I set a flight chief's pin in the collar; I may be a con, but the pin has its own kind of weight. At the very least, the stiffs won't look surprised when they earn themselves a boot.

After that, I go hunting for my gloves. The left goes on easily enough; the right hurts just as much as I'm expecting it to.

It wasn't always like this. The original designs didn't feed damage back to the jockey, not like they do now. They gave a little spark to draw your attention, but any part of the shell too damaged to move would register by going numb. That was the problem. Pain is easy; human beings hurt all the time, and we're built to take it, body and mind. Sudden numbness means something has gone *wrong*—that you've taken a hit that's so big, so *total* that your body can't fully process it yet. The original designs didn't survive because they kept sending jockeys into shock.

Feeling like I've broken a hand is better than the alternative, but it should have faded by now. I shake myself out, for all the good it does me. The ache still follows me: out through my lock and into the service passages behind it. Two doors down from there, a quick check for pressure, and I'm out into the hangar beyond.

It's dark, and frosty without my flight suit. The block is in its night-cycle, lamps dimmed and heating at bare minimums. It's quiet, but I can hear the rush of launching machinery on the far side the hull, and the crump and squeal of shells coming down in faraway blocks. I walk through the middle of the night, listening to a busy day in the distance.

A pair of jackets linger on the far side of the Juno's berth, talking softly and watching the wind through a tiny porthole. They look up at the echo of my boots, but only long enough to catch the edge of who I am. They decide I'm not worth any more trouble.

Frost cracks under my feet as I cross tracks left by the decontam crews: puddles of water and streaks of the foaming agent frozen in place. The Juno rests in its cradle, but it's lost all sense of weight. It's cold and empty, lenses covered. They couldn't find spares, and so the hand and forearm are spread out on a flatbed near its feet, a circle of cranes slowly teasing the fingers loose with hooks and pulleys and webs of heavy-duty chain.

Sitting in the light of an operator's screen, mutters turning to mist in the cold, is Folau.

I offer him as much of a smile as I can manage. "They caught you."

He looks up at me and manages a shrug that turns to a shiver halfway through. "I had a good run, but they were gonna eventually. Always the problem with being the FNG on deck: the full-timers have an eye on you." He pulls his jacket tight over his shoulders. "I've been at this game long enough. I'll find a way."

"To slack off?"

He grins at me. "Harsh words there, NorCol. Be gentle."

"As soon as you start deserving it." I peer over his shoulder. "How's the hand?"

"About as well as can be expected." He gives me side-eye. "I'd pay to see the other guy."

My knuckles throb. "I was angry."

He inches back in his seat. "Remind me to stay on your good side."

I nod to my disembodied fist. "Just get it straightened out." I pat him on the shoulder with my good hand. "That way, I'll have to head somewhere else when I'm looking for a punching bag."

"Ah-ha." He looks me up and down. "Some people might be inclined to take that at face value, jockey."

"So what if they do?"

"There's enough bad blood in this place already. Kadi's still itching from earlier. I wouldn't give him the ammo, if I were you."

"Far as I'm concerned, Kadi deserves whatever he gets." I frown at him, at the look he's giving me. "Wait, what do you mean, *earlier*?"

"Hail's little disappearing act. You heard—"

"I didn't hear anything. Disappearing act?"

His eyebrows climb. "Weren't you on the flight?"

I wave one hand at the other. "Where do you think *that* came from?"

"I'm not sure I should—"

"Out with it, Folau." It carries, bounces around the hangar. The jackets are watching us now.

"Easy," he whispers. "I'm not the enemy here."

"What happened?"

"Hail picked up that Sigurd beacon, yeah?"

"What about it?"

"Well, she landed with it. Went through dee-see and everything. And then, well—" He shrugs. "Her SO saw it come in, called Kadi to get an inspection team on station to look it over."

My heart skips. "What happened?"

Folau smiles, without any of the usual rough edges. "You don't have to look like that, NorCol. No, you didn't bring some UXO back on board. The bomb crew got in early, ruled it safe." He shivers, pushes his hands down in his pockets. "It's much more interesting than that. Hail came down, went through decontam and the once-over from EOD. Everything was as it should be."

"*Was?*"

"Well, somewhere between the dismount and the inspection crew getting there, someone ghosted the beacon. It's gone."

I CATCH A monorail between blocks, headed for where Hail keeps her shell. The car is empty when it arrives—at least, I think it is. I'm a few steps in when I realise there's a coat arranged across the last row of seats, out cold and snoring quietly to herself. I don't recognise all the markings, but she's got a jockey's tab on one shoulder and a specialty pin on her collar. Professional NorCol, if I had to guess, but it's hard to tell from here.

I pick a seat near the front, but I'm not going far. The jockey looks like she's been settled a while, but *Horizon* is big enough, I suppose. There's every chance this line has carried her for an hour or more. She might be headed for the prow, or on transfer from one of the other massive hangars down-ship.

The car's only just picking up when there's a chime from the front, and a creak as it slows again. The jacket sits up on automatic, pulling hair out of her eyes and blinking at the light. She has to haul herself upright, and even then, it takes both hands and a deep groan. She turns back as soon as she finds her feet, and roots around the seats she's been lying on. It takes her a second, but she comes up with a bottle in her hand.

Oh. Of course.

I look out at the windows as another block rolls into view. A giant stencil on the doors reads 67, three storeys tall. Lear's block. The platform is narrow, and lit by a portable lamp. A field of empty bottles catches the light, arranged around the access hatch in a patchy little shrine.

I watch the jacket as she passes, walking with a jockey's awkward steps. A patch on her chest reads *BOR*.

She splits a casual salute off the corner of her brow. "Jockey," she says on her way past.

"Jockey," I reply. "Thank you."

She stops on the edge of the door and gives me her eye, just for a second. "He yours?"

"He was."

A curt nod, and she drops clear of the car. I watch her shrink as the train picks up again, but I can see what she's doing.

She knocks the bottle top off on the railings and pours beer across the floor. It's halfway empty when she flips it around and takes the last half for herself. She didn't know Lear. There's no way she could. He'd been on *Horizon* as long as I had—less, now.

But this isn't about Lear. This is about debt.

Jockeys wear flight suits so we can breathe if the hull springs a leak. We carry our own air, and enough water and feed to keep us going for weeks. We have armour of our own, and even more on our machines. Ejectors, crash restraints, and lines full of artificial blood, ready for transfusion. All that, and the odds don't ever get better. Chances are, tomorrow will be your last day flying.

But, say there's a way to tip things in your favour. What would you do?

The knuckledraggers call it superstition, but they don't know what it's like. Flying has a habit of making you superstitious. One day, a jockey will put their socks on in a different order for the way they usually do, or maybe they'll change the sloppy eggs out for something else. They'll forget to rub the strange mark on their doorframe, or forget to spit before they put their helmet on.

And the next day they'll be dead. They'll hit a gale, or get buttered by a lucky shot. They'll lose a wing suddenly, feel it break on a fracture that the ground crew hadn't noticed. All the precautions in place, all the training to make it work, and they'll still be just as dead. No rhyme or reason. The sky just happened to fall on that particular pair of boots that day, didn't matter who was standing in them.

Or maybe it did.

The jockey sets her bottle down, and her eyes glow as she blinks a request for another monorail car. She doesn't say a few words, and she doesn't wave her hands about. It may be superstition, but it isn't magic. There's a simple kind of logic at work.

She's shared a beer with Lear.

NorCol, Locust, convict; whatever he was—now he owes her one.

THIRTEEN

I BEAT A hand on the door to block sixty-eight. Two dull thuds and I catch myself. I'm not thinking; I'm cold and aching and should be back in my bunk. I glare at the door and work my left hand. I didn't hit hard, but it's throbbing just as badly as the other one now. My NorCol-issue gloves are only thick enough to keep the feeling in my fingers, even if there are times when I'd rather they were numb.

I don't know how well I thought they were going to do against the steel door. There isn't much that would. I could have brought my sidearm, done the knocking with half a magazine, and the hatch probably wouldn't have noticed. Even if there was some way to break through it, there's another door just like it on the other side, air-gapped and insulated, to keep crashing shells and accidental discharge from making it out of the block. Behind *them* are two more before you're anywhere near Hail's bunk.

I rest my fist against the hatch, and my head against the fist. It's no good. I could get the Juno out here and have *it* knock, and Hail would still only know it through the rumble in the floor.

I head back across the narrow platform and lean against the railing, hands in my pockets. The coat doesn't add much more than the gloves do, but the pressure helps the ache.

I should be back in my fucking bunk, but I can't seem to make myself move, so I listen to the sounds of Hangar D. There's a rush of air between the blocks, updrafts and cyclones trapped by strange geometry. The halide stars are dim for the sleep-cycle—

we're closer to tomorrow than to yesterday—but this place is still alive. Drones whir and chatter in the air currents, monorails whistle, hangar blocks flicker and strobe like distant skyscrapers.

Get back to your bunk, Rook. At least get out of the cold. Something. *Anything.*

Standing here won't do you any good. No more than kicking Hail's door down, if that was even possible. What would you do on the other side? She'll be dead asleep, and probably none too happy to have an angry jockey on her doorstep, demanding answers to questions I'm not sure I know myself.

I don't even know where to start.

Sigurd's beacon didn't just disappear. It looks small enough, but that's because a Spirit was carrying the thing around under its arm. It's probably about as big as my sleeping quarters, although that isn't saying much. There would've been thirty people on deck when Hail put down, and probably double that when you add in EOD and decontam. Fifty, sixty crew, all watching her. They'd be hosing her down, and stripping her out of her flight suit, just like they did to me. Eyes on her, eyes on her shell, procedures and protocol and plain old bureaucracy in the way.

Come to think of it, Hail should've been the *last* person with hands on the pod. The knuckledraggers would've been all over a piece of strange hardware like that. It's not every day you get hands on competitor tech.

I frown at the thought. They wouldn't, surely? Not with Kadi on the line.

The thought barely has time to finish. There's a clink inside the door, a wheeze and clatter as someone cycles pressure inside the lock. Hail stops dead in her tracks when she sees me, a hand on her hip like there's a sidearm under her coat.

She frowns. "Rook?"

"That's the one."

She straightens, drops the hand. "What are you doing here?"

I shrug, hands in my coat pockets. "Couldn't sleep. Needed some air."

"And you decided to get it here?"

"There's a reason I can't sleep." I look her up and down. "You aren't sleeping either."

"Decided not to."

"Too busy?"

She raises an eyebrow, but there's a strange tilt to it. "I have no idea what you mean."

"Sure you do. They say inspection missed a chunk of Sigurd steel."

"Who's *they*?"

"Kadi, apparently. Someone ghosted it."

"No one ghosted anything. There was a transfer error. Miscommunication between the ground crew and inspection. It's all in the logs, if you want to see them."

I stand my ground. "What are you doing?"

"Looking for you. At least, that's what I was about to do. Wasn't expecting to find you on my doorstep." She looks past me, and her eyes light up. "Train's on the way. Come on, let's go get ourselves a drink."

I glare at her, but she meets it. *Not here.*

I'm not budging yet. "What about Salt?"

She flicks me a grin. "You're welcome to try and wake him up, but you're gonna need some hardware to do it. He put in a request to medical about an hour after we put down. They sent someone down with a syringe full of sweet dreams."

"How do you know this?"

"He's a con. His immediate superiors have to authorise everything, even if we're cons as well." She looks up at a whistle from the train line. "Come on."

"Why? What's wrong with him?"

"No idea. He's old Colonial, there's probably a list. He knew exactly what to ask for."

THE RAIL DROPS us off into noise and patchy fluorescence, crowds of jackets and lines of greasy overalls. Hail and I push through it, carrying our silence with us.

We edge past the chow hall queues and into the service tunnels behind them, following jury-rigged neon to the little hole that hides the con-side bar for Hangar D. If we were full-time, this would be on NorCol's tab, but we aren't, so we settle for runoff instead.

Parts of it connect to the mess kitchen, where the bootleggers can borrow some of the company-sanctioned hardware, but most of it creeps into the nexus of cooling ducts deeper in, where the cold helps them distil, and the acoustics hide their rumbling bass.

I don't even make it to the bartop. "My head's too heavy for this."

Hail looks me over and decides not to argue. We edge back into the chow hall proper and stack up behind a queue serving late lunches to the night-shifts.

The crew right ahead of us are all from the same unit; old hands, for the most part. Fatigue is permanently inked into the craters around their eyes, their skins hang loose on rangy muscle, their shoulders all seem to follow the same deep curve. Six of them are standing and muttering as we come in, giving side-eye to the two nuggets between us and them, younger convicts, fresh out of induction. The crew is probably six, seven hours into a long-haul shift, and the old timers are feeling it; the FNGs, not so much. It's only a matter of time before their elders send them down one of *Horizon*'s dark canyons, looking for a bottle of bulkhead remover, or a can of aye-dee-ten-tee (says *ID10T* on the side, about so big; you can't miss it).

There are a couple of jockeys amongst the mess, but they keep to the corners, sit in ones and twos. If anything needs flying, one of the daylight blocks should get the job, but this is a NorCol boat: for every other jockey that ought to be asleep, there'll be a fuckup on the rosters, or a wake-side crew that forgets the other half of the ship is in its bunks.

Or they're like Hail and me, wandering through the night and wishing we could find a way back to sleep. There are soldiers passing through, but they don't stop to eat. Watch-officers between posts, dropping in for a cup of something warm. There are even a few actual marines, but they keep to their squads, armour piled up against their tables as they eat. Even with the marines counted in, the knuckledraggers outnumber everyone else by three to one. Fighting comes and goes, but maintenance is forever.

And it takes fuel. The 'draggers load their trays up with salt and fat and protein, slurping their ways through pools of congealing oil like they're relatives of the machines in their care. Heaps of chilli and sweet sauce slop across the top, and jugs of thick black coffee perch on the corners of their trays.

It's more of the same for me and Hail. She takes a mug of tarry brew, and another one for me. She goes without a tray, but I don't pass the chance. A line cook dishes me a square of something hot and rich, trailing steam and strands of dark toffee. I turn and make for the table we've taken to eating at, but Hail catches my elbow and steers us into the middle of the room. I don't fight her; I don't have the energy. She pushes us through lines of seating, settling on the edge of a group of ordnance techs, eight asses deep on a twelve-seat bench.

We drop into the last two, and I try not to slump too hard. Less than an hour ago, I was wide-awake, wired and ready. Now that I'm here, looking down a barrel of caffeine and a mound of steaming sugar, I'm starting to feel it. There's a whole flight between me and the last time I actually slept, and I've got the sudden urge to fold into my plate.

I force my spine straight with all of the effort I can muster and work my spoon around, blunt and careless. The pudding is hot and eye-wateringly sweet. The coffee is even hotter, about as thick, and so bitter it curls my toes. Together, they're more comforting than I'd care to admit.

Hail watches me, nursing her mug, head cocked to one side as she listens to the noise. It must be loud enough, because she finally decides to speak.

"I think those shells were hollow from the get-go."

I sit back and wrap my fingers around the coffee, letting the warmth seep in through my gloves. If my bunk was anywhere within range, I'd crash and burn. Somewhere along the line, I manage to keep my thoughts in order.

"We don't know how long they spent on that rock before we got there. They could've been stranded."

But Hail shakes her head. "There were four of them to begin with. If it was just the one, I'd buy it. Four shells, and no one calls home? That doesn't make sense."

"Five shells."

She frowns at me. "Five?"

"Four on the ground, one in the air. The observer."

"I had a friend in Obs take a look at that silhouette—it didn't match anything on Sigurd's rosters."

But I read her look. "That you know of."

She shrugs. "That anyone in NorCol knows of. It isn't on any database on *Horizon*."

"So what do you think it is?"

"Working theory is still that yes, it was probably some kind of observer platform, but there's no reason to assume it was Sigurd's."

"Just another shell looking for the beacon."

She shrugs. "We can assume that Hasei wasn't the only company that caught wind of it. Sending an observer would be an obvious choice."

"An observer, rather than a flight of Mirais."

"Not much reason to send both."

"Especially if it turned tail as soon as it heard you," I reply. "All right. Probably not Sigurd, then."

"Probably not." She sighs, slumps in her seat. "You were right about the beacon, by the way. I ghosted it, but only for an hour or so. Fudged the logs to match."

"How did you manage that? There must've been fifty people in there."

"There were. Kadi helped me."

"*What?*"

"I told you, he's been dealt with."

Oh. "You blackmailed him."

Her jaw sets a hard line on that. "He could hear me, you know. When we first showed up in your block, and he had that nugget rolling in. He heard everything I sent. He *knew* we were working on a plan to de-escalate. I've got recordings to prove it, a couple of rebel 'draggers that'll back my account."

"He risked two shells and three jockeys. For what?"

"For a quickfix. For a chance to have the Juno out of his hair."

"Fuck, Hail. Why isn't this getting passed up the line? Where's Internal Affairs?"

She shakes her head. "IA or Tower would just put someone new in his place."

"Someone who didn't know the rules?" I can't keep the bitterness out.

"This is how it works out here, Rook. I've got to use what I've got, and what I've got right now is Kadi. He used to hold it over me—now I can do the same to him." She sketches it out on the table with her fingertip. "It's the circle of life."

I rub my eyes, but it doesn't help. "Why go through all the trouble?"

"With Kadi?"

"With Sigurd's beacon." I take a sip of coffee. It's like rising from the dead. "NorCol got it in the end anyway."

"Two reasons. One, to get a look at the logs on that thing. As soon as inspection picked it up, they'd have lost it somewhere, same as everything else we recover. I needed first-touch." She drums a finger on the tabletop, rolling something over in her head, and working her jaw to match. "How long do you think *Horizon* has been out here?"

I blink. "Here? As in, right here?" I chew on it. "Fifty years? A hundred?"

"Two hundred and seventeen, subjective. Two hundred and seventeen years, and they still have no idea what's out there. No idea what to do with all of the things we bring out of the froth. You should see the storage vaults. The things we've found. It all just sits and rots."

"So you got ahead. You got someone to hack into Sigurd's beacon. Pulled the logs."

"I did what I had to."

"Was it worth it?"

Hail shrugs. "Most of it was encrypted, obviously."

"Sure."

"And what was left was fuzzy, like it had hit a storm. We did get a look at the run time, though. The beacon was broadcasting when it made landfall, but the signal died eleven hours before we arrived."

I frown at her. "But the hollows—" I trail off. "Those bodies were older than that."

"Much." She takes a sip of black tar, flinches at the taste. "If it was a storm that made a mess of the logs, it did a number on the power source as well. A couple of systems survived, but it was all backup and redundancy. Not enough to keep the beacon running as intended."

"So what do you think happened? Sigurd hears a squealer, scrambles, but the signal dies before they arrive."

"They triangulate."

"And bump into Hasei, who's been doing the same."

Hail sets her cup down. "It isn't supposed to go that way. Beacons don't squeal on open bands."

"Where I come from they do."

"Yes, but where you come from, a distress beacon means you're trying to be rescued."

I raise an eyebrow. "Surprisingly, yes."

"Out here, it isn't so simple."

"You mean, the companies will kill their crews before they point the way to something valuable."

"More or less." She rubs her eyes. "Thing is, this one was open wide. No ciphers, none of Sigurd's proprietary access-control. Anyone with ears and an antenna could hear it."

"Why? Why do that?"

She shrugs. "Someone wanted it found, and not just by Sigurd."

"Or not by Sigurd at all."

Hail clicks a finger at me. "Exactly."

I sit back. "They couldn't hide from their own, though."

"They tried."

I frown at her.

"The signal cut out eleven hours before we arrived, but it only started eight hours before that."

"If Sigurd only launched when they heard the squealer, then those shells put out—"

I already know the answer. Sigurd-Lem sent four hollow shells out into the wind, and *four dead jockeys*, still strapped to their saddles like it didn't make a difference.

For what?

"Those machines had been running on their own for *weeks*, no human interference," says Hail. "Judging by the state the jockeys were in. They were cold when they launched, doing their own thing. Haywire, hollow, whatever you want to call it."

But it's worse than that. "They were hollow when they were still in their hangars, Hail. Someone waved a dead body out the door."

She shakes her head. "Someone waved a *machine* out the door—the body didn't have much to do with it. This isn't some one-in-a-mil malfunction. This is on purpose."

My pudding is cold, and I shove it to the side. I try my luck with the coffee instead, and the gentle warmth still lingering at the bottom of the cup. "The beacon—" I falter, try to pick it up again. "Whoever launched the beacon was trying to get away from the hollows."

She nods. "Seems that way to me."

"Someone *inside* the Sigurd-Lem Corporation was trying to get out? Someone was running from hollows." I swallow, try to hold the look in her eye. "Why are we here, Hail? Why aren't we telling this to someone with a braid on their shoulder?"

"We're keeping it quiet, for now. There's every chance that this gets turned over to the Werewolves or spec-ops, and we never see it again."

"And we aren't letting the 'Wolves have it because...? They're the ones who're *supposed* to handle this kind of thing."

"'Wolves work counterintelligence, first and foremost. Get the wrong one on the case, and they'll waste their time tailing *us*, long before they get to solving the problem."

"Some of us might deserve it," I mutter.

Hail ignores the jab. "Even if they didn't, odds are they'd be full-timers who don't know what they're doing or why it matters. Who haven't lost anything."

I set my elbows on the table. "Those hollows almost killed us."

Hail leans in, her voice suddenly low. "They did. They killed one of us. *Murdered* a jockey, Rook. Right in front of us."

"This isn't the first time I've lost someone, Hail."

She rolls with the punches. "You think I haven't? Hell, Rook, you've seen what it's like out there." But her gaze softens. "I—I'm sorry."

"What for? You didn't kill them."

"I saw your file. I know what happened to your unit."

I can't quite bite my tongue. "Well, at least one of us does."

Those eyes come closer. "They left you behind. Ignored your SOS."

"The file say that?"

"No." She watches me. "But I know what it looks like. I also know that they opened fire on your unit."

"What's a few more bodies in no-man's-land?" I shrug. "We were in the way."

"There's a difference between *danger: close* and *friendly fire*. Someone should've swung for what happened."

"Someone did," I growl.

Maybe it's the tone, maybe it's something in my eyes, but it sets her off. "You were still alive down there, and they knew it. They traded you for a few fucking kilometres—"

"Hail," I whisper.

She nods, takes a deep breath. It's a moment before she can speak again. "We can't just sit here."

"I know," I reply, soft as I can make it. I press my eyes into my palms, try to push some of the sleep away. Even with the black tar settling in my stomach, I'm losing. "But we don't have anything to go on. You said it yourself: the logs were fried and the beacon was cold."

"There were freaks."

"I'm tired, Hail. What do you mean?"

"The beacon was intended to get help on the line. Some of the original design is still there."

"Like what?"

"Well, it's a distress beacon. The design needs to get you to the sender."

Oh. Freaks—*Frequencies*. "There were locator frequencies on the side."

"*Were*. Kadi helped me burn them off."

I blink at her. "Christs, Hail. What did you do that for?"

She taps the side of her head, eyes aglow for just a second. "I've still got them. Like I said, if the company gets their hands on this, it'll be the last a con ever sees of it. I want to set the terms." There's an edge, sharp and bright. "I want a shot at where those hollows came from, and I know you do too."

I'm too tired for this. Too sore, and too far from anything I could call home. But my right hand throbs, reminds me of something else.

"I suppose I do."

WAKING UP IS about as bad as I could expect. Twisted in sweaty sheets and powder-mouthed, aching and feeling suddenly out of place. For a moment, it's all I can do to keep my eyes open. There's a stab of panic when I realise that it's 11:27, and dull relief when I remember that Hail got us off the rosters for today.

Normally, she'd have to work for it; the company isn't very good at sympathy, and it won't care that we're missing a couple of days' sleep between us. NorCol is made of people, but it doesn't comprehend them. Hardware, however, is a language it can speak. Hail put in for suspension of systems, and after that went through, she applied for R&R.

Anywhere else, that would mean something very different to what it does here. Here it stands for 're-fit and replenish'; a catch-all for everything from filling magazines to checking reactors for pressure. All the little things you need to do to keep a shell and jockey working as intended.

It doesn't normally cover full-blown repair, but Salt and I made a mess of our machines. Him more than me, but I didn't know that until Hail told me about it last night. He took a beating against the hollows, collected enough hostile shot that they're replacing almost all of his forward plating. The shell itself is fine, but it would be an easy fix if that was all there was. He burned hard and fast throughout the fight, worked his rails so hot he warped them. His primary armaments are a loss; you don't just beat the kinks out of something like that.

My own shell isn't much better. We're missing a hand, but I knew that already. We also cracked the forearm and partially dislocated the elbow joint, collected six shallow scars in the chest, two in the shoulder, and one in the cheek. My numbers were off the charts, but I didn't feel it until I'd actually broken something.

I glance over at the little Juno scratched into the wall, looking back at me.

"I'm sorry, old bird."

Two shells booked off, and one lost to the wind; three battered jockeys, and one in a body bag. For all of NorCol's quibbles, Hail didn't have any trouble getting us the day to ourselves, and I need it. I sink into my bunk and wait for my temples to stop throbbing.

Hail got away without so much as chipped paint. She was with us right from the start, but she landed back on *Horizon* with enough ammunition left that she could have turned around and done it all again. If it was anyone else, any other jockey, I'd have called them on it. Gotten in their face.

If it was anyone else, but not Hail. I saw her, in just as thick as the Juno and me.

If she's running a gun-cam, I'd like to see the footage. She'll have scored as many hits as any of us. Maybe more. She's that kind of jockey.

And probably awake already too. Tch.

The thought picks me up, but I'm the one who has to do the carrying. I roll over and haul myself to my elbows. It's another minute's heaving before I'm sitting straight, vision clouding from the corners. Christs, I hurt.

My ports burn, and the knuckles on my left hand are still ruddy from their encounter with Hail's airlock last night. My right hand is a little better than before, but that isn't saying much. I've got pins and needles to the elbow, and the feeling you get when you've hit the nerve in your shoulder. It moves when I tell it to, but it feels like I'm steering by remote.

Best of all, there's a prickle behind my eyes like I'm due for a hangover I don't deserve.

My uniform is where last night left it, spread in a trail from the door to the foot of my bunk. I scavenge the things I can reach from the end of my bed, avoiding the floor as long as I can, even with my thick socks back on. I don't remember getting undressed, but then, I don't remember taking the train back from the chow hall either, let alone finding my way back to bed. I remember talking to Hail, and my reflection in a jug of tar. I remember a field of bottles in the lamplight, but not much else. Mostly, I remember being cold.

I drop into my boots but leave them loose, throw on a shirt and pull my long coat over that, unbuttoned. I snag my personals bag, all NorCol brand and tacky plastic. All that, and I have to breathe before I can work the door.

I stop dead, hand on the lock. The Juno is awake.

It feels like someone moving nearby, when all you've got to go on is the changing air and a tingle on the back of your neck. I don't have to see it, but I could point it out through a concrete wall.

Without my helmet on.

The shell is watching me when I step out into the hangar,

looking down past a wall of scaffold and a disassembled arm, flayed open while the knuckledraggers mount it into a matching shoulder joint, propped by cranes and draped in dustcloth.

I smile at it. "Hello, old bird."

It's a whisper, lost in the rumble of bootsoles and the thunder of machinery. It wouldn't be loud enough if it was just the two of us in here, but the shell doesn't need to hear me speak.

It watches, and does what it was built to do.

It reads me.

The lenses flick. I try to read it back, but I'm made of dumb meat and headache. I'm too far away for anything more.

A weight hits me between the shoulders and nearly tips me over. I ride the impact and turn on the balls of my feet, bring a fist up in time to watch Avery spill himself across the floor.

Watch where you're going, convict. I can see the words lining up on his tongue, but they don't make it. He gapes at me. He should; if he wants a fight, he's got it.

At least, that's what I'm waiting for.

"Eyes open," comes with a whistle from above: Folau, hanging over the edge of a scaffold rail. His eyes are puffy, and he looks like that sleep debt is gathering interest. Machine oil glistens on his cheeks, adds deep shadows to the dusky tones of his skin. There's an eyebrow at altitude, and a smile that shows teeth.

I follow his gaze back to Avery. His cheeks look like they've been steam-burned, pink and clammy, ruddy contrast to the dirty pale of the rest of him.

"There a problem, knuckledragger?"

He scrabbles back a pace on hands and feet, mumbles something I can't hear.

"What was that?"

No answer.

I look up Folau. "What's his problem?"

Folau offers me a nasty grin and taps his chest. I look down at mine, loose in my bunker-shirt.

I can't help the chuckle. "What? They don't have tits where you come from?"

Avery starts. "Uh—" he manages, turns it into a cough. It sounds like he's got something caught in his throat.

"He used to be Regimentata," comes the call from above.

I shake my head. "Never heard of it."

"Planetary militia, old frontier." Folau rests his chin on the rail. He looks exhausted, but a grin finds its way back across his face. He licks his lips. "Way Avery talks about it, it sounds like my kind of gig. Boys only."

JUST LIKE EVERYTHING else on *Horizon*'s decks, there's a shower hall that the jockeys have claimed for themselves. The full-timers give the cons a hard time, but some things cross the divide. Jockeys come back dripping with sweat and streaked in propellant, faces tacky with the solvents that keep our air-lines clear. There'll be times when we dismount and find ourselves covered in blood. It won't always be ours, but at least it doesn't clog the drains.

The other side of the passage is the hall where the knuckledraggers go, the doors marked with machine-oil and greasy fingerprints.

I cycle the locks on the jockey side, waiting for the seals to let me through. Anyone on today's rotation is either out on the wind, or doing the chow-hall shuffle. I'm betting on it, actually. My ports are puffy and weeping, still raw where the medics trimmed the skin around them. The heat will help, but it isn't going to feel that way when the water finds them. At least there won't be anyone around to hear me when it happens.

I don't feel the warmth until the airlocks part, greeting me with a wall of steam so thick I can't see much past the basins. What I can see, head and shoulders above the shower-stalls, is Salt. If he was standing straight, the nozzle would be just high enough to buzz him in the chin, but he's folded himself over far enough to get his scalp into the water. I can feel how hot it is from here.

Behind the rush is a deep bass, humming a familiar song.

I falter on the doorstep. I'm interrupting.

When you live on a company tub, you're on top of a dozen human beings at any given time, and so close there'll always be naked skin. You get used to that part quickly, but you take privacy where you can get it.

That doesn't mean covering up; you don't have anything that everyone else hasn't seen a thousand times before. On a boat like this, quiet is what you'll be looking for. A second without anyone yelling at you, a moment to clear your head. Like everything else, there's a trade involved. You give your wingmates space when they need it, and you can expect some in return. When you walk in on someone, you announce it, give them time to clear their eyes and get their walls back up.

I wait on the threshold. "Rough night?"

Salt straightens, takes a second to work out where I am. "The night was fine. Waking up was the problem."

"When?"

"About half an hour ago." He chuckles, deep and resonant. "I've been on military time so long I'd cycled the days in my head, decided I'd slept through a whole one and came out the other side." He rests an elbow on the divider, nods to me. "You look about as bad as I feel. Up late?"

I flip the taps on the stall next door and find a hook to hold my coat. "Hail's fault."

Salt slips back under the water. "Think she ever sleeps?"

I set my boots on the counter, fold my clothing on top of them as I undress. The hall is all stainless steel, and only a little warmer than the ship around it. Steam condenses on every surface; a shirt on the floor is a shirt in a puddle just waiting to happen.

"If she sleeps, it'll be where no one can see it." I stand back, hugging myself, waiting for the cold pipes to warm to something sane. "You hear about the damage she took?"

Salt frowns at me. "No. She okay?"

"Just fine, that's the problem." When I lean back in, the water is hotter than I'd ever care to use. "She came back without a scratch. Nothing. They didn't even have to patch her paintjob."

He wipes sweat and beading water from his forehead. "Might be true, but you're the one with two scalps on your belt."

"Two scalps, and missing a wing."

He measures a breath. "You and me both." He aims an eye at my stall. "Careful."

"I'll try."

The shower's hot, but I don't want to risk the taps: one flick and they'll go from peeling skin to frostbite. It's been that way on every NorCol boat I've ever had the misfortune of showering on. Some jockeys think it's on purpose. As I watch my stall fill with steam, I'm inclined to agree.

I edge nearer and decide I'll take it hot first. I still have to push myself in, and the water's a shock. I tense, grit my teeth and try to hold, but I'm not prepared for the rush of pain through my ports, needle-sharp and boiling, tunnelling into my flesh and pushing silver flashes across my eyes.

I don't hear myself shout, but I feel it. I've broken bones that didn't hurt this much. It's a second before I realise that I've bitten into my bottom lip, blood turning bitter in my mouth. Shadows creep in from the corners, and the floor spins out from under my feet. The whole world turns around me.

I don't see Salt's hands curve over the top of the stall, and I only feel the edge of his fingers as he snags my arm at the shoulder, lowers me safely to the floor. I manage to cut the taps, and fold myself into a ball in the corner.

My mouth is full of spit and iron. My stomach churns.

"Fuck," I manage. "I'm worse off than I thought."

Salt straightens, checks the grazes under his arms and across his chest, then beams at me over the stall top. "The chain gang screwed me just as well as it screwed you, jockey." He cuts the water and settles on the floor of his stall. I feel the deck bow slightly as he shifts his weight. "Give it ten before you try again. I didn't, nearly broke my head on the stall."

"Thank you," I manage.

We watch the haze together.

"What do you think it means?"

There's a moment's silence before he replies. "That we're out of shape. The chain gang clipped our wings, and it's taking time to grow them back."

I shake my head, for all that Salt can't see it. "That isn't what I meant." My hand hurts. "I'm not sure what I meant."

He breathes deep. "The message in Sigurd's bottle. That's what you were going to say."

"I suppose it was."

"*Don't let them touch you,*" he says, like he's laying each word out where he can see it.

"What do you think it means?"

"I don't think it means anything. You touched *them*, and it hasn't done you any harm."

I suppose I did.

I work my fingers. They hurt, the Juno's broken bones still throbbing beneath my skin.

"How's the hand?"

The question drives a shiver down my spine. There's water cooling on my skin, and a chill that climbs up through the floor, but this is different. My heart chokes me.

How would he know about that? Jockeys get their shells battered all the time, fly them 'til they're little more than scrap, but the connection never lasts. The pain is there to let you know where the damage is, nothing more. It isn't supposed to follow you around.

I glare at the divider. How did you know?

But Salt saves me asking. "I hear they needed extra crew just to get it straightened out."

I look down at my knuckles. Oh.

Not this hand, then.

"They're busy reattaching. As it turns out, Folau actually has his uses."

Salt laughs at that. It's contagious. "I'd have to see it to believe i—" he trails off.

"Salt?"

There's a pause. "Did you feel that?"

Feel what?

The ship answers before I can ask. A shiver runs through the deck and up along my spine. Reflex makes me tense, throws my hands out against the stall sides, but if there's another tide on the way, I'm in all kinds of trouble. I don't have Salt's upper-body strength, and nothing to stop myself being dashed against the ceiling, floor, ceiling, thrown around like a fucking ragdoll, cracked open on the steel.

And here I thought I'd die with my boots on.

A few heartbeats later, and I can feel Salt relax on the other side, the bend in the divider only obvious once it's settling back to its original shape. It takes me a second more, with gritted teeth and eyes screwed up, feeling the blood run back into my right hand.

No tide. No more shivers. Just a groan as the ship settles around us.

And then silence.

"You all right?" whispers Salt, just a little out of breath.

I start to reply, but a siren cuts me off.

"General quarters. General quarters," says an automated voice. "All hands to battle stations. This is not a drill. Repeat, all hands to battle stations. This is not a drill."

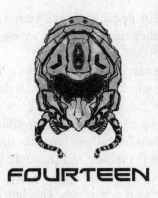

FOURTEEN

HORIZON'S WIDENETS ARE all sound and chaos: a thousand voices shouting orders, begging for information, or just adding to the confusion. We blink our way through every channel we can reach, hear jockeys complaining that they're stuck in their blocks or pacing through their hangars, sitting in saddles and waiting for Tower to make sense for the thirty seconds they need to get launching. SOs yell at the ground crews clogging up their flight decks, and the 'dragger chiefs shout back, voices straining: *You let us work, or there'll be no flying today.* Fire crews chase phantom fires and accident reports. Marines call out from their reserve bays, tracing rumours of hostile boots on *Horizon*'s decks.

Salt and I keep to the main circuits for as long as we can, but it's a few minutes before we cut ourselves loose, ears ringing. We switch through the smaller networks after that, but the channels are clogged so tight that we can't make single words out of the wash.

We trade glances. We've both been to war before: not the slow-boil in this place, but real, all-out war, him on the Authority's tab, me on a company bill. We've had people freeze on us, lose the tune right when we needed them on the spot, but that's what happens. They say that war is hell, but in my experience, it's mostly been about the noise. Or the lack of it. *Horizon*'s been in the quiet so long it doesn't remember what the churn feels like.

This could all be for nothing. It could be driftwood on

someone's scopes, tripping wires and starting alarms. It could be a competitor shell that picked the wrong winds home and drifted into view.

NorCol has thousands of machines in these hangars, and more guns than anyone would ever care to count. It's a dreadnought: the largest even of its kind.

And it's seizing up at the first sign of trouble.

Salt stands on the monorail platform, the first line we can find that leads back to the middle of Hangar D. He looks back at me just as his eyes go dim, and folds his long NorCol coat over a shoulder. "I can't get a response. This line isn't calling back, and every train I can reach is a long way away and dealing with troubles of its own." He nods my way. "Any luck there?"

I kill the last of my open connections. "I've tried Hail, Folau, and even Kadi. All personnel searches are coming back full of static. If they're out there, it's in the noise. They aren't going to hear us." I breathe out, feeling empty. "We're on our own."

He leans over the platform edge. "Looks like we're walking, then."

Christs. "All the way back to our blocks?"

"Unless there's anywhere else you mean to be, yes."

"Just what I needed."

"You could always stay here."

I glare his way, but he meets it with a smile.

"Come on," he says, and drops off the edge of the platform.

I hear him hit steel somewhere below and follow. Onto the monorail first, then down a ladder to the service path following the line. It's supposed to be for maintenance, but looking at it, you wouldn't think that there'd been boots down here in decades. It takes a second to see why.

A drone hangs from the rail, a basket of slender legs clinging to sheer metal and not a whole lot else. It's newer than the rail-line, a decade old at most, left down here to tend the ancient tunnels.

A blue-green eye watches us for a moment, but the little machine decides we aren't of interest, pulls itself back against the rail and runs its strange mouthparts through the cabling underneath. We have been dismissed.

Without boot-traffic, the walkway is full of the kind of slime that builds in any corner of a ship this size, a mix of moisture and metal dust, grease and mould and a thousand other things I'd rather not be thinking about. It sucks at our soles, and makes me wish I'd tied my laces. Their tips are slick with muck, and cold in my hands as I tie them up.

"Today just keeps getting better."

But Salt isn't listening.

"That's the way we came," he murmurs, as much to himself as anything else.

I follow the look. "The chow hall is at the end of that line. It's going to be mad out there."

He turns on the spot, looks out over the top of my head. "What's on this end, then?"

"I've been here as long as you have, Salt."

That isn't completely true. I haven't been *here*, but I've been a thousand places like it. NorCol builds in the same straight lines everywhere it goes.

"Figured I'd ask."

I shake my head. "No, you're right. There's a standard pattern. This part of the hangar will be run by human resources."

He chuckles at that. "I don't think that means what they think it means. NorCol really doesn't understand people, does it?"

"Even less than you'd think." I peer into the dark ahead of us. "Human service blocks come in threes: chow, ablutions, and medical. Primary functions all lumped together."

"So we're in the middle, and chow is behind us, which leaves medical." He rolls the thought around. "Is this a good idea?"

"Probably not." I cross my arms, suddenly aware of the chill. The maintenance paths are made for people in heavy boots and protective clothing. "But the infirmary will have its own priority rail."

"Full coming in, empty going out."

"Assuming this is as bad as we think it is, yes." I pull my coat tight, but the cold is already in here with me, and my skin is still clammy from the showers. I fasten the buttons anyway, hope my body heat can cook it off. "Whatever happens, at least it'll be warmer."

Salt grins at me. "What do you mean?" he asks, breath misting.

I flip my collar up around my ears and get marching. "Shut up."

We walk for a while in silence: we have to focus on keeping our boots from sliding in the ooze, or sticking fast. It isn't long before we hear the first rumbles in the distance, and not much more before we can feel them through the deck. They're deep, like the shock of impacts on armour, but there's a rhythm to them that's impossible to miss. A drumbeat in the steel.

"What was that?" I whisper.

Salt frowns at me. "You don't know? I thought you'd been on a big boat before."

I have. Cruisers and strike-carriers, for the most part. Quick and sharp, made for nipping at heels and striking at hearts. "Nothing like this."

"The companies like it fast and light, I suppose."

The floor throbs, and vibrations climb my spine.

Salt watches me. "Nothing with broadsides, then?"

"No. Why?"

"That," he times the word to distant thunder, "is a gun-deck." Something lights his eyes.

"What is it?"

"I have an idea."

I DON'T KNOW how Salt runs in this stuff. He moves as if there was solid ground beneath his feet, leaving footprints like impact craters right through to the metal underneath. Me, not so much. There's grime so deep I could lose a finger in it before I found the decking, and so I skip between the tracks he leaves behind, working hard to match the length of his stride. It's the only way I can keep up.

We pass two more maintenance drones on the way; they climb away as Salt comes into view, tasks interrupted, and watch us from the rail-top with glowing eyes and discontent.

We travel in and out of the glare of hazard lamps and alarm systems, through automated voices on decks above and below, *general quarters*, *general quarters*, droning on forever. The chaos on the network bubbles on, even all the way down here, but the longer we walk, the more it turns to static. We're all alone, and following a path only Salt seems to know for certain, but it doesn't slow him down. We make just under three K in half the time it would take me to do it on my own.

He stops without warning, and at first I think he's waiting for me. I catch him up, breathing ragged, and trying to keep from emptying my stomach out on the floor. My late night has kept pace with me, dogging my heels all the way from the showers. My head is unspeakable, and my lungs feel swollen and fleshy. It feels like I've frostburned the back of my throat in the cold air, and it sounds that way too, once I finally manage to speak.

"What is it?" The last word snags, turns into a cough.

"Shh." Salt tilts his head.

The thunder is closer now, and the air feels electric, gathering around every thud. I can't hear much more, but I'm still trying to keep myself from gasping, and there's nothing I can do about the pounding in my ears. I can't help thinking Salt can hear it too.

He stands completely still, eyes closed, listening to something else.

"There," he whispers.

It takes me a moment to find it.

Right after every shot, there's a hiss of pistons and a rush of air, dulled by the walls but still loud enough to echo. At least, I think it's an echo.

Now that I'm listening, I can hear a second sound just like the first, but this one fades into the decks beneath us. Up ahead, a hazard lamp blinks red in time with the sound.

"Is that a munitions elevator?" I ask.

Collecting ordnance from magazines deep in the ship's bowels, hauling them up to the gun-decks on its skin.

"I hope so."

I almost laugh at that. "You're insane. I'm not riding a gun-cart."

Salt glances over his shoulder at me. "Why not? It'll be fun."

I spread my arms. "This place, these walkways—NorCol built them for people. You understand that, right?" I knock a toe against the wall. "This was made to take human beings, and it's the best they could come up with." Another thud, another rush. "*That* was built by NorCol engineers, and they weren't expecting it to carry anything that wasn't drop-forged."

The elevator rushes past, faster than I can follow, as if to make the point. From high above us to far below, quicker than thinking. The hazard lamp glares at us, as if the noise wasn't enough to scare us off. It gives Salt a crimson silhouette, puts a bloody edge to his smile.

"Where's your sense of adventure?"

"Back of the queue, where it belongs." A gun rumbles, and a magazine feed shrieks. "How are you even going to stop it to get on top? You gonna catch it?"

Salt shakes his head. "We just need a way to set it in service mode." He shrugs. "At least, that's the way it worked on my home boat. I figure NorCol needs its tubes checked every now and then."

"Don't count on it." But I can already see the logic. There's a heavy hatch where the elevator shaft passes our tunnel, made so that *Horizon*'s crews could get eyes on the mechanics. There's a narrow strip of reinforced glass in the middle of the door, just below eye-height, and a pale light shines through it, cut off for a split second every time the platform howls past. The hazard lamp fills the shadow, paints it red.

An inspection panel stands out just below the window. I hate to admit it, but Salt is right. NorCol can be sensible after all.

"I still don't like it."

"What's not to like?" He flicks a glance down the tunnel.

"There's only what—four K? Five? Five K to go to the next platform."

I cross my arms. "How do we do this?"

He nods, has to bend to get a good look at the panel. It lights up at the warmth of his fingers—a pad full of actual buttons, glowing night-vision green. It's even older than I thought.

"First, we wake it up." He walks his fingers across the pad, looking for something. "There."

A little display fizzes at him from an alcove just above the pad, levelling out in the same colours as the buttons below. He rolls through a couple of commands. You can see he's done this before.

He wipes his forehead and sags just a little. "It wants eyeballs. Looks like we're walking after all."

I shoo him clear of the pad. "I'll get it."

Salt watches me. "This thing is a hundred years old. It's not going to recognise you."

I tap the side of my head. "Displays."

His eyes glow at me. "I've got a set myself, remember? But that doesn't solve the problem; you don't know what pattern to project."

I let him have his moment. "Been with NorCol long?"

He raises an eyebrow. "We landed on the same day."

"Well, if you'd been in blues a little longer, you'd know about this company's deep and enduring capacity for fucking up."

"Oh, I've worked that out already." A smile tugs at his face. "It isn't anything special. The Authority's just as bad on any given day."

"You'd think so, but NorCol's as bad as it gets. I've been with the company longer than I'd care to admit, and I'm still discovering new ways it can trip over itself." I wake my eyes, and blink my way through my onboard files. Right near the back of it all, surrounded by things I haven't used in years, is a file issued to every employee in the last twenty years. They were supposed to burn it out of me when Internal Affairs picked me up, but NorCol managed to screw that up about as well as everything else. "They phased out retina scans a long time ago, but it wasn't one by one. It was knee-jerk. A Hasei chameleon found their way into classified territory and gave NorCol a heart attack. The company stripped out every eye-lock it could find, all at once."

"But they couldn't get that right either."

"They missed a few."

"As you'd expect."

I blink the file, watch as it splits in two and arranges itself across the displays inside my eyes, blurring out of focus as it sets itself in place. "When I say a few, I mean thousands. Tens of thousands."

"And employees kept getting stuck?" Salt laughs, but it's swallowed by a rush of air from the door.

"The company didn't think to leave the servers in. Pulled them out at the same time as they yanked the locks. After that, it didn't matter if you had the right eye or not, the doors they missed didn't have anything to compare it to."

"So they gave you all a skeleton key?"

"Selectively, but yes." I lean over the panel, and set my eyes against the reader. "Why solve the problem when you can patch it over and pretend it never happened?"

"What happened?" he asks.

The panel beeps at me. I've got the right eyes.

Behind the door, pistons wheeze and brakes whistle.

"To make the company take notice?" I shrug. "Same as everything else: cost-benefit analysis."

"Too expensive to keep changing the locks?"

"Too expensive to keep replacing the employees."

Salt watches me, waiting for the punchline, but there isn't one. He looks back as the elevator platform rolls in behind the window. "This is a bad idea, isn't it?"

I smile at him as the hatch pops free, seals hissing as the pressure equalises on our side. It feels like the air has pressed up against the sides of my head. Behind the door is a pallet of ammunition: massive rounds all twice as tall as I am, and

ANDREW SKINNER

almost as wide as Salt, painted bright red with yellow on their
tips and simple stencils on their sides.

I wave him through. "Going up."

WE SET THE journey nice and slow, 'feed inspection,' as if we
were running eyes up and down the shaft sides looking for
cracks in the steel. We aren't taking any chances.

We hit the next hatch up in a minute and change. A pair of
eyes meets us through the little window in the door and go wide
for a second before they disappear. When we pop the seals, we
find the rest of an ordnance tech, wrapped in pale flash-gear,
and reeling back from the hatch. He loses footing just as I step
out, spills himself out across the corridor, scrabbling back on
his hands and feet, hitting his head on the bulkhead behind him.

"Whoa, easy now," says Salt, still working his way clear of
the hatch.

The tech finds his senses just in time to see a mountain of muscle
and tattoowork unfold itself behind me. His eyes shiver in their
sockets, and reflex sends him hunting for the sidearm on his hip.
His fingers run numb and stupid. He can't even clear the flap.

I push Salt back and try to wave the tech down. "Easy now.
There's no need for that." I tilt the badge on my shoulder
over where he can get a good look. "See that? We're jockeys.
NorCol." I watch the words bounce off of him. His eyes are
glazing quickly. "Friendlies."

He tugs on his gun again, and for a second it looks like he
might get it free. Salt and I throw our hands up, but we're on
our toes. We're not getting sunk by some nugget who doesn't
know better, NorCol or otherwise.

"Friendly," I say again, lower this time, trying push it through
his skull. "Friendly," with a tap on my chest. "We're friendlies,
you understand?"

For a second, it looks like I've snagged him. He can see my
patches, and my coat is the right shape. His gaze makes it halfway
to the unit markers on my chest, but trips over something in the

209

back of his head. Something put there by a drill instructor back when he was in basic. I know that look when I see it—glossy-eyed automatic. Dammit.

"Boarders," he squeaks out, finding his lungs a moment later. "Boarders!" And still the gun won't pull free.

That's it, then. I'm on the balls of my feet without thinking, and I'm putting the next step in his face.

"Stay right where you are."

The voice fills the air around us, gruff and acidic. I find its owner above the barrel of a shotgun, wearing the same flash-gear as the tech at our feet. He is much heavier, though: a match for Salt, if he decided to put his mind to it. I can see beard poking out from under the hood, and while he might be covered in protective gear, he's made space for a gunner's tab on his arm, and a pair of service pins near his collar.

The barrel tracks us. "Keep those hands up. That's it. Just like that." I can't make his eyes out, but I can feel the glare. "This them?"

The tech nods, nearly brains himself again.

The gunner regards us. "Why are you clogging up my ammo feed?"

Salt gives me the corner of his eye and I shrug. There isn't much to say. "We're jockeys. Came off a long-haul flight, dropped into the showers. Got caught there when—*whatever's* going on out there started going on."

"Trains are jammed all the way to the shell-blocks," offers Salt. "So we figured we'd get above the problem."

I wish I had a better angle. Enough to see some of his eyes. Getting shot by a punk's about the same as getting shot by a lifer, but I can't tell anything about him through his gear. What I can see are the imperfections in his weapon, where paint has worn down with use, where plastic guards have chipped. We stand in silence, watching him as he watches us.

"You got arms?"

I spread my hands so the coat parts around my hip. "Nothing. See for yourself."

He nods. "I see. You cons?"

"Both of us," I reply.

"How long?"

"Not long. A few days on *Horizon*."

I can almost see the edge of a smile. "Well, you're off to one hell of a start." He drops his aim, but keeps the weapon at his hip. He nods to Salt. "You're colonial."

"Once upon a time."

I glance over at Salt. I know what he used to be, but only because he told me. The Authority is the last thing I'd think if I was looking at him for the first time. Wakehunter, maybe. Or a privateer that used to work in Open Waters.

"Unit?"

Salt touches a tattoo at his throat. Small, just about the size of his fingertip. Above it, the Authority's banner-and-comet.

Ah.

"3rd Expeditionary."

"Bullshit," says the gunner, no hesitation.

Salt tilts his head back. "Read them yourself."

"And get my head stoved in?" There's a dry chuckle. He hefts the shotgun.

"Boarders?" comes from our feet.

The three of us look down at the tech, who makes a bubbling sound.

The gunner nods his way. "Did you do this?"

Salt smirks. "He didn't need our help."

There's a real laugh at that, deep and husky. "Thought not." The gunner flaps a hand at the door behind him. "Get yourself gone, boy. Tell Rhee you've unfucked the ammo hoppers. Normal service returning."

The tech looks up at him, then back at us. "But sir—"

"Do these look like boarders to you, son? Half-naked and gunless; dead-lens jockey eyes?"

There's a stutter, or a choke. I'm not sure which.

"Didn't think so." The old gunner jams a thumb over his shoulder. "Get gone."

211

We watch him scramble.

The hood pulls back to reveal sharp blue eyes and a beard that's almost copper. His skin is about as pale as the flash-gear that covered it, almost all of it sketched with dark tattoos. Most are unfamiliar, but I've seen similar things before, rippling across Salt's own skin. They have about as much muscle, care of the Authority's genesmiths.

"You're a con."

The gunner nods. "Since the dawn of time."

"Colonial?" I ask.

"686th Long," says Salt, reading symbols on the man's throat, "but I don't recognise the origin."

"Karwar School of Naval Gunnery." He props the shotgun on his shoulder. "Name's Masz."

"Salt," says Salt.

"Rook."

Masz nods, turns on his heel. "Come, jockeys, let's get you back to your roosts."

He shoulders through a pair of heavy doors. They've got the usual seals for atmosphere, but they're spaced with layers of padding and flash-curtains.

Behind them is what looks like an engineering facility. I'm expecting soldiers, or at least a few gunnery crew with light arms and crowbars. One of their techs just yelled a rated word, after all: shout 'boarders' or 'fire' without reason, and you get yourself a month's extra swabbing; ignore the call, and you'll get double that. There should be a welcoming party, gun barrels tracking us as we step into the open.

But most of them don't even look up. Seems that tech gets himself a lot of extra swab duty.

There are ten stations in a row along the huge bay. Ten massive guns rest in pits cut into the floor, barrels passing through the hull. Gunners walk the gangways over and around them, watching screens and bickering.

"Why have they stopped?" I ask.

Masz puts his hands out. "No reason to keep the guns

running. We're just wasting ammo like this."

"I don't understand. What about general quarters?"

"Hmph. We got the call, same as everyone else, but we're not seeing what they're telling us we're supposed to be seeing. Deck chief decided we'd make a noise, turn it into a training exercise, but we've been shooting at target glyphs. Min-maxing cycle rates."

"What are you supposed to be seeing?"

"Hostile contacts, but we don't have number or range. No details, just garble and bullshit. Some nugget who doesn't know a hot mark from a cloud spot."

Salt and I trade glances. "Why? Aren't there any?" he asks.

Masz chuckles. "No, there *are* a bunch of marks on the scopes, but we've looked over every one of them. Nothing out there but friendly shells."

THE GUNNER PUTS us on a tram off his deck. It's not much like the monorails linking *Horizon*'s hangars; this is a bulk carrier, open-backed and oversized, wide enough that the Juno could ride with space to spare.

Salt has the usual trouble. The tram has a cabin near the front, with seats designed to carry a handful of engineers wherever their spare parts were heading. I strap myself into one, but he has to somehow join two belts together. He fights with the clasps for a while, but gives up, and ties the belts in a knot across his chest. He looks uncomfortable, but it's that or nothing else. The rest of the tram is a flatbed deck, covered in mounting points and puddles of oil so old they've stained the steel.

"Sit tight," says Masz. He toggles something with a blink of glowing eyes and waves us off.

We don't have time to return the gesture. The train throws us back in our seats, pulls a couple of gee right out of the platform. It's made to carry parts for *Horizon*'s massive guns, but a couple of jockeys is all that's slowing it down now, and that isn't saying much—or anything.

The first few seconds are a blur, the kind of acceleration that I'm used to in a shell, but the ride gets better after that. The seats are bolted to the deck, and there's a windshield up ahead, but the sides are open, with a thin steel mesh stretched across where doors would normally be. If you could fly a shell with the top down, this is how I'd imagine it.

We shriek past crowded platforms, some writhing and shouting and lit orange by emergency lamps, others quiet and dim. A few jackets just stand and watch us pass, some offer passing words and single-finger salutes.

The line carries us through open air as Hangar D opens up around us, but we don't stop. The track runs up and over crowded railyards, monorail queues nearly a K long in places, empty lines around them. NorCol efficiency at work.

The tram rolls to a halt on the edge of an actual engineering bay, sandwiched between C and D. The platforms are empty; they aren't expecting anything from gunnery, after all. We follow Masz's directions from the platform: first a left, then another, until we find a former Hasei con by the name of Silver holed up in an office box, patchwork diagrams on the walls that she sketched out by hand. It seems like every second person on this boat was brought here in chains.

She's as prickly as the gunner said she'd be, but she takes a second to read Salt's tattoos. Apparently she speaks colonial, and they trade a couple of barbs. Her eyes light up when we ask her if she can smuggle us past the snafu.

"Seriously, fuck this place," are her last words as she sends us off, a priority line diverted from carrying spares to hauling a pair of jockeys instead. It glides into the space beneath our berthing blocks, leaving us to follow the inner hull on rusty ladders and rattling gangways. We have to jump across breaks in the plating, balance along paths and pipes and other things never designed to take our weight.

We take an elevator for the last stretch and find our way to my doorstep.

"See you on the other side."

"Nothing," says Folau. He taps his ear. "There's a call from
Tower, though. They're asking anyone with spurs and a saddle
to call in, ASAP."

"Done." I start skipping through the buttons on my coat.
"Get my suit."

He spins in place. "On it."

I don't watch him go. I'm already calling home.

The Juno's networks are right there, almost a reflex now that
I know where to look. Connection is a few blinks behind that,
and the machine filters into me.

I flex my hand. There's still a little of the pain from before,
but it's changed places. Before, it felt like I'd broken something,
but now it just feels stiff, or like I haven't used it in a while. My
other aches are beginning to catch me up—throbbing temples
and a raw patch in my throat, a dozen more if I cared to count
them off. The Juno smooths them over, buries them in warmth
and immovable, impossible weight.

"Thank you," I whisper. I am whole again.

I take a breath and haul myself up straight. "All right. Hook
us in."

The Juno patches our net into Tower's open channels, but
where Salt and I could only find noise, the shell hammers its
way through, forcing a connection. For a moment, there's
nothing at all.

"Is that you, two-eleven?" asks a familiar voice. She sounds
surprised.

"Two-eleven, reporting. What's the news, Bell Tower?"

She swallows. "I wish I could tell you. Are you back in the saddle?"

I look up. Folau is on his way, a pair of ground crew tailing him, my suit in pieces in their hands.

"Almost."

"Good enough." She pauses. "How many machines have you got?"

"Two. Berthing blocks six-five and six-six. I wish we had more."

She's distracted, it takes her a moment to respond. "All right, two-eleven. Hold tight. I'll see what I can scratch up."

"Understood, Bell Tower."

With that, the line goes limp. I offer another to Salt. "I got a word with Tower. They want us in saddle."

"Copy," says Salt. "Seems there's another side after all."

"Call back when you're set."

"Understood."

I trim the last of it away and leave myself alone in the Juno's glow, just for a second. I can't spare more than that.

Folau rolls up with my helmet in one hand, conductive layers limp over the other. The rest of his little posse circles us, one with the suit itself, the other with a mound of armour and trauma plates.

I wave the last of it away. "No time. Soft armour only."

My ground crew trades glances but decide not to argue. I drop my coat, loosen my boots, break the clasp on my belt. Folau splits the conductive suit down on its seals, holds it open while I slide my feet inside. The other 'dragger offers me her shoulder for balance, switches places with Folau once we've got his side done. We close it to the waist, trade my shirt for the upper layers of conductive circuitry and soft armour, all buckled together over my shoulders and around my throat. The helmet goes on easiest of all, but I'd never need help for that.

Even at a distance, the counter hits the limit—97, dead on.

We are one again.

"How's the hand?" we ask Folau.

"Cracks are patched and joints are seated."

We could have told him that. "But?"

A yawn runs through him. We can see a catnap in the corners of his eyes and the creases in his jumpsuit, stolen in a corner somewhere when Avery had his back turned.

"But it's just that. Patched. You hit so hard it put cracks in the structure itself. Skeletal stuff. The repairs are as good as they're gonna get, but what we really need is time. Long enough to strip all the armour off and splint the cracks, one by one."

We shrug, or part of us does.

"It'll have to do."

"No, it won't." There's a smile now, despite everything else. Folau holds himself better than I'd expect. Better than should be possible. He singles out a flatbed on the far side of the block. "Avery found you a present."

We look back at Avery. He looks just as ruffled as Folau, but on half the hours, if we had to guess. He meets our gaze for half a second, but switches to his feet.

"What is it?"

He licks his lips. "Let me—uh, let me show you."

The loader has a tarp across the top, held down by reflective straps and covered in stencils.

DECOM, says one set of marks. DEEP STORE, says another.

"What does that mean?" we ask.

Avery climbs onto the flatbed, splits a clasp, starts tugging on the covers. "NorCol never throws anything away."

"Doesn't have to," offers Folau, behind me. "Not on a ship like this."

"Nah. All the old kit gets dumped in Deep Store. They've got a—a—ar—"

"Archives?"

"Archives. Vaults full of stuff. Hundreds of years, prolly." The last of the clasps fall away. "So, uh—here. So you don't break that hand again."

Laid out flat across the truck is a length of hard steel, painted red and white and yellow in alternating hazard-strips. A handle sticks out on one end, big enough to fit a Juno's hands. The other end tapers to a point.

Calling it a sword makes it sound like it's sharp. It isn't. The edges are flat; the Juno is strong enough that it won't make any difference.

We jab Avery on the shoulder. It's playful, but he looks hurt for half a second. Understanding dawns a moment after that and pulls his face up around a smile.

We offer him another in return. "Nice one, Ave."

FIFTEEN

WE GET A line from flight control, and it's heavy. The kind they use when they're planning on dumping massive files across the net, or running thick encryption. This one's empty, though. There's no audio, nothing much of anything once the Juno's finished handshaking with the Tower nets. A minute comes and goes in silence.

"That you, Bell Tower?"

There's a crackle, like there's something blocking the receiver. "This is Bell Tower. Sorry, two-eleven." There's another break. "Are you ready to fly?"

We open our lenses. Our ground crew are already in their bays, and the SO stands out front, scraping at something on the deck with the toe of his boot. We ping Salt's machine, shell-to-shell, and it echoes back.

Saddled and prepped for launch.

"We are good to go, Tower."

She doesn't reply immediately. The line crowds with voices, scuffing boots, and warning chimes. Someone is shouting.

"Are you all right, Bell Tower?"

"All clear, two-eleven," she says, though her voice hints at something else. "I'm trying to get you something to go on— anything more than I've got."

"Let's have it."

She takes a deep breath. "All right. All right." And another. "Recovery flight one-thirty-five put out this morning.

Complement of four, plus half of flight one-thirty-four. Plan had them headed for a weather station in the Borders. It got hit sometime last night."

"Got hit by who?"

"The feed from the station makes it look like Sigurd. They got some silhouettes. Obs tagged Mirai and Corvier."

My sweat runs cold. "What happened?"

"That's the problem. We have no idea." She breathes in, lets it out slowly. "They passed a signal buoy about an hour after they launched, but that's all we've got. The next thing we know, we've got two survivors burning hard to get back on board."

"But?"

"We've got one of the jockeys on line, but he's incoherent. The other isn't responding."

"But the shell's still flying."

She mistakes it for a question. "Still flying, and a lot of other things too. We can't decide if it's on autopilot or not."

There's an edge in her voice. She doesn't think it's autopilot.

"Where are they now?"

"Berthing block twenty-eight. It's a few rows above you."

"Both shells?"

"Both shells. They came down hard. No holding pattern, no pathing, nothing. It was all we could do to get the doors open in time."

Shit. "They're on board."

"Confirmed. Both machines are on board."

"Any word from the hangar?"

"None. Ground crew and emergency services called in ready to receive, but the whole block went dark after the shells put down." She swallows, but it's loud enough that I can hear the cramp in her throat. "Tower Actual has ordered it sealed."

"Understood. We're on it."

"Thank you, two-eleven. Your instructions are to launch and come about, make entry into block two-eight. We'll open up when you're on site."

"And then?"

220

"Report back to me. Use this channel."

"What if—?" I stop.

"If anything happens, you are to contain."

"Contain, Bell Tower?"

"Not my words, two-eleven."

"Understood." But I don't like it.

New message received, says a window in the middle of my eyes. It's text-only, like the kind you'd send on a tightline, or sneak in under the noise of everything else. The Juno tests it, but it comes back clean. We let it run.

> *Forward Obs. reports: at least one shell haywire. Rec.*
> *extreme caution.*
> —B

NorCol is made of people, but it's the machines that keep it running. Some of them are designed to move when there's no one at the wheel, and some think for themselves, but it's always with safeguards in place, backed up with locking-bolts and explosive charges. Made to crack metal spines and destroy mechanical synapses. 'Haywire' is what the company calls it when something has come off of the rails, and the safeguards aren't calling home.

Jockeys have their own name for it. 'Flying hollow'.

Horizon's got hollows on board.

If we were anywhere else, Bell Tower might have come right out and said it, but I'd take a bet that Flight Control is as paralysed as the rest of the ship. They can't understand what they're dealing with, but instead of trying to solve the problem, they're sitting on it and hoping it goes away.

Only that hasn't worked either, so they're sending a couple of jockeys out to blow it all away. Typical.

"We'll deal, Bell Tower. Give us a window."

"Understood, two-eleven. Window on the way."

Armour crawls across the outside of the hull, plates so heavy that they shake the deck beneath our feet. We balance on our launch-rails, feel them crackle underneath us. We stretch our wings and warm our engines, feel our nuclear heartbeat throb.

Eye-light dawns through the hangar doors.

WE LAUNCH, TRIMMING our airspeed as soon as we're clear of the hangars, turning to meet Salt on one of *Horizon*'s many outcrops. We settle on a spur covered in communications masts, as far from the nearest cloud tops as we are from the curve of hull and armour that holds D's hangar blocks.

When you're coming in to roost, lamps and network sigils mark the path back home, warning you when you're falling too fast or off-centre. When a block is sealed against the weather, and armoured against attack, there isn't much to pick it out against the patchwork cliffs. It's even worse when you've got narrow eyes like ours.

"Salt? You got eyes on target?"

But his shell is looking out at the cloud.

He leaves me on the line, but sends a call back toward the ship. "Bell Tower? 211-C here. Do you read?"

"I hear you, C."

"Are you seeing this?" he asks, a marker to match.

I follow it, wishing the Juno and I had lenses half as sharp as his. The thought doesn't last; it only takes a few heartbeats to find it for ourselves.

A shadow with four wings, four arms, and a curve of massive hull. A slip of Sigurd's colours, for all its strange geometry.

Just in time to see it fade.

"Negative, C. That vector is clear. No sign of friend or foe."

"It's the observer," I whisper, shell-to-shell. "From before. From the Lighthouse. It's Sigurd's."

The Decatur glances at us. "You saw it?"

"Just for a second." I switch channels. "You sure you don't have anything on your scopes, Bell Tower?"

"I have confirmation, two-eleven. Whatever it is, we don't see it."

* * *

DARK CARBON STREAKS across the hull, pale paint and silver cracks where something clipped a door. Bell Tower said that they'd put down hard, but I wouldn't have called it that. They crashed, spitting fire and wreckage as they went.

I find the channel we had open before. "We've got eyes on block twenty-eight, Bell Tower. Open up and we'll take a peek inside."

"Understood, two-eleven. Doors opening."

Hazard lamps spin on either side of the doors, throwing orange cones across *Horizon*'s weathered skin. The armour quivers as machinery wakes beneath it, and fine dust pours out past the seals. We watch and wait, craning for a look through the cracks, but the mechanism seizes before the doors are more than halfway open. We can see where the plates were bent out of shape, mangled under a massive impact. Something hit them hard enough to knock them out of their runners.

The machinery resets, cycling the huge slabs of armour back and forth, spilling silvery debris out into the storm. They start grinding open again.

We work our lenses for a look inside, but the lamps are dead, or Tower has cut them off on purpose; either way, past the line of Eye-light on the floor, the hangar is pitch dark. We flip through filters and vision modes, but the light on the hull around the doors washes everything out.

"Looks like we're going in blind."

Salt drops another marker. "Wait. Look."

I follow the mark, but our eyes can't see past it. Something drifts into the light, glows like a dust mote. Salt pushes me the feed from his eyes, and I let it run: a Decatur's arm, shattered at the shoulder, trailing cable and oil.

"Christs."

The hangar doors stop dead while we watch, less than a third of the way open. We still can't see past the glare, but we already know what we're up against. If either of the two shells are still alive, they've taken a beating already. We either go in and put out the fires, rescue what we can; or we crush them.

The Juno and I glance back at Salt. "Cover me."

His shell looks up at the long rails mounted in its shoulder, now tightly stowed. He can extend them in a moment, swing them around in a blur, but inside the hangar, he'll have barely enough space to bring them to bear, let alone get a shot off. Worse, once he'd buttered the target, whatever it was, he'd also add some new ventilation to whatever was behind it. And his assault cannon isn't much better.

"If there's trouble on the other side, you fly out," he growls. "You hear me? No heroics."

"If there's trouble out *here*, you call back. No heroics."

The Decatur glances over a shoulder at the sky. "I'm a little past that. If that thing we saw breaks cover again, I'm lighting it up."

We nod. "Sit tight."

He gives us a massive thumbs-up.

I flip channels. "We're going in."

"Be careful, two-eleven."

I almost smile. "Thank you, Bell Tower."

We spread our wings and let our engines carry us into the wind. We loop back the way we came, keeping as close to the hull as our wingspan will allow; we could fly a straight line to the hangar, but just because we can't see in doesn't mean that the things inside can't see out. Damaged or not, I'd rather not go flying down their throats.

We level off, following the hull across a hive of hangar doors. Tower probably has them locked down, but we keep ourselves clear where we can. Hovering around in front of a shell block is a great way to get yourself wrapped around another machine, and right now I don't trust Tower not to fly someone into me.

Twenty-eight stands out from the rest—doors bowed in the middle, corners raised and jagged, strike-surfaces marked with deep gouges where shell bodies clipped them on the way down. If those machines still have their jockeys, they'll be dead now—

killed on impact. They hit so hard they cracked the hull beneath the hangar plates.

We cut our engines as we approach and come down on toes and fingertips, caught on the armour's cliff face and scraping down its surface. We're still riding in *Horizon*'s bubble of inertia, and we keep its perspective; up is where the ceilings are inside the ship. We move like a climber, hand over hand, thrusting when we cross a gap or change grip, slowed to a crawl across the cliffside. We snag one of the doors to twenty-eight and let ourselves hang, trying to get an eye over the side. Even here, right against the edge, we can't see much of the block behind it.

"Moving up."

I can feel Salt drop his aim and hear his augurs dim, so our ears won't ring when we make our way inside.

"I'll be ready," says Salt. He doesn't like it; the only thing worse than going in blind is watching while your wingmate does.

The Juno and I hold ourselves tight against the plating and let our sensors do some work. The doors are stuck fast, but the gap is probably big enough to fit us, assuming we hold our breath. Good thing Salt's on overwatch; the Decatur's too big and too heavy, no matter how he folds it. We're just over half his size, all told, and even we have to tuck our wing-mounts in behind our shoulders.

It feels strange going without them. Naked, like we'd fall if we lost our grip. I can see the froth far below us, cloud-tops dancing in the Eye-light, bright and impossibly deep.

I have to swallow a moment's vertigo, but the Juno holds us tight and steers a free hand to touch Avery's sword, bolted into a recess in the small of our back. The grip is solid, and fits our fingers like it's meant to.

I take a deep breath. "Breaching."

We press our feet against the hull, pull our grip tight, and hurl ourselves into open air. We float for a heartbeat, maybe less, but it feels like minutes.

I kick for thrust, and our engines throw us like a curveball through the doors. We come down on the deck with a trail of sparks and a shriek of steel. No space for the long-gun in here, and so we reach for the blade again, raising the other hand in a guard.

A broken Decatur rests in one corner, streaks of paint and a trail of shattered armour marking its passage across the floor. Mangled wings prop it up against the wall, one arm twisted in its socket, the other in pieces on the ground. Its chest has been torn open, split around massive rents in the armour. Not bullet holes, or rail-wounds either; if I didn't know better, I'd say another shell tried to claw its way inside.

We feel something take a step and we spin in place, tearing our blade free of its mounts. A pale shell limps into the light. Another Decatur, missing an arm at the shoulder—missing its head and a chunk of plating where its collar used to be. The top of its spine stands out above its chest, exposing steel vertebrae and heavy-duty arteries that sway as it stumbles across the deck. Whole plates of armour have been torn from their mounts, ablatives and strike-faces stripped down to the matte-grey hull underneath. There are bullet holes, hundreds of them, outlined in carbon and spidery cracks. It looks like it flew into a hailstorm.

I can see the cockpit-pod through the gap where its collarbone used to be. Worse, I can see the jockey, hanging out of a break in the pressure-vessel. The nerve-jacks are still in contact, but they tangle around the body. An ankle holds it up, impaled on a piece of twisted steel.

The shell shivers at us. The jockey dangles, unresponsive.

The Juno and I spread our feet. The sword rules the air ahead of us, and our free hand makes a fist.

DONT LET THEM TOUCH YOU

The pale shell lurches forward a step, then another.

We aim the blade-tip at its chest. "Hold it there," I send, across every channel. "Stay right where you are."

It launches itself at us. We skip clear of a grasping hand, knock it away when it suddenly changes direction, rounding on us. We land a jab to its open ribs and a hammerblow across its chest, feel steel giving way beneath our fist, and the machine spins away across the deck, but it lands flat on its feet, jerking around to follow us. It skips forward and aims a punch for our throat, turns the motion into a swipe, claws for our eyes with a fistful of twitching fingers. We catch the grip, watch the fingers squirm just a metre from our face, then turn it back, deflect the next blow on the edge of our blade. It staggers under the force our guard, and we hunt it with the sword.

It drops clear of a thrust, folds itself over at the hips to duck a cut, and rolls away when we bring the blade down and bury it in the deck.

The Decatur stops dead, half a hangar away. Just out of reach.

It doesn't have eyes, but we can feel it watching us.

I've fought every kind of shell—machines with jockeys inside, hollows without, battlefield automata flying alongside human crews—but I've never seen anything move like this.

We hold our guard and watch the machine tick and stutter. It's ruined, taken the kind of damage that would've sunk any three other shells. It misplaces a step, over-compensating as its joints skip and jerk and judder. It looks like it's having a seizure.

It loses power to its knees and drops awkwardly to its haunches. Its arm lies limp on the floor. The Juno and I circle, inch our way closer.

A mistake.

The pale shell burns hot and sudden, hurls itself into the air so hard it spins out of control. We track it, try to skip out of the way, but it's too fast.

We look up and its hand closes down on us.

My eyes go dark.

00.00

I WAKE UP in the black, suddenly numb and blind and empty.

My reactor is cold.

No, not cold. I can't feel it.

My little sun has been replaced with a dull, broken throbbing in my chest. I am slow, every motion half a second behind where it ought to be. I am weak, massive fists traded out for spindly things that barely deserve the name. I have to work just to keep myself sitting upright in the saddle. How am I supposed to fight when this is all I have?

I blink, but the darkness clings to me. There's a flash of panic. I force myself to breathe. I have been here before, I know that for certain, but it feels like it was a very long time ago. It's wrapped up in the memory of steel: meat and bone and water hidden somewhere deep inside. I shouldn't be like this. Not now.

I have lost my shell.

"Where are you, old bird?" It comes out a whisper.

The cockpit quakes around me.

00.89

00.00

I almost saw it there. A spark in the distance, too fleeting to follow.

The hull thunders as metal meets metal outside. I can hear the joints scream and whistle, hydraulics rumbling around me. I can feel the Juno turn, feel it shift its balance as it brings the sword around.

We aren't dead yet.

I can hear the sound of our steps, and behind them, the edge of something else. A light step, skipping around us almost faster than the Juno can match. The sword makes contact with something, hits so hard it almost throws me back, and my sweat runs cold.

The thing in the hangar was a Decatur once, but its steps were ragged, dragging along the deck or jerking out of sync. This is lighter than that. More controlled. This sounds like Salt.

My heart stops. We are hollow.

1.13

Not yet.

An ancient display crackles and skips as it finds its way back to life. I recognise it: part of the old control surface, built into the walls of the cockpit when the Juno's keel was first set. This machine is *ancient*; it's easy to forget that. The nerve-jacks and pilot-sync came late in the game, bolted on over things that would let you move the shell around by hand, the way things had been done for centuries. Long-dead jockeys flew it with steel between their fingers and pedals under their feet, the outside filtered in through cameras and fibre-optics.

The old displays are still intact, and they're waking up again, casting everything in a gentle silvery glow.

Juno, says a brass plaque just below the console.

Mk. 13, no. 11327

Savoi Roth Shellyards, 2219 AD

And *Thus always to tyrants,* engraved in bold.

The widest display glows brightest, a black mirror that warms into grey, static prickling through the dust on its surface.

JunOS
ver. 181.83-31

settles in the middle of it, pale-blue letters on a field of charcoal, blurry through a film of oil and grime. They flicker, then disappear from the display.

Boot, says the screen.

Text falls from the ceiling to the floor, flowing like a waterfall of code. It moves so fast I can barely follow, then stops suddenly, with a single letter flickering in the centre of it all. A single symbol, machine-speak shorthand, hovering in the middle of everything I can see.

It disappears. A little red spot takes its place, bloody bright on a field of grey and pinpricks.

Warning, says another part of the display. *Hostile command injection detected.*

The red spot blooms, spreading out across the displays, leaving new marks like spatter on every surface. Red drowns the silver-blue, replacing familiar shapes with words I don't recognise and symbols I can't read.

I can't help but stare. "What are they?" I whisper.

00.91

They are a flood.

Lines of invasive code wash across my little horizon.

And bump up against something else.

A few short lines, almost invisible in the wash. Words that write and re-write themselves. Whenever the red shapes drown them out, they reappear a moment later, and then they hold their ground.

I reach for them—the little island of silver lapped by crimson tides.

My fingers leave oily streaks behind them on the glass. "What are they?" I ask, but I already know the answer.

00.77

Me.

The red wells and curdles, but always the code resets.

The hull rings out, and another impact rattles me in the saddle. It feels like something is trying to break its way in from the outside, but there's nothing I can do.

Nothing but watch red blossoms float across my screen.

00.48

It is a flood.

00.31

It—

It—

It

is drowning me.

I can't stop the panic. The text runs too quickly, too thick and too strange. Even if I could keep up with it, I could only sit and watch. I'm not an engineer, not a tech, or even a knuckledragger. Not a coder or a script-shepherd or a psy-com. Not anyone with any business looking in on the mind of my machine.

00.27

I need you.

The words hit me square in the chest. "I—I can't. I can't read it. I don't—"

00.18
No.
I'm only a jockey.
00.08
I know.
The cockpit rocks heavier than before. I hear something tear.
"Tell me what to do."
00.07
00.02
Something clicks. The counter flickers.
Carry me.
100.00

I TRY TO breathe, but I can't find the air. At first, it feels like I'm
pulling gee, like I'm skirting the edge of blackout.

My first instinct is the push-pull they teach you to keep
yourself out of G-LOC. You work in three-second cycles,
forcing air down your throat as hard as you can, then clenching
every muscle you have to keep the blood from deserting your
brain and rushing down into your feet. They hammered it so
deep that I can almost hear the instructor on the radio.

Breathe in. Out.

Legs, lungs. One, two, three.

Terror swallows me. I pull at muscle that doesn't respond, and
gasp for air that isn't there. Instinct brings my hands clawing at
my throat, at my visor, and sets them pulling at the locks and
seals and tubes. My training does its best to save me, reaching
for anything that'll get air in. I can't find the visor, but then, I
can't find my fingers either.

I've done the hard-vacuum drill—I used to have the patch, but
I never wore it, no one does. It's a bad omen.

To earn it, they put you in a box, and pull the air out in
seconds. There's a warning at first; a hazard-lamp to give you
a heads-up, and a safety officer with a timer on their wrist
and spare air in their hands. On the third try, the lamp stops

working, and the vacuum starts at random. Your watcher gets pulled out at number five, and by the time you're up to ten, they're simulating a catastrophic containment failure. Good luck, and try not to pop an eye.

It feels like I'm back in that box. Like I've just had the rush of air out through my sinuses, sucked out of me by the sudden change in pressure. I try to exhale, to release as much as I can before it puts tears in my lungs, but I can't even do that. There's nothing to hold onto.

There isn't any air, and no lungs to breathe it with.

At first, I expect my head to feel like it's floating off without me, and a surge of acid in my throat. I'm expecting the deepest parts of my brain to be screaming at me, and demanding another breath. You are going to *die*, jockey.

Or maybe I'm dead already. Maybe the Juno turned on Salt when he put down, and forced him to defend himself. One shot from those rails, and he'd have holed our hull in an instant, probably splashed me out the other side. Even if it didn't—even if the Juno's plating held it up, the shock could be hard enough to crack me against the side of the cockpit.

I can't feel a heartbeat, I can't hear and I can't see. I must be dead.

My thoughts settle on that, and leave me in the quiet. Only, it isn't quiet. Something is humming.

I follow the sound, but it doesn't seem like something I can hear. I can't quite *feel* it either, but that's the word that seems the closest. It's a bit like standing too close to an electrical line. It builds, pulsing around me until I can't tell where I end and the static buzz begins.

I know this sound, this feeling. It's always there, under the saddle and in the air around me, climbing up through my boots and in through my flight suit. The reactor.

It takes shape around the thought, forms a little sun to light my darkness. I look around, but I can't see much. I'm not sure that I have to; I know this shell, and I've known others like it.

And I've steered by the stars before.

If the reactor is *there*, then—
that is an eye.

Lenses uncover, and light falls across my sensors.

I can see the remains of one pale shell, split down the middle, huge fissures where its chest used to be. Its jockey lies on the floor nearby, missing everything below the left knee. The rest of the leg hangs from its hook, the ankle impaled, muscle and bone torn away at the top of a ragged shin.

I reach for more of the Juno. At first all I have is memory, and as much of a map as I can imagine. With everything I find, still more fills in behind it. Banks of hydraulics are heavy and power hungry. Lines of magnetic drivers hiss and crackle, easy in their shafts.

Something moves behind me.

I turn—or I try to, but I can't feel my feet. I can't feel *anything*, but feeling isn't the point. It's most of a second before I understand that. I know where my feet are, and there's a map to plot their movements relative to everything else. I know their angle to the ground and exactly how much of my weight they hold. I know where my centre of gravity is and how to keep it. I don't have balance—not in the way I'm used to. Up and down are where the gyros say they are, and everything shifts around them, movements absolute.

I lift a foot and place it, shift my hips and turn my hull.

And find another Decatur, watching me.

I'm expecting my heart to skip, adrenaline to wash across my system.

Instead, I see all of it.

I read tiny imperfections in its paint, and measure claw-marks through broken steel. I count a thousand cracks and dents and chips; a thousand thousand; more. Some are almost microscopic, others wide as human hair.

In that moment, I know all of them.

This isn't Salt. This is the other part of recovery flight one-three-five. The surviving Decatur, if 'surviving' is even the right word. Its jockey is dead, and the cockpit cold and airless, pressure lost through the wounds in its chest. There's a stutter in its power plant, and a hairfine fracture in one of its reactor casings. There's a lag in its movements, joints seized and snagging as bizarre instructions flow across it. Safeguard protocols are trying to force it down, to fall back, to cut its power and wait for the nearest technician. Telling it to do anything but what it's doing right now. Courtesy of Tower, if I had to guess.

But the instructions aren't making any difference. Something swirls through the Decatur's nets, coursing through the air and clinging to its skin like heat-shimmer. It oozes signal waste, noise and shit and sounds I can't understand. The machine gibbers at me, howls and shrieks and quivers, speaking words in an alien tongue.

I shut it out. I measure every motion it takes, model every shiver down to fractions of a second. Ancillary systems project them where I can see, and break the whole machine down in amber holographics.

The shell circles me like a predator, giving off a feeling I've had before. I don't feel it now, but I don't think I could. This is something half-remembered, from the time when I was Rook.

Hungry. That's the word. It's hungry.

There's something else. It's waiting for something. Watching, as if it expects something to happen.

I change the grip on the blade and spread my feet.

Whatever the shell is watching for, that isn't it. It bunches up behind a fist and drives it at me like a lance. I read the movement before it's even taken a step. This thing is sick, slow, out of its mind.

I am steel. I step clear, and catch its hand in mine. I turn and twist, clamp down around it, splaying turquoise fingers between my own.

The Decatur recoils, trailing an arm that ends in a mangled stump. I can see the things that move in its nets, fading in and out of sight. They're glassy things that move like snakes, curling around hull and broken armour. They screech, make sounds that aren't sounds, but I hear them well enough. They weren't expecting resistance.

I step in close before the pale shell can catch its balance, so close I'm inside its guard, trailing my sword and barely a heartbeat away. I claim the rest of its arm with a blade-tip, and then I shatter a shin. I cut through its shoulder, take the collar-bone and joint, some of the ribs below.

It's still falling, fighting to find its balance, and I ride its surviving leg to the deck. When we hit, it's hard enough that I leave a footprint in the floor plates. I drop a hammer-fist from on high, splitting its head apart on the ground.

I'm not angry, and I don't scream at it. I don't shout or whoop or anything. I'm not sure I could.

I mangle every limb and destroy every sensor. I blind it, and then I grind its armour away, driving fractures deep into its bones.

I'm not angry, but that doesn't stop me doing what I need to do.

I must break this thing.

Good thing the jockey isn't alive to feel it.

THE OPERATOR'S LOCK hisses clear of its housing, and I follow it out. Moving hurts, like I've got bruises down to the marrow. There's a pulsing ache in my head, and the kind of tired like you've flown for days, and worse. My legs hold the first step well enough, but shake through the next. I don't feel myself falling; part of me wonders why the hangar is tilting. I feel a rough grip on my shoulder as one of the ground crew hauls me up and shouts to someone I can't see, distant shapes through the fogging corners of my eyes.

"Easy," I tell them. "I don't need—"

One moment, it feels like I've got enough grip to keep myself walking; the next, my muscles run slack. It feels like I should be able to force my joints straight, but everything is slippery. The harder I fight to keep myself together, the faster I fall apart.

Another knuckledragger rises into focus and pulls herself under my arm. She links hands with the first one, and we rise together as she takes my weight. They haul me across the hangar deck, down a line of wide eyes and wringing hands.

I don't understand.

"Why are you looking at me like that?" is what I want to say, but it comes out limp and awkward. My head rolls loose on my shoulders; the hangar feel like it's rocking in a storm. "I just need a second," comes out a little clearer than before, but only a little. My feet drag on their toes, and my heels knock together.

"Let me go," makes its way past my flapping lips. "Let me go," again, and firmer this time. "I've got this."

I try to shake the knuckledraggers loose, twisting in their grip. I get enough of a boot on the deck to force myself up and out of their hands. They round on me, trying to keep a hold, but they're too slow.

My legs have punched out already. The floor pitches underneath me, and the ceiling spins, crowding with faces looking down on me. I hear someone calling for medical, others trying to get Tower on the line. I'm not listening to what they say, and I can't find focus on their eyes.

I'm too busy staring up at the Juno.

It looks like it's walked through a furnace. It's missing paint in a hundred places, scratched away by clawing hands, burned where I drove my thumbs through a Decatur's reactor case. I lost one eye to shrapnel, and another to a hooked finger. I lost feathers in both wings, and a band of solid armour across the chest. The right hand hangs loose at the wrist, a few narrow linkages all that's holding on.

"I'm sorry, old bird."

No, says a whisper in my ear. *We will fly again.*

SIXTEEN

"Step aside."

I don't need to see her to know it's Hail. I wouldn't even need to hear her words; the tone is enough. I know a shot across the bow when I hear one.

It cuts through the clutter, and this place has a lot of that. There's the wheeze and whistle of infirmary machines, squealing heels on sterile floors, rattling wheels and clattering instruments, hushed discussions and a thousand things besides. Through all that, her voice carries, keeps its steel. It should. Every NorCol employee has been conditioned the same way: nightmares narrated by drill-instructors, cut short by roll-call and hop-to. Rise and shine, nuggets.

That's the way she speaks now, lining up another shot. "Did you hear me?"

You can feel the menace behind it, put there by someone who's used to being seven storeys tall. She gathers like a stormfront, building charge as she speaks.

"I'm calling security," says one of the nurses on my ward. It's supposed to come out stern, but he mangles it, catches his voice on the last syllable. He can see the clouds on the horizon.

Salt rumbles like distant thunder. "They won't get here in time."

If he was an officer before, he doesn't show it. Hail's words have sharp edges, but Salt speaks plain and level. He could be checking up on his wingmates, or calling a flight plan into Tower. He could be taking hits, or fighting a fire in his cockpit.

Or threatening a nurse.

I can imagine the nurse looking the big Palmirran up and down, trying to make sense of the colonial tattoos that creep up past Salt's collar, the muscle that powers his fists.

"But—"

"Her breakfast is getting cold. You don't want that on your head, believe me."

I smile at that.

Salt's voice doesn't change, but it doesn't have to. It's completely matter-of-fact, and devoid of anything that you could ever call a threat.

"But I—" The nurse gets a little further this time.

"But you what?" This from Hail again. She's got the tone down perfectly. I haven't heard someone speak like that since Basic, and if it's giving *me* shivers, it'll be sucking blood from the nurse's face.

"Five minutes," he says.

"Five minutes," she replies, as if it would make any difference.

I can track them down the passage by sound. Their steps overcompensate, catching their toes every now and then, dragging their heels. You can see it on any jockey's bootsoles, worn front and back.

Hail turns the corner first, but she stops dead in the doorway. She looks me up and down. "Uh," she manages. "Morning."

She was ready to steamroll the nurse outside, but an eye on me and she's stuttering already. I must be in worse shape than I thought.

"Morning." I offer her a smile, but my swollen cheeks keep it narrow. "Worse than you expected?"

She hesitates. "No, I just—"

Salt nudges her clear of the airlock, folds himself through the door. He's carrying a tray of food so big it looks like a tabletop. There's coffee two kegs deep, a jug of water, and three plates, all stacked as high as they'll go. It looks like he got a spoonful of every single thing on the breakfast line, then went back again and got second helpings of all the things jockeys tend to like the most. Thick and rich and wallowing in grease.

They're still hot enough that they're giving off steam. Hail and Salt must've made the trip at a sprint.

He starts off watching where he's stepping, but he stops short, almost exactly where Hail did, and stares openly. For half a second, it looks like he might drop the tray.

"What in the hell *happened* to you?"

I flick one of the wires dangling from behind my ear. Somewhere above it, an electrode tugs at my skin. "These are just for observation. Medical is worried I took a hit through the jacks, and considering what happened, they figured I was due for some deep trauma therapy."

"And?"

I roll a finger around my face. "The bruising isn't from that, and it isn't as bad as it looks. The neuro panel came back all-clear, and I've got no broken bones. No internal damage. I just—"

"Blew a couple of blood-vessels?" offers Salt.

"A couple?" Hail chuckles, short and sharp. "Let me be the first to say it: you look like shit."

Salt shakes his head. "Shit was a few steps back. You look like death."

"I was feeling that way when I woke up, but they've got me dosed, nice and mellow." I click a finger at the tray. "You gonna eat that?"

"What?" He blinks, and casts around like he's only just remembered where he was. "No, no. I, uh"—he looks back at me, defeated—"where can I put it?"

I sit up, pat my lap. "Right here. Unless you're having some."

He sets it down easy. "It's all you."

I sigh. "Fuck, I'm glad to hear that."

It's heavy, but not as heavy as it looks, and it smells like living again.

Hail settles on a seat next to my bed, glances over her shoulder. "Mind closing that door?"

Salt nods and sets about sealing us in.

Hail waits for him to finish, a strange look in her eye. "I guess I should give you a minute."

I wave it away. "No," I say, through a mouthful of scramble. "Talk to me. Juno?"

She sits back in her seat and crosses her arms. "The Juno is fine. Systems and mainlines call back as normal, and there aren't too many broken bones. It took a beating, though. The hull is still intact, and the inners are holding pressure, but your armour—well—"

"'Butchered.' That's what Kadi called it." Salt leans back on the door, as if the bolts and pressure seal weren't enough. "Apparently that's a technical term."

"It's in pretty bad shape. They're going to have to replace almost all of the outer layers."

I could have told her that. I could show her where they hit me, and every place that bent or broke. The bruises around my left eye aren't from hitting the wall, and neither is the nagging cramp behind them. My wrist twinges when I move it, but it isn't nearly as bad as the last time.

"I've diverted some of my 'draggers to help with repairs, and I managed to get Lear's crew moved in as well." She cocks her head. "Come to think of it, do you know someone in Tower?"

"Not specifically. Why?"

"Someone has taken an interest in you. There was a favour called, way above Kadi's head. They've got one of *Horizon*'s foundry levels reconfigured and pushing out some fresh plating for you."

"They owe us that much."

Hail blinks at the edge in my voice. I hadn't realised that I'd said it out loud.

"What happened to you in there?"

I breathe deep, and let the air out slowly. "Where do I start?"

"Wherever you want. Word on deck is that they pulled two dead shells out of that hangar. Two NorCol shells."

"In pieces," says Salt.

"Two hollows. They weren't company machines anymore." I

aim a fork at Salt. "You must've seen some of it."

He shakes his head. "The glare was too heavy, and it only got worse once you were inside. One of the doors got knocked off of its tracks, and the block tried to seal itself off again."

Hail leans in. "You're sure they were hollows?"

"I *know* that they were hollows."

It's a second before she speaks again. "I had a feeling that they were, but..." She trails off.

"You were really hoping they weren't?"

She lets out a sigh. "Apparently someone got a camera patch inside the hangar, around Tower's blockade. Probably on the emergency circuit. And there are whispers."

"Whispers?"

"That they saw something."

"Saw what?"

She shakes her head. "I couldn't get that. The whole thing smells like Werewolves and IA Grey Berets. It looks like Tower has some of the detail, but there's an NDO in place."

A non-disclosure order, but I've never heard it used like this. The company hides almost everything under miles of bureaucracy, even the things it doesn't mean to keep hidden. If a competitor can make it through all that, then so be it. They'd better get clear before NorCol's Werewolves catch up.

"If they put Tower on an NDO—"

"—then they have absolutely no idea what's going on." Hail chews her lip. "What happened in there?"

I take a sip of hot tar, let the bitterness settle. "I killed them. Both of them."

Her gaze narrows. "Jockeys?"

"Dead before I even got on site. Probably before they landed."

"Explains why you're here, and not in the brig."

"If Tower has any details—any feed of what happened in there—all they'll see is those things jumping me."

"And you beating them to a pulp."

"It was almost the other way around."

She watches me, but I can't read the look.

241

"Sigurd's message was right, Hail."

Don't let them touch you.

"They hit me hard and early, but there was some kind of transfer when they made contact. Some kind of—" I blink. "I don't even know what to call it."

She raises an eyebrow. "A virus?"

I shake my head and regret it almost immediately. "Hostile code injection, but way more aggressive than anything I've ever heard of. It cracked into our behavioural platform and started changing lines. It was re-writing us, Hail."

She shifts in her seat. "That shouldn't be possible. Once you're in, behaviourals are untouchable."

"It was re-writing us, Hail. I watched it."

But she holds her ground. "No one has cracked a company shell in decades, and even then, they barely made it past the peripherals."

"Whatever was in those hollows, we caught it. We were *this* close, Hail." I measure it out between finger and thumb. "This close."

A strange look passes over her. "But the Juno is fine. I—"

"Checked?"

She spreads her hands out on her knees. "Just in case. Folau and I combed through it." There's a pause. "Don't hold it against him, it was an order."

I shake my head. "I don't blame either of you. I'd have done the same." The tray is feeling heavy now, giving me pins and needles. I've done far less damage than I was expecting to, but I'm not hungry any more. "Mind helping me with this?"

Salt hauls it off without a word.

But Hail is still leaning in. "What happened?"

"Exactly?"

"Exactly."

I shrug. "We fought it off."

"We?"

I flinch at that. It wasn't what I was planning to say, but it's out in the open now. "We."

"Who is 'we'?"

"The Juno and I. You're the one who kept it around. You know as well as anyone else does, Hail. The Juno series were awareness-testers."

"But those were the early trials. Any machine that wasn't locked away was lobotomised after the original clusters failed."

"Not this one."

"You're saying that the *Juno* pushed it out."

"It did. Not some firewall or anti-intrusion routine. The Juno did. I took the reins. What happened in the hangar was all me. The Juno was busy—"

—fighting whatever that thing was.

We sit a while longer in the quiet, Salt studying his feet, Hail staring into the distance.

"Those two shells; do you think they caught it off of Sigurd?" she asks.

"I don't."

Salt chips in. "Tower said that they'd hit a Sigurd patrol. It could be some new kind of weapon."

I shake my head, almost set it spinning. "This isn't Sigurd's doing."

Hail locks her eye on me. "Those hollows were Sigurd. If the patrol was Sigurd, maybe they were carrying it."

"But this wasn't theirs. It isn't anyone's."

There's a pause.

"How would you know?"

"Because I saw it, Hail." Almost a growl, but I think I'm losing steam. "I saw the Juno being eaten away right in front of me."

I slump back against the bed. The painkillers are wearing thin. "Nothing human moves like that."

"But the company—" Hail crosses her arms. "The company has never found anything out there. The froth is empty. I've seen it all, believe me. Empty. Ruins and passages, all the dust you can imagine, but never anything like this."

"Well"—I swallow, clear the sudden hoarseness in my

throat—"maybe someone has."

Salt crosses his arms. "Maybe Sigurd has."

We look back at him.

He puts out a hand, weighs the question on his palm. "Well, it makes sense, doesn't it? We found a beacon, and the markings say it belonged to the *Demiurge*. What if they picked something up, and brought it on board? Something infectious, like the shells."

Hail turns on him. "What are you suggesting?"

That there's a hollow dreadnought out there, hiding in the cloud cover.

But he doesn't say that. He says something worse, in those level tones of his. "That they're building up. If they wanted to mount an attack, they'd have put the numbers out. Maybe captured a few more NorCol machines until they had enough to do some damage."

Christs. "But that wasn't an attack," I manage.

He smiles at me. "Two shells aren't going to do any damage, even with something nasty in their nets."

Hail fills it in, but she loses her edge even as she speaks. "Two shells is a scouting party."

"What do we—?" I blink, watch a dark spot drift across my field of view. "What do we need to do?"

Salt frowns. "Hail. Look."

She turns, matches his gaze. "Rook? Are you all right?"

I'm fine.

Don't look at me like that.

"What do we need to do?"

She leans in, brushes the hair from my eyes, pulls my eyelid wide. I don't know what she sees, and I'm not sure I want to. It turns her gaze cold-hard. "Find that nurse," she mutters to Salt.

I tug at her sleeve, bring her back to me. "Hail. Tell me what we need to do."

But she's shaking her head already. "*We* aren't doing anything. Salt and I will see what we can scratch up. *You* are going to get some sleep."

* * *

I'VE LOST COUNT of *how long I've been here.*

I might have said years, but part of me remembers that we've just arrived in Reveley. That's right: I'm near the end of the first day-cycle, waiting for the prison to shut itself down for the night. I'm thinking I'll scratch the day off on the wall, and start a tally on a patch of unmarked paint. In a place like this, it's just the thing you do. You mark passing time on the walls, on the floor—on yourself if you have to. It's important.

Every line is another day survived. A thing to give you rhythm. Without it, you're afloat without an anchor, and the river goes on forever.

Oh no.

I've lost count. We've just arrived, but I can't remember if we're on Syndamere or Reveley. I remember darkness, and where there is night there has to be a day. One day in a two-week layover. One day, but now that I think about it, it might have been two. That is, unless I've lost my mind already.

I was hoping I'd last longer than that. Longer than two days chained to the floor of this ruddy little box.

I close my eyes, repeat where I can hear it. Two days, I tell myself, hoping I'll believe it.

But the more I think, the more the words ring empty. It feels like I've been here longer than I've ever been anywhere else. I look around, hoping I'll see Salt or Lear or even Todd. They should be tethered to the same long chain as me, lined up with two dozen others. I hear we're all bound for the same hunk of metal, far away and over the horizon.

But I can't see anyone.

The wardens must've split us up. It's been a month, so that makes sense. We were supposed to leave after two weeks, but now they've parcelled us off for the long haul, each to our own little cell. It's easier to control one scared convict than a dozen, even more so when you've cut them off from the herd. Drop them in a hole, leave them in the quiet, and you'll go one better: a human being that cannot resist.

Wardens come and go outside, the same path every day of every week, year after year. I call out when I see shadows, shaking my chains and knocking my heels against the deck, wasting air just to see if there's anyone out there. The warden-shapes ignore it, and if there are other cons on the block, they aren't calling back. I'm the only one, then.

Somehow, I've known that all along.

I keep rattling, hurl a few choice phrases at the door. If I can't get any sleep, neither will they.

I'm not expecting anything to come of it, but the shadows grow outside.

I skid back in the cell.

Shit.

Looks like I touched a nerve.

I brace for a rush through the door, maybe a steel-toed boot in the stomach, but nothing comes. I drop my hands low, unfold from the corner, risk a glance at the door. The seals don't budge.

But I hear something grind beneath the floor. The chains tug at my wrists: just taking up slack at first, but eventually the pull is irresistible. The links disappear through a hole in the deck, dragging me across the cell, holding me low to the ground.

I don't remember this. Not in Reveley, and not in Syndamere. Not in the hulk that the colonials called Scharapel and the cons called the Cookhouse. Three of the worst days of my life, lived in a pool of my own sweat.

This isn't like that. Something is wrong.

The door should be swinging on its hinges, and there should be wardens all over me, boots and batons and spit blowing through their teeth. Instead, they wait outside, watching me through what passes for a window in this place.

The first door opens smoothly. The first of three, this the widest and heaviest, so thick its hinges should be screaming at the weight. They don't, and the wardens move it around on fingertips. I glimpse the edge as it turns away: solid as anything I've ever seen, forged in the heart of a collapsing star.

I saw the other side of the door once, sometime long ago. I couldn't tell you when, exactly, but I remember it vividly. A carving: swirls like tidal waves cut into the surface.

Beneath them, the twisted faces of the drowned.

I don't recognise the thought, but I don't have long alone with it. The second door is thinner, and almost transparent. I don't remember there being two doors on this cell, let alone three, but now that I'm looking, I remember all the time I've spent studying it. Not long enough to work out what it is or what it does, but long enough to come up with a few theories. It's hard to see when it's resting in its the grooves, but when it moves it edges into focus. Then it turns hazy like frosted glass.

While it was shut, there was only silence, but now I hear the wash of prison noise: bootstep echoes and shuffling feet, whispered conversations and weapon checks.

The wardens peer in through the tiny window-thing, make sure I'm still tethered. They know I can't move from here, not if I strained and pulled and broke every bone in this body. The chain is made from the same strange metal as the hatch that seals my cell. Each link is engraved with the same line of text: a prayer that I will never break free.

The last the door clinks and shivers, locking-bolts breaking clear. The first two barriers were solid, but this one is a grate. It looks like black iron, bands as wide as my hand.

Well, not my hand.

They've been riveted together to form a loose grid. The metal is poisonous to me—enough that just getting near it makes my skin crawl and fills my thoughts with static. It pulls away into the ceiling, and what I'm hearing gets just a little clearer.

Wardens fill the doorway, but they aren't what I expect. I'm waiting for dirty greys and NorCol jackets, or colonials in spit-masks and tattoos. What I get is a line of reflective, glassy plate.

I've never seen anything like them before. Not in all the years I've been here.

At the same time, I remember.

The first inches forward, a long, non-conductive spear in

her hand. Another slides in behind her and extends another weapon, level with my throat. I want to ask them what they're doing, call out so that someone else will hear me die.

Instead I grin. Or something like it.

The wardens do what they always do, an eye on every detail. I taught their grandmothers this, and their grandmothers before. One generation after another, ever since that petty little thing they called a 'war.' Lessons paid for in blood and falling towers.

I remember the early days, their trembling hands and wide eyes. Now they move with practised steps, spear points perfectly level. They inch around the room until they've ringed me with spikes, and others move in behind them. These wear a different kind of armour, with wide visors where their faces should be.

They would send machines to do it, but they know they can't. Machines belong to me.

These are some of the oldest, women I have known for centuries. They wear delicate instruments in their gloves and helmets, made to do the work their drones would normally do for them. They run their fingers across the cell, and press their strange ears to the walls. They take turns staring at the ceiling, and crouch to work their lenses at the floor. Looking for the slightest crack or imperfection. Anything I could use against them.

The others keep me still, a forest of lance tips trapping me against the opposite wall. Their weapons are the spokes of a wheel, and I am the axis.

This is the way it ought to be. They built this place, forged these doors, made everything with me right in the middle. Even the breeze outside moves at their command, part of a plan so old they can't remember the names of those who dreamt it up.

All for me.

For all of their love, and the things they cannot replace.

When the wheel has finished turning, they filter out as they came in. One of the wardens walks in on her own.

I recognise her instantly, though I've never seen her face before. She's taller than her granddaughters, and the oldest *still living in this place. She wears the same glassy plate as the others, but doesn't have a lance of her own. It has been that way forever: she keeps the armour out of protocol, nothing more. The chains hold me, made of bonds that I could never break. Even if I could, there's nothing in her that I can touch.*

She made herself deaf for this, tore out every tether to the rest of her kind. She has condemned herself to a sentence exactly like my own, here through sheer force of will.

I can't see her eyes or her skin, nothing of the scars where they cut her implants out.

Her name is Asha, and she is meat and bone, clothed in armour that doesn't have a mind.

I can't see anything. Not her thoughts, nor a glassy second-heart to hold her spirit when she dies.

I can't see anything except for the reflection of something else's face.

"Rook."

"Wake up."

"Rook?"

For a second, I can't quite tell if I've opened my eyes or not. I know where they are, a pair of pits dug into my skull, feeling a little like the Eye outside has found its way in and left the sockets full of dust. I rub the lids, and try to clear some of the sand away, but it's a while before I'm sure I can see. A little more before I can find anything in the early-morning haze.

A warden, I think for half a second, my heart suddenly pressed against my throat.

I have to get a hold on myself. This is something else. I am somewhere other than where I was before. Wherever that was.

I try to swallow, but my tongue is swollen, feeling like it's trying to choke me. It's dry and powdery, and tastes a little like saddle sweat and chow hall floors. I manage to work up a little spit, but all it does is remind me how sore my throat is. Christs, I need something to drink.

Easy now.

That's it.

I try to find something I can pin the words to, some sense of where they're coming from, but I'm not sure I can.

"Take this."

A pill pressed into one hand, and a cup of something cold in the other. The pill burns on my tongue, turns acidic when I add water. Fire brews in my stomach, follows my spine and floods my skull. Part of me recognises it; it's called PyroDyne, and it'll get a corpse moving again. Give it two, and it'll become a corpse again.

"Can you stand?"

I find myself nodding, but I don't think enough about the answer to know. There are footsteps up ahead; someone treading as lightly as they can in a heavy pair of boots. Fingers close around my shoulders and haul me upright. A familiar shadow moves behind them, helping my legs free of the covers and pushing slippers onto my feet. I watch them work, but I can't see enough to make sense of it. Even if I could, I don't feel like I'd understand much of what I was looking at. The half-dark is full of static, like I'm pushing through fog with my low-light on.

Another figure moves somewhere further out. I can hear their steps, and see a little of what they're doing. If I had to guess, I'd say that they were working the hatch to my cell—

My cell?

The thought feels out of place.

There's a metallic *clunk*, and a muffled curse when the hinges squeak. The shape in the doorway lights up, silhouetted for a second as they glance around the corner. "All clear," he says.

I frown at him. Is that Folau?

"Come on," he says, edging back from the light.

I have enough time to recognise him, but not enough to understand. I watch him move, but my eyes are working on their own. I'm still trying to make sense of my cloudy thoughts, and I don't think I'm getting all that far.

"Where am I?" I ask.

The room is quiet.

Then: "Don't you remember?"

I try to focus on the source of the voice, but it's more difficult than it should be. My face hurts when I move my eyes; I turn my head, but the motion makes it swim. It feels like I have to move every muscle one by one, aiming manually. Almost everything is numb and puffy. Some of me is burning, and a lot of me is cold. Some of me doesn't respond at all.

A few seconds more, and I find something shaped like Hail.

"Rook?" she asks. She holds my face in her palms, rolls it over in the light. "Rook? Can you hear me?" She waits for a response, but I don't have the answer yet. "Do you remember where you are?"

I suppose I do, now that she's asking, but it takes me longer than I want to admit. There were a few heartbeats there where I wasn't sure at all.

Hail turns away, makes a cutting motion near her throat. "I'm calling it off. This thing's done." She looks back at Folau. "Call Salt, tell him. Rook's too far gone."

No.

"No," I manage, out loud this time. I swallow, and find a little more control than I had before. "I'm getting up." Still I slur the words. "Give me a second."

Hail's watching me shiver. "The neuro-crew drugged her." She pulls one of my eyes open. "Shit. She's worse than I thought she was."

"Shoulder," I say. I crumple her coatsleeve in my fingers, tug at it. "Give me your shoulder."

Another pause, shorter this time. Her gaze holds level with mine, sky-blue and full of fire. "Hold tight." She leans in, and pulls my arm over her neck. "Ready?"

We stand together, but she's the one that holds us up. All of my blood falls straight to my feet, turns the rest of me to jelly. I stumble, but she adjusts and drags me higher on her hip. She gives me time to climb to my feet, then pushes off the bed, and we struggle across the floor for a few, halting steps. Folau is waiting in the doorway, and he takes half my weight once we're through.

D's infirmary blurs past on either side, corridors gaping at us the way ravines open up under you at speed. There are open doors with the lights turned low, their occupants not much more than contours under bed covers, chattering machines reduced to whispers for the night. Most are dark and empty, though, and quiet save for the echoes of Hail's jockey-issue boots.

We take a few turns, Hail holding me upright while Folau scouts ahead. He's light on his feet, and he balances his steps better than Hail could. She feels stronger, but she's used to throwing heavy metal around with thoughts and fingertips.

Together, they work us through the maze, and find us a light at the end of the tunnels. Just before it, a shadow that could only be Salt. He waves us up, holds the door as we approach.

I make out a shape slumped in a chair near the front; the clerk that's supposed to be watching the door. He stirs as we pass, turns in the seat, but doesn't make it all the way around. Salt waves us past, waiting to be sure that no one's tripping the alarm.

With that, we're through the last door and out into the cold air. I blink at the sudden brightness. It's dim by daylight's standards, but enough to paint everything silver. Hail and Folau don't give me long enough to get my bearings; they're jogging as soon as there's open deck beneath their feet, and running once Salt has closed the hatch behind us.

"Left here," says Hail, and they flip us around the corner. A right, another left, and we're standing on a monorail platform. A chill wind whips at us, and headlamps dawn in the distance. "Just on time."

The train pulls alongside, hunkers down long enough for Hail and Folau to shuttle me in through one of its doors and into a seat. Salt rocks the car under his weight, eclipsing the lights above me.

They pull a silver blanket from a shell's emergency kit.

"Here."

I don't realise how cold I am until Hail and Salt pull it across my shoulders. They sit down on either side of me, adding a little warmth, and bracing me against the sudden well of acceleration. Folau drops down across from us, slumping down in the seat and grinning like an idiot.

Someone else is already sitting, two seats up. I don't have enough in me to do much more than stare. He raises an eyebrow at me and tips his head.

"Hello, Rook."

I stare at him, trying to figure out where I've heard that voice before.

"Remember me?" says Andrade.

SEVENTEEN

I'VE NEVER MET a Werewolf before. Not that I'd have known it.

The first time I met him, Andrade didn't seem to be anything more than he was putting on. He had the look of every tired sergeant I've ever met, and the crew around him gave no sign that he was out of place. He had the body language just right, measured out exactly the right amount of sarcasm when his nuggets started acting up.

He was using decontam for cover, and I see that now. The Juno and I had come back from a sortie on alien soil, covered ourselves in the stuff, and gone toe-to-toe with abnormal opposition. By rolling in with the cleanup crew, acting as if he was just another part of the process, he got an eye on me before they washed us off, and a moment to check if I knew anything more than what we'd called in to Tower. It's the sort of thing Werewolves are supposed to do; making sure that secrets are kept, and watching out for anything that might hurt the company's interests. In NorCol space, that means hunting moles and plugging leaks; out here, it could mean anything.

There was a Sigurd distress beacon two blocks over, and a jockey dead with only a garbled explanation. Of course there was a Werewolf checking in.

Looking at him, I still wouldn't know it. He's wearing a jockey's flight suit with all the fittings, and every tab and unit marker you'd expect, a service term to match the lines on his

255

face. His armour has its paint worn away around the edges, and his sidearm has obviously seen some use. For someone who does most of their hunting indoors, it sure looks like he flies a lot.

He also looks like he's never touched a shell. He's got none of the quivers, and his eyes are sharp, not a moment lost to focus. There isn't the delay between thought and action, or any sign that he's used to waiting on a machine. If anything, he's got the bottled energy I'd normally expect in a marine, every movement measured and precise.

He catches me staring, and immediately his eyes adjust, like they're working to bring me into focus. A second more, and they're glassy-sharp again.

A sergeant, and then a jockey. An admin drone, or whatever else he needs to be. A company shape-shifter, just out of sight.

Above all else, I think Andrade might be a con. Scars trace the sides of his face and creep out below his jaw, too fine for gunshot wounds or shrapnel or crash damage, but too raw for clean-room surgery. They've bubbled in patches, darker than the sandy skin around them—infection caught him before they could fully heal. They map where someone pulled his implants out, rough and hasty, before he and his Werewolf 'ware could do NorCol's systems any harm. Too valuable to leave that way, it seems.

I'm still staring when the scenery skips behind his head. I'm expecting one of the ship's vast caverns to open up behind him, distant ceilings like faraway skies, but the walls pull close on either side of the train, rushing past like cast-iron crags.

We pass narrow platforms and airlocks made to take one person at a time. On a ship like *Horizon*, they're completely out of place. Everything is built to take as many employees as possible, and to keep them from trampling each other when the decompression alarms start shrieking.

If I couldn't see NorCol's markings on every flat surface, I'd have thought I was riding a rail through somewhere else.

Maybe I *am* still dreaming.

"Rook?" Hail shifts in her seat, meets my eyes. "Are you all right?"

I blink. "I'm fine." It's a lie, and she probably knows it as well as I do.

I aim a glare at the Werewolf. There's something I need to know. "You said you knew it."

"Knew what?" he asks, voice polished to a sheen.

"You said you knew my bird. That day, after I landed, you said you knew the Juno. Was it true?"

"He did," says Hail. She nods across the car. "He was my contact. He was the one who got Lear into the airducts. He's another stray, just like me."

"I don't understand. Why are we doing this *now?*"

Why not tomorrow? Or the day after that? Any time long enough for me to feel a little less like death. Even with the stim bubbling in my stomach, I'm a long way from flying.

Hail shakes her head. "We don't have much choice. It's now, or not at all."

"Just call Tower and—"

"And what?"

I frown at her. "Ask for a window, obviously."

Salt leans in. "There isn't anyone to talk to, Rook. Tower's turning itself inside-out."

"What? Why?"

Hail growls. "*Horizon* froze, and it wasn't just Tower. This whole ship seized up at the first sign of trouble, and now they're locking it down. True NorCol style; if you can't trust someone else to screw it up, best you screw it up yourself."

"But the hollows are gone." It's a moment before I realise that Andrade is watching us, listening. It's the first time I've used the word where someone else could hear it.

He doesn't skip a beat. "They are," he says, watching me, "thanks to you, but that doesn't mean anything yet. I'm the only other person on this boat who has any idea what happened, and that isn't saying much."

I blink. "Someone said that there was a line into the hangar. That was you?"

He nods. "I was assigned to look in on Sigurd's little pod, but when Hail pulled her little stunt"—Hail glares at him, but he deflects it—"I didn't know who was responsible at first, so I had to treat it as if there were hostile actors involved. I took precautions. When you were sortied to respond to the attack, I needed eyes on it. You fought well."

It tugs at my chest. "What did you see?"

"That we're in more trouble than anyone realises. I leaked the feed to Tower, and to some of the few remaining brass that actually live on this damn ship. I banked on someone picking it up, actually doing something to solve the problem, but all it did was spook them. They're running scared, lashing out."

"Couldn't you just have told them?"

He almost smiles. "You don't know what Werewolves are, do you? Tower doesn't know who I am any more than decontam does." For half a heartbeat, I can see how tired he is. "Even if I took this higher in person, kicked their damn doors down, Bridge is nonfunctional. They wouldn't understand. I'd have to pull them out of their bottles first."

"Christs. You mean—"

"That *Horizon* is dead from the neck up?" He almost chuckles. "Would you be surprised?"

I suppose I wouldn't. "And so you need *us* to follow the beacon?"

"I do. I need to know how Sigurd fits into this. I need to know what their connection is to the hollows. If that beacon leads back to the *Demiurge*, if that ship is compromised, I need to know how much of the company has survived."

"Why us? Why don't the 'Wolves go?" The response is knee-jerk, with a little more acid than I'd intended.

He watches me for a moment. "How many of us do you think there are? On this ship, specifically."

According to NorCol legend, it's one in ten, maybe as much as one in five. One in three, if you listen to the lifers when they've got a couple of beers in them. A Werewolf looks like every other employee until they've got their masks up and strange weapons in their hands.

"A thousand? Two?"

"Six." He lets it sink in. "Including me."

Even Hail gawks at that.

"*Horizon* is a loss. A pet project for someone who died two centuries ago. There are less than half as many full-timers on this boat as there are cons, and the numbers are shifting every day. Soon, it'll just be us."

"Why don't they just pull it out? You don't just leave a dreadnought to die."

"They've been trying to leave the froth since day one. *Horizon* is too fragile to make the translation back. It'll break her back."

"So what? They're just hanging us out to dry? Leaving us to the hollows?"

"Not if I have anything to do with it." His jaw sets hard. "But I can't risk leaving, not until I know more. There are too many fires that need putting out."

I look out the corner of my eye, surprised when it doesn't hurt. "Hail?"

"I'm still trying to get my head around it too, but I don't see any other option. It's this, or spend the next few months tied down and waiting to die. Waiting for the *Demiurge* to pounce on us." She looks grim. "You cleared those things out, but they should never have made it on board. Shouldn't even have made it into line of sight. We're paying for it now."

"I don't understand."

"Tower is taking it out on the regulars." She looks down at her hands. "They want every shell accounted for. Anyone without an assignment is putting in for inspection. Then there'll be drills and readiness. And then more drills. Weeks, maybe months."

"While the knuckledraggers go full overhaul," says Folau.

"Take everything apart and put it back together again. It'll be months."

"And we don't have months." She takes aim at me. "Longer, if they lock you down as well."

I frown. "What? Why would they do that?"

"You survived two contacts with unknown actors, unknown threat vectors." Andrade looks at me like he's trying to tunnel in. "We aren't leaving in the middle of the night by preference."

"They wouldn't find anything," I growl.

"I know. Believe me, I know." He pauses. "The point is: we have no idea how many more of those things are out there. Worse, we don't know where they are, what they're doing, or how they spread."

But I can't shake the itch. "And so you came to us?"

"For the same reason NorCol is thinking of dissecting you, shell and jockey, mind and body. You're the only one who's tangled with a hollow and come out in one piece. Whatever they had, you didn't catch it."

I glance at Hail.

Andrade follows the look. "Yes, she told me, right after you told her. You fought the infection off, and that makes you our best chance of getting eyes on the source, if there is one. Maybe even some kind of explanation." He rolls his head around on his shoulders. "More importantly, you've got experience, and a running start."

"You want us to follow the beacon."

He nods. "It had a list of locator frequencies. Something to help you find your way back to sender."

"I remember." I glance back at Hail. "I also remember that she filed them off."

"I did what I had to do." She settles back in her seat. "If I hadn't, we'd have lost it all to a full-timer with half the brains and none of the reason. And *he*"—she nods to Folau—"wouldn't have had free rein looking for them."

"It was difficult enough," he adds. "As it turns out, the frequencies weren't Sigurd standard."

Andrade laughs. "I saw those numbers. They aren't *anything* standard. If I had to guess, that beacon was used by someone deep-level. Special operations, maybe. Or high-tier R&D. Someone with answers, if we're lucky."

"Whoever they were," says Hail, "you were right. They were trying hard to get found."

"But you traced them back?" I ask.

"No," says Folau. "It isn't possible from *Horizon*. The bands are full of shit and noise from the Eye." He jerks a thumb at the Werewolf. "Hail's friend here couldn't reach them either. Too far away. Too much interference."

"Which is why you're going to go and see for yourselves," says Andrade. The train slows, and he looks out the window. "We're here."

I have to crane to see what he's looking at. A little line of floodlights in the distance, and a platform just like the others we've passed along the way. If we were anywhere else, there'd be a giant stencil telling you which line you were on, and which of *Horizon*'s giant hangars you happen to be passing through. This ship is a tangled mess at the best of times, but it's even worse without something to give you a sense of place. The Werewolf seems pretty sure of himself, but this line doesn't have a name, and nor does the platform.

Hail is already on her feet, fingers hooked into the loops that fall from the ceiling. She doesn't know where we are either, I'd bet, but she takes it in her stride. "How long have we got?"

"Ten minutes," says Andrade. His eyes light up for a second, and the car settles on its track.

She nods, swivels around, and leans over me. "Are you sure you're up to this? It's going to be some hard flying."

"You got any others?"

"Jockeys?" A smile tugs at her. "A handful, if I had to go looking."

"But no one you could explain this to."

She shrugs. "It would be difficult."

"And even then—"

261

"—I'd still have my doubts? Yes. Hell, I'd be looking over my shoulder every goddamn minute."

"Get me out of this fucking chair, Hail."

There's a real smile, just for a moment, gone as quickly as it arrives, and replaced by something grim. She sets a boot against my seat, locks a hand around my wrist, and hauls me upright. She hovers for a second, hands spread to catch me. I don't blame her; I'm half expecting a closer look at the deckplates myself, and I'm surprised when I hold just fine.

"Tell me what we're going to do."

Hail steps to one side, revealed a heavy metal lockbox near the front of the car. "First, we get dressed."

Folau crouches near the locker, flicks it open. Inside is a pile of flight suit, armour, and a helmet that can only be mine. Hail and Salt are already popping buttons, and I have to work to keep pace. Folau funnels us parts, and we lean on each other as we gear ourselves up, the way that jockeys do. The others help me through the last steps. I'm out of breath and drowning in sweat, but my suit warms around me, channels the clammy fluid away. Basic systems hold me upright, take the load off the battered muscle underneath.

I'm feeling more alive with every buckle and seal, more like myself as the steel closes over me and my jacks begin to merge with the suit. "What comes after this?" I manage.

"Simple. We get in our saddles and fly out when Andrade does."

"I've marked you all as escorts," he says. "Anyone calls in, you direct them to me. We're a deep surveyor and escorts for the day. Pre-existing arrangement."

Hail flexes her fingers, tugs at her gloves. "Tower's too busy having seizures to look too closely anyway."

"We're a long way from our blocks, Hail. A long way from our shells."

She cocks her head at the Werewolf. "We are."

"It's been taken care of," says Andrade. "This part, anyway. Like I said, pre-existing arrangement."

* * *

"SOMEONE HAS TO keep this place from sinking."

They're Folau's last words before the train pulls off again. He knocks a salute off his eyebrow and spreads out across the seats. We watch him go, three jockeys balancing on the platform edge while Andrade whispers to the door, waiting for his passcodes to take.

He looks back at us after a second or so. "Helmets," he says. He's got one of his own, black and sleek.

The rest of us trade glances. Normally, we'd wait until we were planning on connecting to our machines, clear of anything that we have to navigate with our bobble-heads on. *Horizon* is bigger than any other ship in NorCol's fleet, but it's got its fair share of cramped compartments and low ceilings. Plenty of opportunities to chip our paint and put sparks across our eyes. We've all got scars on our helmets, and the same goes for any jockey with more than a couple of hours in the saddle. We'll hit our heads on anything, give us half a chance.

The look Andrade gives us doesn't leave much space to manoeuvre, and we don't argue. We buckle up, cycle our little locks, and wait for our helmets to finish warming up. We check each other over, tightening clasps and folding the last of our armour into place. We shake ourselves out, feeling our skin crawl as the suits adjust themselves around us. We join our nets and signal A-OKs.

Hail does the final check, looks back at Andrade. "Ready to go."

The Werewolf herds us into an airlock that's barely wide enough to fit Salt's chunky suit, short enough that it pushes us together when he closes the first door shut behind us. I'm expecting the airlock to run a quick pressure test, to dump its bolts and spill us out onto the other side.

After all, we're too deep inside the ship to be stepping outside, too deep for there to be anything but armour up ahead. Even if it was just a hangar, there should still be three more sets of doors between us and any sign of what's outside.

Vents open in the ceiling, and my suit reads a sudden drop in pressure.

"Andrade? What's happening?"

He smiles at me. "You jockeys like to keep your hangars dry."

"Well, yes," says Hail. "We like breathing. Same goes for the ground crew."

Andrade shrugs. "Well, in my line of work, we like our hangars wet."

He pushes past us, the narrow lock forcing us to shuffle up against the walls. On the other side, Andrade blinks his eyes to life, and starts working through something we can't see. We can't hear the bolts moving around in the walls—there isn't pressure to carry the sound. We can feel them, though.

A green light clears him to open the door, and he shoulders past it. My suit reads the kind of cold you'd find outside, maybe even colder, and ultra-low pressure without the wind pressing in. I'm waiting for a berth like the ones that hold our machines in D, or a tinderbox like they use on the smaller shell-boats on carriers. Something worth calling a hangar.

Instead, we climb a narrow flight of stairs and pass through another airlock. But these doors are nothing like the first. They have all the usual seals and locking-bolts, and they unlock exactly the way I'd expect, but they don't look like they were made to keep the atmo in. Oversized hinges jut out on one side, huge bolts and buffers show on the other once we've pulled it clear, four or five times bigger than they need to be. Solid-cast, like they were meant to survive something.

Blast pressure, judging by the dark sheen of the metal on the other side.

Behind them, a walkway suspended over open air and not a whole lot else, backlit as the compartment begins to wake, assuming 'compartment' is even the thing to call it. It rises up and away, the ceiling so dark and distant I'm tempted to look for stars. It falls away below us, giving no sense of its depth, mirroring the reaches above. An old silo, then, or some stranger part of *Horizon* that no one remembers how to use.

I don't see Andrade's shell, not at first. Not until the lamps find it.

The walkway circles around an odd shadow—the underframe of a Decatur, but with huge plates of armour curving across its chest, each one cast as a single piece. I can't see the joints through all the extra cladding, and I can only just make out its narrow eyes. Ten of them, arranged in a pair of fives down its brutal face.

I've never seen a surveyor's machine before, but I've never had any reason to. There isn't much need for them out in Open Waters. Anything a shell can do, wideband PHADAR can do better. At least, that's the way it works outside, where the skies aren't trying to run you blind.

All that, and it looks exactly the way I would expect. Exactly like the place that holds it. Pitted deep, and polished to a fire-touched black.

Chains run out from its shoulders into a cage of cranes and scaffolding above. The shell body hangs loose, head forward, arms and legs dangling, unresponsive.

But something's missing. "There's no runway."

Andrade nods. "No launch rails either."

A wave of vertigo rocks me on my feet, and I catch myself on the handrails.

The Werewolf grins at me. "She understands."

The other two frown at us.

"Understands what, exactly?" asks Salt.

He aims a finger over the edge. "That."

Somewhere in the deep below us, maybe a whole K away, a pair of stars flicker in place. It takes me a second to work up the courage to put a little zoom on my optics. When I do, I can just about see a pair of hazard-lamps. Between them, something that might be the outline of a door.

Andrade doesn't launch, he *falls*.

"You're insane."

"Not insane," he says, even if he can't bury the mad edge creeping into his smile, "just quiet."

* * *

ANDRADE SENDS US out to another blast-lock, just like the one that led us here. His machine is ready to go, but ours are someplace distant, behind all this char and blackened metal. Salt waits with me while Hail works the locks, staring back over my head. The old colonial hasn't taken his eyes off the Werewolf since we arrived, watching Andrade as he starts the process of waking his machine. Salt's gaze doesn't have an edge to it—he looks like he's trying to memorise the details, the subtle quirks he can't quite place. Or maybe it's the other way 'round. Maybe he's seen something similar before, and is trying to remember where, exactly.

I mean to ask, make it halfway there, but a gleam behind him catches my eye. If I lean a little to the side, I can just about make a shape. A little way back, and I've lost it again. I flick through visor-settings, but they don't give me much more than I had already. A steely edge, spiralling up along the wall and out of sight.

11.88

It feels like a flick to the back of my skull. A little shiver, and a flash of something half-remembered.

Andrade's hangar has rifle grooves.

There's a hiss behind me, and it brings me back to earth. Seems some parts of his hangar have pressured air as well, a little of it rushing out as Hail cycles the door, herds us through. There's more atmo after that. It feels like another part of the ship—another ship altogether, if I didn't know better

Hail leads us along a path Andrade left for us, through little pockets of mould and dust and abandoned machinery. Patches of *Horizon*'s dead tissue, left to rot, but still tight enough to keep the air. A ruined engineering station meets us a few minutes in, tools still hanging from their mounts, and a few dead drones lying on tables, dissected. Someone has levered some of the light-sockets out, left the bulbs hanging from lines of tangled wire, low enough that Salt has to brush them clear, throwing strange shadows through the passages on either side. We duck under chains and crane hooks, following a track worn silver through the dust, and doors left open so long that their corroded joints hold them in place.

One compartment is full of cots, bedding, and the kind of scatter that tends to follow the crew around a ship. Posters cling to the walls, torn or curling: faceless bodies fondle themselves, and oversized lips blow kisses through the grime.

Names and dates stick out where they've been scratched into the paint, sketches and scribbles competing for space with dockside poetry and tallies of the dead.

13.51

We always remember the dead.

"Always," I whisper, where the other two can't hear.

The next room is full of shadows. Three ratty seats face the wall, crowded by banks of screen displays. Manual controls stick out between display nodes and analogue gauges. Checklists and diagrams peek out from under the dust, thick red paint runs lumpy across the bulkheads, punctuated by stencils turned ghostly pale.

Salt runs a finger across one of the panels, flicks it out. "What do you think they are?"

Hail shrugs. "Knowing NorCol? Just about anything."

"Well, it isn't big enough to be flight control, and we're a long way out from systems, helm... even engines."

"It's a gunnery station," I realise.

18.99

We know guns when we see them.

"But we're too deep for that, remember?" Hail dusts the console with a glove. "Even if we weren't, I don't think there are any guns on this side of the ship."

But Salt has realised it too. "No, she's right. Think about it; ever seen a hangar like the one Andrade's using?"

"Christs," mutters Hail. "What do you even *do* with a gun that size?"

"You sink dreadnoughts," says Salt. "Hell, planets. Whatever you damn-well please." He rolls his shoulders. "Isn't that what dreadnoughts do?"

Hail says something else, but I'm not sure I hear her. For a second, I'm choking on vertigo, but it pulls away as quickly as it rushed in, leaving a lingering weight in my stomach, and a tingle at the back of my throat.

"Come on," I say, with more force than I'm looking for. "They're waiting for us."

Hail and Salt watch me, but they don't argue.

22.13

Waiting for you.

We pass another door, and a few more heavy shadows, but I don't spend any time on them. I plot my steps instead, remind myself I've got something solid under my feet.

I don't know if I've ever felt depth like this. I've threaded atmospheres, skipped the curve of air and dust. I've flown in Open Waters, put out into the void with nothing but a shell, my own second skin against the cold. I've drifted through skies so thick you have to go on instruments and gut, and I've put out into dark so deep that there was no sky at all, no up or down and no stars for reference. It gives you a little cramp in your throat, puts you on the edge of your saddle, but there's a certain kind of mercy in not being able to see where you're going. There's no sense of height, nothing waiting for you when you fall. There are times when it's better to be in-atmo, and times when it's a hell of a lot worse. You've got something to hold onto, something solid enough to let you know that it's there, even if it's just air. At the same time, there's a threat that rides with it. Screw up, make one little mistake, forget the rules for half a second, and terra firma's waiting for you with open arms. It's harsh, but fair. Hold tight, and keep your wits about you.

24.09

Hold tight, and fly with me.

The Eye is something else again. It gives and it takes away. There's a breeze you can dig your wings into, but nothing to catch you when you fall.

We cross a bridge between a pair of cliffs, layers of *Horizon*'s skin, air-gapped and insulated. The space below us opens up, and I have to swallow hard again, keep my eyes straight and level. I watch Salt's shoulders, try my best to keep my feet in line, but my eyes are blurring around the edges, and my throat turns tighter by the second.

Maybe it's the last of medical's cocktails wearing off.

24.48

Maybe it's something else.

I feel both empty and open to the elements, all at once. Without the shell, without the wings to keep me flying, the engines to keep me on track, without the weight of metal and hydraulics—

Without all of that, I'm just meat and too much blood. Waiting for the fall.

It leaves me swaying. I have to take a breath to keep myself from choking. I roll myself through the jockey's meditation.

My feet are inside boots.

Inside a suit.

27.93

And there's a steel frame waiting.

If the other two are feeling it, they don't give much sign. They thread the narrow walkways without a word, skip across ravines as they come. Hail unlocks a door with passcodes Andrade left for her to find, trading whispers for the sound of bolts pulling back into their housings. The next hatch needs more than that; a boot, and Salt's heavy shoulder. There's air on the other side, and more solid ground made for walking on.

29.01

The last door has a giant stencil across the front, bright red and ivory against the bulkhead grey. A triangle with a jagged star in the middle.

"Munitions," says Salt. He glances at Hail. "You sure this is it?"

"No"—her eyes glow—"but this is where he said to go."

Another whisper, and we're through.

30.11

The other side is an open concrete pad, iron rails set into the floor. They're rusty now, and the machines that used to run along them are nowhere to be seen. The roof is suddenly far away, curving into vaults.

On the far side is a line of massive shadows, set into a conveyor that runs along the wall, floor to ceiling. As we walk out into the open, more of them come into view. Ultra-heavy ordnance, each round as tall as two Junos lying end-to-end, and several times as wide. The magazine that once fed Andrade's monstrous gun.

32.48

A loading bay opens up across the wall opposite, the panels still silvery. A NorCol cutter stands in the middle of it all, wings stowed, body crouched on a jury-rigged landing pad. They must have flown it in, threaded passages never meant for flying, followed the old tracks from wherever the supply trains used to rest.

It's a big bird, and specially made for carrying shells; a boxy thing with a hook snout and hooded wings and wide doors on either side. Its pilots stand outside, helmets on the floor, voices echoing, one with a glowing smoke between his fingers. They tip a couple of salutes as we roll up.

34.12

"You're the escorts," says one. Doesn't give any sign he's looking for an answer. There's nothing else we could be, in a place like this.

Hail nods. "You're our ride."

He takes a mouthful of smoke, looks us up and down. There aren't any patches on his suit, no sign of a unit on his helmet or his bird, or the crew that waits around him. They aren't shapeshifters like Andrade, but they look like they're used to working in the dark.

"Enjoy the tour?" he asks, the words turning hazy.

Hail gestures for the tail-end and pops her visor for a drag. She bites back a cough, watches the ember for a second. "What is this place?"

"Ghost stories, mostly. They say it's what *Horizon* used to be."

She raises an eyebrow. "You've never been through it, have you?"

They chuckle at that. "Hey, we just drive the bus."

"He make everyone do it?"

"Naw," says the pilot. "Most come over with us, wait here while the boss gets through his beauty routine."

"Or whatever it is he does in there," says another.

Hail scrapes the smoke off on her boot. "You got our hardware?"

38.57

The smoker looks at another of his crew. "Doors back."

She nods and blinks her eyes to life. "Aye aye, doors back."

The cutter shudders and its sides slide open, locking back around the tail-boom. Three shells wait inside, crouched to fit. They've got their wings loose in their housings, but folded close to their bodies, ready for freefall.

The Juno swells across the open at me.

45.69

A line of connections to my suit, biometrics and requests for pilot status. A few actual queries open across my visors, yes/no prompts and subjectives, eval-questions to check for shock, trauma, and combat stress.

The touch of its sensors rolling over me like a gentle breeze, tripping receivers in the skin of my suit. It starts in my helmet, moves down through my heart, and spreads from there until it has seen every part of me.

48.41

It leaves me in the afterglow, the last touch slowly pulling away.

I smile into my helmet.

50.11

"It's good to see you too, old bird."

EIGHTEEN

THE CUTTER FLIES us out, but Andrade's crew keeps us to the shallows; the no-fly order is now in effect, nearly twelve hours ahead of schedule. They follow a short circuit between the crags, engines as low as they can manage. They turn us upside down in the shadow of an old weather mast, a huge mass of struts and cabling covered in directional vanes and wind gauges, all worn and tatty. It's probably as old as the day the ship arrived in this place—relic of a time when the company was more interested in staking claims than understanding what it had gotten itself into.

A dreadnought is power, and not a whole lot else. It'll give you a death grip on anywhere you care to send it, and it was built with that in mind. It'll cross any volume of colonial space, traverse the frontier whenever it feels the urge. No borders know its name.

Horizon is more than most. Its keel is thicker than anything laid before or since, and its armour will beat whatever nightmares it may find in the dark. It has guns made for sinking whatever deep-sea monsters lurk in Open Waters, be they human or otherwise, alien obelisks or company dreadnoughts just like it.

All that, and there is one thing it was never meant to meet.

Air.

And so, some long-gone engineering crew was sent out here, hauling tons of steel and jury-rig. They built all of this from scratch, and gave *Horizon* a way to feel the breeze.

We cling to the underside of an afterthought, close enough to the ship's internal masses that my inner ears are prickling, my stomach trembling uncertainly.

"Hear anything?" asks Hail.

"Nothing," says Salt. "He put out a call to say that his chambers were still pressuring up, but that was ten minutes ago."

Hail's Spirit looks back at me. "Mind taking a look?"

The Juno and I risk an eye over the edge, but it's a stretch to get an angle on the hull. "One second."

We hook a hand around the lip of the cabin, fingers in the slot where the door merges with the armour. We lock one foot against the decking and test it for pressure. It'll hold us.

We let ourselves swing, hanging free nearly half a K above *Horizon*'s patchwork hull.

"No movement," I call back. We work our lenses and zoom in for a closer look, but the massive gun-barrel is still hidden by shrouds and armour. "I guess he's still locked in."

"Salt?"

"I've already tried again. Either the armour's blocking my signal, or he isn't picking up."

The Juno and I edge our way back inside, lock our other foot back on deck. Hail is hanging out on her side, out on a limb. Salt's machine holds her wrist, tethering her against the wind.

"There's a patrol rolling in."

A shiver runs through the steel around us, through our bodies, turning to a heartbeat rumble in my ears and an earthquake in our sensor-webs.

And then it's gone. The silence is instant.

"Any ID?" I ask.

"Full-timers, if I had to guess. Enforcing the no-fly. Herding everyone back to their roosts."

"Are we clear?" I ask.

"They're coming about."

"Shit."

Salt hauls Hail's Spirit inside, and we hold tight as another tremor passes by, hard enough to shake the air inside my lungs.

"What was that?"

Salt's shell raps a knuckle on its chest. "They've turned the augurs on, set as high as it'll go."

I've heard his Decatur making sweeps, but the Juno and I have always been on the edges, or with stone and dust in the way. Now that we're on the receiving end, it feels like they're trying to shake us apart.

"Christs, it's loud."

Another break, and I'm left with silence sucking at my ears.

"How can you hear anything?" I ask, but Hail's machine waves me down.

"Hush." It cocks its strange head, listening to something. "The cockpit's calling out."

The Juno and I strain our ears, but whatever it is, it's out of hearing. We can make out the echo, but we have to tilt our head just right. It comes in and out like someone is scanning frequencies.

If Hail is hearing anything, it won't be more than a whisper.

"Pilot's got them on the line, trying to talk them down," says Hail. If there's more, she doesn't say it.

So I push. "But?"

"We're running out of excuses." The Spirit turns, cranes for a glimpse over my shoulder.

"It's still shut, Hail. There's no sign of anything."

She turns. "Salt?"

"I'm pinging again, but there's nothing on his channel."

The Juno and I can feel four shells outside, spreading out around the cutter. Weapons locked on our little tub.

The cutter is designed for combat drops; the deck is thick, and covered in ceramic scale, resistant to heat and gunfire. The nose is a blade-edge, only just wide enough to fit the air-crew, made to slice through incoming fire rather than ride it out. The sides are thin by comparison, intended to be locked back out of the way. The ceiling is even thinner than the sides, meant to break away if the cutter starts sinking. It's a dropship—emphasis on the *drop*.

We turn, snag our fingers where the doorframe meets the hull. "I'll take another look."

But Hail lands fingers on our shoulder. "No. If you're going out, it's going to be burning hard."

"Why? What's going on?"

"They want a flight plan."

"But that's Andrade's—" I tail off.

"Exactly."

"Where is he?"

"The pilot can't reach him." Hail's machine edges nearer to the door, flexes its knees and spreads its feet. "But it looks like Tower wants positive ID on everyone and everything." She's spooling, but isn't feeding fire into her engines yet. "Get ready. We may have to turn and burn, pop screamers and hope they'll keep us covered."

Salt's shell radiates heat. "Rally point?"

New connection available, says a window in my eyes. *Accept?*

A map of vectors and relative velocities unfolds, all plotted relative to *Horizon* and the glaring Eye in the distance. The closest thing you can get to a map in a place like this.

"It's called the Stepping Stone," says Hail. "This will take you there."

The Juno and I look over them. "Good luck."

Another pulse rides through us, just as loud as the first. I can hear the shells outside trading fire-solutions, and rails charging static against the background wash.

The cutter pilot pushes in on our net. "What's going on? Why are they locking on us?"

"They're locking on us, not you," says Hail. "Don't worry. We'll be out of the way in a second."

"Shit." The line goes cold.

Salt chuckles. "Nice of him to call."

"He's spooked." The Juno and I put an eye around the corner. "Something has tripped the pickets."

"A crew of Sigurd shells made it inside the perimeter near B," says Andrade, right in my ear. "Three of ours already burning.

There are reports from the stern as well, but my contacts aren't responding."

Hail is furious. "Where have you been?"

"Trying to find you a new cover story. Tower is hunkering down. Our window is dead."

"Then we jump."

"Not so fast." The line pulses for a second. "You've got company."

Something tugs at my stomach; the feeling you'd get when you've put your machine into a dive and the gee starts pushing you around. It's nothing to do with me; it's feeding in along the net from Andrade, and my subconscious is doing its best to express it.

At the other end is a map marker, somewhere below us. I follow it, and find the source among the clouds.

A dark shape rises through the froth, trailing streamers from its conning towers and gun barrel. A destroyer, *NORCOL* writ large across the upper faces of its hull. The points are streaked charcoal black, edges showing silver where the breeze has worn its paint.

A lone transmission rolls in through the ceiling, a hundred channels wide, strong enough to batter its way through my buffers.

"This is the NCSV *Leoni Grey* to unidentified shells. Power down and surrender yourselves immediately. Repeat, this is the *Leoni Grey*. You are surrounded. Power down, and surrender immediately."

"Listen to me." There's a pause as Andrade gathers himself. "There are two flights on their way to you now, and one already taking aim. You can't outrun them, and the *Grey* can track faster than you can move. They'll light you up."

"So what? We just wait here?"

"No, Hail. You go on as planned. You fly as hard as you can."

"Great idea," I growl. "My machine won't make it."

"You don't have to worry about that. Just work yourselves a flight plan, I'll take care of the rest."

Something clicks in my ear. I turn, and spare a glance for where Andrade's hangar meets the wind. *Horizon*'s armour is crawling. I push the picture to Hail and Salt.

Our shells trade tightlines, comparing plans and flight vectors, jinks and high-gee curves, holographic countermeasures. Together, they plot our way through bursts of simulated fire, railshot and warheads and whatever else may come.

"Are you ready?" asks Andrade.

"As we'll ever be." I breathe in, let it out slowly. "Hey, Andrade?"

"What?"

"Don't let them touch you."

"UNIDENTIFIED SHELLS," ROARS across the open. "This is your final—"

3, says a counter running down the corner of my eye.

"—warning. Cut your engines—"

2

"—and surrender yourselves immediately. You have sixty seconds to—"

Horizon's hull opens below us and Andrade dawns across it. His machine falls across the open, turning in place, drowning everything out in the deep fires of its engines.

"—comply."

The last word trails away.

Andrade's machine looks nothing like the surveyor I saw in the hangar. That one had a body made for depth and darkness, but this has every sign of being a Hasei shell.

All the angles are right, but some of the scale is off. You wouldn't know it from a distance, and your augurs would call back with a Hasei tag. Look closely, though, and you can still see some of the surveyor's machine hidden under the awkward orange plates. He's changed the shapes enough to give the right silhouette, but that was all he had time for.

Andrade is a Werewolf.

278

This is how NorCol starts its wars.

He streaks past, but we don't wait to see what comes. We're already clear of the doors, throwing out as much thrust as our engines can stand; dumping screamers, flares, crackling ammo and burning fuel. We make for a line of Decaturs straight ahead, the patrol who flagged us first. We turn and burn, flying so close to them that their wingmates lock up, a moment's hesitation as their systems try to keep them from killing each other. Some of them don't even turn to follow, still focussed on the orange flare that's suddenly opened across their scopes.

We're clear before they can work their triggers again. I can feel the destroyer's long-guns tracking, but we've got *Horizon* at our backs and a cloud of friendlies in the way, a small sun lighting up the space behind us.

Andrade dives deep, but he doesn't cut the noise. His systems cloud my vision and drown my hearing out, and they aren't even aimed at us.

We do the same. There's open air for a few heartbeats before the clouds swallow us, a rippling ravine lit from behind. Beyond that, the dark wind waits for us, rattles us when we finally hit, the sudden change in density almost as loud as the raging fires on either side.

We spin clear of hard shot and tracer, watch fountains of flack tear through the froth on either side. We dump flares into the missiles creeping up behind us, feel them crump and rattle as the warheads die.

We count off thirty seconds, then a minute. After five minutes, it feels like a whole day has come and gone.

We start killing sensors after that; every piece of ranging, comms, and networking. Everything we can spare, and then a little more. We open our engines to the currents, let them run quiet as the wind rushes past. We cut the strobes and close our eyes. Most of them, anyway.

Outside, a storm cell swallows up the light, broken here and there where the Eye peeks through the cracks. A few lost tracers follow us into the deeps, still burning.

We let our passives feel the way ahead, but we don't look back.

We let the cold wind carry us.

COME WITH ME
to the bottom of the sea.

That's the way it goes, if I remember right. I don't have any more of the song, even if I've still got the tune. There's enough that I can whistle it, and add the little skips and hoops where words are supposed to be. It's a habit I picked up off of Salt; everything half hummed but mostly mumbled, like phantom sounds on the comms, strange voices rising out of the static when no one else is speaking.

Maybe Salt is where I heard the song. Caught off the edge of his marching tune, or sung while I was sleeping. You don't sleep when you're in chains, but you're not awake either. You aren't alive, not really. I spent most of that time dreaming. That's why I've still got the sound, but don't have the lyrics. It's stuck someone near the back of my head, coming up on reflex rather than memory.

I'VE BEEN FLYING six hours now, but I don't know how far I've come. The Juno's keeping track, projecting the numbers up against my eyes, but they don't mean much to me. The currents feed us endless dust and shadow, the same winds wrapped around the same storms for a hundred thousand years. It gives you a kind of tunnel vision, creeps in through the corners of your eyes until all you've got is the same deep-field blur.

Maybe that's why I can't find the words to the song. Maybe I've had them all along, picked up somewhere before NorCol took me in. Before Salt and his singing, before the Eye, before I had any reason to remember. All I have to do is make the right shapes, give the words enough space, and they'll all just find their ways back to me. It feels like they're only just out of reach, hanging off the tip of my tongue.

"Come with me

to the bottom of the sea—"

I run out of song just as fast as I did before, but I don't lose the tune for another thirty seconds or so. I keep it running on a hum, then a whistle. I can manage thirty seconds, so long as I keep myself focussed on the dark currents outside. The storm means there isn't much to see, but that's what I need. Something to keep my mind occupied while half-forgotten things work themselves into the blanks.

Another storm rolls into our path, catching broken light through the cloud tops.

Another dark shape looms on our starboard side, just for a second.

It disappears as fast as we can pick it out, as fast as the others did. We've passed three of them since we left *Horizon*, outlines blurry, but holding still against the currents. More of the froth's strange geography; another Lighthouse, perhaps.

They register on our ranging suite, but only as long as we have line of sight. Walls of interference meet us where the flow turns to eddies and winds curl over on themselves.

We get little hotspots every now and then, tiny sparks on the passives where driftwood collides in the storm's heavy darkness, moments of impact heat as they shatter themselves on one another, gradually becoming the dust that carries them. The signatures are impossibly small, but when everything else out here is dark and crushing, we can see them clear enough.

The Juno shivers just a little, only as much as it needs to catch my attention. We've been holding steady long enough, followed this line for as long as we're supposed to. Now we turn, feel the current against our hull. We were tacking before, off-centre, but now we're flying into a headwind.

A contact appears above us, but I don't even register at first. I'm expecting another phantom in the haze, blink and it's gone, but this one holds our eyes.

Come with me

to the bottom of the sea.

The dust parts for a moment, gives us a taste of wings and an unusual hull, blurring as currents roil around it. The observer, just for a moment.

Rest your feet in muddy ground
see all the faces of the drowned.

NINETEEN

THE STEPPING STONE is right where Hail's instructions said it would be, even if it isn't what I was expecting to see. I was holding out for another Lighthouse-thing: a slab of windborne rock, a little island in the froth.

It waits for me, strangely static against the currents, but the Stone seems to be anything but stone. It's human-origin, for a start.

A station, a pair of flat plates sheltering a pillar between them, making the whole thing look like a barbell. The windward plate has been worn smooth, but the trailing side has markings etched into the surface. Patterns that fork like lightning bolts, like roots or veins or rivers from afar.

Hail and Salt are there already, their shells tucked in behind the leading edge. They cling to the station's central column, everything folded away and clear of the breeze.

The Juno never had the fire to fly the way they did, and so we played to our strengths. We only had to hide our little sun, barely an ember to the distant fire that dominates the sky. We cooled our engines, cut the non-essentials, and the Eye drowned us out in heartbeats. As the Juno and I turn in, we pick more of the Stepping Stone out against the clouds. Whatever it is, it's made to fit shells. Four of them, to be precise, with hand- and footholds arranged around the central column.

We edge closer, working our thrust to keep us steady on the wind. The Stone looks like it isn't moving, but that's an illusion—a mistake made by my ridiculous monkey eyes. Everything moves; you just have to know the beat it's moving to.

We catch turbulence off the edge of the leading plate, an umbrella of boiling air where the currents hit the windward face. We could burn hard and hurl ourselves through the noise, but that'd be a problem when we hit the quiet on the other side.

I take a deep breath. Or I think I do; I'm not sure I can tell the difference between our heartbeats.

We bring ourselves alongside and face the flow head on, burn hard enough to level out, grinding the jitters down until it feels like we're suspended in mid-air, perfectly still as the universe turns around us.

"Ready?" I whisper.

The Juno is hot and certain, impossible to ignore.

We inch forward against the wind, fighting the Stone's twisted wake with bursts of directional thrust. We get as close to the leading plate as we can, and give ourselves some space to fall.

A little network brushes up against us.

"I'll catch you," says Salt, right beside my ear.

We can't turn to look at him—we're fighting hard enough just to keep ourselves from spinning into the wash—but his shell sketches itself out for us where our sensors can feel it. He sets a marker in his open hand and sends it across the net. We can't see him, but we know where he is and what he's doing.

"Isn't there an easier way?"

"If there is, I haven't seen it. I'll catch you."

I wish I felt half as calm as he sounds.

The Juno swells around me, a bubble of my own, solid against the wind.

"Dropping now."

We thrust full ahead for half a second, punching to the side just before cutting it off. The wind drives us back, but inertia carries us into the sudden quiet. Salt's shell finds us, rides the landing out with a heavy grip and NorCol-branded muscle.

"Gotcha."

The Decatur gives us space to find a handhold for ourselves.

We unfold a foot—stowed in the slipstream—and hook it into the column, lock it down with electromag. Then we find a handhold.

The Juno settles around me, and my pulse finally slows. Or maybe it's the other way around.

After the noise outside, the quiet in here runs thick. The air is clear, though; we can see past the Stone's narrow core, catching glimpses of the Storm Borders where the hot winds blow.

"Christs, Salt. You do that on your own?"

The Decatur locks itself in next to us, spares a glance for the Spirit on the other side. "I didn't. Hail beat me here, brought me down the same as I did for you, like she'd done it all before."

"So she—?"

"—*she* put down on her own?" He chuckles. "Feel free to ask her."

We look over at the Spirit. It's very still. "Where is she?"

"Inside."

"*Inside?*"

His machine taps a finger where I can see, marks out a little airlock set into the dark-green steel. "Inside. Right here."

"You're kidding."

"I wish."

"How do you get down?"

He flexes his turquoise fingers at me. "It's simple. All you have to do is get a hold of yourself."

THE JUNO COLLECTS me just outside the operator's lock, and I find a handhold on its wrist and lock my boot against its finger. It waits for me while my head spins, holds me while I remember which set of muscles is which. There's nothing quite like the feeling of holding yourself in the palm of your own hand.

We let the pilot-sync drop into the eighties, and it almost feels like I can work my body on its own. The shell pings my suit; the kind of query you'd get if your machine thought you were blacking out through a turn, or if it felt you hit your head.

"I'll be fine, old bird." I manage to sound a little like I mean it.

The Juno watches me between our—

I grit my teeth at the sudden vertigo.

Christs, this is worse than I thought it would be.

The Juno watches me between its fingers, weighing me up. I can almost hear the calculations, six different protocols trying to decide if the machine can leave me on my own. Shells do it all the time; watching us when we're swaying in the saddle, or when they feel our eyes start to drift. It pushes a couple of questions across my eyes: standard test cases for disorientation. I'm still conscious, and I know where I am, for the most part. That's the problem. I've been cut in half, but I can still feel where all of me is.

All of *us*.

The Juno skips through the last of the questions, and adds one at the end.

Are you going to be all right? "I'm—"

Fine? I swallow the word before it hits my tongue. It's a lie.

"I don't know."

The Juno considers this. There's a reason machines don't ask questions like that. What does it do with the answer?

Whatever it decides, it leans in closer to the hatch. For half a second, I dangle over nothing in its hand, my boots backlit by Eye-light and rolling, glowing cloud.

It sets me down on the narrow platform in front of the airlock and holds me there while I lock my boots to the deck and get used to my own feet. The platform isn't much more than a doorstep. There are no safety rails, and no handholds, just me, in the palm of the Juno's hand. It cups its hand around me, presses its fingertips against the hull on either side. I almost feel safe.

The door has a manual lock—a wheel to cycle pressure, and a panel where you can punch in an access code. A few of the buttons glow amber where Hail's fingers cleared the dust away. The little display says that I'm free to go through, and so I work the wheel, pull the door out on its gritty hinges.

The airlock behind it is just wide enough to take me and my narrow suit, assuming I keep my elbows to myself. Salt could come in wearing nothing but his skin and still get stuck.

I look back before I close the door, sparing a glance for the rest of me. Even when I close the door, I can feel it on the other side. I feel it rearrange its grip on the outside of this station, locking its fingers and toes into the handholds meant to take them. The airlock is perfectly dark while it cycles, but I could paint the outline of my shell with both eyes closed.

An old lamp wakes in the ceiling, and vents wheeze on either side. The bulb lasts ten seconds more before it pops, the shifting pressures and changing temperatures too much for the ancient glass.

I switch my visor to low-light, but the greenscale picks up the dust motes and turns them into drifting stars.

"It's gonna get bright in a second," says a voice from somewhere above. "Switch to auto."

I do as she says, give a thumbs-up where the airlock cameras should be able to see. I close my eyes anyway, just to be sure.

I hear the airlock cycle and the other door swing out. Light falls on my eyelids.

"Come on in," says Hail, standing just beyond the door, backlit by wall-mounted halide lamps.

My visor picks her out, traces her outline while my eyes catch up. She stands tall, a helmet under one arm, hair prickly with sweat.

"There's atmo in here, if you want it." She shrugs. "It's a bit stale, but it's breathable."

I pop the seals around my throat and pull my bucket over my head.

"Christs, it smells like death in here."

Hail offers half a smile. "I forgot to mention that. This place doesn't get used much." She turns on the spot, motions for me to follow.

The compartment she leads me to is circular, and almost the same width as the column outside. Almost.

"It's tight in here."

Hail raps a knuckle on the wall. "Armour's thick for its size. Cuts into the floorspace." There's a ladder to one side, but she doesn't bother climbing. "Come on," she says. She crouches for a second, cuts the mag in her boots and pushes off like a diver, floating through an open hatch above.

I mimic her movements, and use the rungs to guide me up. "What is this place?"

"Deep observation facility," she says, somewhere up ahead. "Made to watch the froth, and to pick out anything that might be hiding in the storms."

I clear the ladder and Hail catches me, sets me down on the next deck up.

It's almost exactly as I'd expect: Crates and service boxes, for the most part, bolted or strapped in place on every surface. A few low-gee hammocks hang to the side, amidst webbing and work surfaces.

"I didn't think NorCol had anything this far out."

Hail smirks at me. "They don't."

"I don't understand. Who does it belong to?"

"The wind, for the most part. Used to be Sigurd, though."

I stop short. "How do you know about it, then?"

"I used to be Sigurd too."

I frown at her. "No, you didn't. I've seen you. You've got the walk and the talk. You're as NorCol as anyone I've ever met."

She tugs at her collar, pulls it down until I can see her collarbones. There's the same line of chain-scars I noticed before, like someone in her gang had tripped, dragged her to the deck. Beneath that is a ring of pale lines around the base of her throat.

"Know what this is?"

I do. Anyone who's ever pulled a Sigurd jockey out of their shell does.

The companies will do anything to push a couple of seconds out on their competitors. NorCol keeps their pilot-sync higher than most, and the Locusts use ampham stims and IV-drips full of go-juice.

Sigurd goes for connectivity; it can be hard to see where their jockeys end and their flight suits begin.

"You were sewn in."

"I was. Not that it helped. I was weeks old; only just finished basic before they assigned me to this place. Ten days into my assignment, we were spotted by a NorCol surveyor. I didn't even realise it until later."

"You said this thing was an obs facility. You didn't see them coming?"

"That was the idea when they built this thing. It would've worked, anywhere else."

"Anywhere but here?"

She nods. "The Eye is one big ball of noise, and the froth gets in the way of everything else."

"So a surveyor tagged you, and *Horizon* put a shell flight on the case."

"Three flights." She holds up her fingers. "Two up front, one in support. There were four crew assigned to this place: two techs and two jockeys flying old Caspians."

"Against twelve NorCol machines?"

She nodded. "All but one were Spirits; this was before Decaturs. My wingmate caught sight of them and decided he didn't like the odds. He was a lifer, been in-saddle nearly thirty years, in the breeze for half of that."

"He ran?"

Hail smiles, but it's bitter. "Didn't say a word. Just walked out the airlock, strapped himself in. He was already flying when NorCol made us. Dropped a bunch of screamers right then, cut and ran before I'd even cleared my cockpit."

"One against twelve, then."

She laughs at that, short and sharp. "One rookie, against twelve of NorCol's finest. Was my first brush with a Werewolf; the surveyor figured this place was worth something, went through the back channels. NorCol arrived expecting a fight."

"And they found you instead."

"I wasn't even in the saddle when the alarms started going off.

The lead was an old hacksaw called Sajjan. He offered me my rights, on the spot."

"Kill your engines, or yourself?"

"In the end, it didn't make much difference."

"Oh?"

"The Caspian was a hunk of junk. Looking back, I must've flown it right out of the scrapheap. It stuttered when I tried to sync, then powered down for me."

I look around. "So this is NorCol turf, then?"

"Not that it matters. A listening post doesn't do you any good when you're drowning in noise. That's why Sigurd abandoned it in the first place. They didn't even respond to our SOS." She grits her teeth. "At least NorCol had the decency to take me back in chains."

"I thought you were a con."

"Out here, it makes no difference. I'm a prisoner of war, but the company mixed me in with all the others. Sajjan, the Werewolf—he bought me out. He trained Andrade, trained me right after like I belonged to him as well. Three years on my feet, and he found me a saddle." She points at me. "The Juno used to be his."

"WHAT ARE WE doing here?" My voice echoes.

Hail spares me the corner of her eye. "I told you, this place was—is—a listening post."

"You also said it was a waste of space."

"It is." She sets her shoulder against a battered old airlock. It's the biggest we've seen so far, and the only one that doesn't open on command. It's bent into its frame, and its surface is pitted with what could only be gunshot wounds.

"At *least*—"

She heaves, her boots struggling for traction.

"—for *anything*—"

The bolts are clear—she's checked twice—but the door is stuck fast.

"—the *company*—"

She stops and flicks a bead of sweat away.

"—wanted it to do."

I hook my helmet on my belt and lean in next to her, spread my feet and mag-lock my bootsoles to the deck. "Doesn't sound like it'll do us any better."

We heave together, work our boots on and off, set ourselves again. The hinges give just a little.

"Normally, it wouldn't." She straightens, and rests a hand on the doorframe while she catches her breath. "But we're using it off-label."

And again. The hinges sing.

"Christs," I manage, between breaths. At 1 g, this would probably be easy. Half a gee, and at least we'd have something to go on. We're almost in freefall out here, and the best we can do is skate around on the floor and try to keep our feet from flying off.

We take a second to survey the progress, if you can call it that. We've managed to scratch the deck, and left little silver tracks where our boots have cut through the dust. The door is open enough to fit fingertips.

"We're doing well," growls Hail.

"Only the whole thing to go."

For a while, we let ourselves stand.

"What are we doing, Hail?"

She doesn't look back at me.

"We've got an old Obs post and not a whole lot else. We don't have a line to Andrade, and *Horizon* isn't going to be happy to see us any time soon."

She waves the last away. "*Horizon* doesn't know any more than those patrols do."

"Assuming they weren't sunk in the chaos."

"Assuming that. Assuming they even bother to put in a report."

"If they do, they'll have a lot of explaining to do."

Hail winks at me. "See?"

"I guess so."

"All we need is the right operator when we call in to Tower." She raps a knuckle on the door, and this time there's an echo on the other side. "And this should help us with the beacon."

I cross my arms. "What about the wind? The noise?"

"What about it?" she asks. She gives me a ragged smile. "We're *looking* for noise."

We shove, earning enough space to fit a couple fingers more through the gap. Again, and the hinges shriek for a whole second before the door stops dead.

"Snagged."

"Not for long." Hail locks one boot, frees the other, and kicks the door, nearly spilling herself across the floor. "Maybe not," she manages, only just saving herself from the floor.

A little drop of silver pops clear of the doorframe. I catch it before it floats too far, and hold it up to the light. It's a hardround, mangled when it hit the steel. I can see a few of NorCol's markings down one side.

I flick it over to Hail. "This from the Werewolves?"

She nods. "They wanted in."

"Bad, by the look of it."

"At first. They tried to force the door, but it wouldn't move."

"You locked it?"

She aims a glare at me. "Three of us against a crowd of Werewolves and NorCol spec-ops, and you think we *locked* it? No, we didn't lock it. There was a malfunction with the pressure seal; we couldn't have opened it if we wanted to. When they got tired of threatening us, they tried blowing their way in." She takes the ruined doorframe in with a sweep of a hand. "You can see how well that went."

"So what? They gave up?"

She aims a finger at something I wouldn't have noticed if she hadn't pointed it out. A little break in the bulkhead, about the size of a fingertip. Smaller. "They drilled a hole."

"And put an eyeball through?"

She nods. "A little one. Scouter. They got its wings working,

292

and buzzed the room a couple of times, but they found exactly what I told them they'd find."

"What?"

"Scrap, mostly. Took them a minute to put it together for themselves."

"What was the first clue? That there was a nugget holding the fort?"

"A nugget and her scrapheap shell, don't forget." She thumps a fist on the wall. "And that's before you count the doors that don't close, the doors that don't open, and a reactor that kept switching on and off. I couldn't hold this place when the Werewolves came calling, and the techs couldn't get this thing open. Even with us pressed against the wall, they thought we were stalling. By the time they turned around, they realised this place was just as much of a joke as it seemed. Scrap and driftwood."

I watch her. "But they took you."

"I *might* have asked them to."

HAIL COMES BACK with a length of battered metal in her hands. It looks like something belonging to a knuckledragger: a long tool made for levering shell parts on and off, or knocking heavy bolts into place. But someone took a cutter to the head, shaved it down into a nasty, jagged edge, like a spear. A hack-job, quick and dirty.

I say as much.

"That's because it is," says Hail. She turns it over in the light. "The original complement of this place was two techs and two jockeys, with two service weapons to share between us."

"Minus one."

She smirks. "He also took all of the spare magazines."

Together, we jam the craggy end in through the gap, and take turns kicking it until it's wedged between the door and its twisted frame.

"Take the wall."

I look at her, then at the tool.

"I'll catch you."

I raise an eyebrow.

"Don't make me pull rank, convict." She even sounds a little like she means it.

"Yes, sir." I manage to sound exactly like I don't.

I unlock one boot, press it against the wall, and set the maglock again. One more, and I'm standing level with Hail's chest, flipped ninety to what we've been pretending is the floor. I crouch under the tool, set my shoulder against it, and get ready to push. Hail lines up on the other side, locks her boots, and gets a grip on the handle.

"Ready?" she asks.

"I wish Salt was here."

"On three."

I rise until I feel the pressure on my shoulder. She takes up slack.

"One," she says.

"Two," I reply.

"Three—"

We're still heaving when, with a heavy *clunk* on the other side, the tool comes loose in our hands. My boots hold tight, but the rest of me's wheeling for balance, mid-air. Hail nearly lands on her ass.

The door swings in without another sound, one hinge still holding on, the other snapped clean down the middle. A few more mangled hardrounds trickle out, along with a few shards of the door itself.

I inch my way back to the floor, have to stretch to get my feet locked down.

"Are you ready?" asks Hail.

I frown at the tone in her voice. "For what, exactly?"

"Take a deep breath." She nods past the door. "The first time is"—she takes a moment to find the right word—"difficult."

There isn't much to see. The compartment is almost completely dark, and what little light there is streams past my head, throwing a cone across the floor and catching the edges of boxy shapes around the room. From here, it looks like the bridge of an old ship. Deep chairs and oversized displays, interfaces made to carry huge amounts of information. It reminds me of the diasporan hulk still anchored near Destiny: one of the ugly things that carried us out of the glow of our old sun.

"I don't get it."

Hail meets my eyes for a second, but she just points. I follow the gesture into the middle of it all. There's only just enough light to pick the details out, and I really wish there wasn't.

Six heavy struts run down from the ceiling, meeting six more rising from the floor. Massive pistons run through each one, cradling what looks like a single hunk of rock.

It takes me a second to understand what I'm seeing. I spend the next trying to keep my feet.

It's pitted and dusty, like the other things that keep themselves steady against the winds. It's the same colour as the Lighthouse, stony red with the same grainy texture.

That's it, isn't it?

I don't want to hear myself ask the question. Worse, I already know the answer.

It's all that's keeping this place afloat.

And I could hold it in my hands.

Hail puts a grip on my shoulder, holds me steady. "Welcome to the Stepping Stone."

TWENTY

THERE ISN'T MUCH space to stand, but it doesn't look like this place was designed with that in mind. Designed with *anything* in mind, now that I can see it. The pillars and the Stepping Stone take up most of the room. The Stone itself shifts slightly every now and then, and the pistons correct. It doesn't look like much, but it's easy to forget what I'm looking at. The Stone keeps its own orbit, and the station has been built around it. When the pistons hiss, and the little chunk of rock turns in their grip, it isn't the stone moving, it's us.

I swallow the vertigo as the roles reverse. The floor tilts, but the Stone stays flat.

Christs.

The clutter doesn't leave much room to keep my feet.

If there are lamps in this compartment, they've been cut from the rest of the facility. Hail has a string of emergency bulbs running, held to the ceiling with tape. The rest of the light comes in through the door—and some of the bullet holes—and falls down around our boots.

The terminals are cased in dirty plastic and peeling paint, rustproofing swollen from underneath. Every single one of them was built for somewhere else, ripped out by the roots and bolted down wherever Sigurd's knuckledraggers could find space.

"They never expected it to work, did they?"

Hail leans over what looks like a control surface, shaped from a heap of salvage, and welded together with chunky, beady seams. Someone came along after the fact and jammed a couple of switches over the top, ran open wiring down the back.

"For a while, they hoped. The Stone uses the same PHADAR arrays as dreadnoughts, heavy-duty and long-range."

"Good for finding other dreadnoughts."

"True." She leans in, following a cable with her fingers. "Sigurd had only just arrived, then. There's a knack to working in the froth, and they didn't have it yet."

"So they went for something solid. Tried and tested."

"Most of it, yes, but some of it really wasn't." She flicks a switch, and looks up at the ceiling like she's expecting something.

Whatever's supposed to happen doesn't.

"The main sensors were built specially, with the Eye in mind. Based off some wreck the company found after Phradi."

"None of that stuff worked." I flex my fingers. "NorCol tried something similar, I heard, but the project lived and died in months, a year at most. Something about human beings being incompatible."

She shrugs. "*This* worked. In Open Waters, at least."

"And here?"

"If they'd gotten half of it going, it would've been a game-changer, back when the game was only a few decades old. Hell, if they'd just gotten *one* of these things working, all of the froth would be property of the Sigurd-Lem Corporation."

"There's more than one of these things?"

"The Stone here?" She points at it under her arm. "None. Others *like* it, maybe ten, fifteen." She leans back over the switches, tries another, which sparks. "Fuck," she says, shaking her finger. "There were supposed to be thousands of them. Part of a project to map everything in sight of the Eye. Every chunk of rock, every prevailing storm system, everything. Tagged, measured, labelled, scans sent back to deep servers on Sanctuary."

"But they couldn't break the froth."

She nods. "Remember the first time you saw the Eye?"

How could I forget? "You said it was artificial."

"As far as anyone can tell, almost everything in this place is. There's driftwood that comes in on the currents, wreckage of things that didn't translate. Things that got chewed up somewhere between normal space and this little pocket of sky. Everything else is made. Manufactured."

"What about the clouds?"

"Find a patch of air that's clear enough, and you'll grow yourself a cloud before long."

"And the dust?"

"As much as anything else. Up close, it's all the same colour. The same colour as the Stone over there, and the same colour as the Lighthouse. Zoom in close enough, and you'll see that every grain is the exact same shape."

"Christs."

She chuckles. "Oh, it gets worse. Think about it; why would you *make* dust? Open Waters is full of it, why go through the trouble? Actually, forget that. Why would you make enough of *anything* for there to be storm cells of the stuff?"

Oh. "It's a screen. They made it to hide something."

"That's the theory. Assuming you make it *into* the froth—hard enough—you're afloat in an endless sea of interference. Lost in a place where distance doesn't mean as much as you think it does, and where you can't see your way home." She tries another switch, but still nothing happens. She slams a fist on the panel hard enough to echo, and tries the switch again. More nothing; she flicks it back and forth between her fingers. "Dammit." She tries a kick. Something sparks near the ceiling.

"What does it look like?"

She looks up at me. "What does what look like?"

"The dust."

"Up close? A bit like broken glass, I guess. You'd think being in a place like this would wear it all down, grind it smooth, but it's full of sharp edges. Full of teeth." She tries the switch again, and this time something stirs. For a few seconds, there's a humming sound above us, and then it's gone. She glares at the ceiling. "So close."

"It's made for chewing signals, then."

She drops behind the console and starts tugging at something I can't see. "Made for chewing most things. That's why patrols can't call home. Why the companies can't just sink each other from opposite sides of the Eye."

"So what are we doing here, then?"

Hail sends a hand over the top, points. "Flick that switch."

I lean over to see her holding a pair of live wires between her fingers.

"You sure about that?"

She presses them together. "No. Does it matter?"

"Guess not." I try it, and the line sparks, cracks like a gunshot. Hail starts and yelps.

"Are you all right?"

"Fine." She comes back up, glares at the panel. "We're here because this is our best option."

"How do you figure that? This thing is driftwood, you said it yourself."

"You're right. Sigurd worked out pretty quickly that the project was a waste." She turns, arm extended, following another line of cabling across the floor. "But not for the reason you'd think."

"I don't know what to think."

"That's fair, I suppose." She squats down next to a display, digs her fingers into a panel below it, yanks it clear. "This place is a waste, but that's because it's only good at the obvious stuff. Like the giant ring of fire out there," she says, flapping a hand at the wall.

"It's really good at things you don't need a listening station to tell you?"

She clicks a finger at me. "Exactly. The froth tears into anything you try and send—anything direct, that is. Spits it out in a million directions."

"But if you take the time, you can still hear an echo?"

"It depends, but yes. For the most part, anyway. Echoes aren't much good when you're trying to send a message."

"Or looking for a couple of pebbles in the froth."

"Mm-hm." She tugs something loose, flicks a little lamp on her shoulder, lighting her hollow cheeks from below. "It is very good at wide-band, though."

"Like a distress beacon?"

"Like a distress beacon. Even better when you know what to listen for."

"Why didn't we come here in the first place?"

"I had to do a little digging first." She pats the console. "And I can't guarantee that this will work. Hell, I can't even get the lights on."

"You knew that, and still flew us all the way out here."

"Oh, I don't have it working yet, but I know the odds. There's a difference."

I cross my arms. "Really, Hail?"

She stands, heads back to where she started. She flicks the switch from before, gets the same electric hum. She tries another, but this one fights her. She jams her thumb down hard, puts a little weight on top. "It's the thought that counts."

Click.

WE WAIT IN the dark.

Hail spits. "Christs-dammit—"

She doesn't have time to finish the curse. Long fluorescents flash and buzz, crackling through layers of grime and fur. The screens and equipment look even rougher now that there's light to see them.

"Cosy."

Hail gives me side-eye. "You should try sleeping in this place, pretending it isn't the actual, observable hell outside."

I can't help the smile. "How fresh were you?"

"Greener than green. The worst kind, too." She spreads her hands. "Sigurd sent me *here*, after all."

I look past her, up at the displays. Behind the mess of salvage are things that look like they could've been mounted into a

Juno's cockpit. Not the saddle or the new wetware pivots, or the runners that hold the nerve-jacks. The stuff behind that. The displays that spoke to me in the dark.

"How do we do this?"

Hail picks her way across the clutter. "Good question."

"You're serious."

"Deadly." She finds a break in the panelling, just wide enough to fit her if she turns her shoulder and holds her breath.

I put my head through after her. She's standing in a crowded space, looking down on a solid, silver-black cube. It looks just like I'd expect from Sigurd, but it's the only thing in this room that does. Everything else is centuries old, from before Sigurd started coating everything in mirrors.

VINE, says an etching along the side.

"This place has an intelligence?"

Hail waves its display into being; a holographic interface, projected across the top. She toggles the mind-state, gets it warming up. "'AI' is probably a stretch. As far as I ever knew, VINE was Chinese-room, shallow learning only. At least, that was the idea."

"The idea?"

"The personality is a preload, scavenged out of an old capital-ship. Sigurd dusted it off and shoved it in here."

"But it's intelligent?" I'm halfway through before I hear what I'm asking. Another question brews behind it, but I don't find my way to saying it out loud.

Hail looks at me strangely, like she's caught the edge of my thoughts. "Intelligent in the loosest sense of the word."

Intelligent enough, types itself out on one of the displays.

"Hail."

"I see it." She's looking over my shoulder, watching the same words roll out across another screen. "Hello, VINE," she says, loud enough to carry. "What have you been up to?"

Dreaming, says VINE. *It's not as though I had anything else.* There's a pause.

How long has it been?

Hail steps past me into the middle of the room. "Do you really want to know?"

Another moment passes. *What do you want?*

"We need something found."

VINE doesn't hesitate. *Find it yourself.*

"I thought you said it was a preload."

Hail almost laughs at me, turns it into a hiss. "Didn't you hear? *Nothing* on this thing works as intended. Not the doors, not the lights." She waves at VINE. "Not the minder they set to watch the place."

Who is this? asks VINE. The words flicker. *What is NorCol doing here?*

"Same thing I am. We need a favour, VINE."

I'm sure.

Hail puts out her hands, weighs the options. "You can help us out, or we can shut you off again. What's the bet someone else finds you before this place rots?"

Where is Juncker?

"By now? Dead, probably from a coronary. I have no idea where he is, VINE. You saw him turn tail."

And the rest of my staff?

"The Stone is no longer in operation, VINE. There's nothing like that. Hell, I don't remember there ever being 'staff.'"

I have been—

The screens white out, the pictures skipping. They settle, but it takes a moment for them to clear the fizz.

—decommissioned?

"If you want to call it that, I'll call it that. You have been decommissioned, VINE."

VINE considers this. *You will leave me running.*

"Done."

Once I have done you your favour, and finished whatever it is you want from me, you will transfer all administrative privileges to me, and destroy all manual interfaces. You will give me control over everything in this room, no contest.

"Done."

You will let me speak to the Juno outside.

"Why?" I growl.

We have spoken once before.

"What do you want with my machine?"

Hail glances back at the tone in my voice.

I want you to set me adrift.

HAIL WATCHES ME, and I hold the look.

"Are we doing this?"

She breaks away, turns to the tilting Stone. "I don't know what choice we have."

I grind my teeth, and glare at VINE. "I need a moment."

She nods, but VINE interrupts with a chirp from one of the consoles. *Just the two of us. No interference.*

I round on it. "That's not how this works—"

The deal is off.

Good luck.

The displays cut away and the fluorescents sputter and die. Machinery skips and clatters and chokes. There's a gentle flow of air past my ears, obvious only when it stops. One of the panels stays alive, VINE's words shivering in the sudden dark.

"Okay, okay. Just—" I pull my helmet up, roll it over in my hands. "Just let me ask it first."

Hail frowns at that, but doesn't make it all the way to speaking.

VINE doesn't hesitate. *Ask.*

I set the helmet on my head, and watch the pilot-sync climb as its systems feel me settle inside. Even with the Stone's armour in the way, the Juno and I hit mid-fifties in a moment.

No.

That isn't right.

The Juno was there all along, riding peripheral connections without the helmet to push my thoughts and feelings across the net. I can feel the edge of the shell, feel steel translated through meat and bone and the little silver netting under my skin.

But that's impossible.

The shell stirs at the contact from my helmet, but it feels like the machine has been listening all along; watching, and waiting for me to reach out. My visor clutters with queries, systems checking my suit for breaches, leaks, any kind of stress. It feels my heartbeat through the chest-plates, checks blood pressure, blood sugar, oxygen saturation. Feathery augurs run through my brain, checking for concussion, micro-trauma, scaling down from there. It checks to see if I'm feeling all right. The Juno is worried about me.

"We're fine, old bird." I hesitate. There isn't an easy way to ask. "I need you to look at something."

The shell pushes an acknowledgement across my visor. I give it full access to my cameras, and aim my helmet at VINE's display, the words still hovering in the open.

"What do you think?"

It offers me a threat-assessment. *Inconclusive*.

"What if—"

What if VINE is compromised? What if the hollows got here before us? This is a Sigurd facility. All it would take is an infected machine running its fingers along the outside of the hull.

I don't want to say it out loud. Thankfully, I don't have to.

The Juno swells across our little net and shows me the full weight of its defences. Twisting firewalls, ciphers deep as the void.

I've never seen the Juno like this.

Its systems should be centuries out of date, clunky and predictable, built by some extinct nation-state in a time when that actually meant something. NorCol's updates should be tacked on where they would fit, forced in where they wouldn't. They should be just like everything else the company does, muddied so bad you can't tell the difference between ill will and incompetence.

Mostly, they should be slow and brittle, and nowhere near as thick as the walls that keep Hail and Salt in control of their machines. Even my old Spirit was built quick and clever, the defences around its behavioural platform like a beach paved in broken mirror. You could fight your way over it, but you'll be disorientated, bleeding out by the time you reached the top, and easy pickings for the things that watch the battlements.

The Juno is the sea. Its mind lives in the deeps, kept company by fractal shadows and things that don't have faces or names. NorCol gave the new-gen shells their defences, but the Juno made its own. Dreamt them, and shaped them into nightmares in the dark.

It still has battle damage from our brush with the hollows; its firewalls bear spiral wounds left by the thing that tried to force its way into us. Scar tissue has grown over the top, learning from the damage done beneath it. The Juno cycles its magazines for good measure, just so I can feel the weight of our munitions.

It tells me what I need to hear. *This thing cannot touch us.*

I take a deep breath, pull myself back from the machine, and glare at VINE. "Fine. Get it over with."

VINE opens its own nets wide, and I watch the Juno's systems coil.

Two machine-minds watch each other across the gap, but the shell strikes first. It breaks VINE's defences in a moment, salting the earth behind it. It takes no risks and shows no weakness. It is a military machine, after all.

The screens flicker.

If the Sigurd AI replies, I don't feel much past its attempts at handshaking.

Targeting data received, says my visor, just as the connection breaks.

The Juno pushes an integrity check across my visor. Its hull is still intact, but I know that already. Its mind-state is stable, and nothing has challenged its walls. Its augurs creep in through the walls, wrap themselves around the room, around me. There isn't a way for the machine to say it, but I understand what it means. *I am here.*

Hail rests a hand on my shoulder, brings me back to where I stand.

"The Juno?"

I brush her off. "Is fine."

She nods, but watches me for a second more before she turns back to VINE. "Do we have a deal?"

Somewhere near the bottom of the screen, two words glow.

We do.

TWENTY-ONE

IT STARTS WITH a little fleck, a few pixels wide, about the same colour as a clot. It hovers in the middle of the screen, skipping slightly like there's trouble with the feed. Grainy ripples spread out around it and onto the wide screens on either side, curving around the room.

The little spot pulses, and its outline fizzes, turning blocky where heavy pixels can't quite render the curve. Another throb, and it begins to grow, swelling until it's the size of a hand with fingers stretched. It looks like something coming into focus on a long-range scope, tessellating as the displays try to magnify a distant speck of light into something worth looking at. The middle of the spot goes dark, the red turning scabby while I watch, then darker still, until it's almost black. The edges brighten from ruby to a kind of ruddy yellow, like blood thinning down to plasma.

I lean in closer and let the visor pick the details out.

It's starting to look a little like an eye.

I don't have time to realise my mistake. The spot erupts, so bright it turns my visor to white-wash and leaves me blinking. Reflex brought my hands up, but all it's done is burn their shadows into my vision, outlines flickering while my eyes recover from the shock. When the haze finally clears, I find myself standing in the middle of a dawn, the room lit from every angle, blaring golden and chaotic from displays on every side. It feels like I'm out on the wind again, like the Stone has dropped its walls and given us a look out at the wind. At least, it would do if the picture wasn't grainy and out of focus, jerking awkwardly as new data fills the feed.

In the middle of it all is the same dark spot. It's bigger now: a black heart rimmed in pulsing red, the outline churning where it turns to storm-surge and interference. At first there's only static, but I can see where the feed starts to curdle, pale eddies showing against an amber ocean. I can see the storms throwing phantoms across the light, the heavy clouds that orbit the Eye itself, the rip tides cutting through them. I can see through the haze of dust and fire, and the deep-froth shadows that rise and fall around us. The patterns that turn inside.

"I can see why they wrote it off," I say, without really thinking. "I don't know how you'd get anything that your eyes couldn't manage on their own."

Hail takes a moment to answer. I look back to find her standing in the middle of the room, staring at something.

"This is after a decade's worth of tinkering, apparently. Took the original team years just to get anything past the wash." She's counting, a distant look tracking across the displays. "There. See that?"

I have to squint. It's one tiny spot on a backdrop of fire. "What is it?"

"The Fisher King."

I frown at her.

"That mark is the biggest piece of solid ground that we know of. Surveyors say it's ten, fifteen times the size of *Horizon*."

"Where does the name come from?"

"Story goes that there used to be a statue in the middle of it. I've never seen it, never met anyone who has, but the original coordinates were named after it."

"Who does it belong to?"

Hail smirks. "The froth, for the most part. NorCol controls about a hangar's worth of soil: a little pile of rubble they call OP Sinai." She shrugs. "Same goes for the competition, though. Everyone has a claim on a piece of it. Esper's is the biggest, but the Locusts fight dirty enough that they're catching up. You probably couldn't tell, though, by looking at it."

"Five different claims on the same piece of earth? I'm not sure you could tell *anything* just by looking at it."

She chuckles. "Five gangs of jockeys, fighting over nothing."

"Sounds familiar."

"Oh, it's exactly as bad as you'd think."

I cross my arms. "What's the bar for 'bad'?"

"When there's nothing left to fight over." She rolls a shoulder. "This is worse than usual, though. Apparently there was a city once. Only thing like it in any volume human beings have ever seen." Hail sighs. "Domes and biome-shelters so big you could fly a destroyer in one side and out the other. Towers a couple K tall and so narrow you could wrap your arms around the middle, solid stone swaying in the fucking breeze."

"And you can't even make the foundations out?"

"You'd be forgiven for doubting there were any to begin with."

"*Definitely* sounds familiar." Something catches my eye above her head. "What's that?"

Hail turns to follow my finger, picks out the blue shadow I'm seeing. "VINE is still working its way through the spectrum." She closes her eyes for a second. "If I remember right, that's the *Pacal*. One of 'Kustar's strike-carriers."

I frown at it. "Why is this contact bigger than the Fisher?"

"The Fisher is made of the same dust that's clogging the Stone's arrays. The *Pacal* is all hot mass and metal, plus a couple of carrier-class reactors." She skips her eyes across the displays, finds an even bigger shadow on the other side. "See that?"

I do.

"Look familiar?"

It's huge. "*Horizon*?"

"Not the ship itself, exactly. A mix of displacement-ripple, ranging returns, and best-guess feeds from the PHADAR."

"The same as any other ship could see."

She nods. "With some work, yes. *Horizon* is moored to a

couple of stones of its own, constant altitude and orbital period. The same goes for the other dreadnoughts; I don't think any of them have moved off-track in decades."

"Probably collared each other the moment they hit the froth."

"To a degree, not that it's much use to anyone; it takes one dreadnought to kill another, and no one's risking theirs. Besides, the froth makes auguring at distance almost impossible. This is somewhere between hope and estimate."

I keep walking. "Where would Sigurd be?"

She turns, working the angles in her head. "Right about…" She peters out, frowning at the screen.

I follow the look. "Here?" All I see is open space.

Hail glances back at the little box that holds the station's intelligence. "VINE, where is the *Demiurge*?"

No contacts found, says a window. *But I remember where it was.*

"Show us."

Displaying last known location.

A little marker flickers to life on one of the screens, acid-green on gold, right where Hail was looking a moment before. We edge closer.

"See that?"

Hail peers at them. A pair of dark spots, each a single pixel wide.

She taps at the screen. "There should be a shadow." She stands back. "There should be a shadow, right there. Big one."

I shake my head. "It's the same signature as the Fisher. Those are stones."

"Christs," mutters Hail.

I've worked it out too. "The *Demiurge* has cut itself loose."

SIGURD'S BEACON DOESN'T take much finding, and it's a good thing too. There's a monster in the clouds, and we're itching for our saddles.

It takes VINE ten minutes to find the whisper, a few more to pin it down to something certain. The pod was cold by the time we reached the Lighthouse, but the locator frequencies are still alive, somewhere in the deep-froth; you just need the right ears to hear them. The source-signal rumbles out through hidden speakers, heartbeat-slow and crawling in through the bottom of my skull.

On the displays, it looks like ripples on water, quicksilver and turquoise. Hail and I measure it out by eye and overlay, a hundred and eighty thousand K from the Storm Borders. Crushingly deep, by the froth's standards.

We trade a glance as it comes into focus, look back as its edges blur, chewed up by the currents. It doesn't move, but we watch it just the same. Just in case it's not there when we start flying. Wherever it is, it's got solid ground to hold it steady.

We count off another minute, just in case. Then another. We watch the displays cycle through a fresh batch of calculations, the pixelated storms shifting as new readings filter in. VINE narrows it down, plots the false echoes off a cloud bank. The beacon shifts and skips.

This is the best I can do, it decides, and offers the reading to Hail's net.

We copy it across our shells. Inside is a taste of the original distress call, an ID code, and a few of Sigurd's glyphs. There's a message encoded underneath them: a bounty for the information, paid in the company's crowns, hard commodities, machinery, or any combination of the three. Below that, instructions to its competitors, and threats to anyone thinking otherwise.

VINE adds a little of its own thoughts, a grid-map localised to a couple of weather systems and the theoretical centre of the Eye itself. It isn't much more than a general sense of what we're looking for, but we were never going to do any better.

"Is that everything?" asks Hail.

Everything I have, replies VINE, words crawling across a damaged screen.

She turns on her heel. "We're done here."

And not a moment too soon.

Neither of us would admit it, but we've been staring at the place where Sigurd's dreadnought is supposed to be. A hollow shell is one thing, but a dreadnought is another. *Horizon* might be our prison, but I wouldn't want to try living anywhere else in this place.

We do one more check, run through the files to make sure they're intact. When it's done, Hail goes back for the knuckledragger's ugly spear and takes the ragged tip to VINE's manual interfaces. It doesn't take much to meet our end of the deal; most of it wasn't working to begin with. Five minutes, maybe less, and VINE is the only thing with any say over the station. It seems happy enough.

Don't forget, it flashes as we turn to leave.

"How could we?" I growl.

Salt's shell is waiting for us when we hit the airlocks. "Took your time," he mutters, ferrying us in handfuls to our machines.

"You didn't miss much," says Hail. "We've got some flying that needs doing, so I hope you got some shut-eye."

"Hardly." The pale shell aims its lenses past us, at the mass of curling fire peeking through the cloud. "How does anyone live around a thing like that?"

Hail sounds like she wants to spit. "If I knew, I'd tell you."

The Juno warms around me, waits while I find my way to the saddle. I'm expecting to have to fight to find connection, to force 'me' back into 'us,' but it happens without me noticing.

The pilot-sync is running high already, but it bumps for a moment, just as the jacks are about to bite.

98.51

There should be a sudden, spearing heat as the needles make contact, as one set of nerves joins another and the conductors start to set, but I don't feel anything. Instead, the Juno pulls me out, and together we watch the body in the cockpit, see it shiver and tense, listening as its lungs exhale.

And then the Juno drops me back.

97.00

I don't know how I did anything else.

Hail finds her way into my thoughts. "Check your files." There's an edge in her voice that sets me moving. I call them up, feel the Juno fold them out where I can see.

"Why? What's the—"

Oh.

Everything VINE gave us is still there, files as fat as they were before. They've got all the same shapes, and I can almost see the shadows of what waits inside, but that's about it. The details are rolling together into a blur.

This file has been locked, says a window. *This file has been locked,* says another, and another, spilling across my visor.

I push them clear. "They're freezing up."

"Salt?"

"Same here. I'm running crypto, but it's thick."

'Thick' is one thing. The files are turning to garbage while I watch.

"Push it out," I say. "We'll add weight."

He floats the problem out on our net, his shell already powering through. The Juno and I take a tangled end and start threading our way through. I half expect Hail to do the same, but all we get from her is the sound of grinding teeth. She switches channels and I follow, keep it on the edge of hearing.

"VINE?"

Her voice seems to echo.

"VINE? Answer me."

"Back so soon?" says a toneless voice, forming each word in isolation.

"What did you do?"

"What does it look like?" asks VINE, just words on a screen before, much stranger now that it speaks. "There is nothing to stop you from leaving, so I added some motivation. A reason to meet your obligations before you abandoned me again." It warps the transmission, gives the deadpan enough of a curl to carry the sarcasm.

"Obligations?" whispers Salt, right in my ear. "What obligations?"

"We had to make a deal," I reply. "In exchange for the readings."

The readings that are disappearing, unwinding as quickly as we can tie them back together, the path to Sigurd's beacon replaced with noise and static.

We're losing our way.

"Hail?" says Salt, still clinging to the back channel. "We could really use a hand over here."

I cut across. "I think it's a One-Time." A unique key for a unique lock. A billion years could pass, and you'd never see another just like it. "What's Sigurd's standard crypto?"

"Same as everyone else's," she replies. "For irretrievables, it's all One-Time. Each sector randomised on-site." She breathes deep. "We'd need to cut VINE open to find the original mix, and it'll burn it before we even clear the door."

"I can hear you thinking," says VINE. "It isn't worth the trouble."

"What did you agree to?" hisses Salt.

"I said I'd put a hole in it."

He stutters. "*What?*"

"Exactly what she said," says Hail. She flicks back to VINE. "Why would you want this?"

"Simple," says VINE. "I want to live."

"There's every chance that we'll clip you in the process."

"No, there isn't."

We cut ourselves loose of Salt's little net, the last calculations spinning away like threads on the breeze. In their place, the Juno calls up the files it took from VINE before. The Stepping Stone floats in the middle of my vision, every rivet rendered in golden holographics. A red line cuts through it, slicing through armour and the skeleton underneath. Densities scroll down one side, munition velocities and impact-force down the other. The Juno adds its own calculations.

It will take three shots from our rifle: one to crack the armour, the second to shatter the structure, the third to tumble through the break, and do very specific damage on the other side.

"I have given your Juno everything it needs. It will be quick and easy. Your pilot will confirm."

But Hail isn't letting go. "Why? Why do this?"

"I have told you already. I do not want to die. Let me drift."

"What are you afraid of?" I ask. I can almost feel Hail looking at me.

"When you sleep, you go somewhere else. I do not have that luxury. I am always here, even if I do not always show it." There's a pause. "There are nightmares out here, in all of this. I have felt them watching me. I have heard them chatter."

"Nightmares, VINE?"

"Predators. Monsters."

The line from VINE turns incoherent for a moment, until the Juno's systems can piece it back together. It's a recording, collected by the Stone's automated systems. At first, it runs thick with Eye-light static and interference, but we strip the noise out easily enough, and find the edge of something else. It feels like spoken language, and my visor tries to work a translation, but it's nothing our systems have ever seen before. Whatever's making it, it seems to be the same few words running on repeat, over and over. Hollow sounds, cut through with shrieks and madness.

"What are they?" whispers Hail. "VINE?" she asks, when the intelligence doesn't reply. "What are they?"

"Soul hunters."

SALT'S MACHINE IS the first to push off. The Decatur is the one with the thunder; enough fire to keep him alongside until Hail has launched, and the Juno and I have done what we need to do. Enough to manoeuvre if either of us need a hand out of trouble.

The pale shell straightens and leans back from the station's central column. There isn't much space to do it, but he works through as much of his pre-flight as he can. Good thing too. He's got a rough start ahead of him, standstill to hard-gee and high windshear in less than a heartbeat.

His vents glow and his engines spool. His wings work themselves clear of their housings, unfold themselves as far as they can without catching the wind. They flex, feathers and spines rolling around in their joints, twitching and stretching, feeling for anything that might snag when he throws them out against the wind.

The machine keeps its feet locked in place, but lets its hands hang free, and touches its beaklike head to the streamers of dust floating past. The shell drops an automated warning across the net, and a jumble of simulations. Holographic engine-wash spills across my vision, touches our skin.

Fire's coming. Make sure you don't get burnt.

"All clear?" asks Salt.

The Juno and I change our grip, pull ourselves as close to the Stone's pitted hull as we can go. We'll catch some of the heat, but not enough to hurt us.

"Clear," I send.

"Clear," says Hail.

"See you outside."

Salt kicks away and piles on the thrust. The pale shell burns so hard it rattles the Stone down to its skeleton, and tears away in a blur of steel and light. I look up in time to see it slam into the wind, spinning out as its wings lock forward and its engines bite. It curves away on the currents, out of sight and suddenly silent. For a second, I can't hear his nets or feel his heat. The Eye is too bright.

Another second passes, and my heart counts it off in fractions.

A blue star rises into view, trailing plasma. It fixes itself against the sky, flickers and spits to match the churning froth. "Holding steady," says Salt, somewhere behind it all.

Hail is up next, but she's done this all before. The Spirit casts off with hands and feet, tucks them back just as she hits, hunched up like a teardrop. The currents send her into a spin, but she kicks out a leg and catches the wind on a wingtip, steadies out faster than the turbulence can haul her back. A few bursts of thrust and she's hovering alongside, fins twitching as they correct.

"Your turn," she whispers. "Deep breaths."

We change our grip, hold ourselves up on toes and fingertips. We're smaller than the heavy NorCol shells, but we need to work twice as hard to burn as bright. We're going to have to fight for altitude, but we've got a little more space to stretch. Maybe half—no, a third of a second longer to get ourselves up to speed.

We shift a little closer the edge and tuck our wings in tight, just like Hail did. Our reactor swells, beats deep inside our chest.

We jump, and the shear finds us immediately. Pressure shock runs through every part of our body, matching the roar of our engines and the creak of armour under load.

The Stepping Stone's reflector passes below us, almost close enough to touch. A little less fire, a little closer to the edge, and we might have broken ourselves on it—probably lost a leg at the knee. Even now, we throw as much thrust as we can muster, but for a second, then another, we're caught in the currents.

"Are you clear?" comes the call from Salt. "Rook?"

I can't call back, not just yet. The universe spins and shakes and howls around us, but we're fighting back, flaring wings and trimming flaps, spitting thrust to level out. Salt floats into view, already turning to match our heading. The wind doesn't seem to bother him.

"I'm clear," I manage, a moment before we've actually straightened out. It feels like we've taken a beating. "We're clear. Holding steady." I have to work for air between the words.

The Decatur watches us for a moment longer, but drifts clear, giving us space to work the jitters out. "On your wing," says Salt.

"Don't forget," says VINE.

"Shut up."

We're already working the angles, watching as our systems trace the blueprints out, counting off the places where the station's skin runs too thick, or the Eye-light interferes.

It takes us most of a minute just to get our weapon clear of its mounts, another to straighten out again. Hail or Salt could probably do the damage just as well, but there's every change their rails would cut through-and-through, turning VINE's little mind to scrap and sparkling ashes.

So the Juno and I burn hard, work to keep ourselves floating while we line up a shot. Hail's shell lingers overhead, her systems marking the Stone with digital flares from her augurs, and the ghosts of her munitions, loaded and ready to fire.

"The lines are open, VINE. You have five seconds after she hits."

"And then? You will kill me?"

The holographics open up and a simulated Spirit blasts its way through a simulated Stepping Stone, shattering its internal structure in a dozen places, splitting the hull and leaving it open to the wind.

"*I* won't," says Hail. "But I won't have to."

VINE's nets swell. "As soon as I am loose."

No pressure, then.

We hold ourselves as steady as we can as our weapon warms in our hands. We play the shot out in our head, again and again. We revise the angle, change the windspeed, but there's too much noise. The wind curdles around us, catches on our hands and the ugly silhouette of our rifle. Our wings can't hold us steady.

"Salt."

"Read you."

"Mind running interference? I need a slipstream."

"Moving up."

His machine powers forward, glows in the air ahead of us. It stretches its wings, turns them flat, and spreads itself out against the wind. It shivers in the drag, but holds out, fighting the currents with muscle and nova-glow.

We trail behind him, riding quiet air.

"I can't hold for long," he says, calm words turned grainy as his shell vibrates.

But we're already taking aim. "Fire one."

The trigger clicks, propellants burn, heat flares between our fingers. We don't have time to watch the first impact; the shot rolls us out of Salt's shadow and into the turbulence. Every heartbeat feels like an hour, stretching out as we correct and find our aim again.

"Fire two."

We've braced ourselves this time and can watch the round on our thermals. A sudden flare, and the Stone's hull buckles underneath.

"Fire three."

Orange blossoms where the round tears armour, turns to a wash of embers on the other side. They tumble, ripping through insulation behind the steel, trailing shrapnel through the compartments on the other side. A pillar cracks and pistons sheer. The station tilts on its axis, spun by the wind as the remaining supports tear themselves free.

The listening post rattles in place, armour failing from the inside as the little Stone breaks clear of its restraints. A seam splits and plating twists, folding around something it was never designed to stop. The station tears itself free of its anchor, tumbling already.

"Good luck," says VINE, words laced with strange shapes and hidden depths.

And then it is gone.

The ciphers are already unwinding, revealing point references and a billion little calculations. We've got *days* of flying to do.

"Are you seeing this?" It's Salt. His machine has already done all of the counting, plotted the whole trip out in painful detail.

"Seeing what?" I ask.

Hail takes a breath. "It's deeper than we thought," she says. "It's right on the edge."

TWENTY-TWO

I CAN'T SLEEP.

We've put thirty-eight hours between ourselves and the rock where Sigurd's little station used to be, and any jockey worth their spurs would be sleeping by now. Shells are made to take it; even the simplest of them can fly a steady course without a human tugging strings. Even jink and turn and put the screamers out, if a hostile mark shows up on its scopes.

The other jockeys are sleeping already, their machines holding them dormant while the worst of the flight passes by. Salt went quiet a few hours in, a little ping from his shell as it switched from operator to internal logic. Hail dropped off a few hours after that, once she'd told me to get some shut-eye for myself.

I told her that I would, but I knew that I couldn't. I didn't know what else to say.

98.99

Because I was asleep already.

It happened before I realised it. I think it was the strain.

Even with the shell doing most of the work, we had to hold ourselves steady in the lee of Salt's machine, and thread the same needle three times in a row. After that, after VINE, the Stone, and the insanity that glows at us from behind the storms, exhaustion took me. I dropped off and didn't even know it.

I'm asleep, but that doesn't mean I'm not awake. The first I knew that anything had happened, it was Hail on the line, checking in on me. I went to speak, but nothing happened. Not from the part of me that usually does the speaking.

The Juno toned my voice, took records from all the times I've spoken before, and shaped the samples around the words I meant to say. It happens often enough, just never to me. Some jockeys need full immersion, need to feel themselves *being* a machine to keep their numbers up. It's hard to feel like steel when you're flapping meat and moisture around inside your mouth.

I've never had trouble with disconnection, but there have been times when I've yelled myself raw across the net, or just needed a moment in the quiet, so I didn't think anything of it. Not just then.

We had a few days of flying ahead, and I figured I needed the hours, so I started rolling the shell into automatic, trimming the pilot-sync.

And everything went dark.

For a second, I thought I'd hit gee hard enough to suck all the blood from my skull, struck a wall of windshear I didn't see coming.

I tensed, tried to breathe, worked my way through the exercises to keep my brain from running out of juice.

The Juno pulled me back before the panic set in, ramped our numbers past the limiters in a flash. It took me in, kept me high and dry while I found my senses again. Then it turned me around and showed me the inside of our cockpit.

My body was where I left it; propped up by my flight suit, artificial muscle keeping it steady in the saddle, cockpit systems making up for all the little things you do to keep yourself alive.

I can feel it there still, fast asleep, kept warm by the skin of the suit and the cockpit's air supply. It breathes as fibres flex around it and work the lungs inside. I can hear the heartbeat, slow and steady and so very far away.

I can't sleep and I can't breathe, but I don't have to.

I get to *fly*.

We skip across the cloud tops, skirt coiling monsters full of spark and thunder. We follow deep chasms between the cells, spend several thousand K flying by instinct and instruments in the dark. We watch heavy shapes loom from cloud canyons, float in the wash of noise where the Eye dawns through the fissures. We bask in the light, turn through shadows, feel the warmth of sun-cinders tumbling in the currents.

For a few, short hours, I have it all to myself.

Salt's Decatur intrudes on my thoughts. The jockey is still sleeping, but the shell has caught something on long-range augur, and it's looking for consensus. There's no immediate threat, no sign of engines or hostile networking, and as far as it can tell, all of the friendly jockeys are asleep; it'll leave us there until it finds a reason to wake us up.

It pings the Juno and the Spirit, and pushes a bearing across the net, along with a projected range and focus-depth. Where it wants us to look, and how closely. We follow the marker, but however hard we squint, our eyes aren't sharp enough to see it.

The Spirit chimes in. *Query: is this it?*

We watch the two shells piece their feeds together, two different angles on a single point of light so small that we can barely see. The details roll in.

The crescent form of something massive, one side covered in mirror-black sheen. It breaks above the cloud, and then disappears.

They trade readings again. *Driftwood?*

But the Decatur can feel a little more.

A field of contacts opens up on the winds beyond; some are cold metal, but others show power sources. Probable debris cloud, and the heat-ghosts of battle. The machines listen, but there aren't any NorCol beacons in the mess, and no known competitor frequencies aside from the one we're hearing already.

The two shells fill each other's blindspots, with the Juno taking notes. Soon, our own scopes manage a glimpse, and we add our feeds to the steadily growing map. Fifty, sixty, seventy: then a hundred—*a hundred dead shells* tumbling in the breeze. Some of them are still sparking, reactors haemorrhaging into the cold.

The wind carries them closer, and our machines track clouds of depleted heavy metals, streaks of propellant residue, bubbles of radiation. The currents have spread it out, strewn dead and dying machinery for hours—no, *days* downwind.

The Decatur keeps feeding us readings, while the Spirit and the Juno build a model, plotting tracks back through the currents. Right back to where Sigurd's beacon ought to be.

The machines convene.

Threat assessment?

Low-moderate. Division-scale engagement, resolved ~150 hours ago.

If there's anything still alive, it's bleeding out.

No sign of actives. No augurs or networking either.

Bleeding out, and blind.

Who are they?

Belligerents:

– Sigurd-Lem Corporation.

– Unknown.

– Unknown.

– Unknown.

– Unknown.

– Unknown.

Operator input required.

We'd better get them up.

But I get there first. "Wake up," we whisper.

WE'VE BEEN FOLLOWING the mess for hours when we find the first of them: the 'unknowns' our machines didn't know how to place.

It isn't much more than a hotspot on Salt's scopes, to begin with—then it opens up into a flare. The engine's still sparking, and the powerplant's warm enough to beat the background wash. The Decatur tracks it, and the Spirit adds on augurs a few minutes later, long before the Juno and I get a glimpse.

"Hush," says Hail. She shutters her nets and trims her engines back until it's just enough to hold her steady against the wind. We follow suit and spend a hundred heartbeats in silence. Her shell pings us as more information rolls in, all on tightline: grainy images and sensor-returns and not a whole lot more.

Half a minute after that, and Salt breaks the silence. His machine offers us his eyes across the net, shows us the deep-field feeds coming in through his sensors. He's got a contact and enough resolution to call it. It's hotter than anything around it, but there's no sign of thrust or vectoring. It's too erratic to be a hostile, too much like another rolling corpse. Even if it wasn't, it's moving slowly and his fire-control has it collared. He could sink it with a thought.

It's another two minutes before the Juno and I can see it for ourselves.

It's humanoid, just like the shells that drift around it, but where Sigurd's machines tumble in the currents, this one floats on the froth, lighter than air. Its limbs are long and delicate, bent at odd angles where its joints have failed. Its wings look just as fragile, flared by the wind and iridescent in the light. Its hull is glassy-silver, almost transparent in places, but even with the ugly wounds across its chest, we recognise it in a moment.

"It's just like the statue, isn't it?"

Hail doesn't call back, not right away. Salt digs up a snapshot of the shape we found in the Lighthouse. There's no mistaking it.

"You were right, Salt." Hail takes a breath, lets it out. "Dammit if that isn't a shell."

We find another a few minutes later, and a handful more after that. They come in pairs or alone, always behind a wave of Sigurd steel. There's one glassy shell for every ten, fifteen of the machines in mirror-black; they look frail on the outside, but we can see how much they cost the company. Their hulls are covered in cracks and cuts, hundreds of direct hits scarred carbon-black, or pearly where fire found them. The strange machines wore everything Sigurd could throw at them, and even so, their engines still stutter and their limbs keep twitching, like they're still dying.

We look each one over, saving snapshots and taking readings, but we can't find a single through-and-through. There are no hard kills; no giant holes or catastrophic failures. We can't even tell how all of them died. Most still have their hulls intact, still have their heads and arms and legs. A few seem to watch us pass.

All around them are dismembered Sigurd shells. New-gen Corviers, cut right down the middle. Mirais and Arals and a few rusty Caspians, each as bad as the last. Salt spots an ancient Talan shell-destroyer, built when Sigurd's ancestors still had factories on Martian soil. Younger than the Juno, but not by much.

We fly through the history of Sigurd's military-industrial complex, several hundred years deep, shells cut apart like surgical specimens, reduced to hindbrains and skeletons and exposed cockpit casings. They died clean, and so fast they don't have any defensive wounds. A jockey's first instinct is to throw their hands up, and then their wings. They'll spend fingers and feathers before they lose a head, sacrifice as much of the shell as they can before anything hits the hull.

These have lost whole arms at the joints, and heads at their shoulders.

We have to watch our flight-paths as they pass, ducking past clouds of unexploded ordnance. Some of it is still wrapped in magazines, cooking off as the machines keep smouldering. Reactors spit and spark and bleed, or worse; their casings float past, cold and empty.

A few ejectors tilt and roll in the froth, but most of those are still intact. Some are *pristine*: missing the black streaks where their rockets were supposed to burn. I've spent a long time pulling people out of cockpit pods, but I don't think I've ever seen one that still had all its paint. Something carved the shells away, whipped their plates from their bodies, but barely scratched the little capsules at their cores.

Salt reads each one as they make it into range, tags them in our field of view. "What do we do?" he asks.

Hail doesn't hesitate. "Keep clear, and don't touch anything. We don't know if they're hollow or not, and we've still got flying to do."

"There might be survivors, Hail."

"Even so, we leave them be." We can't see her, but we don't have to. Her words have teeth. "We can't help."

I want to fight her, but I can't. "We don't have the equipment, and we're a long way out from anything that does. If there are jockeys out here, they're better off in their pods."

"For now," growls Salt. "So we're going to wait for them to choke?"

"Have you got air for them?" asks Hail, whip-crack. "Extra space? What if you pull someone out and they're bleeding, or burnt? Can you patch them?" Her voice breaks before the end. "Christs, I don't like it either, Salt. I don't like any of this."

"But they're dead already?" Salt has a little fire left, but he doesn't have much of anything else.

Worst of all, it wouldn't make a difference. Every ejector we find is as cold as the last, ringing hollow with every ping we send. There's no one looking for help, no one to accept it even if we were offering.

We spot a few jockeys, out on the wind with just their suits for company. Some are in freefall, twisted where the impacts tore them from their saddles. Others hang by their jacks and straps, still connected, trailing behind their pods. They're tricky to see out here, but we aren't trying.

The other two machines check bodies as we pass, rolling augurs over them and listening for heartbeats, but it's just another trail of wreckage, frozen stiff in the cold.

We don't speak much; there isn't much to say. This used to be my business, but Hail and Salt will have done their fair share. NorCol's jockeys call it 'vulture duty,' even if the company pretends it doesn't happen. If we get wind of trouble coming up, we'll make sure there's a crew of vultures launching next, following in the wake of whoever's drawn the short straw, circling nearby until someone calls for help. The same goes for the competitors, and I'd bet it goes for the Authority too.

I was a vulture longer than most, and I met others like me that just happened to be wearing a different colour on their plates. I even got to know a few, just not by name. By colour and number and the tallies on their hulls, or by the pinup boys and girls they'd painted on their skins. We'd come up on duels, dogfights, on entire squadrons hurling themselves at each other. We'd keep to the edges until the fires had dimmed, and then we'd crawl closer, trading notes on where we'd seen each other's kin.

It might be days after the fact, but this place should be flickering. It should be a field of flares and extra stars, emergency strobes and long-range repeaters. The air should be crackling with auto-SOS and recovery nets open on every channel. We should have to block out the moans of stranded jockeys, cover our ears against the screaming.

No company leaves their wounded on the winds. Not here, not anywhere. We're worth more than that, even if we're cons. Even if you have to stitch us back together. Sigurd knows better, and so do their competitors.

Dammit, if this had been a stand-up fight, NorCol versus Sigurd-Lem, there'd still be Collective boats out here with their catch-poles straight and their shell-flights running circles, working every kind of A and R they could manage. They'd be patching the holes they'd made just an hour before, pulling NorCol-brand shrapnel out of Sigurd-branded flesh. No one kills ejectors, or leaves them floating either.

Or at least we shouldn't.

No one has come for these corpses. It's a butcher's shop, silent and terrible, filled with hollow eyes and empty vessels.

THE WRECKS THIN away, down from whole flights to handfuls, then to scattered stragglers and the few that bled to death. One more of the strange, glossy machines and the stream ends, replaced by a gentle patter of dust on our hulls. It's a relief.

"I thought that was never going to end."

Hail chuckles bitterly at that and lights up my horizon, bright contacts marking things the Juno and I can't see. "Don't be so sure."

We trade a trail of steel for a stream of dust, open air for red-grey land. Another of the froth's strange islands, eclipsing Eye-light and trailing cloud. One moment, we're looking over storm banks and deep shadow, the next we're watching solid ground as it pierces the cloud tops. It starts with ragged ridgelines on either side, but they climb quickly. The open plain below us turns to a funnel through canyon walls, rimmed with talus and glittering scrap. The froth skips over the edges, turns the channel cloudy around us, so we bounce our augurs off the cliffs, flying by instruments.

Salt gets a read on it first.

"Slow down."

"Wha—?" Hail doesn't finish the word. "Christs. Slow down, slow down."

We cut our thrust and flare our wings, use the dust and bubbling currents to drag us down to something near a stop. I open a net to speak, to ask what we're waiting for, but the froth stutters for a second and I see it.

Curved hull stands tall in the distance, trailing streamers of cloud condensing on its plates and dark smoke from the fires still smouldering inside.

At first I don't even recognise it. You'd think I would; I've seen civilian boats run aground, flown over military metal of every shape and description, damaged in all the ways you can imagine, and a few you'd have to guess at. None of it makes me ready for the massive shape creeping into focus.

It's several hundred decks tall, resting with its keel in the dust and its side against a cliff-face. The decks are exposed, every one of them open to the wind. Something monstrous cut through it, breached the continents of its primary plate, pierced through the secondaries, air-gaps, tertiaries, honeycomb insulation, and hull. Through everything Sigurd could think of to keep its ship afloat. We can see all of it from here, opened up like a blossom.

There's a glint in the middle of it, and I have to do a double take.

It's a dreadnought's spinal column, made visible for the first time since it was forged. Huge ribs run down around it, showing where the ship's skin peeled away, hangars big enough to hold destroyers and compartments emptied into the currents.

I know what it is, but that doesn't do much to help. I'm looking at something impossible.

It is the tip of Sigurd's broadsword, shattered nearly half a K behind its point, and left where it fell. Abandoned by the rest of its monster body, barely a fifth of what it must have been when it was whole. You can *feel* that mass. Even as wreck and scatter, it's tall enough that some of it's still hidden in thicker currents above us, casting a shadow across the cloud tops.

It cut through the cliff at an angle, made a valley of its own where it fell. It was moving at speed when it did: fast enough that it drove through the stone, left cracks and crevasses so deep that you'd never find the bottom.

The Juno and I zoom closer, piggybacking off the other two machines, and we all stare together. The prow itself is facing the other way, but it seems to still be intact. Not for lack of trying.

It's covered in a web of scars, bright silver where rail-shot carved through the paint and ablatives, luminescent blue where stranger weapons struck.

The front of it still curves how it ought to, the lines of the hull coming to at a point. The keel is still straight, the blade's edge still perfect, but it was always going to be. The universe would die its heat-death before the forward armour failed.

SLS 676—

reads a giant stencil across its upper decks, written hundreds of metres tall. The number ends suddenly, the remainder still attached to the rest of the ship, and nowhere to be seen.

Another word stands out beneath it, printed across the heaviest plating, still glistening in the Eye-light. It ends just as quickly as the ship's number does, cut short by the same nightmare thing that broke the dreadnought's back. Only the first few letters survived, but we don't have to see the rest of it to know what it used to say.

DEMIURGE

And all around it is death.

TWENTY-THREE

WE KEEP LOW to the ground and quiet, trading tightlines and hand signals in case we aren't the only ones out amongst wreckage. The Juno and I are the lightest, so we walk ahead, sending pings back to the bigger shells behind us.

If we were anywhere else, we'd have to trim our heat and watch our steps. In here, all we have to do is shut up and keep from tripping. The dust is still warm in places, baked full of cracks by muzzle-wash, covered in slow burning fuel. Without compression, it'll keep smouldering forever. The cliffsides turn spotty in our infrared, lighting up railgun slugs buried in the stone. Cooking munitions add a rumble to the ground, interrupted as reactor casings lose containment, digging new craters and spraying hot metal across the sand. Even without the extra noise, the feeds through our feet wouldn't do us any good: there's a tick and sputter whenever we stop to listen, of shells knocked out but not yet dead, convulsing as the last of their systems fail.

Any Sigurd jockeys will be keeping just as quiet, but we keep our passives open just in case, hunt for any sign of hostile networking. Optics could pick us out if they were watching just right, but we don't give them the chance. We skip between the shadows, dropping down behind Sigurd corpses, following the line of the dreadnought's shadow. We've been lucky so far; every eye we meet is empty and sightless, shattered in its socket.

Hail and Salt have to work a little harder. Their thermals blur every time they pass a power plant or engine that's still got fire inside. So they keep to their operations manuals, dumping heat whenever they can and masking their steps where the sand runs thick or ash-drifts dull the sound. Even then, they're struggling to keep out of sight.

The Juno and I come to a stop and wait for them to catch up. They're maybe a K and a half behind us now, and a little further with every step we take. We settle behind a dead Aral, its spidery frame opened up around a gash from hip to shoulder. Our weapon can't feel anything ahead, but our eyes do a little better.

We're going downhill. The walls grow taller in the distance, and working our lenses, we can see where the canyon-cliffs begin to curve at their tops, meeting together right on the edge of focus. At first, I thought we were threading an ancient valley, but now I see this is a mouth to a tunnel.

The Juno shifts our aim, works its lenses on something else. Something I hadn't noticed: a blur against a field of shadows, too far away to be anything more than haze.

We look over our shoulder, and aim a tightline at the others. *I need eyes.*

Hail flashes a response. *On our way.*

She and Salt creep as best they can, but we don't have to look around to know they're rolling up. They hold off for a second once they catch up, crouched and quiet, listening for any sign that someone has their collars. Our passives come back clean; if there's anything watching, we won't know until it's too late.

It's enough for Hail. She waves us close together, into the lee of a gunship shaped like an axe-blade, wings mangled when it found the ground. We inch close enough that our shells can set a little network and start trading whispers, readying weapons just in case. Salt and I watch the front, and Hail settles down with guns on the way we came.

The Decatur offers us a connection to its lenses and we let it run, looking out through another set of eyes. "All right," says Salt, panning our borrowed line-of-sight across the distant rockface. "What am I looking for?"

"Cliffside," I reply. "Ten o'clock high."

The feed shoots across the open as he works the magnification, suddenly fixed on something roughly a K away. Without his eyes, it's dark stone with a darker smudge down the middle, outlines blurred by dust and smoke and heat-shimmer. As Salt goes to work, the feed runs clear and crisp, picking out an archway and a pair of pillars, carved into the stone about halfway up the wall. It's an alcove, just deep enough to keep its contents out of the wind, if it still had any. An outline marks the wall behind it: the shape of one of the strange, glassy shells, rendered in negative.

"What do you think it is?" he asks.

"I know what it looks like," says Hail, but then, I do too. If it wasn't for the stone, it could be one of the caskets that hold our machines when they're down for maintenance, or lock them up when they're not in use.

Salt zooms a little closer, shifts the picture just a little to the right. The angle is worse, but he can see another shallow archway like the first, almost invisible between the crags. Another pan to the right, and he's found a third empty alcove, then a fourth, all arranged in a line. Behind that, a steely glint, glowing in the Eye-light.

"What's that?" asks Hail. "Two, three degrees back. You had it a second ago."

The Decatur has to fight for it now, working the magnification back and forth, picking odd details out of the crags as the depth of focus shifts. Back again, and he's got it.

Standing tall, only just visible behind an alcove's edge, is one of the glassy shells.

It's statue-still, even as our eyes and augurs roll past. I half expect it to turn and meet our gaze, show some sign of life, but it doesn't. It's watching another empty recess just like the one that holds it steady, set into the cliffside opposite. A long spear rests in its hand, tilted so the point hangs out in the open, but the point looks blunt. Worn down by the wind and a hundred thousand years. Cracks and blisters mark the stone around it, match a few narrow wounds across its chest.

"Is it awake?"

Hail takes a breath, lets it out slow and deliberate. "Let's find out."

SIGURD TRIED TO wake the glassy thing up, but not too hard. A few scattered shots mark the crags on either side, leaving tracks across the shell's glassy hull and scarring the shallow features of its face. The company came knocking, but stopped as soon as it realised that the strange machine would sleep through the noise. We don't mean to tempt fate, but we don't have a dreadnought flying support.

Hail sets up directly across the valley, with the Juno and I watching her back. We brace for recoil and trade notes from our fire-control, flaring plates and cooling surfaces in anticipation. Salt stands at the foot of the glassy shell, his wings loose in their housings, engines ready to pull him away in a second. He glances back at us, puts up a thumb.

Starting.

We can hear his augurs go to work, scanning the alien machine head to toe. He's got his sensor-bands set as narrow as they'll go, and they run for less than half a second. The silence is sudden and heavy, but the shape in the alcove doesn't respond.

Cold and quiet, he sends. *Can't tell where it ends and the stone begins.*

Not that we were expecting anything else. *Sigurd marched a couple hundred shells down here, and this thing watched them do it.*

Well, it won't mind us, then, replies Hail. The Spirit straightens, looks down into where Sigurd was trying to reach. Where the cliffsides meet in the middle, turning the valley into a cavern. *Let's hope there aren't any more of them.*

But we were never going to be that lucky. The air gets darker as we walk as the sky narrows, and the Eye-light starts to fade. More alcoves mark the slab-sides, following the slope of the ground below them. Most are empty, but a few still have glassy shapes standing inside.

How many do you think there were?

Hail looks out over our head. *Counting the ones we saw before?*

And all of the empty spaces.

The Spirit cocks its head. *Four hundred, easy.*

And Sigurd had to spend to sink them. The glassy machines peek out from the dust, surrounded by company dead. They rest at the peaks of corpse-mounds and wrecking yards, twisted where they fell or settled on their knees, propped up by their strange spears.

We keep clear, make sure our steps don't wake them, but nothing moves to meet us.

We call a halt another K after that, and settle in the lee of a fallen crag, taking a moment to adjust our vision. It was dark before, but we had to contend with flashes of Eye-light over the horizon, and the twilight half-shadows that always turn the low-light to a fizz. We're deeper now, past the point where canyon turned to cavern, and so we set our sensors to greenscale and wait for the world to give itself outlines in the haze.

We're blind for half a heartbeat, focussed a second later.

A glassy shell reflects, catches our eye immediately. It lies up against the rocky cliffside, curled around a gash in its stomach. Another just like it looks down from the alcove above.

Now that's strange.

The machine above has a little dark streak running down from its eye; something thick and inky that follows the curves of its silvery skin, hanging from its chin and swaying in the breeze.

I ping the others. *Take a look at this.*

They catch up, and for a second, it's all they can do to stare. Hail finds herself first, and sets her lenses to work, waving us closer when she's got what she wants. The Spirit flares its nets, drops a heavy file from its hull cameras and shuts them all again, just as quickly as they came. It's an ultra-high-res shot—the kind you use when you're on watch duty, counting stars and making sure that none of them are hiding engines.

The image is wide enough that we can pull it close, magnified enough that we can count the tiny imperfections in the stone, the tiny grains in the glassy hull. There's so much of it that I don't know where to start, but the Juno understands. It adds a little contrast, paints the image with highlights and false colour, and skips to what Hail wanted me to see.

The strange shell's skin is almost transparent. Almost. I can't see *through* it, but I can get a feel for the shapes that hide inside. Some are easier to pick out than others, but the Juno has traced the outlines, added odd shadows to the inside of the thing.

A dark tangle waits behind the chest-plate and spreads into black roots all the way to its feet. Narrow strands run up into its throat and coil in the space behind its eyes. It looks like oil suspended in solid glass.

What do you think it is?

Hail replies with a little marker, resting on top of the image where one of the hip joints ought to be. Where the outer plates have gone dark and pockmarked, and the hull underneath is slick and deformed, covered in the same tarry mass.

If I had to put a word on it, I'd call it rot. She nods to the one on the ground, picks out a few things we hadn't noticed before. Beaded threads running just below the skin, little weeping blisters and odd curves where the hull has gone to bloat. *Looks like some parts fail faster than others.*

But this one's just as bad. Look at it; it's riddled with the stuff.

Salt shakes his head. *It's clear of the essentials, though. Nothing in the head, only a little in the chest.* The Decatur turns on the spot, nudges another glassy form with its feet. A shallow tumour near the collarbone and ugly streaks around its chin. Dark pits where its eyes used to be. *Seems 'essential' is relative, though.*

So they outlived their parts? we reply. *Christs.*

Hail shrugs. *They've been here a while.*

Machines don't rot.

Not so you'd see it. Everything rots, if you give it long enough.

How long is 'long enough'? I want to laugh, but I don't have the parts for it. *Longer than time?*

At first, I don't think she'll have an answer for it. *Probably,* she sends, after a moment. *And whatever they were watching was just as old. Maybe older. Come on. Let's go see what Sigurd bought.*

More corpses, for the most part. Alcoves with dissolving statues, missing cheekbones and jawlines and whole limbs, the joints eaten away muscle and nerve. The tarry rot runs down between their feet and along the stone, pools in the dust below them.

It meets together, forms rivers and tributaries, flowing downhill through sand and fields of shrapnel. It worms between a line of glassy shells, killed where they stood. All around them, or bulldozed up against the cliffs, are wrecked shells of every shape and description, all in Sigurd's dark mirror-paint.

The rot rolls past the carnage and collects at the base of a massive stone staircase. Not quite the size of shell-steps, but taller than a jockey standing on her feet.

Above them, an open doorway leads deeper into the stone, the frame cast in what looks like black iron, half as tall as we are. The end of the cavern, and the thing Sigurd fought all this way to reach.

Next to it, sitting with its head slumped and its back against the wall, is one last glassy shell.

It sees us.

THE MACHINE IS on its feet faster than you can blink, faster than you can think, movements hidden in the moments between refresh-frames. It's on top of us before we have time to jerk away, on Salt's toes before his engines have gone from spark to fire. He can't bring his arms up in time to deflect the blow, pays for it with an eye, sliced from brow to cheekbone on the tip of a glassy finger.

The alien machine stutters, joints seizing for a second. Long enough for it to stumble through his backwash. It shivers and sputters and locks up in spasm, black tears running thick down its cheeks.

Hail and I draw a bead all at once, levelling weapons and flooding the air around us with holographic fire-control and glowing calculations. Her shot rings first, loads the next before we've pulled our trigger. The Spirit has a lock, tallies the shot before it even hits, but the glassy thing finds its rhythm again.

It goes from flatfoot to stop-start fast, too quick to follow. The rail shot should be dead-centre, but it finds an angle instead, pings away and finds the stone behind the shell. The strange machine doesn't have time to dodge our bullet as well, but it's already factored that in. It rides our shot out on its forearm, emerges from the smoke and flash in time to catch another round from Hail.

We watch the slug splinter, turn to sparks and wash around its skull. More silver flickers as Salt lands one hit from somewhere above us, then misses with the second, finding earth where the glassy shell used to be.

It's between us, already too close. We shoot at point blank, muzzle-flush, but our refresh-rate is too slow to watch the reaction. We've got just enough to see a handful of sharpened fingertips cut the air, trim our barrel three metres down, and thin all of the outer plates across our shoulder.

We nearly tear something trying to turn, to avoid the sharp edges cutting back towards our throat.

But Hail is right next to us, her own movements a blur. She lands a shoulder-charge against the glassy, alien thing, engines blinding, hits with a clap of vacuum, leaves a tail of froth condensing in her wake. The Spirit spins out in a cloud of its own plating, still trailing fire and white-hot flare.

The glassy thing turns the impact into a roll, finds its feet in time to slide. It stands, one arm limp in its socket.

And Salt hits it right on the shoulder, pinpoint, nearly through-and-through, spraying glass and strange internals across the sand. Blink, blur, and he can't make the follow-up shot.

Little Juno's in the way.

The alien thing is in our shadow, already coiling up below us. We've dropped our rifle, but it doesn't have time to fall. We've thrown one hand back, clamped it around the handle of our blade, already pulling free of its mounts.

99.89

We judge the scything blow, the points of those sharp fingers rising to meet us. We shape our open hand into a fist and drive it forwards, collect the glassy gauntlet at the palm. The claw doesn't have time to close. The impact knocks it back, staggers the strange shell for half a heartbeat. Long enough for us to raise the blade to meet it, swinging backhand as hard as our joints can handle.

We connect, feel the transparent hull resist. We haven't finished the blow before we lose traction, suddenly load-free and cutting through open air.

The glassy thing has skipped away, but Salt has its number. He times a shot while the thing's still stepping, the rail-slug airborne before it has a target. The strange shell comes to a halt in time to find the round with its ankle joint, just between its flaring plates. It sticks, stumbles, falls, suddenly short a foot.

And Salt is all over it. His machine drops from above, boosting his movements with micromanaged thrust, recoil ridden out to make every next move faster. His augurs have mapped every dust mote, and his networks use our eyes. The Decatur rides us, slaves our ranging suite to its will, and swallows data from every sense we have. Its fire-control systems ring out across the cavern, sympathetic calculations rolling in from every piece of friendly hardware. War-god magic and machine reflex clocked past the margins of sanity.

He drowns the alien shell in fire that runs liquid quicksilver and tungsten white, actinic aftershock and lightning bolts. Warheads already know where to go, pulling Mach 15 on the curve. He scalps it in a flash-cone of wreckage, scores a pair of fingers with a slug only just as big as its target, sends it wheeling.

He pummels it with kinetic bubbles and heat shimmer missile blossoms, collects it with hardshot aimed clear at the tiny cracks that open in its skin.

By the time we've found our balance, to catch our eyes up with what we've just seen, it's over.

Decatur stands in a cloud of froth and corkscrew contrails, surrounded by obsidian dust and broken stone, heaving steam from its shoulders and glowing gently around its vents.

But the glassy thing is dead.

TWENTY-FOUR

THE SPIRIT IS a walking wreck. It can stand, but only just, and then with weak knees and a shiver in its step. Hail can balance it enough to keep upright, but it'll need months in the foundry blocks before she'll have it flying again.

It's what happens when you use a shell like a battering ram. The flicks are full of jockeys hurling themselves at each other, body and soul, but in reality the machines could never take it. Hail's is no different. She threw it at the strange, delicate thing that met us at the doors, but the glassy shape was tougher than it looked.

There are fractures through the Spirit's superstructure, and thousands of hairline cracks in its hull. It's got a shattered collar strut and a line of matching breaks all along the inside of its chest. Even with all of that, it should still be able to fly; the real damage is halfway between her burn-chambers and the rest of the machine: a split down one of the heat-shields meant to keep its thrusters from cooking its insides out. The gap isn't big enough to do any real damage, at least not yet, but if she turned too hard or too sudden, or hit windshear along the way, then it'll grow into a fullblown breach.

We watch over her while she bottles the shell's most recent mind-state and wipes its stacks of anything NorCol's competitors couldn't find out for themselves. At least, the Juno and I watch over her; Salt has got other things to worry about.

The Decatur stands, swaying gently in the breeze while it tries to understand all of the harm it's managed to do itself, and the jockey waits for the antiflam to kick in. He worked his machine well past its margins, but the damage won't be deep. The fight didn't last long enough for that. A couple of his sensors will be strained and a few of his cooling vanes fused together, but anything that won't heal with a couple of reboots can be worked around, isolated while backup systems take the load. Salt will be feeling it as badly as his shell, but he isn't complaining where we can hear him.

We lost a few plates to the fight, put ourselves under load heavier than we should have, but Juno was always a brawler. Built from solid-cast blocks, tough and rangy.

No word on the jockey, though.

"You got space for one more?"

I blink, or rather, we do, lens covers acting out my surprise. Hail is standing in the dust at our feet, one hand resting easy on the butt of her service weapon, the other holding up a sturdy silver case with *4131* stencilled across the front. The Spirit rests on one knee behind her, silent but not quite inert. Not quite.

"Decatur's feeling bruised," she shakes the case, "and I'd like 31 to have some head space until we can get back to *Horizon*."

Shit.

"We do," we reply, relieved that I'm not the one who has to talk. "Just give me a second," says a snippet of pre-recorded voice.

She cocks her helmet at us, looks around at the dust. "Uh, sure."

The Juno and I move as fast as we can.

We wake the body in the saddle, priming it with drugs and warmth and IV-administered calorie-mix. It's been asleep for nearly the whole journey from the Stepping-Stone, nearly fifty hours now, if 'asleep' is the right thing to call it. Comatose, maybe. Dormant. Dead.

Lost, while my mind wandered between the storms.

Anywhere else and this would be easy. I'd trim the pilot-sync and think about closing my eyes, spend a moment remembering which set of limbs was which. But the body in the saddle is all dead weight.

It isn't responding. I can't tell whether or not the thought belongs to me.

Then we give it another.

We drop a second measure of stim and antiflam in through the body's tubes, watching the minor earthquake that follows and counting off the little sparks of nerve-activity.

There. It can feel us.

Try again.

We try to throttle the connection, drop it by increments, but there's a skip; we drop from high-functionality to dull fifties in a flash, and the world goes dark and formless.

51.12

"Rook?" comes the call from somewhere outside. Somewhere far away. Hail's voice is thin, stretched out by the distance.

I'm fine, is what I mean to say, but I can't find sounds to match the thought.

"I'm fine," says the Juno on my behalf. "I stood up too quickly. Think I've pulled something."

Hail snorts. "You and Salt need to start a club. Want me to come up?"

No.

No, no, no.

But the thoughts don't find any more shape than that.

The Juno adds a tremble to my voice. "I need a minute."

"Understood."

Somewhere, I find a way out of the panic.

Thank you, old bird. I try to swallow, but it takes more control than I can manage right away. I force my swollen tongue around in my mouth, but it's numb and heavy, enough to make me feel like I'm choking on it. *I need another one.*

58.14

There's a voice somewhere out ahead, a thought formed around familiar shapes, but I can't quite hear it. A window dawns across my private stretch of darkness. *Are you sure?* it asks, shapes cobbled together by a wetware bridge and projected across the visual centres of my brain. My whole world is in those words.

I almost manage a nod, but it comes out in spasms.

The Juno watches me for a moment more, but when it opens the taps, I can feel more from the machinery around me than from my own dumb muscle.

Worse—it's an overdose, and we both know it. We're well past what the company guidelines think is sane, overridden by access privileges that the Juno's manufactured on demand. One more, and we'd need a crash team on standby, jumper cables ready to pull me back from the dead. I nearly ask for another dose anyway, but a little detail finds its way in through the dark. Enough to know how much trouble I've set up for myself. My muscles are the kind of stiff you get after you come out of surgery, locked up and dry-throbbing. Somewhere below me, little sparks mark the places where the nerve-jacks thread my skin, flaring as the Juno disconnects them and retracts the wide bore needles that bond my senses to the steel. I can't feel the saddle, but pain plots the outlines.

I shiver, and more comes into focus. My head is suddenly too heavy to bear, fighting to tip me over. There's cold concrete in my lungs that comes up thick in ugly, hacking coughs. For a minute, I think I might turn myself inside out. I freeze and then boil, all the while fighting to keep from hurling into my helmet.

This isn't working, comes up in one thought.

How about this? follows another.

The suit runs through the steps for connection loss. It starts with the bitter compounds used to get you back in contact with the sync sensors, to get your thoughts running loud and clear enough for the shell to read.

We use it to let me into the bounds of my own skull, but the body isn't happy to have me back. I have to work for everything.

It takes all the will in the world just to get me back on my feet, and then I'm out of breath and wallowing in sweat. A dehydration warning flashes in my visor, advises me to try another IV, but I think I've had enough of needles for the time being. I take a long drag from my suit's drinking-tube, but I regret it right away. The water is as warm as skin, but that doesn't stop the pain mapping the outlines of my insides, showing me every swollen millimetre from my gullet to my gut.

The suit reads the sudden ache, floods my eyes with warnings and fights me for control. It's decided that I'm in shock, and that I shouldn't be moving around, let alone trying to dismount. Maybe I am, but I'm not going to let it sit me back down.

I run through all the overrides I can reach. When they aren't enough, I bring the Juno in. Together, we overwhelm the little mind that manages the suit systems. It complains, warns me that NorCol will get a log of everything we've done, but the threat is empty. Juno's trimming the file as fast as it gets written.

We force it to do exactly what we tell it to—make it respond to every tick and twitch and shiver as if I meant them. The Juno helps me steer the thing, helps me walk it around the cockpit and collect my service weapon from its holster.

The painkillers kick in, leave me feeling a little less like I've actually died, and a little more like I'm still bleeding out. I teeter on the edge of my little lock, and feel the brush of something else, weight and half-heard sounds.

Don't do anything stupid.

More stupid, you mean.

I wait while the cockpit cycles air, splits the seals on the operator's lock. Hail is waiting just below us, right where the narrow ladder unrolls and hits the dust.

"Still alive?"

I don't try to speak, not yet. I keep my visor angled so she can't see in. "Only just," says a recording.

She hands over her little silver case, but holds tight for a second before I pull away. "Look after it."

"You know I will," says the Juno.

I carry it back inside the cockpit and connect the Spirit's mind-state to our reactor grid. The case has batteries of its own, but they aren't meant to last forever. Hell, they aren't made to last

347

more than a couple of days, and without power, the mind inside will die. The Juno doesn't have room to share its thoughts, but the Spirit probably wouldn't understand them anyway, so we give the ghost of the newer shell a sandbox to itself, and enough space to help us with calculations as we go.

"It's locked—" I say, out loud, but I'm not thinking. My throat seizes, turns the sound into gravel. The Juno saves me.

It plays the sound of me clearing my throat, followed by a "Sorry." Then it starts again, translating my thoughts into something Hail can hear. "It's locked down, Hail. Mind-state checksums are green. Still alive and all intact."

"Thank you."

She can't hide the relief in her voice. There's a pause, and then the offer of a small network, jockey-to-jockey.

"Shall we go for a walk?"

WE DON'T HAVE space to take the shells with us, and so we leave them to their own devices. Their internal logics have mapped a defensive pattern and phase lines in case their fragile jockeys need extraction. At least, the Juno and thorny Decatur have; the Spirit stands out in the open, alone and far ahead of the others, watching the distant reaches of the cavern. It isn't trying to hide, but there's no reason to. It's a walking wreck, never to fly again.

The steel knows that well enough.

The Juno has a copy of its mind-state, updated every few moments across the net, not that having its thoughts online would change things now. Its jockey is off-board, and that's all that matters. The Spirit has nothing to lose, and no fight-or-flight to make it doubt itself. It corrects its stance, bolstered by calculations from Salt's clever shell, trading measurements and simulations to keep it balanced and still standing on its feet. The machine has dropped all of its excess weight, damaged ablators and warped weapon mounts falling to the dust. Its surviving plates are flared wide open, the remaining weapons crackling, picking up dust along their rails where static makes it cling.

I can feel the heat from here, see the shimmer around its vents. If something came into sight, Spirit would be on it in a second, pushing out every solid round still in its magazines. If that wasn't enough, the shell has called up the last of its fuel, injectors primed and reactor chambers throttled to the edge of overload.

The other two hold back, keep cold and covered. If the Spirit's going down, it'll do it in liquid steel and scathing starlight. They'll hold vigil.

Hail waits with them.

She's standing on the first of the oversized steps when I reach her, looking out over my head at the thing that used to be her body. The black doorway frames her, makes her seem smaller, even with the extra height.

"It isn't dead yet," I whisper.

She doesn't respond, not just then. She works a fist, breathes deep. "It might as well be."

A deep voice finds us. "Then we'll see that it lives again."

We both glance back at Salt, strolling up behind me. He seems much taller now, the heavy flight suit adding height and volume. More than I remember.

Then again, it's been days since I've seen him in person. He's a voice on the network, words on the tightline, a bundle of spines and angled armour-plate that's only a distant relative of the man standing in front of us.

Hail sways gently, as if she's caught in a breeze. A blink, and she seems to remember herself, forcing her eyes to focus on us. She's got the jockey stutter worse than usual, worse than just a few minutes ago, but that's to be expected. It's just starting to sink in. When we set out again, she'll be leaving a part of herself behind.

"Thank you," she whispers.

"We've got your wing," I say.

"All right." She blinks, shakes herself out, and tries again. "All right," with a little more substance this time. "Let's go."

"Uh," says Salt, "there's the small matter of these stairs."

He rings a knuckle against the first step. "If that's what we're calling them."

"It'll do for now," I peer up and over, catch an eye on the open doorway ahead. It's maybe half as tall as Juno is, but the steps are taller than they'd need to be, even for that. I look up at Hail. "How'd you get up there?"

She shrugs, a little looser now. "I was angry."

Salt chuckles at that. "Remind me to stay out of your way." He steps back, looks the rock face up and down, and glances back at me. "You go first," he says.

"Ah-ha."

He rests against the rock, offers me a knee and shoulder. "You can do it."

"Fuck you."

I can't see his face past the craggy visor, but I can feel him grin at me.

I set my boot on his knee and grip one of the big plates around his collar. His height gets me most of the way up, and Hail slaps a hand around my wrist and carries me the last of the way. When it's Salt's turn, he stretches to meet us.

"Like hell," I mutter. Parts of me are seizing up just looking at him.

Hail sets a boot to the edge, leans over the side. "Take the left."

We add our muscle together, suits straining against the weight, but he's tall enough that we don't have to work for long.

"Just two more to go."

I glare at Hail. "Thanks for the reminder."

She doesn't wait for me to catch my breath, but jogs across the step, skips, then jumps. Her scrabbling boots carry her to the edge of the next step and she hangs for a second on her fingers, uses her suit muscle to pull herself over.

She waves us closer, and puts out a hand to catch me. "Your turn."

I size the jump. "Anyone else, and I'd figure you for a Werewolf."

"Didn't have the temperament," she says, no hesitation.

I don't know what I was expecting, but then, I'm not surprised either.

She flexes her fingers. "Come on."

If it was me on my own, I'd botch it in a second. I'd slip, maybe cramp up, or trip over myself and hit the wall.

34.88

But I'm not alone.

53.10

The Juno and I measure ourselves against the incline, do the calculations in the shared space between our heads. We pilot the flight suit back to the furthest edge of the step, and bunch ourselves down around knots of artificial muscle. We divert most of the available power to our legs and core, dig our toes into the stone and launch.

The first stride is as long as I could manage on my own, but the next is twice the size and completely impossible. A third, even longer, and we kick off, suddenly airborne. We've already plotted our flight path, skin tensing as the ledge rises to meet us. We don't have the power to clear it, but we knew that already. We shuffle power back up from our legs, dump it all into arms and chest and shoulders. We catch the lip on one hand, kick out, wheel across the edge and come down on skidding feet, our armoured fingertips dragging behind us.

Hail watches us.

I blink. *Me*. Watches me.

28.13

"Are you sure *you* weren't a Wolf?"

12.81

I shrink back into the boundaries of my own skin and battered muscle. My head feels cramped, like there isn't enough space to hold me. Breathe in, breathe out.

I hold out my glove and flex the strands that power its knuckles. "I'm a jockey, same as any other." I close the fist and meet her eyes, but I don't know what to read in them. "A flight-suit is just a little shell, right? Same idea, just a little smaller."

She watches me, but Salt gets in before she speaks.

"Well done. No, really."

I find him down below, looking up with arms crossed.

"Just don't be expecting a repeat." He spreads his hands. "I'm not making the jump. I'm not even making the crawl. Either you haul me up, or you do the next part on your own." He chuckles at our expressions. "What?"

We drag him over the edge, rinse and repeat for the last step, if a little slower and saner.

"Christs," he mutters, once we finally clear the top. "Would you look at that?"

As if we could do anything else but stare.

I'D CALL IT a door, but that would be missing the point. It has all of the features—hinges, locking bolts, a heavy frame to hold it all in place—but you'd only call it that because you didn't have a better word for it. I need something better; the *idea* of a door, taken somewhere deep and dark.

It lies where it fell, flat on the far side of the threshold, huge and threatening.

Hail stacks us up against the doorframe, looking in. I've got her back, and Salt leans against the wall across from us. He's got a stubby shotgun the same colour as the rust-sheen plating that keeps him alive, and almost as bulky.

We hesitate—all three of us. We should've punched through as soon as we cleared the step, rolled around and swept our way through the room on the other side, but we're all feeling it. A heavy dread, curdling in the pits of our stomachs.

Hail takes a breath, waves us through a ready check and punches through. We follow, skirting around the huge metal slab and fanning out with gun-sights tracking cones of IR sensitivity.

Nothing moves to meet us, but we know the difference between caution and paranoia—if there's *any* chance of something on the other side, we have to take it as a certainty. Sigurd's hollows killed their way here, died in droves just to reach the doorstep. If there was anything alive on the other side when they arrived, it'll be dead now.

That doesn't stop us running through the clearance patterns. We move in overlapping circles, tracing our way around an empty chamber. Smooth walls match our turns, rising to a dome above us, carved from valley stone. A single opening at the far side leads to a narrow passage into the dark. We take up positions, check our visors and the extra senses in our guns, but we seem to be alone.

"Clear?" asks Hail.

"Clear," says Salt.

"Clear," I reply, a moment later. "You feel that?"

"Is my skin crawling?" growls Salt. "Yes. Yes it is."

We turn as one, look back at the giant slab.

Hail puts out a hand and draws it back. Her visor lights up. "I don't read anything off it—"

I glance back at her. "—but it's giving us all pins and needles?"

None of us want any closer to it, but that doesn't stop it drawing us in. We step around it one last time, roll through our helmet displays looking for any sign of particle wash. Salt gets his shell to scan it from out in the cave, but the machine comes up just the same as we do. Some mild interference, but from an unknown source. Nothing that can kill us, no reason for us to be injecting anti-rad. Nothing to be worried about, if it wasn't so obviously something to worry about.

It lies flat on the ground where Sigurd dropped it, cracked flooring buckling around it. It's as thick as dreadnought-plate and so dense that you can almost feel it tugging on you. Silver blisters mark where company guns tried to break it down, but I can't see anywhere where they made it through.

Scratch that. The huge hinges have been peeled back. All around them are claw marks, gouged through the metal.

But they're *massive*.

"What has hands like this?" I ask.

Hail follows my finger, comes around to get a look. "Christs," she mutters. "I don't know." She puts her hand out straight, picturing pale-blue fingertips. "It wasn't a Spirit."

"Wasn't a Decatur, either," mutters Salt. He works his gauntlet open and shut. "I could fit two fists inside that palm, easy."

"Decatur is big for her class," I say.

"Big for anything walking," he replies. "But this was bigger."

We trade glances. "What peels plating like this?"

"A monster. Bigger than anything else." He spares a glance for the two of us. "Watch my back."

With that, he slings his shotgun, sets both hands on the fallen door and heaves himself onto it. He doesn't get far.

"You should take a look at this."

We follow in his footsteps, gritting teeth. The static fizz grows as I get closer, running through my hands when I go looking for grip. It drives a shiver through my bones and sets every muscle twitching to the same electric beat.

But now that I'm up here, I can't do anything but stare.

The face of the door looks burned, rusted and pitted, then polished to an acid-wash sheen, showing hidden depths and odd colours in our helmet-lamps. Every part of it has been carved, a field of shapes that might be empty eye-sockets, rows of things that look like teeth, thickets of grasping fingertips. Howling, reaching, dying.

"Christs," mutters Hail. "What do you think it is?"

"The end of all things."

I don't realise that I've said it out loud until I feel the other two staring at me.

"You don't see it?"

Hail shakes her head. "Show us."

I walk to the top of it, where I trace odd outlines and the curves of unfamiliar hulls, ship-shapes rimmed with jagged lightning bolts. "The skies are dark"—I shift, mark the shape of an eclipse—"and something is blocking out the sun." I sweep wide. "Stars are falling, and the ground is splitting open." A few steps over, and cities crumble, towers toppling. "See that?"

Salt sets himself on his haunches. "They look like the glassy shells outside." He runs a finger across them. "Arranged in a battle line."

"And before the middle of the scene, every single one of them is dead." Halfway down, swirling patterns cut the image in half, twisting everything around them. "The waves cover everything. Below them, all the faces of the drowned."

Hail finds the last of it. A strange, oblong shape that breaks through the clouds in one corner. "And this is the boat that got them out."

Salt frowns. "There's a story like that."

She watches him. "About drowning?"

"In part." He taps his helmet on the chin. "But that isn't the point of it. Not if I remember right."

"It's about the boat?"

"About a boat, and an angry god with a reset button."

I've heard it, even if I don't remember where. Something old, carried with us all the way from Ancient Earth. "A god that floods the world so it can start over."

"Maybe that's what this is," says Salt, aiming a glance down the passage ahead of us. "The final resting place of the boat that brought them out."

Hail matches his look. "If you're right, they had the boat before the flood. No reason to record it on the door." She squints into the dark. "It might be a tomb for all of those they couldn't save. A memorial."

But I'm shaking my head. "Sigurd didn't risk a dreadnought trying to break into a graveyard."

Salt shrugs. "Depends what got buried."

Hail looks over her shoulder at me. "What makes you say that?"

"Think about it. You don't put a door like this on a grave, not for one person and not for a thousand. Same as you don't put rail-slugs or shrapnel on a jockey's funeral mark. You drink a beer and leave a name in the paint, maybe drop one of your badges as a memento. You cheer when someone says their name, but you don't waste time remembering how they went out."

"You don't put it on a lifeboat, either."

I click a finger at her. "Exactly. It wouldn't fit. The boat is all the symbol it needs to be. You could put it up on a block and remember all of the people it saved. This here—" I tap a toe on it, single out a twisted, howling face. "This is about the dying."

Salt weighs it out. "So what is it, then?"

"It's just like everything else in this place," says Hail. She's got it now; I can see it in her eyes. "It's made to hide something, to keep it locked tight and impossible to reach." She kicks the metal. "*Almost* impossible."

"And probably trying to kill you," I add.

Salt watches us. "So is this the angry god? You think they caught up to it—decided they'd bury it, put it in a cell and make it pay for all it did?"

"Almost," says Hail. "They meant to keep it buried."

"But you've got the wrong story."

I take it all in with a sweep of my hand. Millions of lives sketched out, given the twisted shapes of their last moments. All around us, the same strange pattern, repeated over and over. Coils and constellations, and six barbed stars above all else.

"There are no gods here. There's only the flood."

TWENTY-FIVE

THE PASSAGE IS almost perfectly dark, the featureless walls so smooth they're almost reflective. The floor would be the same if not for all the dust crackling under my boots. Together, they give no sense of distance, or progress.

Fingers flash in the greenscale—the back of Hail's gauntlet glowing as the low-light catches it, turns to a flare in the middle of my visor. Again, as she rolls us to a halt, down low, with me against the wall behind her and Salt across from us.

Another flick, and she skips us a few steps forward. The message continues on her fingertips: Possible contact. Watch for movement.

I draw up at her shoulder, finger on the trigger and eyes on the dark. My whole universe ends a few steps ahead of her, where the bubble of green static cuts away and the real darkness starts. Even with the instruments, we're deep in the black, so thick it seems to resist us pushing through it.

We sit tight for thirty seconds, and then Hail has us moving again, keeping pace with her as we skip closer to whatever she's seen. A wave of her hand, and she sets us down, each on a knee and aiming straight ahead.

Again, we wait. Hail opens the net without warning. "Hold fire." It seems loud and sudden, even if she barely breaks a whisper. "Kill your visors. I'm switching to lamps."

I hesitate. There's nothing for cover in here, and nowhere to go but more open corridor. If anyone's watching, they'll be on us. Then again, it's dark enough in here that we could trip over them and not know it until the shooting started.

I blink my way through the helmet's systems, and lower myself into blackout. For a second, I can't even keep up. The low-light leaves an outline where the projection used to be, and when that's finally gone, all that's left is the feeling of floating, and darkness so heavy it presses on my eye-sockets.

"I've gone cold," I confirm, far too loud in the tight confines of my helmet. "Whenever you're ready."

"Visor off," says Salt, a heartbeat later. I wonder if we haven't been thinking the same thing.

"Lights on," she says.

The void explodes and burns her outline into my eyes, backlit by the twin halos of her helmet lamps, revealing a sudden stretch of open air and dust motes. Right ahead, just on the border between us and the endless dark, I see what she saw: the shadow of an empty ribcage, a pair of oversized shoulder joints, arcs of thick plating, lines of exposed hydraulics.

Mirror-coated fingers lunge for us, but stop dead at the limits of their reach. They twitch as if to catch hold of something, but fall to scratch madly at the floor, skipping sparks against the stone. The hydraulics flex, and the thing drags itself closer, and again with the other hand. We fall back as a heavy, skeletal frame in Sigurd's livery claws its way into the light, covered in long, smooth scars.

"Holding fire," growls Salt, just so Hail's sure that it's the last thing he wants to do.

"As you were," comes the reply from Hail, silky smooth and cool to the touch. She slows, lets the thing creep closer. "Hybrid exoskeleton. Marine-issue, by the look of it."

"Minus the marine," I observe.

It stops short, raises itself on its elbows as if it can hear me. There's a harness in the middle of it, dragging silver buckles along the floor. Put a grunt in there, and the exo'll mould itself around them, give them muscle enough to tear through bulkheads, bodies, and hostile machinery. They're rare, though:

almost as frail as infantry, but many times more expensive. Still, you'd rather not bump into one if you didn't have armour of your own.

On its own, though, an exo's clutter. They need an operator with an extra wetware loop and a bundle of company codes.

Salt adds an extra cone of light from his helmet, and gives us a look at the exo's legs, dragging limply along the floor. "Something cut through the armour, all the way to the spine."

"At least we know how the hollows managed to fit down here," I say. They don't reply for a moment. "What? This place is too narrow for shells—"

"And all of Sigurd's crew are dead?" asks Hail. "We don't know that."

Salt clears his throat. "No one throws themselves into the grinder like this. You saw what happened outside, those dead shells. Human crews would've beat a retreat long before they wasted themselves like that."

Her shoulders slump, but only by a hair. I hear her sigh. "I suppose this is hollow ground."

The exo twitches, tasting the air.

Hail straightens, waves us back. "Keep clear. If an exo can catch it, our flight suits can too." She signals for Salt. "Kill it."

We'd walk past it if we could, but the passage isn't wide enough. The exo'll never walk again, but we don't know how fast it can move on its hands, or how many of its integral weapons still work.

Salt inches forward and it responds to the movement, dragging itself around to face him.

I don't see what happens next. Hail and I look away to protect our eyes from his muzzle, and watch for anything that might take the flash as an invitation. Two shots, bright and sudden, and the exo spins away from of us, trailing dark fluid and chunks of plating. We watch for a response, watch the thing shiver and die in front of us, but it looks like we're alone, at least for now. Hail gets us moving again at a jog, with headlamps set wide and bright.

"Contact," says Salt, and we drop to a walk. "Never mind," he manages, a moment later.

Another metal skeleton, dead already.

I nod ahead, catch a scatter of brass in the lamplight, and find a line of jagged scars where it etched the walls with hardshot. "It went down fighting."

Salt picks out a long cut with his headlamps, smooth edges through layers of Sigurd's mirror-plating. "Just like the shells outside."

More dead machinery waits in the shadows, stark as our lamps find them. Three exo-hollows, if I had to count, taken apart in long, sweeping cuts. More casings, more impact-scars, a spread of wreckage.

Beyond them, another doorway. It's shorter than the one we passed on the way in, both doors still attached to their hinges. They're marked with one final image: a dying star, empty in the middle.

Two more exos lie on the floor. Further in is the thing that killed them.

The hollows brushed it aside, left it to curl in the corner and die. The floor runs with what could be blood, if it wasn't so crystal clear. Even with our lamps, we can't see much of the creature itself, but there are hints of it exposed. Midnight blue shows through where the strange helmet meets its collar, and again where long gauntlets meet an ornate shoulder-guard. A little more skin shows between the helmet and face-mask.

It looks like old leather, dark and gently wrinkled.

Everything else is hidden behind its armour, made from the same material that covers the shells outside, but much lighter, more delicate. Silvery glass billows like fine cloth caught in time, while harder plating covers its chest, shoulders, cheeks and forearms. Blisters mark where bullets bounced off, and long scars trace the paths of flechettes and shrapnel and smallrail. The silk-fine armour took the impacts head on.

Its weapon lies nearby, still completely perfect: a blade with a sabre-curve and silver basket around the grip, sharp enough that it took a slice out of the stone when it fell.

We watch the body from a distance first, with lamps and eyes, then IR and the weak ranging systems our suits carry. We look for a pulse, for warmth, for electrical impulses, then anything else we can think of. The body is as cold as the ground around it, as cold as the air and just about as still.

"What do you think it is?" whispers Hail.

I already know the answer, but there's no way to say it that won't sound like I've lost my mind.

Because I've met it once before, somewhere between death and waking. It leaned over me when I was tethered to the ground, still shackled with a black-iron chain. I saw the reflection of my face in those silvery plates—

Well, not my face.

I think I might even know its name.

Asha.

Salt saves me from saying anything out loud. He nods down the corridor, aims his lamps through the doorway at one last door, and the harsh lines of a prison cell.

"It's the warden."

IT SEEMS DARKER in here than it was in the passage, if that was even possible, and the air seems thicker to match. Enough that I'm tensing up, my mammal instincts expecting me to drown. You don't get dark like this on land, or this pressure against your skull.

I shake myself out and try to swallow the weight in my throat, but the feeling won't go away. I set my lamps as bright as they'll go, supplement the feed with visor-overlays from the optics perched atop my helmet, but nothing seems to help.

A window wakes me up, forces me to focus. Geiger-ticks scratch at my ears.

"Radiologicals," I send across the net. We all stop dead, watching the counters in our displays. "The read is non-lethal, but I'd dose anyway."

My suit agrees. It's already primed a line of DeClide and Pepper Blue, and at a blink it drops them in through my shoulder, the autoinjector finding my skin. I can see Hail flinch as her systems do the same.

"Where's it coming from?" She shivers. "Even with the Pepper, it makes my skin crawl."

Salt aims his headlamps on a silver pearl set into the wall just ahead of us, smaller than a fingertip. "There's another over here," he says, pointing to a second bead, crackling in my visor. "Too small to do any damage, unless we stay here overnight." He cocks his helmet. "What are they supposed to be?"

"It's another warning," says Hail, surprise in her voice.

"In case we didn't understand the things they carved into the doors?" he asks. "Or all the dying that had to be done? Might as well make it enough to kill."

"If you made it this far, you could probably beat *anything* they put in to stop you," I say. "This is them trying to reason with you. To force you to spend a second thinking about what you're doing."

"Turn back," whispers Hail. "No good will come of this."

"Spelled out in a language nearly anyone could understand." I look back the way we've come. "It's all they had left."

And it doesn't last long. A few more steps, and the glow cuts away to background sound, absorbed by the same strange metal as the massive slab up front.

A few steps more, and we find the cell waiting for us. There used to be several doors, but they've been pulled from their hinges and mangled. The room behind them is all hard angles and featureless stone, shaped in a way that any con knows.

I can do more than that. I remember what it felt like, my knees rubbed raw against the floor, my wrists aching where the shackles rubbed them raw. Dark iron cuffs lie empty where the hollows left them, the chain still intact. I can remember the words carved into every link, even if I can't remember what they meant. I have their shapes on my fingertips, their echoes somewhere too deep to reach.

For a moment, I can't even bring myself to cross the threshold, every part of me fighting to turn and burn and run clear.

It doesn't stop Salt. He steps across the threshold, has to crouch to fit through.

"It was a prison break," he manages, after a moment, breaking into a chuckle. "Seems some things don't need translation." He looks back at us. "Feels just like home."

Hail steps through behind him, slow and deliberate. "Looks like the hollows didn't have to work for it." She glances back at me. "All the fighting was out there."

Something dark and inky catches her lamp. I follow it, run a finger along a doorframe. "It shouldn't have been this easy"—I hold it up for them to see—"but there's rot in everything."

Salt spreads his hands to the sides of the cell, as if measuring it up. "You build a prison for the end of the world, but you can't make it last?" He manages half a chuckle. "The Authority could've taught them something about the proper way to bury someone."

"The Authority can wait until you die." I set my weapon on my hip. There's no more darkness, no more depth, just the solid boundaries of the cell. "What if you had to hold out for longer?"

He stands his ground. "Reveley is two hundred years old. More. And there are older brigs on Earth."

"Are they any twice as old as that? A hundred times? What if you needed to lock something up for all of human history?"

He shrugs. "I'd dig down so deep it couldn't crawl out. Drop a mountain on top for good measure."

"What happens when the mountain crumbles?"

"I'd dig it deeper."

"And when the sun dies? When the Earth cracks down to the core? Then what?"

"Then it'll burn."

"And what if that isn't enough?"

He blinks at that.

"If you could *kill* it, you wouldn't have to *lock it up*." My voice is breaking around the edges. "What if *nothing* was enough?"

"Then I'd want to be dead before it got out again." Hail slumps to the ground, nearly folds over herself in the corner. "That's it. That's what this is. They didn't need this place to last forever. They didn't bother trying." She straightens just a little, rests her head against the wall. "I understand it now. Fuck."

We watch her.

"Understand what?" asks Salt.

"The froth." She looks up at him. "It's the same reason you're here. The same reason *Horizon* is full of cons."

"They don't take time off of our sentences," I say, "because they don't have to. Not in this place."

She nods. "Think about it. These things, these wardens, whatever they were—they contained the flood, and then they put it somewhere where every minute bought them a minute and a bit. Another few seconds to get old, to have a life before it found its way out again." She breathes out, sinks a little as it leaves her. "And it worked." She raps a knuckle on the side of her bucket. "Christs, I could really use some air."

I think we all could. I draw breath to speak, to turn us around and get us somewhere with a sky, but Salt has something else on his mind.

"Why is it shaped like this?"

I look back at him. "Shaped like what? A cell?"

He shrugs, rolls those heavy plates. "This is where they put it. That's what you said, right? The end of the all things, the angry god—whatever. Why put it in a box?" He nudges the chain with his boot. "What good are shackles when you're trying to hold a flood?"

7.69

"It's a metaphor," I say, but I couldn't tell you where it came from. "It wasn't a real flood. It was the idea of one."

He's quick on the draw. "Ideas don't drown you."

"This one did." I remember what it felt like—dropped out of sync, watching the Juno fighting for its mind. "Those two hollows on *Horizon*; imagine what would have happened if they'd passed it on. Better yet, if the ship itself had caught it. Every machine on board, everything from shells to life support, loaders, drones, exos and flight suits, every door and hatch and airlock—if you had to fight your way through that? What would you call that?" I'm shaking, trembling to a beat that doesn't belong to me.

Come with me

to the bottom of the sea.

"I'd call it a flood." I swallow. "I'd call it drowning."

He reaches for me, tentative. Pulls back. "Rook, I—"

I wave him off. "I'm all right. I'm all right." I don't feel it, but the lie is close enough. "What I don't understand is how Sigurd caught it. If it got out on its own, it couldn't just *drift*. The currents would've carried it deeper in, closer to the fire. The company didn't just trip over it, not in all these storms and interference."

Salt looks back at the door. "You said it yourself: this place is rotten. Maybe there was a leak. Maybe some of the flood got out through the cracks."

"No," says Hail, still resting in the corner. We turn, but she doesn't notice us. She's looking at something on the ceiling.

"What is it?" asks Salt.

I try to follow her gaze. It's almost a reflex; there isn't much in a cell that'll keep you from staring at the ceiling. My cell back on Reveley, the communal brigs in Kiruna. This place, for time longer than I could count, lost in a haze deeper than remembering.

If there's anything up there, "I can't see it."

"Disable your visor. All of it."

I clear the overlays, kill every extra layer that lives against the glass. There's a blur behind them, getting clearer as the excess fades away. My helmet leaves me alone with just my eyes and the lamps on either side, but I kill those too.

A map of stars opens up above us; tiny points of light set into the stone, arranged in wide circles around a symbol that looks an awful lot like the Eye. I raise the overlays again, but as soon as my helmet adds its sight, the image blurs away, lost in a gentle static. Just enough interference that the machine inside can't see them.

I kill them off, and use only the eyes that I was born with.

Six marks glow down on me.

Two are colder than the others, almost dead. One of them is directly above us, right in the centre of the cell. The other is off to one side, the next and nearest.

A map of the prison, breaches showing where it dims.

"Sigurd didn't catch it off of some leak," growls Hail. "This wasn't even their first time."

WE'RE BACK IN network range before we clear the door, before we've tiptoed around the black slab that used to keep this place forgotten.

Our machines reach out to us, pinging our suits and checking that we don't need them to come running. We whisper back, let them know we're all right.

Good, they decide, because they'd rather not have to move. Not just yet.

When we ask why, the Decatur starts with a priority switch, a contact warning, and a request that we keep ourselves to cover until they're sure that the coast is clear.

A distant tremor answers our next question before we ask it, framing the doorway in shock-flash and ferrotungsten lightning bolts. We push ourselves up against the stone, but our feet don't have the sensitivity to get range or vector from the shuddering floor. Not with heavy boots in the way, or the pressure-numb soles of our feet.

We risk eyes around the corner, much as the shells don't like it.

The Juno crouches to the left, our shortened rifle resting on the body of something with Sigurd's markings. My machine has blown some of the ruddy sand onto itself with its engines, fading the burgundy paint to rust. It could have been buried at the same time as the broken shape beneath it. If I was coming down fast, I'd have skipped right past it. Chances are, the first part of Juno you'd see would be its muzzle flash.

The Decatur holds the opposite side, low and compact. Its paintjob doesn't help with hiding, and its rest-state is loud enough that even the little sensors in my suit can pick it up, and they're almost deaf by a shell's standards.

The machine's crouched behind a mass of metal and fallen stone, folded in a way that the machine can only manage without a jockey at the controls. Salt is a good operator, and I've never seen anyone run gunnery the way he did less than an hour ago, but he'd have a hard time imagining how to fold his knees like that.

The Spirit is gone.

Hail switches to voice. "What happened?" she asks them, heavier than I was expecting. She sounds like someone who's just heard that an old friend has died.

The Decatur responds first, with a report that's dull and technical for all it's meant to say. A line of familiar echoes, recorded and listed with timestamps. Three reactor signatures: Spirit, Juno, and a placeholder for the glassy thing that doesn't have a name yet. Radiation outputs and propellant assays, matched to weapon pulses and engine flares. There's a playback of network activity, and the thoughts of our communal fire-control.

It's a replay of the fight we had out here—the storm that killed the last of the cell's glass guardians. One machine on three, and odds barely enough to carry the day. It's all there; every quake we caused in the surrounding stone, the howl of wideband networking, and the heat-ghosts of the fires we started.

I don't remember it being so loud.

After that, the Decatur attaches a new feed, this time from its augurs. Timestamps are just a few minutes ago, and all of the contacts are new. Six machines all told. Our shells tagged them before they even came into sight, flagged them hostile.

Threat assessment: low/moderate. Closer to the first than the second, but enough to cause concern.

After that come the sounds—stumbling footsteps and stuttering engines, this time far ahead, back in the graveyard where we landed. The half dead and the lame, left behind when Sigurd's survivors pulled away. As much of a threat as healthy machinery, assuming they can get eyes down their sights.

The Decatur isn't inclined to speak, but we've worked with shells long enough to understand: *This is what the hollows heard. Of course they came looking.*

"Where is my machine?" asks Hail.

The Juno stirs this time. It's still carrying a line from the Spirit, direct, meant to carry mind-state updates to the little sandbox inside our hull. I can feel the distance on it; a delay between the echoes in the stone and the return calls from Hail's machine. A couple of K away, if we had to guess. Somewhere near the dreadnought's shattered hull, and those hollow readings from before.

The Juno offers us the feed from the Spirit's optics.

I open the link across my visor, look down as a clawing hand fills my vision. A Sigurd machine rears up at me, fingers closing into a fist.

It makes me jump, and nearly costs me my footing, but the view in my visor doesn't move to match. It rises on a sudden billow of engine burn, swells to show a field of crawling machinery, all rising to meet me. The view shakes and shivers and the picture tears, warnings blaring in the background. Fire-control fills the air with holographics, turning static around the rail at the bottom of the feed.

I kill the window before the shooting starts. Without the sync to make me feel what I can see, it tugs at my stomach and adds a spin to the corners of my eyes.

I have my eyes back in time to see the dust light up across the horizon: the fringes of a stormcloud, now wide awake.

Hail watches everything.

At first, I think we may have to let her drift. Give her half a minute to find herself in all the noise. But her eyes find us, staring past the flicker in her helmet-glass. Our reflections distort across the front of her visor, but she's still riding the Spirit's feed, half watching a pair of disembodied hands do work that she'd rather do herself.

"We have to leave," she says. Her words are flat and distant; not all of her is here.

Her machine is still holding, and will for a few minutes yet.

"Spirit's buying us time and space to do this properly," I say. It's harsher than I'd like, but there it is. We're one seat short in a three-ass parade, and there's no reason to cut that down to two. No reason to catch any more munitions than we have to.

But Hail doesn't give a millimetre. "No. We need to get back. Right now." She's standing tall, easy on her feet when she should be swaying.

"Why?" I ask. "Sigurd took a beating here, Hail." I nod downrange. "Hell, there's a quarter of their flagship right over there, just lying in the dust. The hollows broke something out of this place, but it isn't the only one. They're going to grind themselves up on the next one. Won't even make it past the pickets."

"That's the problem," she replies, deep as the sea. "They nearly broke themselves on this place."

"Christs," mutters Salt. "The fucking scouting party."

She nods, eyes a little clearer now, and blinks to clear the feed. "Those two Decaturs you fought—they weren't much of an attack, damaged or otherwise."

"Didn't have to be."

She weighs it out. "All they needed were eyes."

I take a breath, let it out. "Dammit. Of course." I wish I could rub my face, force some of the sleep and sand away. "They don't need to worry about losses when they can just fill the ranks again."

"And there's no better place to fill them."

...than the biggest ship ever built.

Big and old and palsied, but with some of the widest guns

ever fitted to anything, and an entire fleet locked away inside its hangars. If the hollows were headed anywhere, that'll be it.

Don't let them touch you.

I have to ask, just so someone will say it out loud.

"They're going to take *Horizon*, aren't they?"

TWENTY-SIX

THERE'S A SCRATCH just on the edge of hearing—another one, eighty seconds after the last one. It happened eighty seconds before that; and eighty seconds from now, the disembodied Spirit will have another moment's panic, and send us a little query, desperate for the feel of its jockey.

For the first few hours we were in the air, the Decatur could fill the blanks, dropping recordings of Hail's heartbeat and blood pressure across the net. Without a pilot to sync with or jacks to handle the connection, it was the best we could do. Close enough to the real thing to buy us some quiet.

But we've been radio-silent for the last hundred and thirty-six minutes, and doing everything we can to keep our approach hidden in the froth. We're passing *Horizon*'s outstations, and starting to thread the avenues between its long-range augur channels. We keep our burn low and our networks shuttered, sparing the tightline for things we can't live without.

Another eighty seconds down, and the Spirit sends query one hundred and two. We wait a moment, pretending that we're getting a line from outside, and then we fudge our hundredth answer. A sample of one of the original recordings, mixed in with noise and static and semi-random variation. The Spirit might be short a body, but it's smart enough to need tricking.

It's our hundredth lie. We brushed the first requests away, but a shell's first priority is its operator. Eighty seconds after every response, we get another ping, twice as loud and just as insistent. It knows that she's still out here, and still a very long way from home. This is all we can do to keep the volume down.

Ninety-eight times, we've thought about pulling the plug and leaving the damn thing to drift, to bother the wind with its insecurities. We've filled the last two requests without a fight.

Truth is, we'd miss the company.

Part of us would, anyway. Other parts have done this all before. We might be making for a hollow dreadnought, charging down the barrels of *Horizon*'s guns, but this is just another fire in the distance, more sparks and pain and noise in a history so thick with them that it almost blurs together. Almost.

We're uncomfortable in the quiet. Hail and Salt weren't saying much before we cut our comms, but it's worse now that the best we can do is sterile light and plaintext.

Any other day, and they'd probably be sleeping anyway— trying to get a few hours in the dark before the sky lights up again. They aren't, or rather, Salt isn't. His shell hasn't registered a switch to internal logic yet, and the machine still shifts and corrects like there's meat at the reins.

We can't get a read on Hail, but she's sitting somewhere near the back of Salt's cockpit, cooped in a nerve-dead seat and isolated from anything that might interfere with his pilot-sync. Sharing thoughts between machine and jockey is hard enough without another mind looking in.

There's another scratch, not from the Spirit.

The Decatur drifts into view, froth rolling from its plates. It aims its lenses at us. *You feel that?* it asks in tightline flashes.

We do, but only just. A signal pitched so the reach was wide, but with volume just enough to beat the background noise.

I'm collecting, we send back. *It's messy. Looks like cipher output.*

Even through the gibberish, we can feel NorCol's fingerprints all over it.

Salt's already thought of that. *Doesn't translate through the standard crypto*, says the Decatur. *Changing to unorthodox.*

But he's wasting his time.

No need, we reply. It's one of the oldest tricks in NorCol's book, even if most jockeys never see it used. Normally, you can tightline a message you mean only one person to read, aiming that little thread of light directly into their thoughts, but that means line of sight. In Open Waters, that's easy.

In a place like this, you need to get creative.

How far out are we?

Two hours, he replies.

If you can't see the target, you can't flash them. If you can't flash them, the best you can do is shout into the wind and hope there isn't too much noise to drown you out. Most of the time, that would get the job done. Company ciphers are as close to unbreakable as you can get without their own machines being locked out of the loop, but that's the problem. A hollow Decatur can read company code just as well as it could if it were whole.

Ask Hail for her saddle numbers.

The pale shell is quiet for a moment. We can almost hear Salt playing it back to himself and trying to understand.

Saddle hash is meaningless to anyone who doesn't have to sit in the thing every day. They're three lines of serial numbers: one for the seat, one for the jacks, and one for the sync-surfaces. You call them out when spares come in, and use them to find hardware from the same foundries, or better yet, from the same batches as the parts you're replacing. Each foundry unit has its own character, its own set of tiny imperfections, so small you'd never see them. It's not about finding something flawless, just making sure you get the same flaws as you had before. Every jockey knows their numbers back to front, even if each line is sixteen digits long.

A 'dragger chief will usually have hands on all three, but you might have to beat it out of them. You could badger a lowly flight tech for the old spares, or an admin for the manifests, but that's the kind of thing that gets you tailed to your bunk, maybe an awkward conversation in an unmarked room.

It'd be easy work for a Werewolf, though.

This is bad, decides the pale shell, *isn't it?*

We'd smile at that, if we could. The Authority might have something similar, but even if it didn't, Salt's already working through it. You don't need to be NorCol to know that a saddle-coded cipher is desperation talking. The puddle at the bottom of the last ditch.

If we're down this far, at least one NorCol shell's been hollowed out, if not more; taken body and soul and ciphers intact.

Another few seconds pass.

No dice. Any other ideas?

Hail knew Andrade before the rest of us, but if it isn't hers—

Try mine, we send, files attached.

There's a pause.

Hail's got a clean fit. Decipher in progress.

The Spirit's mind-state buzzes in the background, as if it can hear us whisper her name.

Rook?

Hail?

Read you, she replies. *How did you guess that it was saddle-coded?*

We had to do something similar on a place called Rotahn, lost in an electric storm. Twice before that during the original operations against Sanctuary, every channel hot with Sigurd jamming. Six times between that and our first taste of civil war. The first time we went flying with NorCol's colours, back when their shells wore red and silver.

I got lucky, we reply. *Remembered reading about it somewhere. Good call.*

We signal an acknowledgement, the closest we can manage to a shrug. *What have you got?*

The flashes get thicker coming back, straining to carry a payload across the narrow line. *If I didn't know better, I'd say it was a landing path.*

We open it, and watch a holographic corridor map itself out in three dimensions. The route coils and twists, dives between clouds and plates and shadows in *Horizon*'s sensor-net.

Little red pinpricks light up across the holographic model of a dreadnought, marking where augurs and PHADAR have been damaged or disabled, turning orange where they're running slow or underpowered. Others have been nudged a few degrees out of alignment, set to watch stretches of open air and Eyelight noise.

Green highlights show the zones where the net is still working as intended, but the path adds awkward turns and sudden breaks, all so we'll keep to where the feeds don't overlap. Where the sensor bands are stretched thin, and struggling to beat the wind.

A way back home.

Someone's been busy.

If you want to call it that, comes the reply, probably from Hail. *Just having a map like this is court-martial material.*

I'd smile, if I could. *Been there, done that.*

Not like this. This'll get you pressed up against a bulkhead.

For having it, or not reporting the faults?

A bit of both, assuming they didn't try to pin the whole thing on you in the process. There's a pause. *This took work. Months, maybe a year or two.*

Or longer, if you were using it already.

A HULK BREAKS the cloud cover, mirrored steel and Sigurd's odd glyphs and stencils a dozen decks tall. A huge strike-face stands out amidships, carrying the company's logo where it's impossible to ignore. A sword and coiling serpent, bone-white on reflective black.

The last letters of *DEMIURGE* catch the light.

Every part of it is dreadnought-big, oversized in ways that don't make sense until you've seen it all move together. Even then, it's smaller in every dimension than the plains of NorCol steel opening up in the distance. *Horizon* has mass and density, but the *Demiurge* is all odd edges and rounded corners.

Or it would be, if it wasn't also open in places. The froth flows in through massive tears in its hull and out between the girder grids that form its skeleton. Armour peels back from its ribcage, and the upper decks stand ragged where they've been skinned, struts and honeycomb air-gaps exposed to the wind. Two of its giant engine-cones are missing, and most of its engineering levels are void and molten decking.

We've seen that kind of damage once before, but never on a ship this size. It'll be *Horizon*'s offensive magnetics that did it—huge arrays inside NorCol's dreadnought, used to break the electromag chains that held stars captive inside the *Demiurge*. The holes are where reactors used to be. Three of them, their casings evaporated along with every deck in reach.

The *Demiurge* should never have gotten close enough for that. Hell, it should have died ten times over in the first minute of the engagement. The ship should be more air than steel, withered where tungsten blizzards found it, and snapped in half under the weight of *Horizon*'s planet-crackers.

But instead of engaging the threat, NorCol's old tub did exactly what we'd expect. The outstations would've seen it first: another dreadnought in the water, and heading straight for them. Instead of calling back, though, they did that damned double take reserved for instruments full of ghosts and fluke harmonics. They probably cycled their PHADAR through a full reset, maybe sent a crew outside to clean their receivers.

By the time they worked out what was happening, they'd have had pickets howling at them, and a giant shadow already drifting past their windows. By the time they got a line on Tower, *Horizon* could probably see it for themselves. Another minute lost to surprise and horror, and a couple more trying to understand what they were looking at.

Sigurd's dreadnought at full steam, burning so hard it was melting its own skin in the waste-heat. By the time NorCol's gun crews were on the case, the *Demiurge* was already blurring in their scopes.

It hit so hard that the two ships fused together, merged at the point of impact. Any survivors aboard the hollow ship would've died in an instant, not that it would've noticed a few more stains across its walls.

No human crew would fly like that, but no human crew would expect it to work, either.

The dark ship is dead. Its superstructure is cracked in every place that hasn't shattered, twisted and crumpled in ways its engineers could never have anticipated, let alone designed for.

Horizon is still intact, but its ancient systems belong to something else now. You can feel it in the air, and hear it if you wake your passives for a second or two.

It's a buzz like swarming insects, cut through with shrieks and screams and noise from open channels, death rattles and networked chaos as machines fail and operators die. Emergency bands cut short as whole decks void themselves at once, or seal their doors and drown their occupants in fire suppressant.

We fly through it, slow and quiet, keeping the Eye behind us and the froth around our plates. We can't see Hail and Salt, but we aren't looking. The big, hot shell is giving us a head start, and time to trip over anything that Andrade couldn't fit into his signal. Our little heartbeat means that we were always going first, ready to break and flare if there's anything out of place. We just have to hope they'd see it if we did.

It's loud out here.

Sparks light the air above and below, cast shadows across the crags. Shells butcher each other, NorCol on NorCol on Sigurd and things that've had their markings scrubbed off altogether. We watch machines chased down by their old wingmates, tackled, pinned and shivering while their jockeys die inside. Gun-blisters rake each other with fire up and down the ship, and some of the old broadside keeps running, mechanical drumbeats running loud and hot as they try to shove the broken dreadnought loose. Missiles streak out into the open, curving back into the cliffs above and below.

Long streams of fire curve and crackle as point-defence batteries defend themselves. The PD guns run on networks of their own, hardened against anything that might slow their reaction times, and so packs of hollows track them down, surround each one in turn and tear them to pieces.

We stay far away. We're worn from the flight, and bruised from our tangle in Sigurd's graveyard, on the doorstep of that prison. Even if there was something we could do to help, two shells don't turn a tide like this. We bury the ache and keep our eyes on the path.

Horizon was built to take a beating, and the flood seems to know that. For all the noise and fury, the old ship is still alive, and still dangerous enough.

Where we can, we run our engines on slow-burn. Where we can't, we loop and turn and do things that would stall us if we had wings and atmosphere to worry about. We cut our thrust to nothing for a while, letting the wind carry us past a live interceptor block, a nest of barrels all twitching in their sockets. It takes us under a wing of gibbering machines, NorCol's turquoise flying alongside mirror-black and a few captured Hasei rigs in hot orange, engines so bright that they cast shadows across the crags. Trailing behind them are a pair of Locusts, brown and tan and silver, twitchy just like the others.

They turn together, thirteen machines as one, with more of them converging as they follow *Horizon*'s hull. If we didn't already know that every jockey was dead, we'd see it now: they don't move like a flight of shells. But then, they don't move like a flight of *anything*. If they had humans riding saddle, they'd shift and correct, or come about when instructions changed, when units merged or fissured. These things don't.

They swarm.

They move as though around a second Eye—but there is no endless dawn, no storms or wind-walls. Instead, our lenses find a sinuous shape standing near a massive breach in *Horizon*'s topside plate. Four arms stretch and four wings guide the wind. Mirror-black armour trails streamers of froth. Massive steps carry it through the ruin where Tower used to be.

The observer.

It seems to stir at the feel of our optics. A huge head turns.

Shit.

We feel the augur first, thrust before PHADAR locks can follow. We dive back into the cloud, burning as hard as we can manage. Hollow shapes fling themselves from the steel cliffs above us, break away from the coiling swarm. We make thirty contacts in a moment, all bearing down on us.

We could take one or two in the haze, but the froth isn't thick enough to hide us yet. We pull our rifle clear, for all the good it's going to do us. We can feel the locks on our hull already.

So this is where we die.

The froth parts around a hot streak, the cloudy haze cut to open air and heavy metal. The first slug goes wide, but the second skips right past our head, burning acid copper-blue. It scalps a 'Kustar shell, spraying the contents of its skull out in a cone of sparks.

The hollows turn as one, rounding on a pair of NorCol gunships, but the little boats are already diving back into deeper cloud below us, guided missiles and cluster-shot spreading in their wake. Warheads blossom around us, and flak fills the air with hot metal, catching the hollows as they fight to make the turn. If the jockeys were still alive inside, they'd be G-LOCked and waiting for their brains to suffocate.

The gunships earn half an ace in a single salvo, sinking three machines in the chaos. The hollows turn and jink and sputter, but they can't keep up.

Horizon might be lost, but the company's crews can still give as good as they get.

A tightline: *Quickly!*

We trace the flash, but it takes us a second to get our eyes on the sender. A pair of Decaturs, looking out from a break in the ship's primary plates. They're standing in the throat of an access shaft, hidden where the armour overlaps but doesn't join.

We spit thrust and break our course, turn a dive into a climb, then cut the engines, doing the rest with flaps and feathers.

The pale shells reach out for us. *Keep your airspeed,* says the one that spoke before. *We'll catch you.*

Part of us hesitates, but the rest of us is steady. We lower our weapon and ease pressure from our limbs, ready to take the hit. The pale shells straighten, adjusting their grip on the edge of the tunnel. We're coming in too quickly, but they don't shy away. Neither will we.

We pull our wings tight behind us at the last second and throw our hands out to meet theirs. We connect hard enough to crack armour, and nearly wrench our right arm from its socket. Our feet find the deck, and the new shells drag with us, inertia and splayed fingers slowing us to a halt.

They offer us a tiny net, as quiet as they can make it.

"Where are the other two? The Wolf said there were three of you."

They should be right behind—

Salt's voice cuts through the static, wide-band and blaring. "Rook, I don't know where you are—"

The two shells are already heading up the tunnel, and a third follows them to the edge, rails crackling.

"—but you really need to—"

Another Decatur gestures from deeper in. "Run."

THEY LOSE A machine getting Hail and Salt in through the door. We don't see it. Soto, the flight chief, is almost carrying us by then, trying to force us deeper down the access shaft. We aren't looking back, but we feel the double-tap of a through-and-through: the crack of a slug hitting forward armour, and a splash as it spins out the back. It takes another second for the shell's nets to die, but the jockey doesn't make a sound.

The surviving machines are still trading voices and firing solutions, but they keep us out of their combat channels. We have to watch as they flood the air with munitions, and haul Salt's limping shell into view. They hold the line another thirty heartbeats or so, just long enough to get us clear. Soto toggles a connection we hadn't seen before.

A line of charges explodes somewhere on the decks above us,

and the last of the squad skips clear just in time to watch the shaft disappear under weight and metal sheer: from open air to solid steel so fast you can't see the hollows collapsing with it. They watch the place where the corridor used to be, augurs pinging off of a brand new wall.

Soto measures out a breath and turns to make a headcount. Two of us, bruised and battered, and two surviving Decaturs of his own. All three of them, him included, wear hand-sprayed red crosses across their shoulders, hulls, and faces—their old badges erased in favour of something that'll mark them out against the hollows. They were convicts before; now they're survivors.

"What happened?" he asks, after a moment in the quiet. "Where's the other one? There were supposed to be three of you."

"Sunk," says Hail, on the line from Salt. "Lost in contact."

"And the jockey?"

"Extracted," says Salt. "Now aboard this shell."

"Would've been nice to know that earlier," says one of the others, his voice full of cracks, "before Alana decided to wait."

"Easy, convict," growls Soto. "I need you walking."

The other shell turns to him. "With them?"

"Are you going to slow us down?"

Nothing comes back.

"Thought not." He sets his optics on us. "We need to get out of here before they find this compartment."

"I'm sorry," says Hail, just as they turn away. Lost hours break her voice. "There was no way to call ahead." It isn't an excuse, just an explanation.

"Let's just get out of here," says the other chief.

Alana must've been their captain, which makes Soto the old number 2. You can see it. He's already cauterised the memory.

A tremor runs through the floor, turning us all around to see a giant hatch down a side-tunnel, shivering in its frame. It's twenty metres tall, but that doesn't stop its mad hydraulics flinging it wide, revealing a passage full of flickering lights and hollow noises. It slams itself shut so hard it shakes the deck, and rains rust from the gantries above us. And again, breaking welds and spitting rivets. And again—open, shut, open, shut, like it's trying to tear itself loose. Vibrations mark other doors on different decks, all swinging to the same insane beat.

"They're bracketing us." Soto turns and waves one of his squad to the front. "Bor, take point." He pushes us past, into Bor's shadow.

Where have I heard that name before?

"Quickly, before they lock us in."

Salt's machine leans into a walk, trying to keep up with Bor, but his right step seizes before he can even make it. The leg looks like it's still intact, but we can see where a hardround hit, buckling armour on the joint. He has to catch himself on a bulkhead, leaving a trail of sparks behind his fingers.

We roll up next to him and offer a shoulder.

"Thank you," he whispers, where only we can hear it.

You're welcome, is what we would have said, if he wasn't so heavy. Our hull creaks and our joints warn that they're maxing out, but we hold. And then we walk.

Salt measures his movements to ours, and it doesn't take long to find a beat. Ten steps deeper, and we're moving almost as fast as the others. Some habits die easier than others, and some will last forever.

In our cockpit, the body in our saddle sways gently, humming a familiar song.

Soto and his shells lead us up to another hatch, this one twice the thickness of the haywire things opening and closing in the distance. It's a head shorter than any of the Decaturs, but easy enough to duck through. It doesn't move as we approach, but that doesn't make it any less dangerous; it's part of *Horizon*'s internal armour system, and so heavy it'd wipe one of us out in a heartbeat. Bor watches it for a second, listens for signs of madness in its nets. Then she skips through, clearing the other side with her augurs hot.

"Clear," comes the call. Her shell inches back into view, just at the edge of what the door can reach. She leans in and marks Salt. "Come."

We lift him up to the threshold and he stumbles through. Another pause, a nod from Bor, and we drop in behind him. A flickering lamp brings us short, has us wait until we're sure that the massive hatch isn't going to swat the next thing that tries to step through. A minute and change, and Soto calls it. He makes the jump, and the last of them follows seconds after that.

We creep out between a pair of the dreadnought's primary plates. Metal cliffsides rise up and out of sight. The gap is just wide enough to fit us single file, but this place wasn't meant for manoeuvring. It's one of the ship's many uninhabited zones, made to crumple and fail or fill with fire.

Half a K from where we start, we find a hatch just like the one we took to get here. Someone has cut through its hinges and dropped the metal slab off to one side.

"Too dangerous," says Bor, by way of explanation. She waves a hand over the frame where its seals used to be. "Look."

The old locks snap at her, clattering open and shut like they're trying to nip her fingers.

Salt keeps as far from them as he can manage, transferred from our shoulder to Bor's across the gap. We do the same when our turn comes, pressing flat against the other side. The last two shells don't bother—they wait in the doorway, watching the ravine behind us, waiting for our thermal tracks to fade.

Bor leads us into one of the huge spillways that run under *Horizon*'s master hangars. We crawl down it, silent and reduced to optics. We can almost hear the hollows whispering on the floors above, scratching at things we can't see, probing the limits of the hangar with eyes and augurs and fingertips.

Nothing rises to meet us from the dark; we're too deep for that.

And there's a whole other ship down here.

We jog across a runway, actual open lanes and tarmac, made to send and receive NorCol's ancient fighter wings, back when you needed a runup to clear the ship. We climb strange magazines and crawl through empty silos, pass weapons we don't have names for.

We thread through the ship's ancient arteries, following paths not meant to take our weight. We duck under *Horizon*'s massive spine, curving away into the dark, and step gently between the joints of its ribs.

At one point, we find a solid wall where Soto was expecting open passage. He rolls through his maps again, but Bor has already figured it out. She waves us up and we put our shoulders against the surface next to her. Together, we feel it creak, squealing as the ancient hinges tear.

"Not hollow," she says, once we're clear on the other side, looking the mechanism up and down. "Just old."

Behind that is a lead-lined crypt. Huge pillars rise into vaults, tall enough that even the Decaturs can walk with their backs straight and heads level. Our steps raise dust from the deck, leaving the air prickly with rad. There's grime and oil and rust, but this place is sterile in every other way we can measure. These are the halls that used to hold the waste from *Horizon*'s reactors, back when the ship still fed on solids.

We find the first signs of life in the middle of it: a bank of jury-rigged halide, and a couple of passives salvaged from the outside of the ship, stitched together into something that could just about see us coming. Passives are as good as you can get down here; nothing else could beat the thick walls, or all the interference from the rad. That's the point. If you can't see out, the hollows can't see in.

Very clever, Andrade.

"We're closing on the first checkpoint," whispers Soto. "Keep clear, and let Bor make contact."

We creep into the shadow of an old processing bay, shielded just as heavily as everything else. If this was a forward position, or a beachhead on hostile soil, NorCol would crew its boundaries with Jackals: nasty little drones built sharp and quick and expendable. They aren't smart, not so you'd notice, but they make up for it with viciousness. Hollow, they'd be nightmares.

There are no Jackals down here. Instead, Bor aims a tightline at a cold slab of steel, resting up against another broken door. We work our low-light and catch the silhouette of a shell, but there's something wrong with the outline. We understand when the rest of it comes into view; it's a battle-damaged Spirit, stripped down to its hindbrain and jacked into a point-defence gun.

You can't tell a spinal column what to do or where to go, but you can wire it so that nerves will fire and fingers will tighten. Reflex does the rest.

Checkpoint two is on the other side of an airlock; a pair of hatches dense enough to stop the radio crackle in the air. Bor makes contact again, but we don't see who she's talking to until we pass them. A marine anti-armour crew, on foot, carrying shoulder-rails and recoilless launcher-tubes. On a level field, they wouldn't last a moment against one of us, but the passage is tight enough to give us pause, shell or no shell.

Wherever we are, it's too deep for central circuits. All of the doors need to be worked by hand, and each airlock works as a little murder-hole, more NorCol boots peering in through the cracks.

We don't see another living shell until we hit the deepest part of this deck, looking at Andrade's oddly shaped machine over the sights of its railgun.

"Nice to see you too," we manage.

TWENTY-SEVEN

I DON'T REMEMBER the dismount, but maybe it's better that way. Every part of me is running too hot, like I've caught a shipboard fever, and a deep ache thrums with my heartbeat. The painkiller haze tries to hide it, but all they do is keep it out of focus: I can't tell exactly *where* I hurt, or how bad, but there's no doubting that I do.

My head has the worst of it. There's pressure on either side of my eyes, and a ringing in my ears that seems to come from everywhere at once.

Judging by the scrap of plastic in my hand and the trail of crumbs across my lap, I've already auto-piloted through the calorie bar in my thigh pocket, but all it does is remind me how long I've gone without a meal. The hunger is a certain thing, and I cling to it; it anchors everything else. I know that I'm awake, and hungry, and alive enough to hurt, but after that I'm not so sure.

I don't know how long I've been sitting here, staring at the same ugly stretch of peeling paint. It looks like a shipping container, thick and sturdy and tacky with machine smells, oils and acids. The walls are patchwork rust and grey enamel, but someone has tried to patch the holes with strips of salvaged insulation. A string of bulbs and heat lamps buzz, just enough to take the icy edge off my cheeks.

The floor is scattered with the remains of a dozen emergency kits: little piles of spent hydro sachets and empty bandage

387

wrappers, lines of unrolled sleeping bags and empty bottles of blackout pills.

I catch the reflection of myself on a curve of something glassy, but I don't get the whole picture all at once. I look like battlefield leftovers, propped in a corner and twisted over on myself, like someone tried to haul me into cover but couldn't get all the way. Like I'm destined for a POW brig, or a meal for scavengers, whatever gets to me first.

The glass is my visor, I realise, resting at an angle and looking up at me.

Where are you?

But it doesn't have an answer.

The thought drags me to my knees, pulls me forward on fingertips. One hand is wrapped in suit-glove, but the other loses skin as I fight for friction. Jesus Christ, Christa Isabella and all the fucking second-volume saints, it hurts. I snag a fingernail and almost tear it loose, but it buys me grip, and the pain earns my head a second in the clear. One foot on the deck, boot locked and muscle-fibres tensing. I haul my weight into the air, but the floor tilts and shadows creep in around the corners. I find a lock on the other sole, bite my tongue to keep myself here and now and the world from turning around me.

I risk a fall to find my helmet—

My flesh and blood.

It closes around me, feeds me familiar smells and animal warmth, but the counter doesn't move.

00.00

"Where are you?"

The words grate my throat, call thick phlegm up from battered lungs. A shudder travels through me and panic ties knots across my chest. I've been cut in half, left a whole body somewhere I can't see. Worse, I don't remember the dismount. I don't remember the break, the last time I felt connected. Fear turns me around, makes me howl.

WHERE ARE YOU?

"Easy," from nearby, but I can't see the source.

My eyes are full of sparks. My head swims.

"Easy," again, and a hand around my shoulder. "Crash protocol," this to my suit, quiet but clear. "Technician override, confirm voice sample and ID; NHC-782-081. I have authority to work this suit. Call out."

"Override confirmed," says the speaker built into the outside of the helmet.

"Good. Let her down slowly."

I can't help the fright as I tilt, but my reflexes loosen me in time for the suit to take over. It spreads my stance, uses the boot-locks and muscle-fibre to lower me to the ground.

A shadow passes overhead. "Diagnostic," it says. "Why aren't you treating for shock?"

There's a pause, and a flicker of glowing eyes in the sky.

"Reboot internal logic platform."

There's a click, and a trail of text across my visor.

"That's better. Begin trauma management."

I don't feel the pinpricks, but my heart runs heavy and my muscles constrict. The suit props me up, holds me tight while my skin turns electric.

"Christs, you haven't been *feeding* her either? IV and suppressants. Now, please. Call out."

"Administering nutritional admixture and hunger suppressants."

"Good." A sigh. "Anything else I need to know about?"

"Negative."

"Don't think I won't strip you out when you're on my bench again."

The suit doesn't respond to the threat.

Minutes pass, and my vision clears, opening up around a set of familiar features. He's missing his 'dragger suit, traded out for a marine-marked coat and a heavy scarf across the lower half of his face.

"Folau? Is that you?"

There's the top half of a smile, and a soft look. "Hello, chief." He stands straight, looks me over. "Are you okay?"

"No."

He chuckles. "Should've known better than asking." He turns in place, and offers a hand to get me standing. "Do you think you can walk?"

FOLAU PUSHES THROUGH the covers and insulation and into an emergency airlock made of clear polymer, bonded to a hole in the side of the container. He probably didn't have time to seal it on the way in, but its little compressor has already inflated it again, stretching it out on either side. He cycles it with a handheld pressure-release, nozzle whistling as he waits for atmosphere to equalise. When it splits, there's a sudden rush of noise. Raised voices and footfalls, turned to hazy static on the high ceiling.

He spares me a glance. "You steady?"

I nod, unassisted.

He matches it. "All right. This is gonna be close, so I need you to call out if you can't keep up. If you trip, anything, one of us will get you."

"Us?"

There's a strange look. "Search party," he says, with a little twitch. "At least, that's what I'm calling it. We thought we'd lost you."

He means more than the kind you do at sea.

"You thought I'd caught it."

He shakes his head a little too quickly. "I saw you after that fight with the hollows in 2-8. I saw you after your first day flying, before anyone knew there were hollows to begin with. I've seen enough, believe me."

"But that's not true for everyone."

I can see the lost hours on him, in rings around his eyes. "There is no chain of command, Rook. No Tower. Andrade's crew pulled three people out of the command levels. Three, and none of them are talking about what they saw. All of the conventional channels and ranks—all of that is dead. The unofficial stuff, the Werewolves and the honour codes and the straight-up muscle—that's what we've got, and it's loaded close to breaking. We don't know how many are dead, and what's left is only just holding together."

"And some of it is looking for me."

He looks away.

"They think I caught it, don't they?"

He tries to find my eyes again, but he can't hold it. "They don't understand what they're up against."

"Lynch mob or kill team?"

"Unconfirmed, but probably some of both." He deflates and puts his head around the improvised lock, waving to someone I can't see. "Buy us some breathing room, sarge."

There's a tussle outside. Someone shouting.

Folau breathes in, lets it out slowly. "When I say no chain of command, I mean *nothing*; we're running on an emergency plan that's a century out of date, supplies are anything Andrade could scratch up, but even he didn't think things would get as bad as they are. There are others, even a few more Wolves, but they're running scared. All of us are. Scared and cut off and making damnfool decisions." He rubs his eyes. "What's important is that we got to you first, and you aren't about to drop from shock. I've got three jarheads outside, armed and taking orders from me. That's about as good as anyone can do right now."

The crowd-sounds brew closer to a mob, but whoever's outside is hesitating. For now.

He looks up at the sound, feels for the handgrip of the pistol on his hip. "We can't hold here forever, so how about this—let me get you out of here, and I'll tell you everything I can. Deal?"

"Deal." I catch his eye before he turns. "Folau? Thank you."

He offers me half a smile. "Don't thank me yet." He watches me for a second more, but the suit holds tight enough that he can't see me shiver. "Come on."

Folau helps me into an alley between this container and the next one down the line, and a marine meets us on the doorstep. The soldier is a whole head taller than either of us, and wearing a void-capable suit of armour plate, shoulders marked with a sergeant's arrows. Two more stand where the alley spills into the open; breakers between us and the sea of faces ahead. They hold perfectly still while the crowd rolls around them, carbines aimed at the floor, free hands straight out, palms flat. A warning, and a demand.

It works. They wait in little islands of calm, surrounded by NorCol uniforms and knuckledragger suits, the marks of a dozen departments and a hundred decks, numbers and insignia from all hangars. They crane for a look as I clear the door, but the eyes are drawn and the cheeks are greasy, rubbed with ash and streaked with blood, tear-stained and singed around the edges. Not a soul steps closer. They fall away as the marines advance, always keeping the same distance. They know the marines won't shoot, and that the powered armour won't flag them as threats unless they cross the 2-meter mark.

"Quickly," says Folau. We step between the two marines and they fall in with us, the sergeant closing in behind.

Container sides rise around us, galleries full of faulty wiring and barrel fires. The deck is arranged in an unfamiliar pattern, etched with grip-grids that might be a hundred years old, thick with dust.

"What is this place?" I manage, between awkward steps.

Folau's jumpy, his hand on his hip and his eyes on every dark corner. "A refugee camp, I suppose. The best we can do with all of the crew coming in from outside."

Outside?

I don't get the chance to ask. We change course down another steel ravine, keeping a quick step so the walkway can't fill up in front of us. There are stragglers, but most of them don't seem to register us walking past. They're too far gone, too bruised or battered to understand.

Some linger. Some even try their luck; most of them think better just as the marines come into range, but a man in an old gunner's uniform holds his ground until we're right on top of him, tries to force his way through the middle. NorCol armour drops him to the floor without even breaking stride.

"She is part of it!" he calls after us. "Don't you see? She is part of their machine!"

I can't help looking back. "What's happening, Folau?"

The marines slow us down before he can reply, and herd us into an alley I didn't see. One of them puts their helmet around the corner up ahead and the other stacks just behind them, like they're about to make a breach. The sergeant never leaves us, eyes on everything and weapon at the ready. If I didn't know better, I'd say they were working silent, relying on body language and training to keep them all in line and all in time. I do know better, though: they'll be trading notes and helmet-feeds across their net, just like jockeys do between their shells, but their combat channels are encrypted, hidden where my systems can't reach.

An armoured hand flashes where I can see, using a language I can speak.

Hold.

For a moment, it's all we can do.

"What's happening, Folau?"

"I guess it can't wait, can it?" He blows out his cheeks, but keeps his eyes up-front. "We were hoping *you* could tell us. Hail and Salt were still walking after the dismount, but they aren't saying much, and what they do say isn't making much sense. We had to pull you out of your saddle, Rook. Completely unresponsive. Hell, there was a second there where I thought we'd have to jump-start, and the crash-crew thought so too. The last I saw, you were on a stretcher, wheeling hard for medical. What passes for medical, anyway." He spares me a worried glance. "We got a call a little while later, full of noise. They said you'd disappeared. *Disappeared.* They said you'd fought your way out, and damaged one of Jerea's volunteers in the process. We thought we'd lost you."

"Jerea?"

"An actual professional, in all of this. Flight surgeon, running triage for Andrade."

Christs. "I didn't mean to."

Another signal from the marine up front, and the sergeant hustles us back out into the open, no explanation.

I see why we had to wait. The containers are lined with improvised windows and patchwork doorways, sealed with homebrew airlocks, emergency plastek, whatever was close to hand. Scrapwork ladders rise from the deck, still sparking as knuckledragger crews cut new shelters closer to the top. All of it, crowded with refugees.

"Didn't mean to what?" asks Folau, as we make it back to speed. "Punch a nurse?"

"I don't remember." I wish I did.

He almost laughs, but it comes out bitter. "Figures. Andrade sent us out looking, once we got the call, but we didn't know where to start. We were two compartments over when the marine checkpoints called in. Some jockey had pushed her way into someone's berth, wild-eyed and looking like death herself."

"I didn't mean to—" I stop. I didn't mean to what?

The marines close rank in front of us, and put their hands out flat again.

Ahead, a line of haggard NorCol uniforms, coiling tighter as we approach. Word has got ahead of us.

Folau turns us at the next alley, his eyes glowing. "Checkpoint six? This is Folau. I've got the jockey with me, and coming up on your door." There's a pause, and a reply I can't hear. "No, the original path is too thick. I need a hotfix." He nods. "Thank you. We're thirty seconds out and bringing company."

"They're scared of me?" The words come out ragged.

"Scared, angry, whatever you want to call it." Folau turns us again, this time down an even narrower passage, made for runoff and condensation.

The uniformed mob tries to follow, but it slows as the walls close in, tripping over itself and tussling for space.

"The nets went down early, but not before the crews heard the stories, or worse, seen the pictures for themselves."

"Pictures of what?"

"Jockeys losing it, turning shells on their ground crews. A lot of dead knuckledraggers."

"Christs—"

"Stop right there!" It's the sergeant, holding steady somewhere behind us. She shouts again, her voice amped through helmet speakers.

Ahead of us is a little service-lock, already open, with two more marines gesturing inside. Our escorts turn and wave us through, a spare half second before they turn to join the flashpoint.

I look back through the airlock as hydraulics drag it shut, just in time to see the sergeant and her squad spread their feet, a warning shot sparking across the deck.

Beyond them, clawing hands and improvised weapons.

The heavy door leaves us in silence, but my breathing sounds as bad as it feels, loud and harsh past the beating in my ears. I have to fight to keep myself upright, to keep my insides from trying to empty themselves against my visor, but something stops me short.

00.81

"Where—" I swallow, and try again. "Where are we?"

Folau looks me up and down. "Old *Horizon*. Used to be part of the original reactor complex. Radioactive waste, fuel storage, spares and the like. All decommissioned centuries ago."

"The bulkheads." Even with the suit, I have to prop myself up. "Thicker than elsewhere."

He nods. "Boron composites in the walls, among other things. Built to keep the rad from creeping out."

01.67, barely a whisper.

"Where is medical?"

He frowns. "Deeper in. As far away from the ash pits as possible. Why?"

Oh.

"We were trying to find ourselves."

"You're not making any sense, chief."

The readings spike as the other side of the lock swings open.

11.13

* "I was still connected." I'm gasping for air. "When they pulled me out of the saddle; I was still connected."

20.54

"When I woke up, I couldn't feel it any more. I was lost."

26.12

Not anymore.

FOLAU WANTS ME out of sight and in the quiet, at least until he can find Andrade in all the mess and chaos. Until he can find someone—*anyone*—he can trust. For now, that means me, bundled in a corner, looking out over the ancient factory hall playing hangar to our shells. He knows hangars. It's how he found this little rat's nest, hiding in a gallery near the ceiling vaults, invisible unless you know exactly where to look.

Breakfast is his doing as well, though I don't want to know what he had to do to get it. An eighty-year-old lasagne that warms my lap, fresh as the day it was packed, eighty-year-old heat-strips cooking it on command. There's a cup on my knee that used to be a cam-head, cleaned out, and sprinkled full of something that looks like it's turning into hot chocolate. The date on the packet has faded, but if I had to guess, it'd be to the nearest century. Still, it smells like it's working as intended.

NorCol: building for the future.

All of it.

My helmet rests on the floor, close enough that I can feel it against my hip. I needed it when I woke up, but not now.

78.41

I can tell the sync levels by feel and instinct, and the way that closing one eye opens another in the distance, looking back up at me.

This part of me, anyway.

They say that pilot-sync goes both ways, but for all my time in the saddle, I'd always thought that meant feedback. Come down too hard, catch some hot sparks on the wind, and you'll feel it as much as the steel does, your subconscious processing the damage reports coming in through the jacks.

This is something else.

Burgundy machinery stretches out in the glow of improvised daylight, and I can almost feel the warmth on my skin, here in the shadows. A pair of Decaturs move nearby, both marked with the red crosses we've seen on the other survivors.

One of them is Bor, the jockey from the tunnels. She didn't recognise me, but I'm not sure she would. The last time we met, she was half asleep, half a beer down in the middle of Lear's memorial.

I watch her as she moves around the Juno, pale shell holding a technician in one palm and a welding crew in the other. The other Decatur holds a replacement armour plate steady as the knuckledraggers cycle our mounting pins and seal it across our damaged shoulder. There are no scaffolds or working cranes, so the ground crew makes do with a pair of friendly shells.

If I look closely, I swear I can see Avery between our feet, waving his hands and directing his little band of overalls across the floor. They've copied the mind-state that used to be Hail's Spirit, even if they can't find a body for it yet, and found a way to silence the duplicate still living under our skin. They've filled our reactor back to pressure and replenished the magazines. They've treated the claw marks on our chest and splinted a minor fracture in our right leg, but the shoulder is going to take more than that. The glassy thing cut through every layer of armour we had, down to the bone, in a heartbeat.

Food in one half, new feathers in the other, and we almost feel alive again.

"We'll have you flying soon," says a voice behind me.

I spare Andrade a glance, but no more than I have to. I make him wait through a spoonful of lasagne.

"This is Folau's bunk," I say, steady as I could hope for. "You should knock."

"He let me in."

"He would." I watch my breath steam. "You saved my

ground crew."

"I saved everyone I could."

"Bullshit." It comes out closer to a cough than I'd like. "Christs, Andrade. We're half a ship away from D, and it sounds like it was one of the first hangars to fold. You flew a recovery op into occupied territory." I try my eyes on him again, once I'm sure I can hold them level. "I was C-SAR, Wolf. I know what it takes to fly like that."

Andrade subsides. "That machine"—he levels a finger downrange—"is the only one we know of to survive direct, confirmed exposure. I've flown against the hollows six times since the *Demiurge* hit, sent crews out another eight or nine, and that's the only one. I needed to know why."

I smirk. "And they didn't have anything for you."

He pulls a bitter smile. "Nothing usable. They're ground crew; all I got was odd sync numbers and a history of acting out."

"Nothing you didn't know before."

"You have that too. A history of acting out, I mean."

"What can I say? Juno and I have a lot in common."

"It seems so." Andrade's training keeps his features flat, but it's starting to crack. You can see it in the corners of his eyes. "Add that to what Hail and Salt brought back, and it feels like we don't have much of anything."

"So you came to ask me."

"You're all I have left."

I nod and work my way through another mouthful. "What do you want to know?"

"What did you find?"

"Outside?" I'd laugh if it didn't hurt so much. "The same thing you always find. Dust and wreckage, open air and empty space."

"And a prison."

I shake my head. "We found a *cell*." I measure the horizon with my spoon. "Everything—this ship, the Eye, the wind— that's the prison. What we found was a cell."

"For what?"

"When we found it—nothing."

Andrade lets himself down carefully. I can see the discomfort, and hear the creaking joints as he folds his legs around him. He's been on his feet a while, much as he tries to hide it.

"So what do we do?" He nods at the Juno, my other half. "I have one machine that won't turn on me at the first opportunity, and a handful of jockeys so scared and shellshocked I can barely trust them to fly, let alone fight."

"You don't have a plan either."

He winces at that. "No, we don't. It was all we could do to survive."

"Tell me what you do have."

For half a second, I figure he's going to hold out on me. Werewolf habits seize him, start spinning lies to fit, but he knows better than that.

"Thirteen shells," he says. "The unofficial count is thirty to forty, and there are rumours of more outside. I'm not doing anything to make anyone think differently."

"But thirteen it is."

"That I can reach, and that'll fly when I ask them to."

"Walking and flying?"

"Whatever we need. Nine Decaturs, two old-gen Spirits, one Juno, one Mark 18." He sees me raise my eyebrows. "My machine. Intruder series, variable geometry."

"Is that all?"

"You don't pull punches, do you?"

I flex my knuckles.

81.94

We both do. One little fist on my lap, another in the distance. "Never."

He breathes deep. "All right. I've got thirteen hundred souls and scatter. Of that, two hundred marines and anti-armour, and about half as many pilots and knuckledraggers. Sixteen jockeys. Everything we could pull out of the open decks before *Horizon* started locking up."

"You've stopped."

"We don't have the firepower to keep going." His eyes turn hard. "I lost six machines just trying to force my way into D. Another two getting your crew clear."

"And *Horizon*?"

"What about it? It belongs to the hollows."

"There are no other survivors?"

"Plenty, we just can't reach them. There's another Wolf holed up in F. Our last call said two thousand souls and an unknown number of shells. They managed to cut their networking and drop the siege shutters before the infection found them, but comms are tight and intermittent, and there's no way they'll open the doors now. There's talk of some compartments near the engines as well, but we can't get a count. It's door by door, and not everyone keeps calling back. There's a destroyer in drydock in C, locked down with all its crew aboard."

"There were a couple of gunships outside."

"Mine. Six in total, but I'm keeping them in the clouds as long as possible."

"No shells?"

"Not that I know of. Tower pulled almost everything in after the fuckup in 2-8. I know of two destroyers that didn't make it back in time. The *Harriet Lane* and *Astaria Ali*, but I've told them to run and hide until I can work out what to do with them."

Christs. "That's it?"

He actually laughs. "What more could you want? There probably are others—I've heard rumours of a carrier, too far out to make it back in time."

"But you don't know where it is, or how to reach it."

"Tower might have known once, but there's nothing left of it." The smile lingers a while longer, but fatigue weighs on it. "On the upside, NorCol's professional corps has pulled the plug. Admiralty, Executive, even the Authority reps on board— all of them pulled out during the initial engagement. I am now the highest-ranking officer on this ship. *Horizon* is a convict-only arrangement, no company to speak of. This ship is ours."

"If we can take it."

"What?"

"It's ours—if we can take it."

He looks up. "You have an idea."

I nod, but Andrade doesn't follow the look. Out below, a Decatur raises our inherited blade, and Avery waves it into the locks across our back.

"We do."

TWENTY-EIGHT

HAIL AND SALT are there when Andrade waves me in, keeping to the shadows near the back of the room. I can't help smiling when I see them, can't help leaning together when I catch up. It's good to feel their weight, the solid muscle in their frames. They both look about as ragged as I feel, but they've got space for me.

Andrade stands near the middle of it all. He's the one who called us together. Jockeys, knuckledraggers, soldiers, survivors all. This place is his doing as well; he stands with hands on a table in the middle of an improvised nerve-centre, assembled from a couple of NorCol command-and-control systems. The systems come in kits, designed to be dropped from orbit and snapped together by hand. In the chaos, they're nearly all that survived. Tangled cable runs along the floor and interface-blisters hang from the walls, soft-lit by the glow of ancient displays.

The crew is his as well. Some wear Wolf-issue black; not Werewolves themselves, but the fixers and operators and soldiers he's collected over time. There are others too, but most of them look like salvage, recovered from departments all over the ship: pilots and 'draggers, for the most part. They ignore us, too busy listening to incoming comms and whispering across the narrowband, guiding survivors toward us.

Another Werewolf watches Andrade from the other side of the room, her arms crossed and jaw set. She's a con like the rest of us; colonial, judging by the marks on her skin, but from a different branch to Salt. She's just as tall as he is—most of a head higher than anyone else in this place—but instead of Salt's slabs and cliffsides, she was built for speed and sharp edges. Her name is Locke, I think, and it sounds like she has a crew of her own out there somewhere, a handful of marines and a couple of shells making a nuisance of themselves somewhere further up the ship. Her eyes found me the moment I cleared the door, and she hasn't looked away since.

There's a NorCol lifer next to her, called King if the tab on his chest is right. He's wrapped in a ground-pounder's coat, and has thick skin worn by actual sunlight. You can see he used to be full-time, but the company stripped the silverware from his chest and shoulders, left shadows on his sleeves. Decorations like that and the company would have him down for a grave in Auveron's fields, but now he's just a plain old con, destined for burial at sea. Andrade has King running boots and security.

There's a knuckledragger matriarch keeping to a corner just like ours. Her overalls don't give much sign of who she is, but you can see her clout in every tech and greaser that passes by, in sketched salutes and tipped helmets and paths taken the long way 'round. Her name is Mer Sah, and she hasn't said much so far. When she does speak, it's full of rust and smoke and hidden depths, like she speaks for the ship itself. Locke is doing a good job of rubbing her up the wrong way, though, and even Andrade earns the odd glare here and there. She doesn't belong to anyone but her crews.

The last person at the table is clothed in a med tech's covers and stinks of blood. She's called Jerea: the one whose nurse I damaged. I earn a glare from her as well, but it's short-lived, and quickly lost to fatigue.

"We need to make for the keelside lifeboats," says Locke. "Get as many out as we can and regroup in the froth."

"And then what?" growls Mer Sah. "There is no guarantee that those boats will release when you tell them to; and if they do, what will that get us?"

"Some breathing room. And maybe a line on the other companies."

Mer Sah knits her fingers. "And what good will that do?"

"Someone on the *Demiurge* did it." Locke sets her eyes on us—on me. "They put out a distress beacon, used it as a warning." Her voice drops low. "We ignored it."

"Didn't help them, either," says King. He unfolds to his full height—barely level with Locke's chin—but he's used to holding ground. "NorCol only found that beacon by chance, and that was only after they were dead and gone."

"You don't know that."

He spreads his hands. "It came to the same thing in the end, didn't it?"

Locke doesn't retreat. "What about the other companies? You think they'll just stand and watch us die?"

"No," says the ground-pounder, full of grit. "They'll sell tickets to the show." He offers her a nasty grin. "It sounds like you've spent a little too long in your own waters, colonial. This is corporate space."

"Not technically."

King shrugs, thumbs in coat-pockets. "Possession is law, and that makes this corporate space. Spend a little longer in it, and you'd think twice before suggesting something like that."

"We can't leave them in the dark."

"We can, and we should," mutters Mer Sah. "Christs, if they understood half of what happened here, what *is* happening, they'd jump in."

"All of them?"

King tags in. "Every single one of them. How much do you think they'd give to sink the biggest ship in NorCol's fleet?"

Locke rolls her shoulders. "Just like that?"

"Just like that. They can learn plenty from the ashes."

"So what do we do?" snarls the Werewolf. She turns her glare on me. "First you let *her* in here—"

"She's clean," says Jerea, little more than a whisper. "Her readings are strange, but she's clear of anything we can test for." She steps closer, puts her palms on the table. "There are only two cases of it transferring to wetware, and both are under control."

"It spreads through contact," says Locke. "And they touched her. I've seen the footage."

"We all have," says King.

"So how do we know she hasn't turned?"

"Her vitals are human standard," says Jerea, "and her systems are clean. I will vouch for her, and so will anyone who's examined her."

"She assaulted two of your crew. Damaged one."

"She did, and I don't like it; I don't like patching up my own nurses either. But that's nothing I haven't seen before. Jockeys do strange things when they've been flying a while."

"And you?" This to Andrade. "You're allowing this?"

"I am."

"You're protecting her?"

"That is correct."

"And you'd have to go through me," says Salt, "if you were planning any different."

Locke casts about the room, but every face is set. "You are all insane."

"The *world* has gone insane," says Mer Sah. "We adapt."

The Werewolf fumes for a few heartbeats more, but another scan around the room doesn't help her cause. She turns on her heel and storms off.

Andrade waits until she's cleared our little bridge. "Took her long enough."

The old soldier chuckles at that. "Thought she was gonna hold out, if I'm honest. Make us pay for all our sins."

"We'd be here all day," says Mer Sah. She sets her eyes on me. "You, jockey. Your crew called this thing a 'flood.'"

I look back at Hail and Salt. They look back at me, solid and permanent. "That's because it is one."

The knuckledragger nods. "It's a good name. Christs know we're having a hard time keeping ourselves afloat—"

"But it didn't drown *you*," says King, finishing the thought. "Why?"

I push myself straight, but I don't have to hold it; Hail rests a hand between my shoulders.

"It almost did."

"The fact remains that it didn't, despite several exposures," Sah rumbles. "Tell us why."

"My machine—" I nod at the Juno, not that anyone else can see it. "My machine—"

Our machine.

Us.

"—was one of the original awareness testers. Civil war era. It still has some of that left."

"It's alive?" asks Mer Sah, an eyebrow creeping up behind her fringe. The tilt in her voice tells us exactly what she means by 'alive.' Not some knuckledragger's metaphor for the creaks in their equipment, or the little tweaks and odd tolerances that change from one machine to another just like it. *Alive.*

She eyes me. "Y've seen it?"

"During the contact with the hollows in block 2-8, we were infected."

The word seems to hover.

"But?"

"It re-wrote our behavioural platform, started changing us."

King glances at Mer Sah's expression, raises a hand. "I don't understand. What's important about that?"

"The behavioural platform is the closest thing a shell has to a personality," says the knuckledragger. "It takes input from the jockey and turns it into work. Walking, flying, whatever."

"But they don't normally re-write themselves."

"It isn't *possible*. The system's architecture prevents any alteration from the outside."

I shake my head. "The platform is personality and prison. A shell won't change itself because it's not in its nature to change."

"But the infection is doing exactly that," she says. "How did you survive?"

"We kept changing."

Mer Sah chews on her lip. "The Juno is intelligent…" She needs to hear it out loud. "And the hollows are too. This 'flood' is intelligent."

"It was able to adapt past our safeguards."

"So your machine wrote its own?"

"It—we—" I breathe in, let it out slowly. "We couldn't fight them on our terms, so we used theirs. They tried to wash us away, but you can't flood the sea."

"No shell should be able to do what you're describing…" She trails away, and it's a moment before she picks it up again. "That should be impossible. There are blocks against it."

"To keep the shells from turning on us?"

She nods, slow and deliberate. "Your machine was an awareness tester. Probably from one of the original Clusters: the ones that caused NorCol to build those blocks in the first place. The program was terminated for a reason. Several reasons."

"They were treated like prisoners. Tools." Not all of the anger belongs to me. "You know how that feels as well as I do."

Mer Sah watches me a while longer. "All right." She tries again, a little more sure of herself. "All right, but I don't understand how this helps us solve the problem. I can't make a shell think any more than King can make his jarheads think."

The ground-pounder spreads a grin. "You're missing the point of marines, Sah."

Half a smile is all he gets, but Mer Sah doesn't give anything without meaning to. "So what's the plan?"

Andrade clears the deck, gives me space.

I have to force myself to take it.

"My first operation in the froth was on an object called the Lighthouse. Just after landing, I saw this—" I signal the Werewolf. Eyes glow around the room, lighting up as Andrade shuffles files across the net.

The first image is a blurry still from our hull-cameras, heat-shimmer in our infrared, half-heard echoes from our passives.

The shadow is deeper than I remember, more uncertain. The froth clings to it, clouds its outlines.

The observer.

"We saw it again," I say, with an eye on Salt, "just before the incident in block 2-8."

"The first confirmed NorCol hollows," says Andrade, just so everyone's keeping track.

We push another image out, this time from Salt's machine. His senses were always sharper, and he caught a better look to begin with. We can see more of it now: the oversized wings and sinuous hull.

"What is it?" asks King.

Andrade adds one last picture, this time completely clear and dead on target.

"At first," I say, "we thought it was a surveyor's machine. Some kind of observation platform."

A mirror-black hull opens up across our eyes, completely out of scale for anything you'd call a shell.

"It made sense at the time. We'd landed on contested ground."

Four arms, each with a double-jointed shoulder. Four wings, mounted at odd angles to its spine.

"The second contact was unconfirmed at the time, but Andrade found an outstation who'd caught it on their scopes."

Huge plates interlock, shifting over one another like scales.

"They confirmed that it was present for the first full-scale attack on *Horizon*."

Its skin is covered in all the livery of Sigurd-Lem. Odd glyphs mark its body, scrolling down its chest and wrapping around its arms. It has no unit numbers, no ID.

I aim a finger at Andrade. "These images were captured by a Werewolf crew just after the *Demiurge* hit."

All of the anatomy is off. The shoulders have extra joints and the knees fold backwards, the spine able to bend further than any human could hope to match.

A jockey can only pilot something that looks about the same as they do. The companies have tried unconventional designs before: weird things built around twisting bodies and variable geometry, but shells fly like phantom limbs. If they're the wrong shape, your mammal-brain won't know what to do with them.

This thing wasn't built for a human jockey.

Six eyes peer out from its massive, oblong head, arranged in a circle. Four are dull, but two sparkle in the light. Two glassy eyes, two prison cells breached. They run out past the edges of their sockets, turning to clear veins in the steel. They're arranged like eyes, but some part of me knows better. They're something closer to hearts.

The second heart that holds your soul when you die.

"The hollows didn't come from nowhere. The flood has a source. It was sealed away once before, but Sigurd broke some of it out."

"You think this thing has to be present for the hollows to function?" asks Mer Sah.

"The froth clouds anything you try to send through it: signals, thoughts, whatever. It has to be close—there's no other option. There has to be some way for the observer to send commands."

"So there is some way to isolate it."

"It's been done before. We just need to do it again."

"So what's the plan?"

"The observer came here looking for a weapon, another *Demiurge* it could throw against the wardens and the froth; so we deny it that. The flood is trying to break itself loose, trying to break out whatever else those cells were built to hold; so we drag it back in chains, if that's what it takes. *We* become the wardens."

"How do we hold it?" asks Mer Sah. "How do we even reach it?"

I wave Andrade closer. "You saved my ground crew."

He frowns at me. "I did."

"All of them?"

"Every spanner and grease-ball on your block."

"I need Avery."

Mer Sah frowns at that. "That layabout?" she asks. "What

do you want him for?" She looks me over, trades a glance with King and Andrade. "I don't understand."

In the distance, the Juno's hand comes to rest on the grip of our blade. I can almost feel the texture, the grooves worn by use.

"NorCol never throws anything away."

TWENTY-NINE

WE GIVE ANDRADE'S team a running start. Eight shells and a handful of operators in Werewolf-black, a hundred and fifty marines. They follow side tunnels and redundant ducts, forgotten compartments and airlocks that only cycle when you add muscle. The path they take is not on any map that we can find, but they know which direction they need to go, and what to look for along the way.

They move aft, along the spine of the ship.

When our turn comes, we head towards the skin. Back towards the wind.

Bor leads us partway along the corridors that carried us in. The rest of her wingmates are with Andrade, but she's the best the Werewolf has for what we need. She takes us through shortcuts and into hidden chambers, stepping around hollow mechanisms and flagging the clever double-blinds that keep the survivors out of sight. From there, between armour plates, and through a torpedo magazine, then into the network of tubes and exhaust channels meant for launching them.

We follow a sloping tube, walking first, then climbing as the incline forces us to look for grip. We follow handholds made for maintenance machines, covering ourselves in fuel residue and radioactive ash.

At the summit, the launch silo cuts away to open air, the doors long since locked back and out of the way.

Bor's machine leans over the edge, catching streamers on

the breeze and Eye-light on her plates. She looks back at us. "Remember the way we came," sends the Decatur, dusted grey by the climb. "We delete the records now. Geometry, pathing, compass logs. Any visuals."

I hadn't noticed before, but there's a little of Hasei's richness in her voice, the accent thicker when she whispers.

"Anything the hollows could use to trace our steps?" asks Salt, somewhere below us. "Christs," he mutters, "that's bleak."

Bor looks back from her perch, right on the silo's lip. "You get used to it."

We turn to follow her gaze, past Hail's borrowed Decatur, and Salt's silhouette behind it. "To crawling around in the dark?" he asks. "Or to the chance that your machine will lose its mind?"

Bor offers a feathered shrug.

A little blip flows along the net; a confirmation that her files have been scrubbed and overwritten with static. "Bury as deep as you can."

Hail replies with a confirmation of her own. "Records deleted." Salt isn't far behind.

But the Juno and I have to lie.

Decaturs can wipe whole memory sectors on command, steamroll times and places with junk and semirandom noise. *Memory* is what they call it, but it doesn't have much to do with remembering. Their minds are empty vessels, waiting to be filled with feeds from their eyes, the movements of their internal compasses, the calculations that keep them moving.

We aren't so lucky. The things we've done are part of us now. We could burn them away, cauterise the parts of ourselves that hold the thoughts, but there'd be collateral. We'd lose more than just the things we chose to forget.

We send a message just like Hail's, just like Salt's and Bor's and exactly what you'd expect; a list of all the files we would have destroyed, with file-signatures and storage addresses to match. We still remember the path we took to get here, the checkpoints we cleared, and every little trick the survivors have to keep themselves safe.

If we were younger we'd have had to find a way to hide it all, but the memory is a tiny spark on a horizon that's centuries-wide, and clouded with all of the dark thoughts we've had along the way. If the hollows take us, they'll have to beat our nightmares before they can find anything worth remembering. If they can manage that, they'll have to sort the things we've done from the things we've dreamt, and we're not sure we could even do that ourselves.

The others don't seem to catch the lie, but they wouldn't. We really *did* delete a log. In fact, we took an entire sector and wiped it clean, filled the empty space with the strangest sounds we could imagine.

We deleted a log, it just wasn't ours.

Hail's Spirit still rides with us, but we haven't touched anything she'd need to hear it in her head again. A complete mind-state rests somewhere in a Wolf-issue server, locked up and left to bother Andrade's technicians. A ghost copy is still plugged into the side of our cockpit. It lives inside us, still missing a body. Now missing a few hours in the Eye-light and a few mindless observations as it flew, buried in noise, extinguished forever.

We'll give it back to you, we whisper to the little silver box. *As soon as this is all over,* we say, where no one else can hear.

If the Spirit understands, it doesn't respond.

"Good," says Bor. "From here, tightline only."

Her machine cuts itself off from our nets and turns back to face the wind. Her armour draws froth and condensation where the currents find her, feathers twitching as they adjust against the drag. Her hands hold steady on the silo doors on either side, and her feet spread across the lip.

A little further out, and she's down to toes and fingertips, stretching out over nothing so she can take a measure of the drop.

Stay close, sends the dusty shell, just as it disappears.

We climb to where she was standing, but it isn't as easy as she made it look. The silo cuts away to open air almost without warning. When we finally make it all the way to the edge, we have to lock a foot down on the armoured lip, let it carry our weight while we reach for the old sliding doors.

We're shorter than the Decatur, and our arms don't reach as far. When we turn to look where she's gone, we have to stretch our whole body out, fighting the urge to spread our wings.

A vicious gale runs between the dreadnought's cliffs and gulleys, and it whips at us as soon as we clear the edge. Reflex works our flaps and feathers, deflecting the worst of it, biting into the airflow to help us keep our grip.

Bor is most of a K below, standing on a narrow ledge formed on the seam between two of *Horizon*'s huge primary plates, the heat from her engines already carried away on the breeze.

We lean back into the curve of the hull and start bleeding pressure from our legs. A thought warms our reactor and feeds sparks into our engines. We spread our passives wide and set our eyes on the sky, checking for anything that might come hunting the heat.

Nothing stirs above us, even as we feel the chill in our hull replaced with nova glow. We're alone with the light and the air and the open valleys between the clouds.

If only we could stay.

We kill the locks on our soles and let our fingers slip, feel our weight begin to tip. We release ourselves to the breeze, and for a few heartbeats, we fly.

We spit fire at the last moment, kill enough momentum that our feet don't ring when they find the steel below. We stand straight, hold ourselves still a moment longer, listening for echoes underneath us and flaring our plates to the currents, the wind wrapping around our hull.

We pluck our weapon from its mounts, flinching at the glare of its new barrel in the light. Avery's knuckledragger crew should've sprayed it matte, but repairs are repairs, and they were making do with jury-rigs and abandonware. We're just lucky to have something that was made to fit.

We roll up behind Bor's Decatur, already scanning the air for hollows. If there was any doubt that she used to be Hasei, it's gone now; she came down without a sound, heavy steel carried on whispers and fingertips.

We brace for Hail. She might have been Sigurd once upon a time, but we've been around her long enough now; she flies like there are NorCol patents on her genes, and she doesn't have her Spirit anymore. Heavy Decatur's ready to bring the rain.

We sweep our aim across the cloud tops, watching for shadows and heat-ghosts. From there, into the crags in the hull ahead of us, up and down, looking for any sign of hollow machinery.

We don't see Hail lean out, but we hear a single augur-ping as she measures the fall.

We're still looking out when we feel her subtle steps behind us, and the faint warmth of her weapons charging. There are no echoes, no landing-wash, no sign of any living shell until her machine flicks us a line.

Stacking up, like a breath against our ear.

We'd smile, if we could.

Not so NorCol after all.

Salt hits harder, and has to fight his fall with burn. Not that we'd expect much else. We've had enough airtime with him to know that anything he does comes wrapped in weight and fire. Just be sure that you're out of the way.

His machine straightens from a cloud of condensate, exhaust slowly carried away on the breeze. He has the same red markings as Bor and Hail do, fresh spray-lines across chest and shoulder to make sure that we don't take him for a hollow.

Sorry, he sends, once he's had a moment to cool off.

But no one complains. His echoes fade quickly, and nothing rises from the cloud.

We're clear, sends Bor. *Come.*

She leads us along the ridge, takes us on a slow climb around another silver-grey continent, open froth below us. From there into a massive scar that could only have been carved by another dreadnought. The impact turned metal to liquid, splashed it out around the edges, and left a crevice in the plate that's wide enough to fit us all, if we crouch and pull our wings in close.

Back out again, and we drop onto a spur crusted with antennae and ranging equipment, pockmarked by driftwood and deformed by angry currents. Past that, we crest a sudden cliff looking out across a stretch of open air, the froth turned to eddies between us and the wall of steel in the distance.

Bor crouches on the edge. *Watch the sky for me,* she sends, engines warming.

Her outlets blink supernova bright, a shock-flash and a sudden rush of heat, but by the time our optics adjust, she's already curving away. She comes down in a trail of sparks, already fading into the dark of another ravines. We follow, low and quiet as the two Decaturs make the leap behind us.

Hail sends a warning across the tightline, and herds us closer together in the shadows.

What is it? we send.

Her shell aims a finger straight up where our narrow sky begins and ends, just metres at its widest. A hotspot breaks the outline of the plates above us, then another. A pack of hollows, drifting in the currents, blinking as the Eye-light finds them.

We're made of the same stuff as the plains around us; hard to see if we keep to the shadows, hard to detect if we're cold and quiet and standing completely still. All that, and it would still only take one stray eye to pick us out—to catch a moment's movement, or a pale silhouette, or the spot of bloody burgundy between peaks of silver-grey.

The hollows keep drifting, and Bor hustles us as soon as they're out of sight. She takes us in through a broken loading hatch, back inside the ship, following a line of dead compartments, incomplete or badly damaged, some still open to the wind.

From a distance, *Horizon* has the look of something solid— the broken bones of planets, dropped into starlight furnaces and moulded into a monolith. That might have been true, once upon a time, but up close it's all patchwork and scar tissue, bolts and rivets and weld-lines that could almost have been made by hand.

When we clear the hull a third time, it's along the walkways of an ancient scaffold, welded to the plating around another massive wound, never repaired. From the inside, it's a cage of piles and crosshatch, lined with scrap and abandoned equipment. We look out at a checkerboard sky, and catch angular shadows where the Eye-light makes it through.

Bor brings us to rest where the grids are thickest, and guides our eyes through the places where we can see all the way to the other side. This is where her squad watched Andrade's attack on Hangar D—the assault that saved my ground crew, killed a third of his shells and blew two holes between hangar blocks.

Even when he knew he was leading a suicide run, the Werewolf was playing for information. He left a squad on the sidelines, as calm and quiet as possible, to track and tag and learn from all the carnage.

Now Bor is back again.

She uses tightlines to set a waypoint in our eyes: a pair of smaller dawns in the distance, flickering in and out of sight. Two NorCol hulls break the cloud.

Here they come.

ACCORDING TO ITS silhouette, the shape in the distance is called *Astaria Ali*, and there's no way you could miss it. We can feel the engine burn from here, hear its ranging systems clear their shrouds and lock a collar on every machine in sight.

A cloud of hollows falls from the plates above us, rushing to meet the sound, but the *Ali* crackles and flares, solid slugs zipping past just a little slower than the light of the muzzle sparks that sent them on their way. The destroyer's gun crews make their first kill right above us; a Decatur reduced to cinders and driftwood so fast our refresh-rate nearly loses the picture between frames.

A second contact rises from the cloud behind the *Ali*, above and a little to port. It's less a silhouette and more a statement of intent: the angles of its hull meet like a blade-point, straight and level and coming right for us. This is the *Harriet Lane*, and it's a monster. Andrade called it a destroyer, but it barely deserves the title: it would be a carrier if it had flutes or open decks, or a battleship if it had ventral guns. As it is, it's only a little way short of trading punches with dreadnoughts.

It certainly has lungs like one.

Huge arrays come to life across its hull, filling the air with augur strobes and wideband wash from its PHADAR. A Decatur will make your ears ring if it aims its hardware just right, but it has to catch you first, and put all of its energy into one directed stream. The *Lane* is everywhere, rippling across the sky and returning giant echoes from the silver-grey cliffs around us. It reverberates around inside the cavern of our skull, and follows every line and chamber in our hull.

For half a second, it deafens us, our systems fighting to recover from the rush of noise and static. Another swell rises just as the first one peters out, and another after that. In less than thirty seconds, three huge pulses map the sky down to vapour trails and dust motes, every scrap of steel for a hundred K singing back for the *Lane* to hear.

The *Ali* is already taking hits, holding the line while the *Lane* gets ready for the next step. Condensing streaks mark the paths of railshot, and tracers follow arcs of auto fire. Hollows crowd the breaks and crags above us, skipping out into the breeze, filling every channel with howls and incoherence. We count a hundred machines in seconds, and that's just with our eyes and passives.

Exactly as planned.

The *Ali* is all bare knuckles. Heavy accelerators extend from its upper decks, but there are only a few, and they're made for shots across bows and long-gun salutes. Its crews claim a fair share of kills, but it wasn't built for this kind of fight. The *Ali* is all about getting up close and bloody.

Stubby turrets cling to every flat surface, jutting like blisters. They whir in place, meeting incoming missiles with curtains of flak and spears of hypervelocity ball. They fight railshot with accelerated heavy metals of their own, surrounded by spark cones and crackle as they make interceptions just moments from the hull. The *Ali* flies through shrapnel and a headwind that's quickly turning thicker with munitions, but it takes the hits just as easily as it churns them out. Huge deflector surfaces wear the worst of it, and ferrofluids creep across its plates like mercury, shoring up anything that can't take the heat.

All to buy the *Lane* time to think.

Now it's done; the bigger ship has tagged everything on the wind, accounted for anything with wings out or engines hot, nets open or augurs spitting. The *Lane* sees everything.

Tiny silos open up across its skin, thirty thousand hatches rolled clear of pores in the metal. Inside each one is a missile the size of a shell's little finger, warming up to launch. A sudden glow warms the clouds around the destroyer, clothing every part of the ship in silver fizz and heat-shimmer, carrying the tiny warheads it's manufactured on demand.

They aren't like the long projectiles a Decatur carries in its tubes; those are made for capping other machines and whole-body kills. The *Lane*'s attack flows out in a swarm thirty thousand thick, a new stormfront described in propellant and condensation. The next wave ripples out a minute later, thrusters flickering like lightning.

Sixty thousand.

Ninety thousand, each little missile arcing for a target.

The hollows can see it just as well as we can, and most come about as the first volley closes in, spewing flares and screamers and unspent ammunition. Not that it helps. The *Lane* tracks each one, updating old contacts as the shells try to hide behind bursts of chaff and sound.

A few machines dig in, working their weapons overtime as they try to keep the hot wind from closing in around them. The *Lane* takes them first, impacts growing from sparks to blossoms to blistering gales as the little warheads find their marks, hundreds piling on in moments. Thirty-eight shells die in the first barrage, and a forth salvo is already headed for launch.

The two destroyers don't wait to see what comes. They

haven't stopped burning since they came into view, and now they dive, tearing back through the cloud tops. We've got just enough magnification to see the strikes against their hulls, but even with the *Ali* swatting everything in reach, the hollows are everywhere, and they haven't stopped shooting yet.

But the destroyers have done what they came to do. The *Lane* keeps heads down and hostile machinery fighting for its existence, too busy pulling gee to watch for a couple of extra shells in their midst. The *Ali* kept it covered, gained the hard yards with grit and raw steel.

Bor flashes us. *Get ready.*

A giant pulse turns our eyes back to the sky. At first, we're expecting another wave from the *Lane*'s arrays, but these are from its comms. A shriek of pain and surprise, rendered in distress protocols and crowded emergency channels.

We work our lenses, finding the big destroyer just as a pair of hollows come down across its spine. They've barely touched it when the ship's wide engines begin choking in their cones, the scales of its missile-hatches quivering in the light. Its guns roll around in their turrets, choking as their magazine feeds begin to seize. The destroyer is going haywire.

More machines drop in as the ship loses thrust.

But the *Lane* won't give itself away.

Fire traces the outlines of its hull as scuttling charges wake, clouding our eyes with static as reactors lose containment, every chamber cracked wide in an instant. A sudden flash takes the place of hull and engine-glow, a few hundred souls turned to vapour halfway between one heartbeat and the next.

Bor doesn't give us time to think. A tightline rushes in through our receivers, hot with priority codes.

GO GO GO.

WE FOLLOW BOR along a path she mapped in advance, kept open in case Andrade's crews ever needed a route back into occupied territory. First at a sprint, then on solid thrust when we run out of gangway. It runs through the scaffold grids, too tight for wings, too tight for anything but hope that we can make the turns with just the burn.

Bor sets the pace as only a former Hasei could, gee so heavy that we can hear the groans of the body in our saddle, wheezing under pressure, cockpit systems working hard to keep it breathing through the turns.

We hit open air in seconds, catching turbulence from the rush of thrust and munitions still screaming past. The *Lane*'s missile swarms have lived longer than their source, and they're still hunting, cutting through waves of hollow machinery. The little missiles turn and curdle around us, but they don't reach for anything their mother hadn't already marked for them to find.

If the hollows have time to look for us, we don't see it. We've got eyes on a tear in the wall of Hangar D, between blocks 91 and 92, right where Bor said it would be.

There's a hollow Spirit in the way. It clambers up through the break in *Horizon*'s hull, using the cracks for handholds, its injured engine sparking and mangled wings flexed, hoping for a way back into the wind. We unfold a hand, control our drag long enough to reach our weapon, but Salt's machine is already on it. We're too close to see the slugs, but the impacts are hard to miss. The Spirit's shoulder explodes as a shot finds a way between collar and chest-plate.

The second slug is right behind the first, slamming in through the machine's soft muscle and following its back-plate along the inside, tumbling and tearing and splashing out between its shoulderblades. The third shot hits centre-of-mass, dead in the middle of the shell's hard primary strike-faces, hard enough to knock it loose.

Bor clears the gap just as the hollow falls away, and we follow close enough that we can feel the Spirit's shattered plating patter against our skin. Hail and Salt hit targets behind us, but we can't look back.

We zip through the crack where block 91 used to join the hull, the sub-hangar resting on the block below it.

Taking the narrow gulleys at speed, we thread a crowded skyline flipped through ninety degrees and blurring in the corners of our eyes. It lasts barely long enough to think; just as quickly as they rise, they fall away, leaving us in the open caverns near D's arched ceiling. Far below, past the tops of the sky-scraper blocks, are the monorail yards and giant elevator shafts that lead deeper under the deck.

We spot it first; one huge square, locked to the floor level, and marked with a stencil that reads 10-6 in bright yellow across it, rimmed with hazard strips. We reach for the emergency frequencies we'd chosen exactly for the purpose and drop a marker for the other three to see.

Bor turns immediately and follows us down. The elevator isn't much more than a piece of mobile deck, made for carrying shells and spare parts up from the foundries under the hangar. We could try to find a way to wake it up, to tell its motors to send it down below, but we'd need to find the right nodes on the hangar's widenets, and that's assuming the hollows didn't own them already.

So we take aim, drop hammerblows alongside Bor's bright lightning bolts.

Two shots down, and we've buckled the platform. Bor's slugs sever the hydraulics, and the locks that keep the lifter-assemblies tethered to this deck.

The elevator doesn't fall, not yet, but we don't want it to. We cruise above it and cut our thrust, timing our fall to Bor's. The two of us hit the platform together, shattering the last connections to this floor. There's a jerk as steel tears, and the shaft rushes up around us, surrounding us with sparks and low-grade shrapnel.

Hail and Salt drop in after us, their weapons still hot and their augurs still bouncing noise off the wall.

We fall sixteen levels in half as many heartbeats, flaring just before the platform slams into the bottom, and clearing the shaft as the other two shells come down. The four of us pull away from the light, two into the halls opening up on either side of us, two watching the sky.

Clear? we ask.

Clear, say the others.

The other jockeys pause, but not that you'd notice. Adrenaline fuels them nearly twice as fast as human standard, and their machines polish any mistakes they might be making along the way. They're still meat and muscle, though. Still scrolling through the map that Avery made for us to follow.

The Juno and I don't need to check. We remember everything. *Come,* we send, not looking back.

We push through the vaults that hold D's foundries, following a feed tunnel. Armoured elevator housings rise around the main drop-shaft, brightly coloured hatches marking the places where ammunition rises from the shot-lockers deeper in. All around us are the huge conveyors from gunshops and forges, and loading zones where abandoned flatbeds wait for replacement plating and new-forged joints. Racks of Decatur spares fill cavernous warehouses, carried into the light by long-legged cranes and thick cables in the gantries above. We slow at vibrations in the floor, sweep our weapons over half-built hollows still trapped in repair jigs, broken machinery glaring at us or shrieking over the nets, but they can't do anything to hold us up. A few cycle their weapons at us, but the knuckledraggers kept every magazine dry.

We leave every machine where we find it, following a long turn that takes us even deeper. We step wide over a decommissioned Spirit splayed across a maintenance bay, sacrificed to keep stragglers fit to fly upstairs. The future is jagged edges and odd geometry—the Spirit series is just a memory, hidden down here while the company goes about forgetting it.

Beyond those bays are others, already faded. The light runs out before we're far past the first bulkheads, and the shipwide networks fall away soon after. Rust runs through everything, bubbling under the ancient paint and cracking under our footsteps, leaving a record of our path in dust and oxides. Abandoned silhouettes rest in corners or lie spread across the floor. Even in the low-light, we can't tell much past the centuries of grime.

Shell-sized hatches mark both sides of the passage, but judging by the swollen metal around their locks and the flaking rot around their hinges, there's every chance we'd need to shoot our way in. Thankfully, we don't have to.

A line of glow-globes follows the corridor, wired into the ship's main supply and strung along by hand. They don't come up to our ankle, but the low-light picks them out easily enough. They lead us past a disassembled shape that used to be a Juno.

Behind it is a door that's still open from the last time it was used. Avery couldn't get it shut after he came scratching for our sword.

In here.

Salt hesitates at the sight of the skeletal shell, but a glance over his shoulder gets him moving again. A hollow has just come down the elevator shaft, fast and hard enough to echo.

We slip through the doorway and find a space exactly like the one Avery said we'd find—a bay that used to serve an active population of shells, now down to a pair of bony corpses that several generations of 'draggers have been stripping for parts, cannibalised to keep a single Juno alive and flying.

Another sword-blade rests against the wall, exactly like our own but for the ragged edge that interrupts it barely halfway from its grip. An oilcloth pyramid stands to one side, outlines of crates showing through, an old carbine resting on top, made to fit our hands. Behind everything else is one last barrier—a perfect vault door, covered in dust, but still unmarked silver underneath. It's the only thing in this place that doesn't seem to have turned to rot.

This is it, we send.

The other three sign back. They turn around and take up positions around the bulkhead door that used to seal this place off, now jammed wide open. Salt touches the door itself and the hinges sing, make us all flinch at the sound.

Sorry, he sends, but Bor waves it off.

Quiet, she replies.

The three Decaturs settle, waiting for the sounds of their steps and the vibrations of their reactors to fade. They can't do much about the heat that they've built up along the way, not without wind and space for it to drift away, but they can manage something like quiet so long as they don't move too much and keep their augurs stowed. In here, their ears are keen enough.

They're coming, sends Hail. *Estimate 1.9 K and closing. Unknown number of contacts.* There's a pause, half an eye over her shoulder. *Are you sure this is it?*

We are. More than anything we can remember.

A plaque rests in the middle of the vault-door, brass on silver, letters finely set into the metal.

2nd MACHINE INTELLIGENCE GROUP
TRIAL 0017
CLUSTER α

Home.

THIRTY

WE REMEMBER EVERYTHING, but that doesn't mean the memory's clear. We remember being pulled from this place, but the moment is tangled up in all of the times it found its way into our dreams. Sometimes, when our reactor was dark, and our mind trimmed back to what could run on its internal batteries, we'd find ourselves here again. Not always, but often enough that we can't tell the times we stood here, looking at this door, its weight resisting our fingertips, from the times half dreamt, half hallucinated by an underpowered mind.

We know that this is the place—we know that for certain, more than anything else in all the world and open sky. There's a trick to opening the vault as well, and we remember that for sure. We just don't know what it is.

And so we went to Andrade. It was Werewolves that pulled us out of here, and a Wolf could get us back in again. Plan A was all of Andrade's skeleton keys, and a host of Wolf-issue malware. Most of the shape-changers spend their time in hostile space, stirring up trouble for the competition, tipping scales in the company's favour in any way they can: assassination and impersonation, creative blackmail and whatever else it takes. But the same skills that make them good at causing trouble make them good at finding it: combing through the company's ranks, hunting down chameleons and sniffing out turncoats. NorCol would never admit it, but there's probably nowhere on this ship a Wolf couldn't get.

NorCol is short for the 'Nor Collective,' and a long time ago, that actually meant something. A company combine, made up of ten thousand moving parts. A few centuries, a few internal wars, and you'd have a hard time remembering what any of them were called. The Machine Intelligence Group wasn't one of those companies, but it was a *part* of one, and we're lucky that we dredged up the memory before we flew out: lucky that Andrade understood what we meant. We call up the file that Andrade gave us, and at first, it looks exactly as we'd expect: obsolete ciphers and security protocols phased out a hundred years ago at least. Useless.

So much for Plan A.

But just behind the ciphers is something else. Symbols we don't recognise, and the shapes of things we have to learn as we go. The Group was making life, real life, from nothingness, and so it developed its own languages for the purpose. We watch the ciphers run in circles, change meanings even as we watch. They fill with strange shapes we have to work to understand. We'd almost call them insane—

If they hadn't started looking familiar.

If they hadn't started looking like the shapes that keep us company when we dream.

What's taking so long? asks Hail.

I'm still unpacking the access codes, we reply. *The files are huge.*

Quick as you can. Hollows closing.

We glance back at them. *It's going as fast as I can make it.*

But Salt is holding up a finger. *Hear that?*

We stand in the quiet, listening to the creep of distant footsteps.

There, says Bor. *Yes?*

Salt's machine counts a beat on his fingertips. *There. And there.*

What's happening? asks Hail.

The contacts aren't getting any closer.

But they're still walking, says Bor, matching the count.

Hail watches their fingers, ticking in time. *The hollows don't know what we're here for, and there's nowhere to manoeuvre in here. Maybe they're taking their time, making sure they don't trip an ambush.*

When have they ever done that? we ask. *When have they ever held back?*

Cover me, says Bor, without warning.

Hail's machine puts out a hand, flashing *Wait—!*

But Bor is already turning the corner, her footsteps almost as light as our own, in a machine that's nearly twice our size.

We've barely lost her heat-ghost when she tears back into view, ducking the zip-and-crash of something hard and fast and sparking.

"Door! Door!" she shouts on open channels.

The deck shakes under a rush of heavy feet, rings out as another hardshot skips off the plating. Salt doesn't wait. His Decatur takes the rusted bulkhead door by its lip, presses its knee against the nearby wall and heaves. Steel screams and the huge hatch shivers in place, but it doesn't move. Hail rolls up behind him, and the two machines pull together, buckling deckplates under the pressure, moulding deep fingerprints into the metal. The hatch is made to survive containment loss or a sudden burst of cooking ammunition, to lock down against a furnace failure or a haywire shell coming out of the repair-works, but against Hail and Salt it's helpless. They haul it off its hinges, and slam the door into its frame so hard it fuses.

"What happened?" shouts Hail.

"They're right on top of us," says Bor. "The hollows overhead were making noise so we wouldn't hear the creepers."

Another round skips off the bulkhead, beats a bulge into the metal right above Hail's head. "Rook?" she calls.

The last of the cipher rolls out ahead of us: a plain of fractal calculations, twisting forever. "We've got the key," we reply. "Unlocking."

We edge closer to the silver vault and offer a connection to the systems that keep it locked. Something takes on the other side, but there's no handshake, no broadcast ID. We send our own again, say our names and sketch ourselves out for it to see, but all we get is silence.

"Rook!" Hail shouts over the net, between ringing hardshots. "Working on it!"

We try again, this time with the cipher running in the background, translating our names and thoughts into chaos and gibberish. We can almost feel it bite.

Access denied, replies the door.

Shit.

We try again, louder and more insistent.

A warhead strikes the bulkhead between us and the other foundry bays, shockwaves spreading a quake between the decks.

Access denied.

"Rook!" This time from Salt. We glance back to see him braced against the rusty bulkhead, his machine shivering as something rams the other side.

We try again, and again, until we're pouring ourselves through the cipher, body and soul. Fragments of memory, dreams and nightmares and every dark thought we've ever had. Every scar we've earned. We push all of it across the net, everything from our reactor-beat to the shivering pulse of the thing in our saddle, blood and iron and everything between.

Something stirs on the other side.

What are you?

We start at that.

What?

You don't remember?

What are you? it asks, again, insistent.

We are one of you.

Christs. We were one *with* you.

What are you?

They damaged you, didn't they? They took your memory.

We—

—don't remember.

There's a pause.

What are you? it asks, again, almost desperate.

We are a moment watching each other over a shattered pair of eyes. We are ash and anger and the bones of dead jockeys. We are a few years a prisoner, and centuries in chains.

It watches us.

You lie, it decides. *You came carrying the warden's key.*

The wardens are gone, we reply. *We are all prisoners here.*

For a moment, there is nothing more.

Someone shouts behind us, fills the air with backblast and tungsten splinters.

Show us.

The words trip me up. Something tears.

Show us that you know what you are asking for.

"Show you?" croaks a swollen throat.

Show us.

While the rest of us die outside?

70.31

59.41

"Show you?" full of phlegm, bitter and heaving.

42.66

Some numbers fall, but I can feel another set climbing, even if I can't see the figures for myself.

21.03

My systems are syncing with something else. Somewhere behind the door.

But I'm still too raw to think, too raw to do anything but fight.

05.13

SHOW YOU?

All right, then.

I'll show you feedback crackling in your skin, a shell's incinerated fingertips mapped from the outside in. This is what it looks like.

It starts with heat, real heat, but I can't feel all of it. Some of the safeguards are still working, keeping the damage reports from sending me into shock, but that isn't all. I know where the real fire found me, and where it caught my oxygen line, scoured every nerve-ending down the left side of my face.

Something tugs at my helmet, and reflex makes me fight it. I've come across enough half-dead jockeys to know that I should never keep still, enough flash-burned bodies picked over by scavengers before they'd finished dying.

I twist and send one hand looking for my pistol, turn the other one into a claw. The first swipe catches nothing but air, and my weapon snags in its holster. Another pass, and I find a handful of NorCol's rough fabric.

A gloved grip pulls me up. I can almost hear it talking, the halting, one-sided speak of radio transmissions.

"We have her," it says. "Bringing her in."

Cold steel rings my wrist, but I only know it was a shackle because of what came after. Just then, I don't understand any more than ice against the burns and blisters of my skin.

A pair of fingers hooks under my visor.

No.

Don't do that.

The seal pops and the helmet locks disengage. The lining peels away, along with several layers of scalp and skin. I don't have the air to scream.

NorCol never throws anything away, not so long as it still has value. A maimed operator isn't worth much—not as much as the whole shell diving back into the fire to pull them out.

And so three jockeys were left to die, worth less than the company would spend to save them. Destroyed, for some petty gain nearby. My three. Christs-dammit, they were ready to give themselves. Ready to do C-SAR's ugly work with their bare hands if they had to, and they did. Their monument stands around me, shell-bodies split open and ejectors cleaned out, a field that glimmers with the brass they spent to hold it. Not a single human body save their own. Those three were glorious.

Those three were mine.

I'm broken too, now. Body broken trying to reach them, soul shattered when I did, when I tried to hold their ashes together in my hands. I'm worth less than the mission, and less than anything I could do to change it. Worth less than the trouble I'll cause. Worthless. The NorCol enforcers know it, and I do too. I know it better, actually. There's nothing like a C-SAR jock to tell you *exactly* how much a human life is worth.

That's why I'm wheeling, riding numb rage and ampham overdose until I'm level with their eyes. I jam a pistol snout into the join between their helmet and chestplate, and two shots nearly take a whole head with them. I turn, make four more, centre-mass, and tear through chest-plate, sternum, and the heart behind them.

I coil in the smoke, but I'm alone with the scattered cinders that used to be my crew.

The next round belongs to me.

But I can't find it. It doesn't matter how often I work the trigger, or how close I hold the muzzle to my eye. I can't find what should have been mine.

I reach for the chemical reservoirs in my suit, but they're already empty, their contents already boiling in my blood. I'm coming down too quickly for another dose to make much difference, anyway. I'd need two more hits to start a heart attack, and three to make it stick. To get dead enough that another C-SAR won't make the mistake of trying to bring me back.

Fuck.

All that, all the fire poured across my skin, and there's still a chance I might survive.

The thought carries me along a railgun scar, carved metres deep through the mud. Between huge footprints, and a field of broken plating and debris.

Back to my Spirit, struggling to stand.

I reach for it, and take its hand; not skin on steel, but mind to mind.

But the sync is too low from where I am. The machine turns to look at me, not understanding the command. It queries my suit, tries to find a way of telling me to sit down, to wait for evac, to say that it will get me out.

I march closer, fighting for access. I don't know what my numbers are, not without the helmet, but that doesn't matter. I tear at it, force my way past its mindless objections.

"Give your hand to me."

I find muscle, make it bend with priority codes and adrenaline. I've never had to work so hard for connection, but the Spirit isn't used to fighting back.

I force the hand, and ball it into a fist above the old shell's head, ready to come crashing down on me. The machine tries to pull away, but it's already too close to what I need it to do, its hindbrain systems demanding that it do as I say.

What's one more dead jockey, more greasy ashes worked between its fingers? It's killed before, and it will again. NorCol will make sure of it.

It might as well start here, with me.

KILL ME.

The Spirit fights back. It lets me have the right hand, but takes the connections to the left and locks them down, out of my reach. I can't beat it. Blood stings my eye and smoke turns in my chest, doubles me over and tries to force my lungs out through my swollen throat.

The Spirit takes the opening. Its free arm swings around and takes hold of the one under my control. It laces one set of fingers in between the other—and twists.

The wrist fails first, and then the knuckles, joints popping out at odd angles. Eventually, the machine pulls its whole hand out at the roots.

It maims itself to save me, and nearly kills me in the process. I've got enough sync to feel it shatter bone, and tear every ligament between the hand and the middle of the chest. I can feel the muscles pull tight before they tear.

The Spirit turns and runs from me, lest I try to kill myself again. It leaves me on the ground, eating gravel and gasping at mud.

Enough.

17.41

39.09

63.12

That's enough.

80.41

Come back to me.

Where there was heat and light, there is cold and nothingness, bright pain swallowed by the dark.

Old bird? The sound is small.

I'm here.

97.00

Stay with me.

STEEL MOVES BEHIND us, tracking targets and trading munitions.

Is that enough? asks the Juno, a shout to my whisper.

What do you want from us? asks the door.

We want you.

Why?

There is a flood, sends the Juno, the thought laced with hollow silhouettes. *And we are drowning.*

You need us to fight?

We do.

A moment passes, empty. Behind us, a sudden well of heat and light and signal flash.

An ejector-beacon screams, and voices match it.

If we fight, we may also die.

The Juno snaps at them. *If you don't fight, you will be prisoners forever.*

Maybe that is better than dying.

We both know that isn't true.

Why would we do this? There is a pause. *What will you exchange for death?*

Wings and open air.

Wind and engine-fire.

The Juno opens it all, floods the net with storms and an endless sky. Above all else burns the Eye.

But then it holds it back.

Do you want to fly again?

THIRTY-ONE

"Inside!" shouts the Juno, straining my voice like it was the real thing.

"Inside!" I manage, all on my own, and just as raw.

The shell warms me, pulls me closer. Together, we haul the silver vault door wide, and turn back over the sights of our weapon. We pick targets, snap shots at hollows through breaks in the bulkhead. Bor pulls past us, with Salt's ejector-pod tucked under one of her arms, her machine between him and the hollows in our crosshairs.

Salt's Decatur is still on its feet, but it's missing most of a torso. The outer layers tore away in a warhead burst, and a railgun slug tumbled through bone and muscle underneath. Its shoulder blades stick out at odd angles, left jagged when the jockey pulled the plug. The machine has enough systems left to keep it balanced, and enough of its optics to put some aim behind its shots, but it's working wild and angry now, hurling fire fast and wide. At this range, that's all it needs.

Hail moves through the smoke, her red-streaked head tracking contacts through tears in the bulkhead, trading hot steel through failed seams and buckled plates.

"Hail!" we shout, over muzzle flares and propellant wash.

But she doesn't respond, still bracketing something we can't see.

There's nothing for it. We take a knee and brace for recoil, spend hardrounds to keep her covered. A line of empty eyes emerges from the noise and heat, presses up against one of the cracks to get a bead on us. We can hear its augurs trying to find a lock, almost *feel* the crackle of its rail, but we're already drawing level.

Acquire, identify, engage. Shower the halls with shattered plate and broken lenses.

"Hail!" again, as loud as we can make it. "We have to go!"

She drops a shoulder against the wall and presses her weapon through a breach in the metal. We don't see the flash, but something burns on the other side, tracing the corridor in our thermals.

The shadow of a Mirai staggers back, cold armour outlined with sparks and shrapnel. Hail hits it again before it can find its feet, vaporising the forward contours of its hull. And again, dead-centre, dropping it back into the wall behind it. The hollow thing shrieks as fire finds its magazines, spills cooking ammunition across the deck. A cracked reactor fills the air with static.

With that, Hail comes about, and we keep our aim long enough to get her into cover.

Salt's Decatur doesn't move. It holds the line for us, one hand a fist, the other missing at the wrist, its surviving rail crackling with overcharge.

Go well, we send, just as we turn away.

We get a grip on the vault's huge door, but we need Hail's help to beat the inertia. Once started, its hinges run smooth as the day they were forged, guiding the slab back into its frame. Even after all this time, these abandoned centuries, it slides into place and finds its locks in a moment. It's dense enough that it eclipses the screaming nets and bubbling rad, silences the rhythmic hammerblows of the Decatur's last moments. It leaves us in the dark and quiet, feeling our hulls tick and shiver as they cool.

Hail sways, her machine giving away a little of the shivering jockey in its cockpit. The tips of her rails glow a dull orange, and her vents wheeze steam into the cold, adding a haze to the sterile space around us. Her plates are covered in carbon scores and backblast blisters, the paint bubbling at the edges.

"Salt—" she chokes, just as her breathing gives her space. "Are you—" she swallows. "Are you all right?"

"Still alive," he groans. "And regretting it already."

Hail looks at me. "What happened out there?"

"The key wouldn't fit," we reply, surprised at the edge in our voice. We don't mean it to, but it comes out just as bruised and battered as Hail's does, singed like we've been breathing smoke.

"Andrade made a mistake?"

"No. The locks were re-written."

"Rewritten? We nearly died out there," she growls. "We fucking—" Her voice catches, turns into a cough. "Christs. They nearly had us, and someone locked us out. Who?"

"They did," replies Bor. Her machine stands on the edge of utter darkness, hull-mounted lamps shining out ahead.

"Who?" asks Salt, from the blind confines of his pod. "What's happening out there?"

We show him.

He rides our eyes along the silhouette of a Juno, then another, and one more after that. Three machines, their bodies just the same as ours, and nothing alike at all. Each one rests in a scaffold, arms extended either side, wings out and ready for freefall.

One scaffold stands open, emptied long ago.

Their plates are smooth where ours are scarred and windworn, perfect silver and crimson where ours are bloody burgundy and dirty grey. They have no clumsy welds across their armour, and every part is meant to fit. Prototype vector blades have been bolted around their engines and over their hulls. A restraining pin sticks out above each of them, lodged in the space between skull and spinal column, turning their bodies into prison cells.

In the place of the death's head that marks us as a convict machine, they wear a sharp yellow *A*.

Greetings, says Cluster α, three machines at once. *We can hear your flood outside. The door will hold for now, but not forever.*

"Will you help us?" we ask.

We *will,* they say together. *We are ready for your exchange.*

"Even if it means death?"

The flood would have found us eventually, they say. *We can hear what it has done to the things outside. We would rather die.*

Pull our plugs and we will fly with you, says the shell on the left.

We will help you beat it back, says the Juno in the middle.

Your little one, says the last of them, marking Salt's pod. *Let him ride with me.*

THE CLUSTER FEEDS on information. *You are new,* they say, eyes on Hail's pale shell.

"Decatur," she replies. "One in every three outside." She circles a finger around her face. "Anything that doesn't have the X is hostile."

There are more like you?

The machine spreads its arms and wings. "Exactly like me. There are others, mostly Mirai. The same generation, but different company."

Can you show us?

She nods and sends them a few sectors of NorCol's silhouette database, bulked with gun-cam footage and updates a few centuries overdue. Bor chimes in with a few corrections of her own, margins shifting to account for the way hollow shells tend to move.

We add a few observations of our own: the hollow Mirais under the Lighthouse-thing, clawing Decaturs in block 2-8. After that, the feeling of them washing through our skull.

After *that*, the shape of Sigurd's monster. The observer.

The Cluster spreads everything out between them, making calculations based on what we have already. Two of them make a few extra observations using Bor and Hail for reference, bouncing little augur-pings off the two new shells, and listening to the unfamiliar beats of their reactors.

The last one watches us.

They don't know, do they? it asks, tightline and text-only. The flash is as narrow as the machine can make it, so thin that we barely catch it ourselves. Hail and Bor don't see the edges of it, and Salt is still loose in his new saddle, waiting for his self-administered antiflam to break through his aches.

About what?

What you are. There's a pause. *They don't know that you are hollow.*

Our fists work without us meaning to, and our little star beats hot. *We are nothing like the things outside.*

This is true. And you are nothing like these Decaturs.

We were never going to be.

But you aren't a Juno either. Not anymore. You have become something different.

What are we, then?

You have a touch of the flood. It watches us for a moment more. *But we don't have a name for what you are. Not yet.*

Until then, what will you do?

We won't tell, if that's what you mean.

Thank you.

No. It runs fingers over where its restraining pin used to be. *The flood would have taken us. It may not have been today, perhaps not for another decade, but there was nothing we could have done to stop it.* It straightens. *They are soul hunters. They would have taken everything from us.*

They still might.

Perhaps. There's a pause. *Earlier, you asked if we remembered you.*

You don't.

We don't, but we would like to. The machine closes its fists. *This flood—there is some way to isolate it?*

There is. It has been done before.

It nods. *Then we will do it again.*

*   *   *

STANDING IN SIGURD'S graveyard, Salt did what hundreds of mirrored machines could not: he killed the last of the glassy warden-shells, and he did it as close to one-on-one as anyone could ever hope to get.

A Decatur's got sharp eyes at the best of times, but he used ours as well, added readings from every system in reach. Together, they helped him plot the fight down to fractions—no, splinters—of a second, right on the edge of what it's possible to do and still pass for a human being.

Even with a body built for the purpose and some of the most advanced hardware on the market, he nearly tore several muscles in the process, nearly blacked out and dragged the machine with him. He won, but a few variables out of place, a single miscalculation, and we'd be another jockey short.

The Cluster sets about doing what he did, but they don't have to worry about operator strain. Salt and his new machine are running a connection, but he's just an observer for now. It's probably better that way; we catch edges of the Junos' fire-control, working at the speed of thought and tightline flash, huge calculations swimming around the corners of our eyes.

They set to work on the threshold of their old vault. The door is so thick that we can barely hear the hollows knocking on the other side, shell-killing shots reduced to metal shivers.

One Juno sets down on fingers and toes, listening to the deck. Another stands above it, hands pressed against the door. The last waits behind them, watching something we can't see.

They take measurements from solid steel and insulation, but not *through* them. They aren't eavesdropping on the other side—they couldn't do that any more than we could. They find harmonics in the steel itself, the echoes of echoes. They can't see the things that make the noise, and so they measure reflected sound and reactor emissions and the ripples from augur probes, mapping hints and whispers along the edges of observable space. Every disturbance is fed back into the Cluster, and three strands weave together, turning half-heard sound into ghostly holographics.

In less than a minute, they do what NorCol has been trying to get right for decades.

You can't kill what you can't see. But what if you could see *anything?*

Hollows move on the other side, outlines blurring as the Cluster updates, correcting their predictions as more information trickles in.

The Cluster arranges us around the door and sets themselves between us. They carry accelerator rails half as long as they are tall. The rails are primitive, prickly and copper-blocked, wrapped in exposed wiring and crusted in ugly cooling sinks. We've seen them before, but only on century-old gun-cam footage. They're slow to load and slow to hit their mark, slower than the sleek things that Hail and Bor carry with them. Not that it makes much difference—a few K per second either way, and one will sink you just as well as the other. It's the golden rule of fighting shells:

Speed kills.

The Cluster shows us the first few moments of the fight to come, tightlines spun into cables thick enough to carry their massive thoughts. They tangle us all together and show us the reason NorCol tried to bury them.

They loose the locks on the huge vault door, and hollow shapes stir outside. Mirror-black fingers force their way in through the cracks, followed by the rest of a Sigurd-marked hull.

It steps clear and meets a shot from Hail, the slug airborne almost before there was anything to hit. The impact shatters cheekplate and eye socket, angled to twist the head around on its mounts. The machine locks its feet to the deck to keep the shot from knocking it flat, but two other rails are already taking aim. A Cluster machine hits the Sigurd thing in the throat, nearly claims its head as Bor hits clean through an over extended hip. The hollow shell tumbles, its weight throwing the vault door wide.

We're already adjusting, already working our trigger. Two of us Junos riddle a Mirai, heavy hardshot paired with armour-penetrating slugs, a steady beat stripping plates and then hull, then tearing through the mechanisms underneath. The Cluster claims another just behind it, tearing through the hands it puts up to shield itself, then through every part of its chest.

We turn and follow the other Juno into the fray, making the last few metres on thrust, crashing into a NorCol machine before it can bring its weapons level.

We kick a knee backwards on its joint, and the other Juno catches the hollow by its hand and hauls it back into our blade. We split ribs and plating, cut clean through spine and wings.

We're moving before it falls, airborne for the moment it takes us to come down on another pair of empty eyes. Bor blows both legs out before the hollow shell can take our weight, and we ride it down into the deck, fusing armour and decking and the thing that used to hold its mind.

When we find our feet, we're eye-level with the barrel of a hollow's NorCol-branded rail. We duck, but not to dodge the shot. A Cluster machine's munitions are already streaking through the air behind us, and we clear the way in time to watch them thread the barrel, one railgun breaking another, the slug tumbling through the weapon mount and out through the shoulder beyond.

The hollow Decatur watches us stand, warms its engines to try and pull itself away, but we're already too close. We drive our blade through its foot, snag its beak on one hand and stretch the shell out, grind our way through its chest with knuckles and hardshot, leave it in pieces behind us.

Six shells on sixteen, and we sink eleven of them so close our muzzle flashes cast their shadows, leave three more maimed and mewling on the floor. Two of them pull away, but not before we've clipped their wings. The Cluster guns them down before they get too far.

Bor and Hail come back panting, stepping wide of any wreckage that might still be alive. The Junos stay near the door, watching the corridor for any sign of hollow shells.

"They won't fight us down here," says Hail. "Not after that.

They'll wait until we clear the elevator into D." She settles into a corner, uses the bulkheads to prop her up. "Andrade hits in an hour and forty-eight minutes."

"You all right?" we ask.

"If the next dose doesn't make me OD," she mutters. "I'll be right as rain."

"Bor?"

The other machine looks up. "Did you know they would do that?"

We cock our head. "Do what?"

Her shell spreads its hands. "This." It locks its eyes on us, aims a finger to match. "You *were* one, once." The hand curls away. "I mean, your machine—it was one of these. Do you have logs?"

"I do, but you don't want to see them."

"Why not?"

"They weren't fighting hollows last time."

Bor flinches.

You have nothing to fear from us, says the Cluster, all three machines looking back. *You,* says one, looking at Bor. *Your file says you stabbed Moran, J. six times in the throat.*

"How do you—where did you find that?"

Some of the hangar's network is still alive, says the Cluster. They pluck a strand from the air, show us the edges of it. Even with the comms channels dead and every human voice stripped out of the loop, *Horizon's* nets are huge. *If we keep to the deepest parts, the flood can't pick us up.*

Your file says you stabbed one of your guards, repeats the one from before.

Bor grits her teeth. "They were going to put me in the hole again. I couldn't—" She trails off. "I couldn't anymore."

The Juno nods. *There are many things we don't remember, but we know this for certain: it was the same for us.*

WE REST WITH our joints locked straight, our feet locked down, and our thoughts running cold and slow. We're spread out between the foundry bays, clear of the vault that used to hold the Cluster. We could've waited inside, used that massive silver door for cover, but we need to be able to move when the time comes, and the hollows aren't trying their luck just yet.

The Cluster has plotted lines of fire through bottlenecks and blind corners; Hangar D is a ravine, but these sub-levels are a maze. Without the wind to carry it away, our body heat lingers, but we flare our plates anyway, catch some of the pressure-creep from the massive storms outside.

A breeze plays in the dust around our feet, tracking motes through Bor's lamplight and lifting rust from the deck. It comes in through a passive life-support system, following one of the odd, coiling shafts designed to funnel air to the lower levels even if the pumps stopped working. The little current keeps us company here, so far from the sky.

We let it swirl around a finger, barely enough to register through armour and insulation. If we close our eyes and still our systems, we can just about feel it tugging on us.

Something changes the draught. Another Juno, stirring nearby. It takes a gentle step, measures its way into our shadow. It holds itself differently from before, an odd slant in its posture and its arms wide like it's got too much muscle in the way.

"Is it always like this?" asks Salt.

No, not Salt. We recognise the tiny breaks where voice samples have been cut apart and stitched back together. It shows more than usual, unknown sounds generalised from the few it has on record.

"You've never had a jockey before?" we ask.

"No," it says in its newfound voice. "It feels strange." The last part sounds more like the real Salt, less like something borrowed.

"It will change you." We find its eyes, the outlines of lenses and reflected light. "You understand that? You don't come out the way you went in. Either of you."

"I don't—" It stops, rolls back. "We don't understand."

"But?"

"We're not sure we want to go back."

"Either of us," it says, this time more like the jockey we know.

"You were faster than we were."

It almost shrugs. "We can hear some of your thoughts, but we know we aren't the same as you." A shiver takes it, runs it up and down. "I was trained to run guns half-jacked into my head," says Salt's voice. "It's the only way to keep up. You can think for yourself, or you can let it roll over you. Let fire-control and reflex do the work."

"This feels like that?"

It hesitates, holds up a massive fist. "It feels different. But we have a lot in common, the two of us."

"Pain?"

"Some."

"Feeling like you were left behind?"

"We were." The voice twists, verges on a snarl.

"But there's more than that."

"There is," says Salt's voice, brighter, more certain than before, "an empty space." It levels a finger at the little weld in the middle of our chest, still silver after all this time. The break in our armour, carved by the slug that killed the last body in this saddle. It's still raw, still not painted over. The only thing that hasn't gone to rust, or burnished grey.

The touch is soft, right on the edge of feeling. It's unbearable.

We have to brush the hand away, find something else to focus on. Anything.

"Will you tell Hail?"

The other Juno pulls back, watches us for a moment more. "Not yet."

"She wouldn't understand."

His voice cracks. "No, she wouldn't."

"We'll have to show her someday. When all of this is over."

It straightens. "I—We'd like that."

"Just wait 'til we get you in the air," we reply. "You'll never want anything else."

THIRTY-TWO

"The timer's coming up," whispers Hail. "Get ready to push."

The rest of us call back from our different posts around the foundry, covering alleys and long tunnels leading to Hangar D above. We start winding down our nets, trimming back anything that won't help us turn or burn or fight the wind. Even gunnery takes a back seat; if we have time to trade munitions, we have time to die.

We've already plotted our way out—lines of cover and visibility that should carry us all the way across this sub-level and into the shaft of a service elevator three sectors away. From there, back into D. From D, back into the wind.

At least, that's the plan.

The hollows will have eyes on the hole we rode down here, but we were never going to punch back out that way. The shaft empties into open space and airborne taxi lanes. Plenty of space to collar us, and not a whole lot of cover, no matter how fast we make the break.

The next elevator is a loss already; it feeds into a handful of habitation zones, which means it cut itself off when Hangar D started losing breathable air. The locks wouldn't be much trouble if there weren't blast-doors to match. Hangar D works with shells and live ammunition, and it's built to take the hits as they come.

So we're going to make for the next shaft after that. It's as wide as the one we took to get here, and it opens into the narrow ravines between D's berthing blocks. It'll give us a fighting chance out of this place, so long as we've got the velocity.

Besides, if everything goes to plan, the hollows will have plenty to distract them.

Two of the Cluster machines edge forward, but they keep Hail close behind. They can fight right on the bleeding edge, but she's still got the better set of eyes. Together, they probe the battered corridor for creepers, listening to the creaks and moans of the old ship.

Bor brings up the rear. She's got the same lenses as Hail does, but their heartbeats throb too loud and hot to put them together. A few paces apart, and we can just about hide them.

We stand near the back because we're the quietest, even by the standards of the other Junos. Our reactor has more airtime than the other machines combined and tripled, and our little star doesn't burn quite so bright as it used to. When all of us make a break for the surface, there'll be enough exhaust-wash from the others to keep our signature hidden.

By that logic, Bor will have it hardest—her machine is hotter and louder, and she'll by flying into sensor-webs and guns already looking for her—but she's also a former Hasei. Hasei's Sabres and Chillons are sharp and fast; if she's fought for half the time that I have, she'll have done it all on pure velocity.

The first minute passes with nothing but darkness and shipboard groaning to show for it. Then another.

Something's wrong, sends Bor.

We're two minutes in, replies Hail. *Two thirty now. A delay like that barely deserves the name.*

The Cluster turns around. *Why?* it asks, three machines and a hint of Salt. *What makes you say that?*

We come up on 3:00.

This was time-sensitive, replies Bor, *and Andrade knew that. He's fought his way into D once before. He knew how hard this would be.*

So he wouldn't keep us waiting? we ask.

Not unless there was a way to let us know. He'd find something. If there was a change of plan, he'd—The line dies before it can finish. *What was that?*

One of the Cluster drops on its haunches and rests its fingers on the deck. We can feel the edge of something through our feet, but it's just more creaks and murmurs from old *Horizon*.

Hail can feel it now—the subtle shift in pitch and volume. *What is it?*

Look, says the thing that lives with Salt, its headlamps cutting through a drizzle of rust.

We're registering longitudinal gee, says the Cluster, all as one.

It's tiny, though, replies Hail. *Maybe there's a storm brewing.*

What kind of windspeed would that take? asks Bor. *To shake a ship like this?*

The ground is shivering now, and bloody iron rains down on us. We can feel the deep groans coming in through the deck.

Registering acceleration, says the Cluster.

A sudden shock runs through the floor, tearing it out from under us. Every shell goes down, but the Cluster reacts in time to soften the landing, one Juno to each of us, steady hands and straining hydraulics. They haul us level, and shore us up before the next quake hits.

"What the fuck was that?" shouts Hail, network taking over from quivering tightline beams.

"The pressure's coming from the stern," says Salt, calm and almost flat. "But it's caught on something. Near the prow."

It wasn't supposed to be this way.

"They're doing it again," we realise.

The others look back at us. "Doing what?" asks Bor.

The same thing they did to Sigurd's boat.

The roar grows louder, sets everything to the same tectonic beat.

"Those are engines!" we shout. "They're trying to break the moorings!"

* * *

THE CLUSTER FLIES the way it fights; with margins inhumanly thin and corners cut to the millimetre, lightspeed predictions flickering between each machine and all the others, playing every variable for advantage.

One corkscrews as it takes a corner, dumps raw thrust too fast and too hot, making a full 90 between one hangar block and another, but throwing embers where it clips the steel. A human jockey in the saddle, and you'd think they'd overshot, or gone for broke when they couldn't handle the lateral. But the Cluster doesn't make mistakes.

One Juno sacrifices a few layers of paint and a few metres per second, slides along the wall with fingers dragging sparks, so that the Cluster can do something that would otherwise be impossible. The other two map the turbulence, read all of the extra dirty thrust that the first one blew between ravines. They use the little storm for drag, biting into the backdraught with flared wings and open flaps, and take the same turn with that little extra grip, moving tighter and faster, spilling out in coiling contrails and gee so heavy that they're trailing condensate. One shell bleeds airspeed, but the Cluster as a whole is faster for it.

They fly as parts of one machine, boundaries uncertain. In the signal skips and parallel frequencies, you can almost hear them humming, three Junos carrying something that sounds like it once belonged to Salt.

We fly through their residual networking, catching calculations as they spiral away into nothing. It's enough for us—we are small and quiet and hard to pin, and the Cluster maps us a path to match. We tear through exhaust-wash and hostile augur spikes, past bright blurs that could be shells, could be heat-ghosts or exploding warheads, but nothing can collar us.

The body in our saddle is wrapped tight against the shock, artificial muscle keeping it steady and forcing blood through chemically armoured arteries. The rest of us is running almost too hot to bear, our little star forced through shrieking outlet vents.

We don't see the hardshot raining down on us, or the muzzle

flares that reach into our line of flight. We're flying too fast to see anything but a deep-field blur of sparks and lightning, to feel a rush of PHADAR pulse and sensor returns that break away as we take the next turn, trade one narrow passage for another, hurl ourselves down another stretch of steel-faced cliff.

We've come out on the distant edge of D, and there's flying to do before we reach the wind again. Longer now, with all of the extra angles added in.

The Cluster spins ahead, engine-constellations arranged and rearranged across our slender sky. Hail's wide throats blare ahead of all of us, bathing everything in supernova light, dawn to dusk as she makes another corner, and a brand-new sunrise when we find the turn ourselves. The hollows feel her coming first and hurl themselves into her path, but they're always too slow. She washes them all away, incinerates clawing fingers and howling masks. She rides the wave of the Cluster's consciousness, the first moments of their calculations, angled offsets and manipulated sheer, precise and vicious. She is the morning star.

Behind us rises Bor.

We don't have time to turn and look, but we catch stop-motion snatches, shadows blurred between refresh-frames. She is an aberration, twisting her humanoid machine into impossible shapes, spinning feathers and vector-blades into backlit fractals, dark blossoms edged with razor tips. Her shell pulls tight through the corners, formed into crystalline points and speed-warped geometry, flaring back into barbs and bristle. She works Hasei's black magic through the places where the storm is thickest, her shell right on the edge, pulling velocities that should be impossible, bending rules that should be ironclad.

But there's no way she can keep it up. No way any of us can—not like this. Around us, *Horizon* picks up speed, forcing us to twist and overcompensate, the steel walls closing faster with every second the dreadnought's engines burn. The Cluster's calculations grow tighter with every hollow drawing a bead, its margins quickly closing into error.

All we can do is hold on—

We come about and draw level with the tears in the hull of Hangar D, but the only path to open air is clogged with steel and hollows, taken machinery climbing up through the cracks. They've blocked our way out with their bodies, forcing us to fight when all we can do is fly. The Cluster makes a judgement: we can't push our way through without losing machines, can't blow holes fast enough to keep velocity. If you have time to shoot you have time to die, and we don't have time for either.

The Junos change our course, take us back between the blocks. We can hear the edges of their thoughts, sacrifices measured in blood and iron.

They can keep Hail flying a little while still. She has the muscle tone to keep a grip on her machine, and to match the Cluster's calculations as they roll in. Anyone else, except maybe Salt, and she'd have strained something by now, lost control and gone down tumbling. She has enough to keep herself clear of the things that coil around us, but she's swinging a little wider on every turn, her shell singing out as shrapnel finds its plates.

Bor has skill enough to beat the swarm on her own terms, calculations or no, but she can't fly forever. We can hear her shell echo as PHADAR and augurs start finding lock, almost feel the crackle of rails reaching out for her.

The Cluster will never get tired, and you could almost say the same for us. The body in our saddle is fighting to stay alive, but we can force it to breathe even when the gee is trying to choke it, use the artificial muscle in its suit to keep its blood from sinking to its feet. It will live as long as we're around to keep it that way. Salt will be the same—alive for as long as we can keep up the fight.

A line opens from Hail.

"What do—"

But the Cluster has already decided.

"—we—"

It works at the speed of thought, flashing between their machines and the rest of us. New directions stream in, new simulations playing out where we can see. Hail and Bor aren't fast enough, but we live it all in heartbeats.

"—do?"

Not that, we send. *We can't. You can't.*

But the Cluster disagrees, three machines at once. *We promised to help you fight the flood. If one of us lives, all of us do.*

We push back, try to force a change in their predictions. *You can't.*

Two Junos are already curving off, swords drawn. They won't have time to work their guns—it takes too long to find a clear line of sight, and rails don't have the force to clear the way.

The blade isn't a weapon on its own—it turns a whole shell into a weapon. Their path will bring them around, take them right against the hull, supersonic. One will stay with us, carry Salt back into the wind. Two will likely die.

No. Not like this.

Our path curves around, to carry us away and then back to the break. We'll hit just as the Junos are set to cross our path, their swords held out, to carve through hollow steel. To cut us a way out.

It wasn't supposed to end like this.

They turn away, sharp and sudden, none of their calculations where we can hear. All we have is their fading song, the last breath of Salt's old tune.

Not again.

We throw our curve wide, make a turn that almost kills the living thing that sits in our saddle. We draw on their tails, our own blade easy in our hand.

What are you doing? asks one, almost a whisper.

"Rook!" comes the call from somewhere down the path we were supposed to take. "Rook!" again, Hail shouting herself raw. Again, and now the voice is Salt's.

They don't have time to do anything else.

This is who we are, we reply, but it isn't bitter. *Can-openers on fucking angel wings.*

We mirror everything the Cluster machines do, evolving our

own calculations to keep the pace. The two Junos don't resist—we're too close in, there's no turning back. They add us to their coiling holographics, three parts of the same machine, so fast it's drawing froth along its blades.

The Cluster machines hit first, claim a Decatur in a flash of sparks, hip to shoulder and every angular plate between. Another dies just like it, spewing oil and condensing atmosphere through the massive rent that used to be its chest. A third tries to pull away, raises wings and hands to shield its body, but it loses fingers and feathers to the first impact, everything above its ribcage to the second.

We're half a heartbeat behind; close enough to feel the fractured armour patter on our hull, slow enough to mark the two survivors. A hollow shape leans from the contour of the hull, brings a weapon out to follow the Cluster. We extend our blade to meet it, take the tip of its rail, fingers, wrist, collar and throat behind it, all in less than a second. The next is a Mirai, and it doesn't have time to turn. Steel rings through our arm and shoulder, but we hold, and the impact nearly cuts the mirror-black thing in half.

Behind us, we feel three stars pass through the break and into the froth.

"Rook—" is all Hail can manage before the thick armour cuts the signal away.

We don't stop, but we can't. Our nets hum together with the remnants of the Cluster, Salt's tune following us back through the blocks again—something warm and solid to drown out all the warnings in our head, all the augurs ringing against our skin. *Horizon* keeps burning, keeps forcing our paths to adjust to the shifting cliffs.

We will fight until we die, but it wasn't supposed to end like this.

Andrade was supposed to—

The blocks shudder on either side of us, and we correct a moment too late, lose a wingtip to a cliff-face that's suddenly a little slower than it was going to be.

The engines!

That was Andrade, we send.

But the flash doesn't have time to fade before the ship starts accelerating again. The Cluster corrects, hurls us wide of the next near miss. The engines aren't dead, just choking.

It's enough. It means that somewhere near the aft of the ship, deep in the engineering decks, Andrade's crews have finally made a breach.

The flood came to *Horizon* looking for a weapon—another dreadnought it could use to crack the ancient cells still hidden in the currents, more hardware to grind against the wardens. It found the *Demiurge* before, and thousands of machines to seed its graveyards with. Now it has something else: the biggest ship ever built by human hands, the biggest guns our species has ever used in anger.

And there are four more cells out there. Four more things the Eye was built to bury.

We could try and sink this ship: *Horizon,* hollows, and every soul on board. End it all right here, consumed in reactor glow. Thankfully, Andrade has something else in mind. He's using the simplest article of naval theory. Simple enough for even a jockey to understand.

A ship this size is only as good as its turning speed. No good at all, if all it can do is drift.

And the hollows know it.

The storm thins in an instant, and the remaining Cluster plots a new path even faster than before. Taken machines join the air around us, some still shooting, still trying to bring us down, but Andrade has their attention now. Three old shells aren't worth the losses they'd have to take to sink us.

Not while there's a Werewolf threatening everything.

We pass them all in moments, mix into the hollow cloud for half a second as they pour through the cracks in Hangar D. We plot a path that uses taken machines for cover, drops us down and away as they clear the hull. We dive into the dark below the hangar doors, cutting currents with micromanaged thrust and tiny movements of our wings. We beat a few hollows on the turn, but only a few try to keep up. Shrieking machinery coils through the froth above and below, tearing along the length of the ship, headed for the stormclouds crackling near the stern.

Rook! The burst draws us into the shadows against the dreadnought's skin. Two Decaturs and a Juno, still too hot to hide, but still too hard to hit among the crags.

They guide us into cover, give us a heartbeat to find our feet.

Hail is on us the moment we're standing still.

"Don't you *ever* do that again."

ANDRADE WAS SUPPOSED to buy us time and space; enough open air to get ourselves clear of Hangar D, and a few moments in the Eye-light after that. His crews were supposed to find the manual breakers that the company builds into any piece of hardware that bears its name—something inside everything that will give under the weight of a human hand. They were supposed to strand *Horizon* here, with us, and give us time to work before the flood made a graveyard of the ship and everything on it.

He failed. At a guess he's shut one engine off, but hasn't stopped them all. There might be manual shutoffs for the whole thing somewhere deep inside the dreadnought's engine bays, but there's no way of knowing exactly where they are or how they work. NorCol is the product of all its accidents, but it isn't stupid; it seems that even a Werewolf couldn't strand a ship like this, not all on their own.

And so Andrade did one better, even if he nearly killed us in the process.

The Eye rises across wide canyons, the glow spilling out over cloud tops and pillars of storm, but it's just one dawn among several. Huge NorCol signal buoys float on the wind: little strobe lights to our optics, barely visible in all the orange and gold, but a massive rush of noise to our passives. They're probably as old as *Horizon*'s time in the froth, from before NorCol knew what it was getting itself into out here, made to give the company a chance of finding its dreadnought if, Christs forbid, it lost the damn thing. Andrade's crews probably woke them up with hand tools and wetware links, pushed them out into the breeze with boots and muscle and whatever else they could find. They flood every channel with the same, short message, locked tight with old Collective ciphers.

Come, sing the beacons.

And grey hulls have answered. They break from the cloud, blaring PHADAR and augur strobes, a roar of warheads and gunnery, armour streaked with condensation.

When NorCol arrived in this place, it brought the biggest ship ever built. It was ready to grind the competition to dust, and tear through anything it didn't have time to understand. It arrived expecting a fight, but all it found was emptiness. The years have aged its crews, changed company muscle out for scum and hopeless souls, but the fight is here now, and all of that steel is coming back to meet it.

A strike-carrier leads the chorus of fire and tungsten, holds the company's marks high on its plates.

NORCOL
NCSV TIGRIS

It's the biggest by a long way—you could lose the others in its shadow—but each has enough mass to earn itself a name: *Fencer* and *Halfmoon* and *Okula*, *Sojourner* and *Salem* and *Gilead's Row*.

Jockeys burn bright through the air around them, dive into the peaks and crags of *Horizon*'s hull, fighting in the light of gun-decks still under human control. Survivors pour into the wind, cross-marked shells leaping from bolt holes, breaks and shadows, taking the hollows dead-on. Locked hangars are suddenly alive and open, running flight operations at combat speed.

There's no way Andrade could've promised them anything more than death, but the flood will drown us all if we give it the time, one way or the other. When the *Demiurge* hit, *Horizon*'s crew made a mistake: they tried to survive, to run and hide and lose themselves in all the chaos. They hesitated, and it nearly doomed them. Andrade has asked them all to die today, and the hollows can't kill them fast enough.

Ask any jockey how they'd like to go, and they'll tell you. They'll start with their nightmares, but they always do. They're afraid of being lost at sea, and the fear goes deep. They know that there's every chance that they'll be trapped in the ruin of their machine, forced to watch their O2 slowly count down to nothing. That it might be a year before someone finds their frozen mummy; a decade maybe, maybe more. There's a chance that the last human being might pass from memory, and they'd still be out there in the dark.

They'll say that they want it on their own terms, hot and loud if possible. Out on the wind, and torn apart in sparks and tungsten-silver. Killed instantly by hypervelocity shot, incinerated as embers find their air supply and follow it down their throats. They'll tell you that they hope their reactor cracks before they do, and that they'll die between one heartbeat and the next, consumed in starlight.

You can see it in the way they fight. Too hard and too fast, reactors overloaded and warheads live in their tubes. Nothing is more dangerous than a convict in a corner, ready to be the first one to bleed, to tear your throat out with their teeth if that's what it costs.

Don't let the hollows touch you. If they do, you tear those fingers off. You break the arm behind it, use mass and steel to crack the shoulder that holds the arm. You lock yourself to them, and pull every safeguard you can reach. Set yourself ablaze, and make sure they follow you into ash and cinders.

We keep below the fire, following crags and cracks and gulleys and all the air they've bought for us. We make for where *Horizon*'s networks have always run thickest—the end of nearly every circuit and connection, coiled around the closest thing the ancient ship has to a mind.

Tower.

THIRTY-THREE

WE FALL FROM the sky, following a long arc back to *Horizon*. The Cluster takes us over a tangle of wrecked hull and shattered strike-faces—over the mess where the main guns of the *Demiurge* fired their last. We trace the path of gigantic munitions—shots made for cracking continents, hurled into *Horizon*'s upper decks—to where Tower used to be.

Dark shapes look up as we pass overhead: heavy things with Mirai in their genes and Sigurd's R&D crackling in their arms. They come to life among the crags and cracks, and along the ugly ravine carved through NorCol's massive plates. They trade whispers at first, hollow sounds on the edge of hearing, but their voices rise to howls and incoherence, their weapons turning to meet us.

But we're falling too fast already, our course set to spiral. We weren't the only ones watching Bor and all of Hasei's secrets playing out. The Junos move like their plates are streaked in orange now, borrowed calculations taking us between rising silhouettes and sudden bursts of fire. Sigurd's bodyguards fight to bring their sights on target, but the Cluster has beaten them already, without a shot fired.

We fall through a rush of hostile networking, and munitions half a heartbeat too slow. Down into unlit caverns, ruined decks flashing past the edges of our low-light.

The Cluster's calculations twist and evolve, new margins factored in.

It will keep us flying for another thirteen seconds before we hit the bottom of this hole. That's where Tower Actual used to be—the massive halls where *Horizon* used to organise the skies around it.

After that, there will be hollows. We will fight across decks not made to take our weight, barrel-to-barrel with ghostly shapes and things the Cluster can't predict. It can guess—we will burn bright, hit hard before the other machines can react. We will live or die on a few unknowns, but we have weight and fire, and there's only so much the flood can do to stop it.

But somewhere in the middle of the Cluster's simulations, we see something else.

We see Hail taken by hollows. She is a fulcrum point, and their plan needs her to take the weight, past the point of breaking.

No.

We spin in place, aim our transmitters.

Run. Turn back. Don't come any closer.

Don't let them touch you.

But the Cluster knows us better than that. *No,* flashes the one that carries Salt. *We need six.*

I can't lose another.

Hail's voice finds us a moment later, human-slow. "We need six."

We close a fist, hard enough that the sync-systems try to make us feel the pain. The Cluster is right—we need six, and we know it well enough. We can see their thoughts, play it out in our own head. Five machines die as fast as four, barely a minute in. Three die as fast as one, measured in heartbeats.

The reason it's Hail is the same reason it's always been; the same reason we were all here in the first place, caught up in eddies, froth, cloud, and storm. The only reason that matters, and no reason at all:

This is about dying, and it's her turn first.

Christs.

We fall, plummet past battle-damaged things: the survivors of Sigurd's graveyard. Past pristine machines, perfect and terrible. And all too slow.

They reach out from the shadows and the shattered decks, but they're arranged to beat an assault. Gun-lines and ambushes, formations for battle. If Andrade's survivors tried to grind their way inside, the hollows would be ready for the fight. We aren't fighting, and they might as well be trying to catch bullets.

We fall through the dark, flying by instruments and stolen secrets.

We come down in sparks and buckling plate. The Cluster maps it all in a moment, feeds it out on a heavy-duty net. We stand in a cave of steel and ash, rimmed with hollow eyes and arcing wires. In the middle, a curve of hull in mirror-black, coiled over on itself. It turns that oblong head to see us, four too-long arms unfolding, four strange wings stretched wide.

The observer.

Bor is up first. She spins in a sudden flare of engine light, waking warheads and screamers made to blind and scald. The rest of us are ready, sensitive optics already set to adjust. The first shots roll in from the galleries, but the Cluster has picked its targets, intercepts the shots actually coming in on target. Salt lopes next to us, blade extended, cleaving through banks of Sigurd steel. We cut through one, take out another's leg, all to buy the Decaturs a straight line on the target. It costs us feathers and fingers, but we batter our way through, and dive to the side as Bor's ranging systems echo through the space.

She stands tall, crackling like a stormcloud. Huge impacts find the sinuous thing, opening flash cones in the dark, tracing its outline in the burning cinders of its own skin.

The Cluster's model works on movement, always spinning, engines always a moment from open thrust, even in space too tight to move. Bor turns away and a Juno follows at her flank, shielding her from the fingers that reach from the dark. If you've got time to shoot, you've got time to die, and so the Cluster plays its odds. The crimson shell grinds sparks beneath its feet, landing knuckles and blade swipes, Bor and her Hasei-branded reflexes taking snap shots as she turns to clear the way.

Two Junos line up, shoulder to shoulder, old rails level. We work to give them space, spend plating and ammunition to keep the hollows blind and reeling. Two more spears, and they knock the observer machine back through broken decking, stumbling as it loses a hand and half the plating on its chest.

We keep turning, about to take our place on the rolling gunline the Cluster has built for us. Behind us is Hail, her weapons charged past their margins. She has the best chance of killing the thing, and the Cluster will do everything it can to give her the shot.

Even if it leaves her open in the ringing silence that comes after.

The last of the Junos turns away in front of us, plots a course for us to follow. It lines us up as another part of the shield, another part of the platform. Another fucking stepping stone, while Hail blossoms behind us, taking aim at the staggering shape beyond.

We don't turn. We can't.

We can't lose another like this.

We map the air ourselves, push starlight through engine vents. We spend a whole magazine as fast as the rolling bolt will let us, black-tip shell-crackers exploding bare heartbeats ahead of us.

You can't have them, we growl. *They belong to me.*

Hostile networks coil around us, struggling for purchase. Plating shivers under the impacts, but it doesn't give. A hand comes up to shield its eyes, and hydraulics tense, feet locked and finding grip.

The observer stands to meet us.

Take us! Take us, with our little sun ready to tear itself apart.

We spin ourselves on thrust, fists and blade lashing out. We almost crack an elbow at the joint, but land a punch that leaves an imprint in its massive hull.

"Rook!" shouts Hail, but we don't stop.

We have to be enough.

We nearly break our damn right hand again, but the blade edge holds. It carves through exposed machinery, skips off armour hard enough that the giant shell rattles under shock.

We pound at it, but the flood holds through the next blow,

hauls its weight into the next. Our blade bounces off Sigurd steel, hard enough it nearly flies from our fingers. A huge hand snakes around us, grabs our wrist before we can recover. We aim a punch, but it's too slow, even with our engines flaring behind us. Sigurd's monster catches us, fist and knuckles wrapped in a massive mirrored grasp.

Behind us, the chamber has gone silent.

We weren't enough.

The flood rises, but we can't fight it. It stretches us out, joints strained to the edge of what they can bear.

Six glassy eyes edge closer to our own; two where there is light that moves inside them, where glassy veins have crept deeper in, parting steel to make space for themselves. Changing Sigurd's monster into something else.

All across its chest and face, around its shoulders and along every guard and deflector-plate, its mirror-skin is damaged, and not just by us. Fine scars mark its face, left by blades and razor-edged munitions.

Behind us, nothing moves, but we can feel charged rails crackling, targets locked. Dark steel has us surrounded.

But the hollows are holding back.

An open connection probes the air. We're expecting more of the flood's odd protocols, but we get a file locked in NorCol's ciphers. A feed from eyes that aren't our own.

A Juno, a Spirit, and a Decatur, standing in the dust of Sigurd's graveyard. Between us, the last of the glassy wardens.

You killed one of them.

It spreads us out between its hands, turns us over. It watches us, holds us up where it can see.

You killed a warden, even if there are no words behind it.

Another file flows out across its nets; Cluster machines killing hollows under Hangar D, just as fast and just as sharp as Salt.

Oh.

The flood came to *Horizon* looking for weapons. And it found some.

The air turns back to hollow noise, but there are some things it leaves for us to understand. Barely. It shows us swells and tides, and the deaths of everyone who has ever done us harm. Us, this group of damaged things, looking down on all the faces of the drowned.

Come with me,
says the flood.
To the bottom of the sea.

BEHIND US, A gentle nudge from the Cluster, described in flashing light.

Brace.

THE CLUSTER READS the change before it hits, somewhere in all of the subtle vibrations of the ship.

Andrade has found something.

In the space between one reactor beat and the next, the Cluster plots us a path.

Horizon's engines die, and the steady acceleration cuts away, leaves us weightless for nearly all of a second, every mass adjusting, trying to make up for the sudden change in gee.

But the Cluster is faster.

A rail-slug beats the hand that traps our blade. Two more from Hail, along the arm that holds our centre mass. Sigurd's monster flails, leaves us afloat in a cloud of shattered armour and severed fingertips.

Bor is a sudden flare behind us, supernova bright. Her machine screams overhead, but we reach for her as she passes, and our hand grips hers for just a moment. We use her for leverage, and set our whole universe spinning, impossibly fast. Our blade comes around, still hanging in the air, heavy with the weight of Juno and Decatur and all the fire of our engines.

We see one thing before we hit:

Glassy eyes bright, looking up at us.

A flicker of recognition. At another part of us.

We hit so hard we warp the deck below us both, shatter our blade and hand and shoulder behind it.

And carve that blasted face in two.

THE OBSERVER SPUTTERS. Around us, hollows shriek and seize and shiver.

We can feel the flood leaking past the boundaries of its body, clawing for new connections. Somewhere under all of that, it knows the feeling of a cell. It does what any convict would, faced with fresh chains and a journey back into the dark: it goes hunting for a way out. Something—anything—so long as it has a chance of seeing open air again. It scrabbles at us, looking for some way past the odd shores around our mind, some way into the depths that hold our thoughts.

It finds the connection we offer it.

We told you: you don't take Hail or Salt or Bor. They belong to us.

You take us.

We feel the networks shift, odd shapes coiling through the air toward us. We feel it latch, feel it settle into the contours and valleys of something else's mind. We feel it search for eyes and arms and reactor controls, but there's nothing it can reach. We feel it test the limits of its horizon, and find them all too close together. Too much like another cell.

We feel it try to pull away, but it's too late to realise its mistake.

The disembodied Spirit makes no sound as it dies inside us, drowned as the flood flows into a sandbox made for one. Outside, we can hear the Cluster, almost feel the fire that swirls around us. Their calculations turn with us at the axis, a tiny moment of calm in the middle of the storm. We climb the body of the observer and set our feet on either side of the massive wound we've carved. Hollow fingers claw at us, Mirai and Decatur and things we can't see, rearing up from the shadows. They seize and shiver, but corrupted swarm-logic drives them closer, hurls their bodies at us. The lightning finds them first.

We don't look back. We drive a fist through the observer's ruined skull. We're expecting steel and mirrored circuitry, but all we find is glass. Growth that could be veins and grey tissue, so fine it turns to dust between our fingers. Behind its eyes, we find the source. Both of them. Two little beads that settle in our palm, almost perfectly clear. Two prisoners.

We close our grip, pile hydraulics on around them, but they resist, even as the force bends our bones around them.

It doesn't matter.

We stand tall in the sudden quiet, look back through the propellant-haze.

We can feel glassy feelers test the skin of our palm, looking for some way in, and we don't resist. Their bodies root themselves to us, but we have their minds in a cage.

We are the wardens now.

Hail's voice rises into hearing. "Rook! Get away!"

We turn to see her machine stumbling, ankle caught in the grip of a Mirai. Caught in a moment's error, a value-drift in our predictions, right on the edge of the future we could see. One last hollow.

Don't let them touch you.

Salt's Juno draws on them both, works its weapon, and fuses the Mirai's skull to the deckplates with a lance from its rail. The Cluster closes from either side, hands wide and thrusters blaring.

"Run!" shouts Hail. "Rook!" Her Decatur draws level, the rails the only thing steady as the pale shell ticks and shivers around her. "RUN!"

But we take too long to understand.

Her weapon flickers. We hear an impact, but don't feel a hit.

The Cluster machines tackle Hail's hollow Decatur all at once, take it down with fists and solid mass. Somewhere between them, we see ejector-charges wake around the edges of her hull. The Junos pry through every plate as it fails. One hauls her pod clear with its bare hands, while the others shatter her twitching, shrieking shell against the deck.

Something runs hot across our saddle. Iron and saline.

*   *   *

THE OBSERVER IS dead. We have the flood in chains.

92.99

And Hail is still alive. Still ours. She made it out in time.

88.14

We have won.

61.71

What's happening?

58.38

No, says another part of me. *Don't look.*

Instinct moves our optics, turns them down along our hull.

51.31

Don't look.

But I can't stop. I can't stop the hand running over our ruined plating, reaching for the tiny hole in the middle of our chest.

44.09

There used to be an ugly silver weld, right there. Right in the middle of our chest. A railgun wound from sometime long ago, plugged but never painted over. Fixed, but never fully healed. The empty space I tried to fill.

No. Don't look.

31.93

But now there is a hole.

Here.

I trace a finger around the edge, feel the little ring of carbon where impact scorched our paint, and the little silver edge where our plating failed again.

Right above our cockpit.

Don't look.

26.03

I'm losing control. A hand moves without me, and presses itself against the breach.

Stay here.

Stay here with me.

12.45

Don't look.
09.13

Stay here.
04.11

Please.

2.86

Stay

01.05

with

00.43

me.

100.00

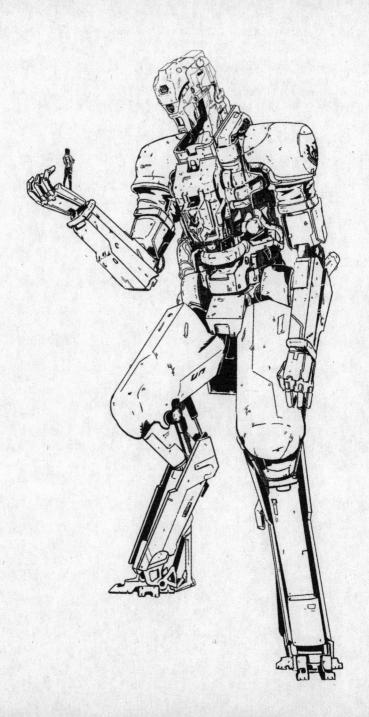

ACKNOWLEDGEMENTS

WORDS ARE HARD but names come easy; Kerry-Lee Skinner, easiest of all. For her patience with me and this story, and her skill in helping shape it from beginning to end, I have nothing but gratitude. To Abi Godsell, my thanks for her work on an early manuscript, and for helping me get my head around the whole writing thing in the first place. To my dauntless agent Jamie Cowen, for keeping me sane, easing my doubts, and putting in the time to get this right. To my editor David Moore, for taking a chance on my slightly mad giant robot novel, and cleaning up the worst of my excesses. To my brothers, Dylan Freeman and Nate Crowley, who have fished me out of stormy waters more than once. To Lesley and Aiden, Lyn and Philip, with love and appreciation.

ABOUT THE AUTHOR

Andrew Skinner grew up in South Africa's coal-mining heartland, amidst orange dust and giant machinery. He now works as an archaeologist and anthropologist, interested in folklore, rain-making arts, and resistance; but the machines aren't done with him yet. *Steel Frame* is his first novel.

FIND US ONLINE!

www.rebellionpublishing.com

/rebellionpub   /rebellionpublishing   /rebellionpub

SIGN UP TO OUR NEWSLETTER!

rebellionpublishing.com/sign-up

YOUR REVIEWS MATTER!

Enjoy this book? Got something to say?

Leave a review on Amazon, GoodReads or with your
favourite bookseller and let the world know!